ALWAY...

"I don't really mind the kissing, you know," Grace confessed softly, "but I think if I were better prepared for them, I wouldn't be so—so woozy afterward."

"You think so?" Jackson asked, both amused and fascinated by her innocent assessment.

She nodded. "Yes. Don't you?"

He reached out his hand. "Come, then."

Grace placed her hand in his and he gently assisted her to her feet.

Savoring the heat of her closeness, the faint scent of her perfume, Jackson stood unmoving a moment. He then used a guiding finger to gently raise her chin so he could feast his eyes on the lush dark bow of her mouth. "Are you ready?" he whispered.

"Yes," she managed to reply with more bravado than she felt. Her inner bells were chiming like Easter morning, her heart racing like a rabbit in full flight.

He lowered his mouth to hers and brushed his lips ever so faintly across her own. "Are you sure?"

Grace's eyes slid closed of their own accord and the initial heat of contact made her walls begin to crumble like Jericho. "Yes," she whispered back.

*Other* **AVON ROMANCES**

# BEVERLY JENKINS

# ALWAYS AND FOREVER

*For Patricia 9/15/00*

*Thanks!*

*Beverly Jenkins*

AVON BOOKS

*An Imprint of HarperCollinsPublishers*

This is a work of fiction. Names, characters, places, and incidents are products of the author's imagination or are used fictitiously and are not to be construed as real. Any resemblance to actual events, locales, organizations, or persons, living or dead, is entirely coincidental.

AVON BOOKS
*An Imprint of* HarperCollins*Publishers*
10 East 53rd Street
New York, New York 10022-5299

Copyright © 2000 by Beverly Jenkins
ISBN: 0-380-81374-2
www.avonromance.com

First Avon Books paperback printing: September 2000

Avon Trademark Reg. U.S. Pat. Off. and in Other Countries, Marca Registrada, Hecho en U.S.A.
HarperCollins® is a trademark of HarperCollins Publishers Inc.

Printed in the U.S.A.

WCD 10 9 8 7 6 5 4 3 2 1

To Ava Williams and Gloria Larkins,
for their hard work, love, and support.
I am blessed by their presence in my life.
And to my eight aunts, for teaching me
style, wit, and grace.

# Prologue

*Chicago*
*January 1, 1884*

**W**earing the ice blue gown she'd planned to be married in within the hour, Grace Atwood stood before the large windows of her late father's study looking out at the beautiful winter day. Across the room and behind her stood the man she'd planned to marry, handsome Garth Leeds.

The sun sparkled on the snow like diamonds. Normally, Grace would've enjoyed the sight, because she loved winter, but because of her mood it might as well have been pouring rain. Less than twenty minutes ago, Garth had come to beg off. He'd lost his heart to someone else, or so he claimed. Were it not for the many guests waiting downstairs in her parlor, Grace would be giving him the loud verbal thrashing he so rightly deserved.

Instead, she'd held onto her dignity. Without bothering to mask the frostiness in her voice, she asked bluntly, "Who is she?"

"Amanda Young," Garth confessed quietly.

Grace's jaw tightened. She'd known the woman in question most of her life. In Chicago's Black representative society, Amanda Young was known for her dour face, her boring dinner soirées, and of course her fortune, or rather, her papa's fortune.

Grace had a fortune, too, albeit a small one left to her upon her own papa's death a few months ago, but the wealth of the Youngs eclipsed all others. Grace sighed inwardly. Her beloved widowed aunts had warned her Garth might be nothing more than a money seeking cad. *Too glib*, Aunt Dahlia proclaimed. *Too handsome*, echoed her sister Tulip, but Grace had been willing to take that chance in hopes that he really did love her for herself. The aunts had been right, it seemed. No decent man would throw his bride over for a bigger catch, but that's what he'd done, and Grace was both angry and humiliated as a result.

For the first time since he'd entered the room, Grace turned from the window to look at him. She'd yet to meet a more handsome man. The light-skinned Garth Leeds had wit, charm, and a smile that could make a woman swoon. Even now, in spite of her mood, she found him striking. "So, when will you and Amanda marry?"

"As soon as the talk dies down."

"Talk that will no doubt center on me."

He had sense enough not to reply. Grace knew that for the next few months every time she entered a room gossips would whisper behind their hands. There'd be looks of pity and well-intentioned words of consolation and advice. How she'd survive it would be anyone's guess, but she'd never run from anything in her life, so it was far too late to begin now. At twenty-nine she'd fallen in love like a silly schoolgirl and been made a fool of, and nothing anyone could say or do could alter that fact. "I'll make the apologies to the guests," she stated emotionlessly.

"What about the gifts?"

Grace paused to turn to him again. She looked him up and down. Surely he didn't believe they should be kept. "They'll be returned. I'm certain you'll want for nothing once you make Amanda your wife."

He had the decency to appear embarrassed. "Whatever you think is best."

*It would've been best had you never entered my life,* she wanted to shout.

Haltingly, he said, "Well, I guess I should be going."

Silence.

He tried again. "Good-bye, Grace."

She didn't reply, she couldn't; instead, she simply stood there at the window until the sound of the door's soft closing signaled his departure.

Once alone, she asked herself how she could have been so blind. Grace knew she would never be considered a raving beauty; she had a head full of thick, copper red hair, was unfashionably short statured, and would be thirty years old in a month's time. Nothing about her would've qualified her to be on the arm of a man like Garth, except her bank deposits, which is probably why he chose her in the first place.

Women like her, watching their youth fade, were susceptible to the grand flatterers of the world because they'd had so little of it in their lives. During Grace's courting years all her suitors had taken to the hills once they'd discovered she ran her father's bank and had opinions on everything under the sun. Even as women of all races made occupational strides in unprecedented numbers, the men she encountered socially found her choice of occupation as baffling as her intelligence. Few seemed comfortable being around a woman like the one her papa had raised her to be, and she dearly wished he were alive today so she could be buoyed by his fatherly strength and wisdom.

After a few more moments of wallowing, she decided she'd moped long enough. She moved to the door, angrily noting that Garth hadn't even apologized for the mess he'd made of her life. Determined not to let her heartache be seen, she set her shoulders to go downstairs and inform the guests that there'd be no wedding; she also vowed never to risk her heart again. Ever.

# Chapter 1

February 1, 1884

Dear Cousin Grace,

Greetings from Kansas. I hope my letter finds you well. As you know, I've joined the Great Exodus and am now a member of a newly founded colony in southern Kansas. It has not been an easy task, trying to carve out a life in a place where none has existed before, but we've done it. We've built houses, cleared land, and put in our first crops. Now, many of the unmarried men wish to start families but lack the most necessary element—wives. We're wondering if you could make inquiries on our behalf as to whether any decent, god-fearing women in Chicago would be willing to travel here and marry.

5

*I'm writing to you because no one else knows of anyone capable of taking on such a daunting task. Our men are stalwart individuals, most are educated, and many like me are veterans of Mr. Lincoln's war. Since new men are arriving weekly, by the time this letter reaches you, we will undoubtedly need between thirty and thirty-five women. If you decide to take up our quest, please reply soon so that the funds you'll need to finance the journey can be deposited in your accounts. I will also be posting to you sketches and information on each of the men wishing to be a part of this plan in hopes of helping the women choose their mates before they arrive. I dearly hope you can assist us. Hello to the aunts.*

> *Your cousin,*
> *Price Prescott*

*March 6, 1884*

*Dear Cousin Price,*

*Your letter did indeed find me well. I've decided to accept your unorthodox challenge. Having given the journey much thought, I feel it would be best to travel by wagon. The insidiousness of Jim Crow makes a train trip too perilous. I do not wish to have us all ordered off a train in the middle of the wilds or forced to ride with cattle. Granted, this decision will raise the costs, but I prefer the women reach Kansas City free of terror and with their dignity intact. I'm sure your men will agree. The aunts send their love.*

> *Your loving cousin,*
> *Grace Atwood*

*April 3, 1884*

"You're going *where*?" Grace's elderly aunts shouted in unison, as they sat in the downstairs parlor of Grace's modestly appointed home.

"To Kansas City," Grace echoed simply. "Cousin Price wants me to find brides for the men in his colony and I've agreed to do it."

Grace watched her aunts, Tulip and Dahlia, stare first at each other and then back at her. She sought to explain further. "You both know I'm not one to cry over spilled milk, but since Amanda's and Garth's wedding, I've wanted to get away, and this seems a golden opportunity."

Both women nodded sympathetically. They knew of the gossiping and whispering that had been dogging Grace's every step since Garth's betrayal and how much pain the whole ugly ordeal had caused her even though she never let it show. Dahlia and Tulip were aunts on Grace's late mother Vanessa's side of the family and had come to Chicago last November to help Grace bury her father, Elliot. They'd intended to stay only until she mastered her grief but the visit lengthened, mainly because they found the bustling city of Chicago far livelier than their home town of Grand Rapids, Michigan, and because they loved their niece as much as they'd loved her mother.

"Who will run the bank while you're away?" Tulip asked. She was the shorter, plumper, and elder of the two widowed aunts. Tulip and Dahlia had been named after their mother's favorite flowers.

"I believe Mr. Rowe and the others are capable of seeing to things."

"You believe," Dahlia echoed skeptically, looking at Grace over her spectacles. The sisters were complete opposites in temperament. Tulip viewed life optimistically and rarely found fault in anyone or anything. On the other hand, the tall, thin Dahlia tended to be more skeptical and opinionated. Tulip often swore Dahlia should've been named *Nightshade* for her sometimes negative opinions, but Grace thought the two women balanced each other perfectly and loved them both equally. "The bank will do fine without me. I wouldn't go if I didn't think so."

Grace had complete faith in the abilities of her employees. Head clerk, Lionel Rowe, one of her father's first hires, had been working at the bank for many years.

"I'd still worry," Dahlia stated firmly.

Tulip's black eyes sparkled with irritation as she told her sister, "Oh, for heaven's sake, Dahl, stop curdling the milk. Elliot wouldn't't've willed her the keys had he not had faith in her good sense."

Grace decided to interrupt before an argument started. Dahlia, for all her contrary ways, had quite a thin skin and her feelings were hurt easily. The aunts loved each other beyond measure, but that didn't stop them from sometimes fighting like the siblings they were.

"Aunt Dahlia, you're right to be concerned," Grace offered supportively, "although I'll be gone for some time, I'm confident everything will go well."

Tulip chuckled, "Grace, you make it sound as if you'll be gone for months. The trains run much faster than they once did. You'll be in Kansas before you know it."

"We aren't going by train. We're traveling by wagon."

"Wagon?" the aunts shouted in unison again.

"Wagon."

"But why?" Dahlia asked. "Why would you want to subject yourself to such hardship?"

"Jim Crow," Grace answered simply.

"Ah," they both replied.

The political gains made by the race after the war were slowly buckling beneath the oppressive weight of the laws and policies implemented by the south's Redemptionist Democrats. As a result, Jim Crow practices were making it harder and harder for members of the race to do even simple things like travel by train. The country's Black newspapers were reporting incidents of men and women being set down on the side of the road, or forced to ride in cars usually relegated to stock or freight in response to protests registered by bigoted travelers, conductors, and ticket takers.

Grace had no intention of putting herself or the other women through such tribulation. Who knew what might become of them if they were asked to leave the train? Being stuck out on the plains, miles away from anywhere, with no one to aid them or protect them against night riders or predators, held little appeal. If they traveled by wagon, they could at least control their own fate.

Dahlia pointed out sagely, "But Grace, you don't know anything about outfitting such a journey."

"I know, but the brides and I can learn. I'm hoping to hire someone who can be both teacher and guide."

"Will you be able to find such a man here in Chicago?" Tulip wanted to know.

"I'm certainly going to try. I've already begun asking around and I've a man named Emerson coming tomorrow. Also, Mrs. Ricks, one of the bank's cleaning women, says a man in her building named Peterson claims to have done this sort of thing before. I'll be meeting him, too, if Emerson isn't suitable. Once that's done I can start canvassing for the brides."

Both aunts looked impressed by the explanation.

"It seems you've given this quite a lot of thought," Dahlia announced, sounding pleased.

Grace considered that high praise. "I have."

"Well, she has my blessings," Tulip told her sibling.

Grace smiled at the vote of support and then looked to Dahlia. "Well?"

Dahlia answered with a merry twinkle in her eye, "Have we ever been able to deny you anything? You know you have mine, too."

Pleased by her sister's response, Tulip reached over and gave her sibling's hand an affectionate squeeze, then smiled up at Grace and said, "Let us know if there's anything we can do to help. Short of accompanying you, of course. We are both too old to go gallivanting across the country in a wagon."

"Amen," Dahlia chimed in. "But we can do most anything else."

A buoyant Grace gave them both a kiss on their smooth but ancient cheeks.

Grace prepared for bed that night more sure of herself and of her future than anytime since the day Garth Leeds left it to her to inform the guests there'd be no wedding. She also felt as if a weight had been lifted from her shoulders, and she had her cousin Price to thank. Had he not asked for her help, she might never have had the opportunity to escape Chicago so she could clear her head and her heart. The days immediately following her "no wedding" wedding day had been a nightmare. Even though she'd wanted to take to her bed and cry into her pillow, there'd been gifts to return, caterers to pay, and honeymoon arrangements to undo.

Having to face her guests after Garth's slinking departure had been the hardest, though. The looks of pity had made her burn with humiliation and it took all she had to stand before them and make her apologies. Although Garth and Amanda had had the bad taste to invite her to the wedding a few weeks later, she'd declined. Word had it that Garth was starting to chafe under Amanda's very short leash and that the only parts of her fortune he had access to were the parts she doled out to him once a week.

Grace took a seat at her writing desk and opened up the packet she'd received from Price a few days ago. Inside were the promised sketches and biographical information on the men. As she'd done upon first receiving them, she studied the faces. They were of myriad ages, sizes, and hues. Some were dark skinned, others light. Some stated a preference for a pretty girl, while others expressed no preference at all, as long as she was god-fearing and clean. A few expressed no interest in a woman with children and Grace found that disappointing, because she knew there were many single women who might be interested in joining the train for the new life it might offer them and their offspring.

Grace set the sketches aside and wondered how it must be to start a new life in a new place, like the men in Price's colony. Price and his friends had been part of the Great Exodus of 1879. Beginning in the spring of 1879, thousands of southern Blacks fled the South in response to the death and mayhem brought into their lives by the Redemptionists after the final withdrawal of federal troops after the Civil War. Most went west, to places like Kansas, Nebraska, and Colorado.

The nation's newspapers dubbed the movement *Kansas Fever*, and it soon became the largest mass migration of the race the country had ever seen. Politicians of all races denounced the Exodus and its organizers because they were losing constituents. Southern planters cried foul, too, as their source of cheap labor began crossing the Mississippi in droves. At the height of the Exodus there were so many Black folks moving west and so much political clamoring, congressional hearings were convened to make sure there was no conspiracy afoot and that Blacks weren't being led astray by nefarious individuals, as some politicians and Black leaders claimed.

The race was content to let Congress debate, but the Exodus continued. Whole congregations from churches in Tennessee and North Carolina added their numbers to the throng of men, women, and families with children seeking hope and a new life on the plains. In fleeing the death and fear being fueled by White Leaguers and kluxers, southern Blacks left the well known for the unknown and never looked back.

Many of the pioneers came prepared, bringing with them all the implements needed to start life anew on the vast desolate plains, but others did not. By 1880, the newspapers were filled with tragic stories of starving, needy refugees. Black churches and aid societies did what they could by sending food, clothing, and money, as did sympathetic societies in England.

Closer to home, the great Chicago meatpacking king Philip D. Armour pitched in by soliciting donations from his wealthy friends and sending beef from his own plants to help feed those in need. Now, five years later, the Exodus had reduced to a trickle. Some colonies had prospered and many had died, but the face of the country had been changed forever as a result of the determination of men like Price and his friends—and the determination of the women soon to be their brides.

At the bank a week later, Grace sat at her desk going over the list of supplies she'd need for the journey when a knock on her office door made her look up. "Come in."

Lionel Rowe, the bank's head clerk, entered. During enslavement, Lionel had been head butler to one of the oldest families in Virginia. He continued to carry that formal air to this day. Today he was as impeccably dressed as always in a dark suit and snow-white shirt. As the aunts liked to point out, the short brown-skinned man was still quite handsome, in spite of his having celebrated his sixtieth birthday last October. "There's a man from the sheriff's office here to see you."

A confused Grace asked, "What on earth for?"

"He says it has to do with that man Emerson you hired to lead your wagon train."

She was speechless for a moment as she tried to figure out how her newly hired guide and the sheriff's office could be connected, but since she had no answers she said simply, "Have him come in."

Twenty minutes later, Grace was seated at her desk with her head in her hands, wondering, *What now?* It seemed Mr. Emerson had gotten himself killed in a knife fight at a tavern on the city's south side two nights ago. According to the man from the sheriff's office, two drunks began brawling over a prostitute's favors and when Emerson tried to stop the fight he'd been stabbed. The authorities found Grace's calling card in his pocket and had come to ask about next of kin, but she'd known Emerson less than a week and could offer up no helpful information.

The news had solved the mystery as to why Emerson hadn't shown up for the meeting they'd had scheduled for yesterday. It also threw her plans for the wagon train into flux. Where in the world would she find a replacement? Finding him had been a hard enough task. When she first began her search for a guide, she'd talked to everyone she knew and posted broadsides in various sections of the city. Once word got around that the man hired would be paid a substantial amount of gold in exchange for his services, candidates descended upon the bank like a hard three-day rain.

Most had no experience whatsoever and seemed interested only in the gold. The few who *were* qualified laughed out loud when she told them it would be an all-woman expedition; they seemed to think women were incapable of mastering the skills necessary to complete the journey successfully, and wanted nothing to do with the trip. Only Mr. Emerson seemed to find the task a worthwhile challenge. Granted, he had the twinkle of mischief in his eye and Grace sensed he'd end up being a handful, but he'd been the only candidate, so he'd gotten the job. And now?

She got up and walked to her window. Now that winter seemed gone for good, the trees were sporting fat brown buds and the grass was starting to green, but Grace's thoughts weren't on the annual renewal brought about by spring. She was too busy trying to find a solution to the problems the wagon train faced as a result of Mr. Emerson's untimely visit to that south side tavern.

That evening at home, Grace told the aunts the sad news. Although they were sympathetic, they had no solution.

The next day, Lionel Rowe came into her office unannounced and softly closed the door behind him. "There's a man named Peterson out here to see you. I suggest you pretend to be busy so that I can send him away."

A bit taken aback by Lionel's unconventional entrance, Grace, seated behind her desk, asked curiously, "Why?"

"Because he's inebriated."

Grace stared. "Drunk?"

"Very."

Her disappointment showed in her tone. "He's the man Mrs. Ricks thought might make a suitable replacement guide for the trip to Kansas City."

"Virginia Ricks should stick to her mops. The only 'guiding' this man is qualified to do is guiding a tankard to his lips. Shall I show him the door?"

"No, send him in. Mrs. Ricks will never forgive me if I don't at least see him."

"Grace—" he began warningly.

She waved him off. "It's all right, Lionel. Your concern is noted, but I'm sure I'll be fine. To be on the safe side, have Mr. Jones post himself outside the door in case I do need assistance." Mitchell Jones served as the bank's constable.

The impeccably dressed Rowe nodded but warned, "Okay, but you're going to be sorry you didn't take my advice."

And indeed, she was.

Grace smelled Lucas Peterson the moment he walked in. The acrid odor wafting from his big burly body burned her eyes and nostrils like smoke. He was dressed in a shirt and a pair of breeches that looked to be made from tanned animal skin. The color appeared to be brown, but due to the stains left behind by perspiration, food, and grime, it was impossible to tell. The shaggy uncut hair was lint filled and gray. Because of his immense size, he'd probably been quite intimidating in his younger years, but now all his musculature had softened to fat. Grace would be willing to bet he hadn't seen soap, water, or a barber in her lifetime.

"You the lady needing the guide?" he asked. His brown eyes were bright with drink.

Grace had been taught by her father to shake a man's hand when introducing herself, but not this time; she stayed right behind her desk. "Yes, I'm Grace Atwood," she stated, trying not to breathe too deeply, "but unfortunately, I hired someone for the position last evening."

Behind him she saw the smiling Lionel Rowe exiting the office. He did take pity on her, however, and leave the door slightly ajar to let in the fresh air.

"Aw, that's too bad," Peterson was saying, in response to her lie about the job being filled.

While Grace wondered how long a woman could hold her breath before fainting, Peterson's drink red eyes scanned her slowly. When he'd looked his fill, he grinned, showing off tobacco-brown teeth. "You're a pretty little thing, all that fine red hair. You know what they say about red-haired women," he stated, then winked lewdly.

Grace stiffened. "No, what *do* they say about red-haired women?"

"That they're real man pleasers—lots of fire."

If there'd been any doubts before, there were definitely none now. Grace wouldn't let this man lead her across the street, let alone all the way to Kansas City.

"Thank you for inquiring about the position, but as I stated, it's no longer available." The statement was a lie of course, but she'd lead the wagon herself before letting this offensive and smelly man anywhere near her enterprise.

As if cued, Mitchell Jones, the bank constable, stepped into her office and Grace greeted him with gratitude in her voice. "Oh, Mr. Jones, good morning."

"Morning, Miss Atwood," he replied, as he discreetly wrinkled his nose in response to the pungent Peterson.

Unlike Peterson, the brawny, brown-skinned Jones was in prime shape. He'd served with the Ninth up in

Minnesota before settling in Chicago and still had the tough, fit body of a cavalry man beneath his black suit. He towered over Peterson by more than a few inches.

"Would you show Mr. Peterson out please, Mr. Jones? We've concluded our business."

"Be my pleasure," the constable responded. "This way, sir."

Peterson didn't balk, but as he walked to the door, he said to Grace, "Too bad you already hired somebody. I was looking forward to sharing a tent with you, Red." He gave her a wink, then treated her to another tobacco-stained grin.

Upon his exit, Grace rushed to the office's lone window. Throwing it open, she stuck her head outside and drew in great deep breaths of sweet fresh air.

The faint scent of Mr. Peterson's visit lingered well into the afternoon. The low-spirited Grace had just about given up hope on ever finding a man to lead the wagon train when Felix Duggan, one of the younger clerks, knocked on her door and told her of a man he'd seen recently in one of the local taverns. To make extra money, Duggan kept books for the tavern's owner. Felix hadn't actually been introduced to the man in question, but had heard the man hailed from Texas.

"His name's Jackson Blake. I don't know if he'll do, Miss Atwood, but he looks rugged enough, and he doesn't stink. Seems educated, too."

The fact that this potential candidate didn't smell pleased Grace immensely, but the sketchy information on his background did not fill her with a lot of confidence; however, at this juncture she had no other choice but to view Duggan's news as positive. "Do you know where I might find him?"

"Last night, I took the liberty of copying his address from his tavern account. Thought you might want it."

Grace took the slip of paper he handed her, and read: *677 Sunshine Lane*. The street name did not seem familiar, but she was sure a hired cabbie would be able to get her there. Grace thanked Duggan for his help, then went back to the work piled on her desk.

When she next came up for air, it was night. Running her hands over her weary eyes, she realized she'd worked through dinner again. The aunts would not be pleased. They thought she worked too hard to begin with and never got a proper amount of rest. But in Grace's mind her father, Elliot, had not built the bank into a successful enterprise just to have his daughter lose everything because she did not give matters the energy and dedication they deserved.

Grace had one more task to accomplish before she could end the day, but as she sat in the back seat of the hack she'd hired and looked out at the dark street, she began to wonder if maybe this task should've been saved for tomorrow morning.

"Are you certain this is the right place?" she asked the hired driver, as she surveyed the torchlit lines of the large house in question. The mid-April night was cold and blustery and Grace pulled her long wool cape closer about her body.

"Yep. Six seventy-seven Sunshine Lane. Says so right there on the fence post."

Under the light of the lantern atop the fence the address could be clearly seen, as could the words above it which read *Sunshine's Palace*. Lively music could be heard emanating from the house's interior and there were all types of carriages and rigs parked along both sides of the dirt road. In the few minutes since her arrival, she'd seen a stream of other carriages arrive and watched well-dressed men of all races step out and head up the walk. "What is this place?"

The driver hesitated a moment then said, "Pardon my language, but it's a whorehouse, miss."

Grace's eyes widened.

The old Black driver turned to view her. "You're not planning on going in there, are you? A lady like you got no business in a place like that."

Still a bit bowled over, she stated, "You're right, but there's someone inside I must speak with."

"Why don't you wait until he comes home? There's no sense in embarrassing yourself here."

*Home?* At first, Grace had no idea what he meant; then, after a few moments, it became clear. She chuckled softly. "You think I'm here to confront my husband?"

"Yes, miss."

She patted him on the hand. "Rest assured, that isn't my intent. I'm here to see a man named Blake."

She then explained why.

The old man smiled. "Oh, well, that's something else entirely, but you still shouldn't be going in there. It ain't proper."

Grace agreed, but had no alternative. She did toy with the idea of waiting for Blake to make another appearance at the tavern, who knew how many days that might take? If she wanted to make the journey to Kansas City before the heat of summer began, she had to get things in motion very soon. She decided she would not be put off; she was here now, and she needed to act tonight, while she had the chance.

"You got anything to protect yourself with, if need be?" the driver asked.

"No," Grace confessed. It hadn't crossed her mind that she might need to defend herself.

"Well you might need something. Here, let me look and see if I can find you a couple rocks."

"Rocks?"

He got down from his seat. Holding one of the hack's lanterns in his hand, he began to search the snowy road edge. "Yeah. Put them in your handbag. It's a trick I taught my daughters. Knock a ruffian for a loop if you catch him off guard."

Grace stared at him fascinated.

A few moments later he presented her with six good-sized rocks, which she promptly placed in her knitted handbag; then she pulled the drawstrings tight.

Grateful for his concern, Grace asked, "Will you wait for me? I'll pay extra for your time."

"Sure will, but if you're not back in thirty minutes, I'm coming in after you. I've a daughter about your age."

Grace smiled. "I promise to be back as soon as I can."

The pact made, Grace left the hack and slowly followed the path the men had taken to the door. Wearing her heavy wool cape over her navy silk business dress with its matching little hat and jaunty feather, Grace clutched her rock-filled handbag and wondered how in the world she would convince the proprietor to let her in long enough to see Blake. She knew that if her aunts ever got wind of this they would skin her alive. Decent women weren't even supposed to walk by such an establishment, let alone venture inside, but Grace had made a promise to her cousin Price and his fellows and she planned to keep her word.

The closer her steps brought her to the torchlit porch, the more distinct the piano music became as it floated out over the night. Grace could also hear the sound of voices and laughter, making it easy to determine the good time being had inside. As she stepped up onto the porch, a large man wearing a fire red uniform stepped out of the dark, scaring her half to death.

"May I help you?" he asked brusquely.

It took the usually unflappable Grace a moment to gather her wits. Grabbing the shreds of her composure, she stated in as firm a voice as she could muster, "I'd like to see Mr. Blake."

"Why?"

The man didn't sound or appear the least bit friendly, making Grace wonder if he'd also mistaken her for some man's wife. "I'm told he might be interested in leading a wagon train to Kansas City. I represent the bank handling the business affairs," she bluffed.

Under the wavering lights of the porch's lanterns, he looked her up and down. His stony manner did not help her nerves. Just when she thought he would turn her away, he announced, "This way."

He led her around to a side entrance and opened the door. "Up the staircase. Third door on the right."

Grace stepped into the dimly lit space and turned to say thanks, but he'd already closed the door behind her and was gone. Looking around, she saw that she was standing at the base of a big staircase. Small votive candles positioned along the thick wooden handrail lit the way up to the shadowy landing and floor above. Where the stairs were in relation to the rest of Sunshine's Palace was hard to determine because Grace could hear the music only faintly, but the staircase seemed to be located on the house's outside wall. She wondered if it sometimes served as a clandestine entrance and exit for those patrons wishing to keep their visitations anonymous.

The carpet looked to be a garish red, but it felt soft and costly beneath Grace's feet as she slowly began the climb. Taking off her cape and placing it over her arm, the swish of her silk skirt made the only sounds.

A well-dressed man suddenly appeared at the top of the stairs. The sight of him stopped her in her tracks. Unconsciously tightening her hold on her handbag, she waited to see what he would do. Smiling, he began his descent. When they came abreast of one another, he politely touched his hat, saying as he passed, "Evening, Miss Lilah."

A tense Grace had no idea why he'd called her "Lilah," but she nodded hastily in response and quickly resumed her climb. He continued on down the stairs and exited through the side door. Her prayers that she not meet anyone else were answered. She found the third door on the right without further incident.

When her first knock went unanswered, she knocked again, this time a little harder. She didn't want to make too much noise. There were four other closed doors on the floor and she doubted the room's occupants would welcome being disturbed.

She knocked again.

Again, nothing.

In a way, Grace felt relieved that Blake was not in, giving her the opportunity to leave this place as fast as the heels on her black kid boots could carry her, but the promise she'd made to Price and his friends pulled at her conscience. Maybe if the door were unlocked she could slip in and leave Mr. Blake a note stating her proposal and a request that he visit her at the bank at his earliest convenience. Casting a quick look up and down the dark hall, Grace quietly turned the knob. It opened. She slipped in, but left the door slightly ajar so that the faint light from the hallway could guide her steps.

The room was dark. As her eyes adjusted to the dimness, the sounds of someone snoring caught her by surprise. Her eyes found the bed in the dark and she assumed the snoring occupant to be Blake. What to do now, she asked herself; she'd never stolen into a strange man's room before. She drew in a deep breath to steady herself. Should she attempt to awaken him, or just leave her note and depart? Gathering her courage, she tipped over to the bed. She was standing there still trying to make a decision when a strong arm encircled her waist. Before she could scream, she was tumbled onto the bed. She landed on her back with her arms gently imprisoned above her head and her body pinned beneath his weight. Several things registered at once: his bare torso, the softness of the mattress, the faint scent of soap and her own shock.

"Where've you been, Lilah?" he whispered against her ear.

She opened her mouth to reply only to have him brush his lips lazily across her jaw.

A mortified Grace began to struggle.

"What's the matter?" he breathed lowly. "If you're mad because I fell asleep, I promise, I'll make it up to you . . ."

He kissed her softly beneath her ear, and when he possessively rubbed his thumb intimately over her lips, the slow, warm uncoiling of something she'd never felt before made her go still. As if she were above the bed looking down on the scene, she saw the shadow of him lean down and felt him touch his lips to her potently, then again, and yet again. Grace'd only experienced a few kisses in her life and not a one came close to equaling this one in terms of sweetness and power. For a moment she almost wished she *were* Lilah so she could fully experience the promise he'd made. Then, all too late, Grace remembered she was sharing kisses with a complete stranger!

Struggling in earnest now, she managed to free a

hand. She swung her rock-laden handbag and whacked him hard against the side of the head.

"Oww!" he yelled, leaning back, clutching his injured temple. In the dark he grappled with her for control of the bag, then angrily hurled it aside. Grabbing her arms, he pinned them above her head and snarled, "Dammit, Lilah, what the hell's the matter with you?"

"I'm not Lilah," she stormed, as she pushed up against his hold. "Let me up, you bounder!"

Jackson Blake was admittedly stunned by her declaration. Looking down through the dark at the hellion struggling beneath him, he tried to make some sense of this. Not Lilah? His head still pounding from her damn handbag, he raised his weight, not high enough for him to scramble away, but enough to enable him to turn up the lamp on the stand beside the bed.

The soft light revealed her face to him for the first time. He scanned the sandy-colored skin, the mussed dark red hair, and the furious copper eyes. She hadn't lied; she wasn't Lilah, but she looked enough like her to be a sister. "Who the hell are you, and what are you doing in my bed?" he demanded coldly.

Grace stared up into the angry black eyes of a handsome dark-skinned man and thought he had a lot of nerve being upset. A thin mustache framed the full lips that only a moment ago had set her on fire, and a short beard dusted his chin and cheeks. There was a small welt forming near his temple where she'd whacked him with her bag. "My name is Grace Atwood, and if I remember correctly, *you* put me here. Let me up."

"So you can whack me again? Not on your life. What's in that handbag? Rocks?"

"Yes," she replied, copper eyes flashing. "The cabbie thought I might need something to protect myself with, and he was right. Now, move yourself." Grace had never had such intimate contact with a man before. The heat of his legs and chest seemed to be burning through the fabric of her mussed clothes.

Ignoring her struggles, he told her gruffly, "Not until you tell me why you're sneaking around my room in the middle of the night. Are you a thief looking for something to steal?"

"Of course not," she snapped. Grace sensed that she was not going to get what she wanted until he got the answers *he* wanted. The displeasure on his face was as apparent as the welt rising near his left eyebrow. Truth be told, she supposed an explanation was in order; she had walloped him pretty good. She faced up to his penetrating stare. "I'm here because I have a proposition for you."

The way he cocked his head at her made her realize she'd made a bad choice of words. They were in a whorehouse, after all. "Let me rephrase that," she offered hastily.

"I think you'd better."

Her temper began to simmer. "I came to see if I could interest you in guiding a wagon train to Kansas."

"For who?"

"Some exodusters my bank is representing."

"How many?"

"Thirty-five or so." She then pointed out, "You're bleeding."

He held her eyes and cracked, "Wasn't that your intent?"

"Well, yes," she replied uneasily.

He let her up.

The shirtless Jackson sat on the side of the bed and wearily ran his hands over his eyes. His head was still throbbing, but at least he'd stopped seeing stars. He touched his finger to the broken skin and saw the small show of blood staining his fingers. Behind him, he could feel the mattress giving as she scrambled off the bed. He thought that a good idea because he wanted her and that damned handbag kept as far away from him as possible.

But his mood deteriorated further when she came around the side of the bed and stood in front of him. Skewering her with a baleful eye, he saw that she'd righted her little feathered hat, her expensive looking navy jersey, and her matching skirt. She had the look of a Black woman about to start fussing, but since he was the one with the aching head, he didn't want to hear it.

"Do you always greet your women with such *enthusiasm?*" she huffed.

"Only the ones who sneak into my room in the middle of the night," he shot back.

Ignoring her, he stood and walked over to the small shaving mirror atop the chest of drawers so he could assess the damage to his face. The glass reflected his bare arms and chest and the red-haired hellion standing behind him with a determined look on her small face, but he preferred to concentrate on the welt swelling near his temple. Had he been struck a bit further to the right, he might be short an eye. Spying a clean handkerchief among his personal items spread out atop the dresser, he used it to staunch the small show of blood filling the injury. The resulting sharp sting did not brighten his mood either. Still holding the handkerchief to his broken skin, he muttered, "Damn woman. You could've killed me."

Grace highly doubted his claim, and she didn't feel a bit of remorse. "What else was a decent woman supposed to do under such shocking circumstances?"

"A *decent* woman wouldn't be in a cat house."

Grace felt the sting of his censure and knew he was

right, but circumstances dictated this unconventional visit. Truth be told, no matter how hard she tried to set it aside, she could still feel his potent touch brushing her lips. That memory, coupled with the remembered scents and intimate weight of him as he lay atop her, made the sight of his bare ebony torso and sculpted arms highly distracting. "May I ask that you put on a shirt, Mr. Blake?"

He looked back at her and drawled, "And bossy, to boot. How do you know my name?"

Grace refused to be intimidated. "By way of someone from a local tavern. Might you be qualified to lead the train?"

"I might."

She could see him studying her with a baleful eye, but she met his gaze with a raised chin. "The shirt, Mr. Blake?"

"How much are you paying?"

"For you to put on a shirt?"

"No, lady, for the job."

Grace felt like a fool but attributed it to her rattled nerves. "The men funding the trip are in a position to be very generous."

"How many men are going?" He walked over to a wooden chair that had a blue shirt tossed over it. Picking up the shirt, he put it on.

Grace was grateful he'd covered himself; now maybe she could handle these negotiations more professionally. She hesitated before answering his question however. Would he laugh like the others when she told him the truth? "There aren't any men. It's going to be an all-woman expedition."

He stared. "What?"

"All women."

He chuckled and said, "No."

"Why does everyone find that so humorous?" Grace demanded. "You haven't even heard me out."

He buttoned his shirt. "Don't need to. These women know anything about driving mules, shoeing stock, or skinning rabbits?"

"Probably not, but they can learn."

Jackson was still chuckling. "Thanks. I haven't had a laugh like this in a while."

Grace wanted him to be serious. "I intend to pay you generously for your assistance."

"You could promise me all the silver in Nevada and the answer would still be no."

"You're being very unfair, Mr. Blake."

"No more unfair than you, sneaking in here pretending to be Lilah."

Her eyes widened. "I wish you'd stop your insinuations, I did nothing of the kind."

"Is that a habit?"

"Is *what* a habit?"

"Throwing around highfalutin words like *insinuations . . .*"

Grace could hear the mockery in his tone, but his dark eyes held something else entirely. They were knowing, and in spite of his bad temper had the look of a man evaluating a woman. It disconcerted her as much as his bare torso had earlier. "And is that a habit?"

"What?"

"Assessing me as if I were one of the house's girls?"

He smiled thinly. "Very perceptive, Miss Atwood. I'll admit, I enjoyed the kiss, but you won't admit it, I'll bet."

"Give the man a prize," Grace tossed back. He was right. No decent woman in her right mind would admit to enjoying the kisses of a stranger.

"See? I was right. A woman like you would rather

die than admit a man could make her feel good."

Grace rolled her eyes. *Men.* "Mr. Blake, you know absolutely nothing about a woman like me."

"I know that a woman like you isn't likely married."

The memory of Garth Leeds passed over her heart like a dark cloud and then slid away. "Why, because I have no ring on my finger?"

"No, because you career women don't think you need men. We're good for carrying packages or driving you places, but that's all."

His handsome face and potent touch notwithstanding, Grace found his views on women quite backward. "Can we limit this conversation to a subject you're qualified to discuss, such as being a wagon master?"

"Bossy and lippy."

"Thank you," Grace responded frostily. Storming out of the room tempted Grace mightily, but she needed him to at least listen to her full proposal. The irritating Jackson Blake could possibly be her last and only hope of getting the wagon train on its way.

Determined to keep her temper under wraps, she said, "Mr. Blake, let's start over. If you'll let me explain why the women are going to Missouri, I'm sure you'll agree to hear my full proposal."

"I don't listen to bossy, lippy women with rocks in their handbags," he replied, wondering how he could make her leave.

Grace protested, "I am neither bossy nor lippy. I'm known to be quite agreeable under normal circumstances."

His eyes were glowing. "Prove it."

"How?"

"Leave."

She stood there stunned. "Just like that?"

"Just like that." Then he added innocently, "Unless

you want to stay and take Lilah's place for real?"

Grace puffed up with indignation. "You are a cad, Mr. Blake."

"And you have a very lush mouth, Miss Atwood, even if you do have the temperament of a fire ant," he replied, watching her with his arms folded across his chest.

The seductive tone of his voice and the dark power in his eyes stirred Grace in places decent women weren't even supposed to think about. *This man is dangerous*, her inner woman declared, *dangerous, dangerous, dangerous*. Grace decided a hasty exit was in order. Remembering the handbag he'd tossed aside, she began a search for it.

"What're you looking for?" he asked, chuckling at her flustered actions.

She snatched up her cloak. "My handbag. I lost it when you attacked me."

"I didn't attack you," he pointed out. "You attacked me. *Now* who's insinuating?"

When her search of the bed and the floor around it proved fruitless, Grace set aside her banker's dignity and got down on all fours to search beneath the bed. She had a strong feeling that he was taking a good long look at her bustled backside, but she ignored him—or at least tried to. She eventually found her bag just underneath the edge of the bed, and as she stood, the light sparkling in his eyes told her she'd been right. "Good evening, Mr. Blake," she said in parting.

"Yes, it has been a good evening. Sure you don't want to stay?"

When she answered by exiting and slamming the door, he was still chuckling.

*I guess that's that,* he said to himself. She was gone for good, and that had been his plan. The last thing he needed was to get involved with a wagon train full of women, even if Grace Atwood did have a mouth sweet as a summer rain. Frankly, he'd been surprised by that sweetness. During that seconds-long kiss, he'd tasted a brief flowering of innocence and fire in her lips. Were she more his type, he might be tempted to determine just how fiery she really was, but he preferred his women less stiff-necked, and besides, he'd have to be out of his mind to take her up on her proposal.

What with clashing temperaments, bad weather, and even worse food, guiding a group of men would be hard enough; a group of women would never complete the trip, and why she wanted to travel by wagon was beyond anyone's guess. By his thinking, women were better suited for raising children than for driving mules across country. But today's modern women thought themselves capable of doing anything a man could do, and Miss Atwood undoubtedly marched under that same banner. He peered in the mirror again at the raw scar on the side of his face. *Rocks*, he said to himself and shook his head.

But truth be told, taking her up on her proposal would get him out of Chicago. He'd been in the city almost three years now, and he hated every day of it. Too noisy, too congested, too many rules. He'd been born and raised in Texas and missed the clean air and the endless vistas, but in Texas he was a wanted man. In Chicago he was just another face in the crowd.

Jackson lifted the small tarnished picture frame from atop the dresser and solemnly viewed the two men it showed. Frozen in time was his smiling adopted brother Griffin and their stern-faced father, Royce, a big man with large muttonchops covering his brown cheeks. By trade Royce had been a carpenter, but on Sunday he preached the Good News. Griffin had been seventeen when the picture was taken. Five years earlier, Royce had found the twelve-year-old orphan Griffin working at an Abilene whorehouse, running errands for the girls and the gamblers there. Royce had brought Griffin back to Texas and made him a member of their small family.

It hadn't surprised Jackson to find himself with a new sibling. Royce had always had a big heart, and it was that generosity of spirit that had ultimately led to his death. Ten years ago, a group of thugs were terrorizing some of the Black tenant farmers in the area near their Texas home and Royce had promised to intervene on the farmers' behalf. When Royce rode out to speak to the men who called themselves the Sons of Shiloh, they hadn't cared that he'd come seeking peace, they'd shot him dead.

One of the men involved in Royce's death had been Lane Trent, the only son of Bill Trent, one of the county's wealthiest Reb Democrats. At the time of the murder, Jackson had been the county's newly elected sheriff and had been trying to build his own case against the Sons of Shiloh. He knew it wouldn't be easy to arrest Lane Trent. Due to the tumultuous times and the rising disenfranchisement of the race, very few men outside the race respected his authority, but Royce had been his father and Jackson wanted the killers brought to justice. So he and his three-man posse rode out to the Trent spread to arrest Lane Trent, but when Jackson stepped up onto the porch, Bill Trent spit on Jackson's boots and said the only thing a nigra could do on his land was pick cotton. He'd then ordered his men to open fire. In the ensuing gunfight, the elder Trent had been killed.

Afterward, Lane, aided by his late father's powerful friends, convinced the authorities that Jackson had no evidence linking Lane to Royce's murder and had gunned down Bill Trent in cold blood. Two days later, warrants were issued for Jackson's arrest, but he had no intention of letting Lane Trent watch him hang for a crime he hadn't committed, so he and Griffin rode north and never looked back.

He and Griffin had ridden together for a while after that, picking up odd carpentry jobs here and there, but they'd soon drifted apart. Last Jackson had heard, his little brother had made quite a name for himself robbing trains. As a former lawman, Jackson found Griffin's chosen occupation disturbing. He disliked the idea of his brother living outside the law, but who was he to judge? So was he.

Jackson set the picture down. The fact that Royce's killers had never been brought to trial stuck in his craw. Not a day went by that he didn't wonder if Lane Trent were still alive, using his wealth and influence to terrorize those less powerful than he. Jackson wanted to go back and clear his name, but according to the newspapers, Texas was no place for a man of the race to be, not if he wanted to live to tell about it. As the south's Redemptionist Democrats continued to gleefully dismantle Reconstruction, burnings, killings, and disenfranchisement were rampant, but the backlash seemed particularly harsh in Texas.

Yet Jackson knew he would always be haunted by his past if he didn't go back to clear his name and avenge his father's death. Before ending up in Chicago, he'd been drifting from place to place, unwilling to put down roots out of fear that one day the Texas warrant would turn up in a bounty hunter's hand and he'd be taken back.

He was tired of running, though. *So what are you saying*? he asked himself. He didn't really know, but it seemed to begin with a bossy redheaded beauty named Grace Atwood and her wagon train of women.

\*     \*     \*

Grace's cabbie had indeed waited, and she fumed all the way home. *The audacity of that man*, she stormed to herself for the fiftieth time during the silent ride through the snowy streets. By the time she got home, her temper rivaled Vesuvius.

When she entered the foyer, the aunts were dressed in their night clothes and their faces were anxious and filled with worry.

"Where on earth have you been?" Tulip asked breathlessly.

A smoldering Grace pulled off her gloves and hung her cloak on the peg by the door. "I'm sorry if I worried you, but I was being assaulted by a man in a whorehouse."

"What?" they screamed.

"Are you all right?" Dahlia asked.

"Did you notify the authorities?" her sister demanded, as they led her to the settee in the parlor.

Dahlia quickly poured a small glass of brandy and handed it to Grace, saying, "Drink this and then start from the beginning."

Grace took a small sip, then began the telling with the circumstances surrounding her arrival at Sunshine's place. She got as far as her entrance into Blake's room before being interrupted.

"So he was asleep?" Dahlia asked.

Grace shook her head. "Yes, so I thought I'd leave him a note, but—"

Grace's mind replayed what happened next: the softness of his mouth, the hot hard feel of his body atop hers . . .

Tulip bent over to look in her face. "Grace?"

Tulip's voice brought Grace back to the present. "Oh, I'm sorry. Where was I?"

"In his bed," Dahlia prompted pointedly.

A chagrined Grace continued, "Well, as I said, I, um, wound up in his bed. He obviously mistook me for one of the girls in the place."

"Obviously." Dahlia again.

"Anyway, I opened my mouth to let him know his mistake, but—" Grace paused again, wondering what her aunts would think.

"But what, dear?"

"He began kissing me."

Both aunts stared. "That must've been awful."

"Well, it wasn't really. I mean, I've never had a man kiss me so—so—"

She stopped and looked to her aunts, as if maybe they could explain the encounter to her.

Dahlia had a mysterious smile on her face. "So after the kissing did you get a chance to ask him about guiding the train?"

"Yes, and the cad laughed."

"Cad?" Tulip echoed. "Did he take any liberties while you were in his bed?"

"No, we ended up arguing and I left."

The aunts shared another look.

Grace knew by the palpable silence in the room that she was in for one whale of a lecture. Admittedly, she deserved it. Decent women did not venture into houses of ill-repute. It simply wasn't done.

Dahlia went first. "Grace Atwood, the next time you think about going into a whorehouse, think about something else."

"You could've been hurt," Tulip pointed out seriously.

Grace knew they were right, she didn't dispute that. "But he may be the last choice. I had to see him."

"It could've waited until morning," Dahlia told her. "When Elliot died, Tulip and I promised him we'd take care of you. We can hardly do that if you're sneaking into men's rooms in the middle of the night."

Tulip added, "The fact that he didn't do anything but kiss you says he knows a little bit about honor."

"He knows nothing of the sort. That fool man mistook me for one of the girls, remember?"

"And whose fault might that be?" Dahlia asked.

Grace chose to ignore that. "He also called me bossy and lippy."

As if she hadn't heard one word of her niece's last response, Tulip waxed wistfully, "My Parker was a good kisser, too, God rest his soul. Made me feel like a church bell ringing."

A smiling Grace shook her head and stood. "I'm going to bed."

She headed toward the stairs.

Dahlia called after her, "Are you going back to see Blake again?"

Grace started up the steps and called back, "Not unless hell freezes over."

# Chapter 2

G race looked out over the sea of women who'd come to the church in response to the flyers she'd posted for bride candidates and was amazed. She'd never expected so many. Women of all shapes, ages, and sizes were squeezed into the pews. Most had come dressed in their Sunday best and the sight of such a colorful display of hats, gloves, and dresses on such a dreary rainy evening filled her with joy. A buzz of voices also filled the church as some of the women greeted old friends and speculated on the meeting to come. A few were seated quietly, hands in laps, while others were gazing around speculatively as if gauging the competition and their chances of being among the chosen brides.

Grace was standing at the back of the church, greeting women as they arrived. She smiled as Tulip and Dahlia

entered, shaking the rain from their parasols. They'd
kept their promise to come to lend her moral support.

After greeting Grace, Tulip looked over the crowd and
said in an amazed voice, "My goodness, look at all these
women. Surely you didn't expect this many."

"No, I didn't. There's enough women here for three
trains."

As Dahlia removed her cape, she asked, "Have you
found a guide yet?"

Grace hadn't, but she was determined to remain optimistic. "Mitchell Jones, the banks's constable, has
promised to ask his friends from the Ninth Cavalry if
they know of anyone. If that doesn't pan out, I've no
idea what I'll do, but I'm determined to get these women
to Kansas City if I have to lead them myself."

Tulip gave her an encouraging pat on the back.
"That's the spirit. Prescott women never give up."

While the aunts moved off to find seats, Grace mused
on Tulip's parting words. Prescott was her mother's family name. The Prescotts were direct descendants of a
seventeenth-century Black privateer the family called the
Buccaneer. The women of the line credited his raucous
blood for their unconventional attitudes, occupations,
and behavior. Grace had proven to be just as unconventional by choosing to be a banker like her father, and as
she started up the aisle to the front of the church to begin
the meeting, she knew she'd need a pirate's strength,
guile, and perseverance if this journey were to be a suc-
cess.

Grace stopped beside the front pew and looked out
over the crowd. As she stood there dressed in her best
black business suit, the hubbub quieted and she became
the center of attention. "Good evening, ladies. My name
is Grace Atwood. Welcome."

She spent the next few minutes telling the women

about the mission she'd undertaken on her cousin Price's behalf and the kinds of mates the men were seeking. "In order to make this selection process as fair to everyone as possible, we'll be using a point system," she told the attentive women.

"There'll be points for being literate, some for being church going, and extra points if you grew up on a farm or already know how to drive a wagon and team. The men in Kansas are looking for stalwart, god-fearing ladies who aren't afraid to put in a full day's work behind a plow, if need be."

"*A plow?*" a woman seated up front exclaimed indignantly. "I'm not traveling all that way to be used like a hired hand!" That said, she stood, snatched up her handbag and cape, and stormed out. Evidently a few other women didn't like the word "plow" either, because they too exited.

A few giggles were heard on the heels of their departure, then someone in the back shouted out humorously, "Scare off a few more, Grace. It'll make it easier for the rest of us to compete."

A chorus of "Amens" followed that remark and the church filled with laughter. Grace grinned, glad that the ice had been broken. They then got down to the business of filling out the applications Grace had drawn up. The ladies were instructed to fill in their names and to answer the many questions that followed concerning their background, age, next of kin, and why they wished to be selected as one of the brides. Grace was just about to say something else when the sight of a man at the back of the church froze her in mid-speech. Her eyes widened. Jackson Blake! *What in the name of Poseidon was he doing here?*

Every woman in the church turned to see who or what had grabbed Grace's attention, and as he walked up the aisle into full view, their eyes widened, too. If his dark handsomeness didn't grab your attention, his height and well built frame did. With his hat in his hand and wearing a black shirt and trousers beneath the rain-dappled long black duster, he looked like a man straight out of a dime store western. Exotic. Handsome. Dangerous. The absolute silence that surrounded his approach was thick enough to cut and serve on a plate, and as a result, the sounds of his booted footsteps echoed loud against the wooden floor.

He walked up to Grace and stopped. When their eyes met, her heart began to tumble. It distressed her to find him even more darkly handsome than she remembered.

"Evening, Miss Atwood. Sorry I'm late."

*What in the world are you doing here?* she wanted to shout. His arrival had her hovering somewhere between anger and a strange sort of elation.

However, before she could speak, he turned to the assembly and announced, "Ladies, I'm Jackson Blake, your wagon master."

Grace's eyes grew even larger. Without giving a thought to the women looking on, she clamped her hand onto his arm and said with a false smile, "Ladies, will you excuse us for a moment? Go ahead and finish your questionnaires. Mr. Blake and I will be back directly."

Ignoring the speculation on everyone's faces, including her aunts', Grace led him back down the aisle and downstairs to the church basement. As soon as she was sure they were out of earshot, she lit into him. *"What are you doing here?"*

"Taking you up on that job offer."

"You didn't want it, as I remember."

He shrugged. "Changed my mind."

"Why?"

He held her eyes captive just long enough for her to

remember the softness of his lips, then replied quietly, "A number of things, but mainly because the money will help me get back home to Texas. I hate Chicago."

Grace swore the room was getting warmer. "How did you find me?"

"I took the chance that you were telling the truth about working at a bank and asked around. Your red hair's pretty memorable."

The way he said it and the look in his eyes made Grace wonder if he affected all women this way.

His voice brought her back. "When I got to the bank this evening, your cleaning lady, Mrs. Ricks, told me I could find you here."

Grace thought Lionel Rowe had been correct. Mrs. Ricks should stick to her mops. "Surely you don't believe I'd still hire you?"

He answered bluntly. "Have you found anyone else?"

Grace paused before confessing truthfully, "No."

"Then I'm your man. Nobody else is going to be fool enough to do it."

Grace didn't particularly care for his assessment. "You believe this is a fool's mission?"

"Yep, but if the pay is as generous as you claim, I'd be a fool *not* to sign on."

Logically, Grace knew she had few options. If she didn't hire Blake, there'd be no telling when or if she'd get the wagons under way. Had she met him under more conventional circumstances, she'd've considered him a godsend, but now, now all she kept thinking about were his irritating ways and his kisses. "Mr. Blake, are you certain you're qualified to do this? I've had many men apply who were only after the gold."

"I'm after the gold too, but I'm pretty sure I can get a bunch of women from here to Kansas in one piece."

"But have you ever led a train before?"

"Yes. Led a group of families from Louisiana to Texas after the war. It took a while, but we got there."

"Do you have any other qualifications?"

The potent smile he ensnared her with made her remember last night, and she raised her chin defensively. "Your kisses have no bearing on this interview."

"No?" he asked, seeming to enjoy the sight of her being flustered.

"No. Stick to the matter at hand, please."

He nodded. "I was a sheriff in Texas at one time. Does that help?"

Grace found that information surprising. "Are you still a lawman?"

"No," he replied distantly.

The tone of his answer gave her the impression that there was more to the story, but she didn't have time to press him for additional details now. "Are you a patient man, Mr. Blake?"

"I can be. Why do you ask?"

"Because you'll probably need a saint's share of it to teach the women all they'll need to know."

"I don't believe that'll be a problem."

They eyed one another silently.

Grace broke off the contact first, saying, "Good, then."

"Can I ask a question?"

She nodded.

"Who's helping you plan this?"

"No one."

He looked impressed. "Ever done anything like this before?"

"No," she answered truthfully, "which is why I need someone experienced to lead us."

"Us? You're going, too?"

"Yes, I'm going, too. Is that a problem?"

"Nope."

Because of his striking good looks, Grace felt safe in assuming he had no problem when it came to attracting women, so she thought it best to address one issue in particular so as to get it out of the way. "May I speak frankly?"

Arms crossed, he nodded. "Feel free."

"The women are not to be preyed upon during the trip. They will be promised to the men in Kansas. Do you think you can conduct yourself accordingly?"

"Promised how?"

"They're going to be mail-order brides."

"Are you promised, too?" he asked, looking directly at her now.

Grace swallowed in a suddenly thick throat. "No."

"Then I can keep my hands to myself."

Grace had her doubts. Even though the kiss in his bed had lasted no more than five or six seconds, the dizzying potency lingered. "Mr. Blake, I'm serious about this."

"So am I. The brides will be left alone, you have my word. And my word does mean something, if that's what's worrying you."

That didn't worry her as much as something else. Grace got the distinct impression that the promise he'd made didn't extend to his interactions with her, but she had no idea how to call him on it. "Then we'll consider the deal done. If you'll stop by the bank tomorrow, I'll have a contract for you to sign."

"Fair enough. Anything else?"

"No."

She turned to sail out, only to have him say, "Hold on a for a minute."

Grace stopped and turned back.

"Found your hat pin in my bed after you left. Thought you might want it back."

The dark eyes were definitely more penetrating than she remembered. Wondering how in the world she could reconcile being attracted to such an irritating man, she asked, "Did you bring it with you?"

He fished around in the pocket on the front of his black shirt and placed the pearl-topped pin on his palm. He held it out for her to take.

Grace walked over. She told herself that retrieving the pin was simply a matter of picking it up, but found the job easier said than done. Because of the way his nearness seemed to befuddle her, it took her two tries to finally get a grip on it, making it necessary to slide her fingers across the warm skin of his palm.

After finally succeeding, she looked up into his faintly amused features and said politely, "Thank you for the return of the pin. Is there anything else?"

"Nope."

"Then I'll see you back upstairs."

Left alone, Jackson accepted the fact that the hellion didn't like having to hire him, but luckily for him and his desire to return home, she didn't have a choice. He was also fairly certain that the two of them would butt heads over everything and nothing all the way to Kansas, but he didn't mind that either. At least the trip wouldn't be boring, and Grace Atwood was easy on the eyes, even if she did have the temper of a fire ant.

Back upstairs, Grace tried to set herself back on an even keel, but found it difficult. She'd just agreed to spend the next two months of her life traveling across the country with a man who seemed able to unnerve her with little more than a look. She had no idea why it was happening or how to combat it.

The women were now done with their questionnaires. Grace collected them and stuck the huge stack into her valise lying on the front pew. She didn't want to contemplate how long it would take to read them all, but they were the least of her problems. Her biggest problem stood six feet, two inches tall and answered to the name of Jackson Blake. He was going to be a handful in ways she probably couldn't even imagine by the time they reached Kansas City. She just hoped she'd live through the experience.

Seeing him re-enter the sanctuary, Grace supposed she couldn't put off introducing him any longer. Regardless of her personal misgivings, she hoped he was qualified and that he and the women would get along. "Ladies, I'd like for you to meet Mr. Jackson Blake. As he told you earlier, he's the wagon master. He led a train to Texas after the war, and we are fortunate to have a man of his experience guiding us to Kansas City."

"He can master my wagon anytime," cooed a female voice on the left side of the aisle. Testimonies of approval laughingly seconded her assessment.

From somewhere near the back of the church, a flirtatious voice called out, "And are you married, Mr. Blake?"

They were treated to his smile, and Grace swore a few of the women melted. He looked over at Grace and said, "No."

That he'd answered the question while holding Grace's eyes made strange feelings uncurl inside herself again, and she wanted them to stop. She'd sworn off men, especially ones handsome enough to make a woman walk through fire.

Pulling herself together once more, Grace told the women, "I'd like Mr. Blake to speak to us about what may lay ahead. Mr. Blake?"

"Thank you, Miss Atwood. Let me start by saying if you're prone to the vapors, please stay home. This isn't going to be a stroll to church. It's going to be one long, hard journey, and the work is going to be backbreaking every step of the way."

He went on to tell them about the wagons they'd have to drive, the game they'd have to catch for food, and the hazards and accidents that could result in broken bones or death. Grace and the other women listened enraptured.

"You could be struck by lightning, drown in a river crossing, or die from snakebite. We may run into farmers who won't want us crossing their land. Renegades who'll think you're ripe for kidnapping. And then there's the weather. We're going to try and reach Kansas before the height of the heat, but there'll be days when we'll bake, and days when we'll have to drive the wagons through bone-chilling rain. If you don't think you can handle what may be ahead, it's best you leave now, because we're not choosing anyone who can't pull her own weight."

A few women squeezed out of the pews and headed for the door.

While Jackson went on to discuss some of the skills the women would need to learn, Grace found herself impressed by his speech and manner. He was proving himself to be more than a rude, arrogant man who tumbled women into their beds. In talking about the dangers ahead, he hadn't pulled any punches, and Grace appreciated that. He'd been a bit harsh in some respects, but everyone, including her, needed to hear the truth. She didn't want any complaining about the conditions once they got under way.

Thinking maybe Jackson Blake wasn't such a bad choice after all, Grace did a quick head count. There'd been seventy-five women at the beginning of the meeting. Sixty-seven remained.

When Jackson gave the floor back to Grace, she asked for questions.

One young woman stood. "Will we get a chance to see what these men look like before we go to Kansas?"

Grace nodded, "I have their portraits. They'll be shown to the final candidates."

Grace pointed next to a woman wearing a sparrow-brown dress and gloves who asked, "What about women who already have children?"

Grace told the truth. "Unfortunately, most of the men have requested women without children. Personally, I believe that's terribly short-sighted, and if I ever do this sort of thing again, I'll insist this attitude not prevail, but for this trip I have to follow their wishes. I'm sorry," she finished softly.

The woman stood. After gathering her things she departed quietly. Ten more women stood, disappointment saddening their faces. Their dignified exits made Grace's heart ache. She glanced over at Jackson and saw a solemnity reflected in the planes of his face as well.

The exit of the mothers seemed to cast a pall on the proceedings, taking the gaiety out of the atmosphere, so after a few more questions and answers, Grace brought the gathering to a close.

"Ladies, it's getting late. Why don't we save the rest of the questions for next time. I urge you to take Mr. Blake's words to heart and honestly ask yourselves if you really have the fortitude necessary to make this journey. In the meantime, I will be going over your papers. On Monday, there'll be a list of names posted at my bank of the chosen candidates. Thank you all for coming."

The remaining fifty-six women left silently. Grace wondered if any would return. She looked back to find Blake watching her. "What?" she asked quietly. She picked up her valise and began straightening the pile of questionnaires she'd hastily stuffed into it earlier. The pain of having to watch those women leave the church still pulled at her heart.

"Maybe next time you can take only mothers and children."

Grace paused and looked his way. She hadn't expected sympathy from him.

"You look surprised," he responded.

"I am. A lot of men wouldn't care two oars about the feelings of those women."

"And you thought I was one of those men." He stated it as a fact, not a question.

She confessed truthfully, "We didn't exactly mesh on our first meeting, Mr. Blake."

"I'll give you that. But don't judge until you know."

Feeling properly chastised, Grace replied emotionlessly, "And will you do the same?"

He nodded. "I will."

Their gazes were locked, and for a moment, Grace found herself wanting to know the man behind the dark, penetrating eyes. Surprising herself with that thought, she hastily looked away, then busied herself with gathering up her things.

She'd forgotten all about the aunts until she glanced up and saw them standing a few feet away, watching her and Blake intently.

Blake seemed to have noticed them for the first time, too. "Evening, ladies."

Dahlia smiled. "Good evening. My name is Dahlia Kingsley, and this is my sister, Tulip Mays. We're Grace's great-aunts. Are we interrupting?"

"No," he said, shaking his head. "Miss Atwood and I were just about done. Pleased to meet you."

Both aunts smiled at him as Tulip exclaimed, "Well,

we're certainly glad to make your acquaintance, Mr. Blake."

Grace's aunts were as unpredictable as they were unconventional, so in order to keep them from saying or asking lord knew what, she jumped into the conversation. "As you see, I've decided to hire Mr. Blake to be the wagon master."

"We heard," Dahlia said, gazing appreciatively up at the tall, handsome Texan.

The smiling Tulip hadn't taken her eyes off Blake since their introduction. She replied, "We certainly did. Mr. Blake, why don't you come and have supper with us tomorrow evening? I'm sure you and Grace have much to talk about, and you can do it over a meal. What do you think, Dahl?"

"I think that's a marvelous suggestion," her sister declared.

Grace noted that no one had asked her how she felt about sitting across the dining room table from Blake. "Aunts, I'm afraid I'll be working late tomorrow night. I have some—"

Tulip waved her off. "Grace, dear, you've been running around trying to get this wagon train under way for weeks. We can eat, get to know Mr. Blake a bit better, and then the two of you can retire to the study to work. How's that sound, Dahl?"

"Sounds perfect," Dahlia replied agreeably. "What do you think, Mr. Blake?"

Grace dearly hoped he'd decline.

"Sounds fine," he answered. His eyes unreadable, he turned to Grace. "What about you, Miss Atwood?"

She was certain he'd accepted just to vex her. "It seems I have no choice," she stated evenly, while glowering pointedly at her aunts. However, they weren't paying her a bit of attention; they were too busy staring up at the Texan.

"How about seven?" Grace asked him.

"Seven it is," he told her.

After being given the address and directions to the house, he told the aunts, "Thanks for the invite. I'll see you tomorrow." He then turned to Grace. "How about I pick up that contract, then?"

"That would be fine."

He nodded her way and headed for the church door.

After he disappeared, the aunts were still staring at the door. Tulip waxed wistfully, "Now, Dahl, that was a good-looking young man. Did you see those shoulders?"

Dahlia nodded. "Sure did. I wonder if his father is still living? Maybe we'll be lucky and learn he's a widower."

"Wouldn't hurt to ask," her sister reasoned.

Grace dropped down into the nearest pew and put her head in her hands.

Grace's afternoon meeting with caterer Otis Hooper and his solicitor about his bank loan did not go well. For weeks now he'd been trying to bully her into lowering the interest. Today, he'd demanded to speak with a *male* bank representative because he didn't believe Grace knew what she was doing. Holding onto her temper, Grace firmly pointed out that *she* was the bank's president and lending officer, and that Hooper would deal with her or no one at all. The confrontation became so heated, Hooper threatened to take his substantial accounts elsewhere, but Grace didn't back down. She knew that there were few White banks willing to do business with Blacks, and those that did charged a far higher lending rate, so calling his bluff, Grace walked over to her office door and opened it wide.

Hooper sat there a moment as if his glare alone would make her change her mind, but when it didn't, he and his man picked up their papers and stormed out.

Later, after their departure, Lionel Rowe stuck his head around her office door. "How're you doing?"

A dejected Grace looked up. "As well as can be expected, I suppose. Could you hear all the yelling?"

"Clearly, but I'm very proud of you. Your father Elliot would be, too. You didn't buckle."

"But he's threatened to take his accounts elsewhere."

"Don't worry about that. He always threatened Elliot, too. He's simply testing you."

"Do you think so?"

Lionel nodded his graying head. "He'll be back in a couple of days, ready to sign anything you want. He may be bull-headed, but he's not stupid. You'll see."

But Grace wasn't so sure. All the way home in the hired hack, her worry about having driven away one of the bank's wealthiest depositors warred with her anger over his insulting attitude. How in the world were women to succeed if they were expected to pick up their skirts and run every time a man bellowed?

Now, up in her bedroom, looking through her wardrobe for something to wear to dinner, she had yet another trial to face: Jackson Blake. Upon her arrival home, the aunts had ordered her to change out of the brown walking suit she'd worn to work, and to put on something a bit more suitable for hostessing before Blake arrived. Grace's arguments that she didn't need to dress for dinner in order to entertain him fell on deaf ears. Tulip informed her that no well-raised woman greeted guests dressed in her work clothes, be she washerwoman, seamstress, or bank owner. Of course Dahlia had agreed wholeheartedly, so a disgruntled Grace had trudged up to her bedroom like a sullen adolescent to change clothes.

The bath she'd taken after coming upstairs had helped to melt away the day's tension, leaving her less wound up and angry, but as Grace continued to search through her dresses, she dearly wished her aunts had spent last evening with their new beaus, the Henderson twins instead of coming to her meeting at the church. Had they done so, they'd've never met Blake, and none of this would be necessary.

Grace finally made a decision and slipped the choice on. She then studied herself in the large standing mirror. The dress, made of grosgrain silk, was charcoal gray and had a line of tiny jet buttons up the front of the close-fitting high-collared bodice. It had long sleeves edged delicately with lace and an upswept skirt. The dress was one of her best, and as she adjusted the fall of the skirt, she approved of her reflection. The black Fedora slippers on her feet were made of the finest Curaçao leather and sported a hand-beaded coxcomb bow across the slightly pointed toe. The little Louis XV heel raised her height by an inch or two. For tonight, she'd abandoned her pulled-back no-nonsense hairstyle in favor of a more femininely curled upsweep, and she let trail two soft curls down her temples. She looked fashionable and self-assured, and vowed that the handsome Jackson Blake would hold no power over her tonight. They'd eat, they'd talk, and that would be that.

Grace leaned closer to the mirror to apply a touch of rouge to her brown cheeks and a dab of paint to her lips. What was it about him that made her feel so at odds with herself? She reasoned that it might be because most of the men in her circle were docile, mannerly gentlemen who didn't dare step on a woman's tender sensibilities, but Blake didn't seem to be cut from that cloth. She still couldn't believe how he'd marched into the church last night and declared himself the wagon master without saying a word to her about it beforehand. He was going to be trouble—handsome trouble, but trouble just the same.

Grace took one last look at herself and headed toward her bedroom door. If she didn't know better, she'd swear her aunts were playing matchmaker, but she was certain they knew she'd sworn off men. The liaison with Garth had proven to be a terrible mistake, and Grace never made the same mistake twice. Blake's visit was nothing more than a business meeting. There would be no murmuring kisses, no tumbles on the bed, and no broad, distracting ebony shoulders. She didn't want or need a man in her life. Not now—not ever.

While the aunts saw to the final food preparations, Grace set the table. The aunts had insisted upon using the best china and silver. Grace thought they were going a bit overboard for such a simple affair, but she knew better than to say anything, and so set the table according to their wishes.

When Grace finished, she stepped back and viewed her handiwork. Overboard or not, it was a beautifully set table. A crystal vase of multicolored spring flowers centered the white cloth and the sparkling place settings, adding an elegant touch.

She turned as her aunts entered the dining room. Tulip held a tray of sliced ham and Dahlia followed, carrying a bowl of her famous potato salad.

"Beautiful table, Grace," a smiling Tulip said, then set the tray down.

"The flowers are lovely, too," Dahlia echoed. "Vanessa taught you well, my dear."

Vanessa had been Grace's mother, and flowers had been one of Vanessa Atwood's passions. From spring to late fall, Vanessa deemed no table setting complete unless it contained a vase of blooms from her gardens. After Vanessa's death, Grace continued the practice because it seemed to keep her mother's spirit close by.

Grace turned her thoughts away from the melancholy memories the flowers evoked and directed her attention to her aunts. They were dressed for entertaining. Tulip had on blue silk and her sister had chosen a dark green. They'd both had glorious heads of lush red hair in their youth, a legacy passed down from an Irish slaveowner, but now, in the twilight of their years, silver had replaced the vivid coloring. Grace asked a question that she'd been wanting an answer to since Blake's visit to her office. "May I ask why you've taken such a shine to Blake?"

"It isn't often such a handsome man graces our table," Tulip replied.

"And if he's a bounder, we need to know from the outset so you can hire someone else," Dahlia added practically.

Grace thought that made sense, but still had a feeling the aunts were up to something else entirely. "So you're not matchmaking?"

Dahlia laughed. "Of course not. This is strictly a get-acquainted dinner. Isn't it, Tulip?"

"Dahl's right. Strictly business."

They both looked quite innocent, but the sound of the door chime prevented Grace from interrogating them further.

Tulip exclaimed, "Oh, he's here. Grace, dear, *you* go to the door. Dahl and I will finish bringing out the food."

They headed back to the kitchen.

When Grace opened the door, the sight of him standing there so tall and handsome with his wide-brimmed hat in his hand made her heart skip a beat. Once again, he was dressed like a man of the West. Beneath his long black coat she could see a gray shirt, a pair of black trousers, and a beautiful black leather vest detailed with silver. His dark face looked freshly shaven, and the devilish beard and mustache had been trimmed. His handsomeness exuded a manly power that commanded a woman's attention. "Good evening, Mr. Blake."

He nodded, saying, "Evening, Miss Atwood."

Forcing herself to look away lest she drown in his eyes, she stepped aside so he could enter the house. "Were the directions helpful?"

"Very. I had no problems."

"Good. Hand me your coat and hat."

She hung them on the peg near the door. "My aunts are waiting. This way, please."

Jackson followed her, feasting his eyes on the soft sway of her walk. She looked fine in the gray dress, mighty fine, he thought to himself. The curled upswept hair made her seem more like a woman and less like the bossy banker he'd been treated to so far. He cast an eye around the surroundings. The modest house with its paintings and good furniture seemed like a natural setting for Grace. She'd impressed him as a cultured, well-to-do woman, and her home reflected that.

After welcoming pleasantries were shared with the aunts, everyone went into the dining room. Blake helped the aunts with their chairs and his gentlemanly manners earned him a smile from them both.

A seated Tulip looked over at Grace and directed, "Grace, dear, why don't you sit there, and Mr. Blake can sit beside you."

Grace would've preferred to sit on the far end of the table, but moved to the chair Tulip indicated.

As she pulled out her chair, Blake came up behind her, enveloping her in his body's heat and the faint spicy scent of his cologne. "Let me help you with that."

Once again finding herself lost in the eddy of his gaze, Grace shook herself free and replied, "Thank you."

As he sat down beside her, Grace swore she'd cut off both of her hands if they didn't stop shaking.

Dahlia took her linen napkin from the table and spread it across her lap, saying "Now, isn't this nice?"

Grace smiled politely.

Tulip said grace, and afterward, everyone helped themselves to the aunts' fare. Tonight's menu consisted of succulent slices of spiced ham, potato salad, and steaming fragrant mustards. Dahlia's dinner rolls were light as clouds and as always seemed to melt in Grace's mouth. Savoring that first bite, Grace sighed pleasurably, but didn't realize she'd made the sound aloud until Blake looked her way.

Jackson wondered if she remembered giving that same throaty sigh the night he'd kissed her. Probably not, he answered himself, and if she did, she certainly wouldn't want to be reminded.

Thinking the look he'd given her was one of censure because of the sounds of pleasure she'd just made, Grace apologized. "I know ladies aren't supposed to make noises at the table, but Dahlia makes the best rolls I've ever tasted."

His eyes were lit with humor. "I understand. They *are* good."

Dahlia buttered a roll and said, "When Grace was ten, she could eat a dozen of my rolls in one sitting."

"Never gained a pound," Tulip added, as she forked up a portion of her sister's potato salad.

Before any more of her history could be revealed, Grace turned the conversation to safer realms. "How long ago did you leave Texas, Mr. Blake?"

"Almost ten years ago. Came east after my father's death."

"Any other family?"

"An adopted brother. Mother died of cholera when I was still young."

"Sorry to hear that," Tulip put in genuinely, adding, "Grace grew up without her mother too."

Grace could see the question in his eyes, but rather than elaborate, she focused on cutting into a slice of ham.

Jackson sensed Grace's withdrawal and wondered how old she'd been at her mother's passing. Jackson had been so young when his own mother died that he had no memories of her. Judging by Grace's silence, she'd been older.

"How long do you think the wagon train will take to get to Kansas City?" Tulip asked, interrupting his thoughts.

"I'd like to try and do it in thirty to thirty-five days," he replied, before taking a sip of the water in the glass by his plate.

They spent the remainder of the dinner talking about the wagon train's journey, but as the dinner concluded and the apple pie and ice cream were placed on the table for dessert, Grace's thoughts on the journey were set aside. Her awareness of Blake took its place. All evening she'd been trying to pretend that tonight's meal was no different from any other meal she'd shared with the aunts, but it was a lie, and she knew it. Her vow not to be moved by Blake's presence had proven to be as worthless as Confederate money. She was as aware of him as she was of her own heartbeat. She found herself covertly watching the long, dark fingers of his hands, the cut of his ebony jaw, the way he smiled at the aunts. She listened to the varying intonations of his voice, inhaled the faint scent of his cologne, and hastily looked elsewhere whenever his eyes strayed her way. At one point during the meal, they'd both reached at the same time to pass Tulip the plate of rolls and their shoulders had brushed inadvertently. Now, nearly twenty minutes later, Grace could still feel the heat of his arm against her own. Jackson Blake was dizzying, powerful, and more man than she'd ever met in her life.

At the conclusion of dessert, the aunts refused to let Grace help them clear the table.

Dahlia told her, "You and Mr. Blake have business to discuss."

"Yes, but I can certainly help with this first."

"Go on, Grace," Tulip said, as she began picking up the dessert plates. "We're fine here. I'll bring you in some coffee in a bit or two."

Grace surrendered and gestured to Blake to follow her from the dining room.

Grace ushered him into the study that had once been her father's. After his death late last fall, the space had become hers. It had taken her weeks to get up the courage to change the room's physical appearance. She'd wanted his spirit to remain beside her and feared that boxing up his things and storing them away would somehow remove his memory, too. She'd loved her father deeply and he'd loved her. He'd been her only parent for over fifteen years, and her grief had eased only a tiny bit.

In the end, she stored most of his personal belongings in the attic, but other articles remained: his spectacle case still lay atop the desk where he'd placed it, and the finely etched globes he liked to collect were still positioned tastefully around the room. His imported Cuban humidor lay in its customary spot atop a small Queen

Anne table, and beside it sat the large white cup he drank his morning coffee from each day.

Jackson took a seat on one of the finely upholstered chairs and glanced around the room. All the dark polished wood gave off a man's feel. This didn't feel like a woman's space.

"This was my father's study," she explained, as she took a seat behind the big cherrywood desk. "He died last November."

Jackson's keen instincts had served him well during his lawman days, and although he no longer wore a star, he was glad to know that his sense of people and situations continued to be strong. "I'm sorry for your loss," he said genuinely.

"I loved him very much," she offered, then gathering herself, said, "Let's get down to business, Mr. Blake. Here's the list of supplies Mr. Emerson compiled before his untimely death. See if there's anything you might want to add."

He wondered if she were really as strong as she appeared, but he took the ledger from her and began to look at the items listed. "Who's Mr. Emerson?"

"The man I originally hired as wagon master. He was killed a few days ago in a knife fight."

"Sorry to hear it," he voiced without looking up. "How much of this stuff do you already have?" Listed were items such as barrels, ropes, tack, cookware, canvas, and many other various items both big and small.

"I've purchased most of what's on the list. Everything's being stored in my godfather's warehouse over in Evanston."

"Looks like Emerson knew what he was doing. Can't think of anything else I'd add, at least, not off the top of my head."

When he handed the ledger back to her, she put it

back on her desk and said, "Tomorrow, I've an appointment to look at horses and mules."

"Do you know anything about horses and mules?"

"Not as much as I need to know, I'm sure, but I'll manage."

"Why do you want to travel by wagon?"

"Jim Crow."

He understood now. "How many ladies did you say were making the trip?"

"Thirty to thirty-five."

She was as poised and as elegant as any woman he'd ever met. With Grace dressed as she was, and with her hair rising softly from her face, he found it hard to imagine her covered with the dirt and grime they would encounter once the journey got under way. "Are you sure you're cut out for this?"

"What do you mean?"

"You just don't look the adventurous type, that's all. There's going to be flies and mud and snakes—"

"You think I'm better suited for what, a drawing room?"

"Frankly, yes. A woman like you should be gracing some wealthy man's table, not traveling across country behind a train of mules."

"Women are doing many things these days, Mr. Blake. Gracing a man's table is not my life's dream." *At least not anymore,* she reminded herself. Aloud, she continued, "I appreciate your concern, but I'll be fine. I've your contract here somewhere."

A modern woman, he thought sarcastically, but admittedly she was a beautiful one. The copper brown eyes went perfectly with her sandy-colored skin and rich auburn hair. He wondered what she looked like with her hair down. Stunning, he'd be willing to bet. He could almost imagine her standing before him dressed in her nightclothes, her hair free and tousled from lovemaking. The high-collared gray dress with its long sleeves fit snugly over her lovely bosom, emphasizing her feminine curves very attractively.

She found the contract and took a moment to write something on the top sheet. As she moved the diamond-tipped quill pen over the paper, he noted her slim graceful fingers and well-manicured nails. Grace Atwood was a perfect example of the educated and cultured members of the race often referred to as "representative Blacks."

Finding himself attracted to her surprised him for a number of reasons. First, he preferred his women tall and statuesque. Grace Atwood was neither. Jackson also avoided dallying with women of good family because they expected marriage when all was said and done, and that was a state of bondage he had no intention of entering, mainly because every good woman he'd had the opportunity to meet seemed to want to change him as if he were a floor that needed to be planed and sanded. Frankly, he liked himself just the way he was. As a consequence, he preferred to share his favors with discreet independent women who didn't want or expect promises or commitments but enjoyed the lusty games of passion as much as he. "Do you have any siblings?"

She raised her copper eyes to his. "No. I'm an only child."

"Were you lonely growing up?"

She shrugged. "Sometimes, if there were no playmates around, but I never lacked for love. My parents kept me too busy to be lonely."

"Doing what?"

"Charity work, school, traveling. My mother's family comes from Boston, and her father and grandfather sailed and built merchant ships. She'd been all over the world by the time she and my father met."

"How much of the world have you seen?"

"Quite a bit. Europe. Cuba. Egypt."

"Which was your favorite?"

"Cuba. I loved the colors, the markets, the music. Our race has had a strong influence on the lives of the Cuban people. Have you ever traveled there?"

"No. I've never left the States."

"I see."

An awkwardness seemed to settle over the room. Grace, at a loss as to what to say next, decided getting back to the matter at hand might be best. She handed him the contract. "Here's the contract for your services. Look it over, if you would, please."

He scanned the document slowly.

After a few moment of silence, Grace asked, "Do you see anything you wish changed?"

"Nope. Everything looks to be in order."

"And the pay?"

"The pay is fine."

"Good, then if you would affix your signature at the bottom—"

He interrupted her, "Before I sign, we need to get one thing clear, though."

His serious tone caught her attention. "And that is?"

"If I'm going to be the wagon master, you're going to have to let me be in charge."

Grace asked slowly, "Meaning?"

"On decisions affecting the train, I have the last word."

She stilled a moment and surveyed him. "On everything?"

"Everything. You're not hiring me to be second guessed, are you?"

Grace had to confess truthfully, "I hadn't really thought about it, but I suppose the answer is no."

"Good, because if you did, we should tear this up now," he said, indicating the contract.

"But suppose I disagree with this, 'last word' of yours?"

"Unless you can bring me around to your way of thinking, then we'll agree to disagree, but my way goes."

Grace wasn't sure she liked this high-handed attitude, but she *had* hired him for his expertise. "Fine, but please know that if and when I disagree, I intend to say so."

"Wouldn't have it any other way. In fact, I'm betting we wind up arguing a lot."

"Why?"

"Because you're probably not used to a man ordering you around."

She wondered if he were deliberately baiting her. "I've no trouble being instructed by someone with more knowledge, Mr. Blake, be they male or female. Now, are you signing on or not?" Grace was trying her best to keep her temperature under control.

He signed, and then signed another copy she'd had drawn up for him to keep for his own records. When the formalities were over, she said politely, "Thank you, Mr. Blake."

"You're welcome."

Luckily, at that moment, Tulip came in carrying the promised coffee. Her entrance seemed to drain some of the tension.

"Here you are," she called out cheerily, as she set the tray with its silver service down on the small Queen Anne table near the windows. "How's the planning coming?"

"Quite well," Grace answered. "Thanks for the coffee."

"You're welcome. The kitchen's all clean, so Dahl

and I are retiring to our rooms. We hope to see you again soon, Mr. Blake."

He stood. "I hope so, too. It's been a pleasure, Mrs. Mays."

"Good night, Grace."

"Night, Aunt Tulip. I'll look in on you when I'm done here."

Her exit left them alone once more. "Would you care for coffee, Mr. Blake?"

"Sounds good."

Grace walked over to the table and poured them both a cup. He joined her and took the cup she offered.

"There's cream and sugar."

"No, I take it black."

He sipped and found it not bad, for "back east" coffee. Out west, coffee had strength, character. Here it tasted civilized.

Grace took a few sips. "How much feed do you think we'll need for the animals during the trip?"

He responded by saying, "Relax for a minute. Drink your coffee. Are you always so diligent?"

Her answer came easily. "I try to be. A woman in business has much to prove. If we aren't diligent, we aren't taken seriously."

"I see. Well, you don't have to prove anything to me. I took you seriously the moment you hit me with that weapon you call a handbag."

She had the decency to look embarrassed. "I was trying to protect myself."

"So you said," he replied, his manner light.

"Well, it isn't often I'm tumbled into a strange man's bed. You startled me."

"I promise, I'll give you fair warning next time."

The promise in his eyes made her hand shake enough to send her coffee sloshing over the top of the china cup.

"Oh dear," she said, eyeing the drops of coffee dotting the bosom of her gray dress.

Blake extracted a clean handkerchief from the inner pocket of his vest and handed it to her.

Grateful, she began blotting the dampness. "Thank you."

"My pleasure." He spoke wondering if she knew how fascinated he was by the sight of her slowly dabbing his handkerchief over her lovely curves. Realizing he was becoming aroused by the innocent yet intimate display, he turned his back and drained his cup. To further distract himself he poured himself another cup and drank it while he focused on the night scene outside the window.

"I'll have this laundered and returned to you," she pledged, indicating his handkerchief.

"That would be fine."

What would be finer, he mused, would be for him to forget about desiring her, because it would lead nowhere. Women like her had no business with men like him. "Do you have a beau?"

The question caught Grace off guard. She raised her eyes to his. "No," she answered quietly.

Her soft-spoken response made him believe there was more to her answer, but he didn't press. By the time the wagon train reached its destination he'd know all he needed to know about the beautifully endowed Grace Atwood. "What made you want to go into banking?"

Glad that he'd changed the subject, Grace replied, "My father founded the bank. Succeeding him was a natural event."

"Maybe, if you'd been a son. Daughters are supposed to marry and give their fathers grandchildren."

"Says who?" Grace asked, her eyebrow arched. "This

is the nineteenth century, Mr. Blake. Women have choices these days, and I chose banking."

"Do men give you a hard time?"

"Is the world round?"

He grinned. "That bad?"

"Many refuse to believe I'm qualified. This afternoon, in fact, a customer threatened to take his money elsewhere because I wouldn't be bullied into lowering the note on his loan."

Because so many men had been killed during the war, women all over the nation were taking on responsibilities and occupations once considered men's work, work like doctoring, teaching—and yes, banking. Grace was certain the country would be better off due to the ideas and diligence brought to the workplace by the female population, but there were many men and women who did not share her view. "Do you think a woman should be able to do whatever her intellect calls her to?" she asked him then.

He shrugged. "I try and stay away from debates like that, Miss Atwood. Most of the women I know are happy just being old-fashioned women."

"And that means what?"

Jackson felt as if he'd just stepped into a bear trap and he didn't know whether to go forward or backward. "Well, you know—serving their men, having babies, that kind of thing."

"And you say these women are happy?"

"Sure."

Her next question was asked softly. "Have you ever asked them?"

The look in her eyes dared him to be truthful. "No," he had to admit, while wondering how much tighter the bear trap would get before she'd let him escape. He made a mental note never to get suckered into a conversation like this again, not with her.

"You might be surprised by their answer, Mr. Blake," she replied, as she sipped at her coffee with a small smile of satisfaction on her lips.

"Why no beaus?" he asked, wanting to bring her down a peg or two.

Grace thought he'd given her a low blow, but she raised her chin and replied, "Because I have opinions and the education to back them up. Men seem to find the combination unsettling."

"At least you're truthful."

"I am that," she agreed, "but men don't care for that trait, either."

He chuckled. She was a handful. It would take a very special man to appreciate all she had to offer.

They spent the rest of the evening going over some of the forms filled out by the candidates and managed to do it without arguing. When the clock in the hall struck nine, Grace thought it best to bring the evening to a close due to the lateness of the hour, and he agreed.

She walked him to the front door and waited while he donned his coat.

As he took his hat down from one of the pegs, he asked, "What time are you going to see about the animals in the morning?"

"Early."

"How early is early?"

"I hope to be leaving here around seven."

"I'll be here at six-thirty."

Grace cocked her head. "I don't remember asking you along."

"Are you the one who just admitted not knowing as much about horseflesh as you should?"

Unhappy about being tripped up by her own words, she replied coolly, "Yes."

"Well, the last thing we need are a bunch of broken down nags that can't even get us out of Illinois."

"Mr. Blake—"

"Six-thirty, Miss Atwood, and be ready, please. I don't want to spend an hour waiting for you to decide what hat to wear."

Grace's eyes widened.

"See you in the morning." And he was gone.

Snarling, Grace closed the door.

# Chapter 3

True to his word, he arrived the next morning at exactly six-thirty. Grace greeted him at the door dressed and ready to go. She stepped back to let him enter and said coolly, "As you can see, I already have on my hat."

Figuring he'd earned that crack, Jackson stepped inside. While she closed the door, he studied the olive green hat on her head, the full green skirt and matching jacket, and the black high-heeled boots. "I thought we were going to look over some horses."

"We are."

"You look like you're going to tea."

Out west, women wore hats to protect them from the sun or to church; here, women wore confections. "How would you describe that?" he asked, holding her faintly hostile eyes.

"My hat?"

"Yes, your hat."

"It's olive colored and made of fine Milan straw. It's medium high and has a round top. The material draped around the brim and crown is made of crêpe, and the ribbons and bow on the front are faced with black velvet and gimp."

"That's what I thought."

Grace didn't care for his sarcasm. "Mr. Blake, I don't care if you dislike my hat. You asked that I not make you wait, and I haven't. I didn't ask you to accompany me in the first place, if you remember correctly."

Realizing she was right on the edge of shouting, Grace lowered her voice so as not to awaken the still sleeping aunts. "Shall we go now, or do I need to describe my walking suit and boots, too?"

"No," he replied.

Neither of them noticed Dahlia standing on the stairs until she forcefully cleared her throat. "Good morning," she announced.

Grace dragged her still angry eyes from Blake and saw that her aunt, dressed in a morning gown and with her hair still in curlers, looked quite perturbed. "Good morning, Aunt Dahl. I hope we didn't wake you."

"No apologies needed. I love being awakened by young people arguing over hats."

That said, she descended the stairs and walked off toward the kitchen.

"I hope you're happy," Grace whispered at him harshly.

"I wasn't the one shouting."

"No, you were simply the one who started this."

Dahlia came back through the front room carrying a cup of coffee poured from the pot Grace had left on the stove. She'd obviously heard them starting up again because she said sternly, "My sister is still sleeping. Don't you two have someplace to be?"

"Sorry, Aunt Dahl," Grace offered, while shooting daggers at Blake. "We're leaving right now."

"Good," she said, climbing the stairs. "Because if you wake up Tulip, I'll have both your hides."

Grace grabbed up her cloak and handbag and stalked to the door with him close behind.

He politely handed her into the covered buggy he'd borrowed from Sunshine. After taking his seat he picked up the reins. "Where to?"

She told him, then withdrew into a testy silence.

The trip took them outside the city. Grace had lived in large cities all her life, and even though she enjoyed the excitement and the hustle and bustle, she always found the open countryside a joy, and she could feel some of her testiness draining away. The pastoral surroundings also reminded her of the horseback rides she'd taken with her parents when she was younger. She'd learned to sit a mount almost as soon as she could walk, and loved riding to this day. Back then, riding fed both her wild spirit and her imagination. Sometimes she pretended to be a member of one of the Civil War's Black cavalry units and she and her mounted companions would be riding hard to Richmond to free it from the Rebs. At other times she would be on a spy raid with Harriet Tubman and they would be racing back to Union lines with vital information needed by General Montgomery.

"Did you hear what I said?"

His question brought her back to the present. "I'm sorry. No."

"I said, I apologize for taking digs at your hat back there. I didn't get much sleep last night and I suppose I took it out on you."

Grace studied him a moment. He looked sincere, and because she'd no desire to spend the day shouting at him, said, "Apology accepted," then added, "I hope your restlessness wasn't caused by the aunts' cooking last night?"

"No, nothing like that."

In reality, he'd tossed and turned 'til dawn's early light because of the redheaded woman seated at his side. Now that he'd made up his mind to return to Texas, he was finding it hard to concentrate on a plan to clear his name due to a rising preoccupation with his lovely employer. Who'd've thought he'd develop a hankering for a fine, upstanding daughter of Black representative society? She was everything he didn't want in a woman, from her short stature to her modern ways, but she drew him nonetheless. It was a distraction he didn't need.

Unaware of his inner battle, Grace said, "This is beautiful countryside. I used to ride out here with my parents when I was younger."

"Horseback?"

She nodded.

He looked away from the road a moment. "You ride?"

Grace smiled at the surprise on his face. "Yes, why wouldn't I?"

"Most city women prefer hacks and carriages."

"Yes, we do, but many do ride."

"Can you drive a wagon, too?"

"I've no idea. I've never driven one."

He didn't know why he found her admission surprising. She was a banker after all, and beneath the fine silk and lace probably lay a woman of many accomplishments.

She went on, "When I was younger we rode quite a bit, but after my father started the bank he had less time.

Then, once my mother died—I kept riding but he rarely came along."

Her parents had loved each other immensely. In an age when arranged marriages were still common, they'd had a love match and didn't care who knew. On more than a few occasions the adolescent Grace had come into a room to find her smiling mother standing in the circle of her father's arms. She'd even seen them sneaking kisses in the kitchen. Watching them bask in their love made Grace grow up wanting to have a marriage just as special, but now she knew it would never be.

When Grace and Blake arrived at their destination, the livestock owner, an old man named Drain, wasn't the least bit friendly. Grace had no idea if his attitude stemmed from race, or if he was just ornery by nature. However, when Grace told him how many mules and horses she'd need, the man all but tripped over himself in an effort to accommodate her, then personally drove them out to view his stock.

Grace knew a bit about good sound horseflesh but Jackson knew more. He looked for youth, strong straight legs and clear eyes in the animals Drain had for sale. He felt the musculature behind their necks and assessed the quality of their mouths and teeth. His knowledge made Grace glad he'd come along.

It took almost two hours to choose and tag all the animals they wanted, but when they were done, Grace knew it had been two hours well spent, in spite of the muddy pasture and the horse pies.

With that portion of the task completed, Grace and Jackson were driven back to Drain's home to conclude the written portion of the transaction. He took them in through the back door to his small kitchen and gestured them to the chairs ringing the table in the center of the room.

After writing up the bill of sale, he handed it to Jackson who immediately passed it to Grace. "She's the one you're doing business with. Not me."

The old man looked skeptical. "Well, I don't know. Never done business with a female before."

Grace had spent the last two hours walking around a mud-filled pasture, pushing and prodding mules and horses that smelled like mules and horses, and she was in no mood for close-minded shenanigans. "Mr. Drain, profit has no gender in the business world. If it does in yours, I'll take my gold elsewhere."

She stood intending to leave.

Drain quickly threw up a halting hand and chuckled. "Hey, hold on there, missy. I ain't saying I wouldn't. I just said I never did. Sit. Please?"

He then swung his humor-filled blue eyes over to Jackson. "She always this touchy?"

Jackson shrugged. "Far as I know. I'm thinking it might be because she's a banker."

"A *what?*"

Grace replied, "A banker, Mr. Drain. Are we going to complete this transaction or not?"

"Yes, ma'am," he said, looking up at her wondrously.

Grace read over the bill of sale he'd drawn up and found something she thought needed clarification. "Mr. Drain, it says here you agree to supply the animals, but there's nothing that specifically speaks to the animals we chose. I'm sure you're an honest man, but the way this bill is worded, you could send me a bunch of half-blind nags and I'd still be obligated to pay."

There was silence as he assessed her.

Jackson thought she had a very good point.

"You really think I'd do that?" Drain asked with a crafty smile on his weathered face.

"No," Grace countered easily, "but I need to be clear on what I'm buying."

He assessed her for a few moments more. "Why do you need so many animals in the first place?"

"I'm putting together a wagon train to Kansas."

"Why don't you just take the real train? Be easier."

"Jim Crow."

He held her unwavering eyes. "I see." His manner turned serious. "Well, hand me back that bill and let's see if we can't put it down clear."

"Thank you."

Taking the bill from her hand, Mr. Drain glanced over at Blake. "She your woman?"

"Nope."

"Well, if I was colored and fifty years younger, she'd be mine. She's something."

"That she is," Jackson responded, looking over at her with glowing eyes. "That she is."

The ride home was rocky over the uneven road, but Grace didn't mind; procuring the animals had been one of the last major items on her list. With Blake's help, the task had been relatively easy. "Thanks for your help back there."

"Anytime. Thank you for the business lesson. I liked the way you handled Mr. Drain. You got some style, lady."

Grace appreciated the compliment. "Being a female doesn't mean I'm gullible."

"I know it and Drain knows it now."

"I simply wanted to make sure he didn't send us a slew of old animals that couldn't even make it out of the state," she said, quoting Jackson's words.

He shot her a look that held a hint of amusement.

Smiling, she added, "Drain might've been an honest

man, but I wasn't willing to take the chance."

"You did right to call his hand."

Grace knew she didn't really need the Texan's approval, but it made her feel good, knowing he appreciated her keen business sense. Few men did.

"Where're you planning on setting up the bride camp?"

"My godfather, Martin Abbott, has some land about a day and a half's ride from the city and he's been gracious enough to let us use it until we are ready to leave. It's in a valley. There's a stream running nearby and an old church on the top of a rise with a working water pump."

"Sounds like you've got everything under control."

"I do. The last piece of the puzzle was you."

Reins in hand, Jackson looked her way. She'd proven her mettle to him in more ways than one today. Her suit was a mess after the trip to Drain's muddy pasture, and even though she'd stepped in enough horse pies to win a farm contest, she and that creation she called a hat still managed to appear elegant. She hadn't whined, complained, or even flinched during the two-hour task. "I'm beginning to think maybe you *are* cut out for this trip. You did well back there in the field."

"Oh, you expected me to spend the entire time tiptoeing through the mud holding my hems out of the way and squealing every time I brushed against one of the animals?"

He turned his eyes back to the road. "There you go, getting all puffed up again. I was trying to give you a compliment."

"Well, did you?" she asked, her eyes twinkling, knowing she'd put him on the spot.

"Frankly, I did. Yes," he confessed aloud, but inwardly he was wondering if she'd bring all that fire to a man's bed.

She asked, "Do you remember telling me, 'Don't judge until you know'?"

He didn't like being bitten by his own words, but she was right: he'd prejudged her in much the same she'd done him that night at the church. "Point taken. You've got mud on your nose."

Unsure she'd heard him correctly, she said, "Excuse me?"

He pulled back on the reins and stopped the team. Turning to her, he repeated, "I said, 'You have mud on your nose.'"

He pulled a clean handkerchief from the pocket of his duster. Pouring a bit of water on it from his canteen, he gently wiped away the spot of mud on the bridge of her freckle-dusted nose. Grace could feel herself trembling.

Jackson knew he had no business touching her, but he couldn't resist tracing a finger slowly over the tiny spots. "I like these . . ."

Grace managed to say, "When I was younger, I hated them. The boys at school called me dot-face . . ."

As their gazes held, it was as if the whole world suddenly went silent. Grace didn't hear the birdsong, or the sound of the breeze rustling the trees. She was aware of only two things: the powerful eddy in his dark eyes and the loud thumping of her own heart. When he leaned over and touched his lips to hers, he paused for a moment, raising his eyes to hers as if seeking permission to continue. She replied by touching his bearded cheek with all the wondrousness she felt, and it was all the answer he needed to lower his mouth to hers once again. When he finally drew away, she felt as if she were floating on air and her insides were humming like the last fading notes of a struck bell.

Jackson knew he had no business doing what he'd just done, but it wasn't anything he'd planned. Yes, he found her attractive, and yes, his desire for her seemed to be growing daily, but he was destined for Texas after escorting the brides to Kansas City and he didn't need to start something with her that he couldn't finish. "Let's get you home."

Still reeling from the moment, Grace thought that a splendid idea.

He pulled the team to a stop in front of the house, then looked her way. "I suppose I should apologize for what happened back there."

Feeling a bit awkward, Grace shook her head. "That— that isn't necessary. I could've stopped you." She finally found the courage to meet his eyes.

"I don't want you to think I'm going to make that a habit—kissing you, I mean."

"I understand, and I don't."

Contrary to his words, Jackson wanted to drag her back into his arms. He hadn't gotten nearly enough of Grace Atwood. "Let's get you to the door." He came around to her side of the buggy and opened it. Grace stepped down with her hand in his and tried to ignore the heat that seemed to burn through the fabric of her glove.

She said genuinely, "Thank you again for your help."

"You're welcome. I'll be in touch."

He touched his hat to her in departure, then got back in the buggy and drove away without a backward glance.

Grace spent Friday night and Saturday reading the questionnaires she'd gathered from the brides. She began by first separating the legibly written from the illegibly. Many of the women had a fine hand, but a few wrote no better than chickens. Some of the reasons cited for

wanting to go to Kansas ranged from the sheer adventure
of such a journey to a strong desire to start a family.
One woman, a graduate of Oberlin, hoped the colony
might need a teacher, while another wrote that she'd
been owned and trained in basic medicine by a doctor
during slavery and thought her nursing skills would be
an asset. Grace set those two aside for further review.

Another potential bride's sheet went into the discard
pile because she'd baldly penned a desire to marry the
richest man in the colony. Discarded too were the
women who listed their current occupation as saloon
hostess. Grace also set aside for further review applications of those who currently lived on farms, or were
seamstresses or otherwise gainfully employed, whether
they were washerwomen, domestics, or store clerks.

She tried to be as objective, yet as selective, as possible because her final decisions would impact the future
of many lives. The only time she applied whimsy to her
process was in her selection of a woman named Loreli
Winters. Miss Winters was a gambler by profession, a
truly unconventional occupation for a woman. Grace
doubted any of the men would be interested in claiming
a gambler bride but found the idea of including her in-
triguing. To Grace's way of thinking, a woman gambler
would have to be fearless by nature and very resourceful
in order to survive in such a male-dominated world, and
as a result, might be a unique asset to the wagon train.
She just hoped it wouldn't turn out to be a bad idea.

By Sunday after church she was bleary eyed from
poring over so much information. She'd whittled down
the pile to thirty-five and held another six in abeyance
in case one of the women chosen changed her mind.

Monday morning, Grace posted her list and then sent
the bank constable, Mitchell Jones, out to Sunshine's
Palace with a packet for Blake. Inside was a note in-

forming him that she'd made her final decision on the brides and that he was to meet her at the church Tuesday evening for the final meeting before the trip began. She also included an envelope that held a bank draft for the first half of Blake's pay. He'd get the balance once they reached Kansas City.

"Ladies, we need to get under way. We have a lot of territory to cover tonight."

The women had been visiting back and forth, but once Grace spoke they broke off their conversations and took seats at the tables set up in the church's basement. The women looked eager to begin, but as Grace called the roll of names it seemed five of the candidates were missing. "Does anyone know the women who aren't here tonight?" she asked.

A woman in the back, a brown-skinned giantess named Tess Dubois, stood. "Elvira Keppler got married over the weekend."

Grace let out an astonished laugh. "Married?"

"Yep. Her fiancé finally saw the light. When Elvira told him she was headed to Kansas to be a mail order bride, her news pushed him right off the fence and into the preacher's arms. She says to tell you thanks and Godspeed."

"Well," Grace stated, "I guess Elvira won't be joining us."

Everyone laughed. No one had any information on the other missing women, so Grace made a mental note to contact some of the alternates she'd chosen. She just hoped they were still interested. At the conclusion of the roll call, Grace invited each of the brides to stand and introduce herself to the group.

The woman who stood first was a short, bespectacled woman named Daisy Green. She was a bit older than some of the other brides but had been chosen for her farm background and her nursing skills with animals. Next stood Sarah Mitchell and her younger sister Molly. Sarah wore an ill-fitting wig, and her barrel-shaped body seemed about to burst from her gown. Molly, the thinner of the two, had features so sharp she resembled a crane. Both women were seamstresses and spoke in such haughty tones, Grace hoped she hadn't made a mistake in asking them along. Ignoring them for now, she turned her attention to the next woman rising to her feet.

"My name is Loreli Winters and I'm a gambler."

Loreli was fairly tall, had ivory-gold skin and a shrewd pair of golden brown eyes. Her bright green dress with its black satin trim had a neckline that was far too racy for the gathering, but the flashy gown appeared costly and she wore it with style. Grace also liked the little black felt hat perched atop Loreli's light brown curls.

Grace could see the Mitchell sisters disdainfully staring Loreli up and down. Evidently not liking what they saw, they immediately began whispering behind their hands. Grace didn't like their cattiness and was now certain the two were going to be trouble, but with five brides already unaccounted for, she didn't want to dismiss them and have to find yet two more replacements.

The introductions continued with Ruby O'Neal, a schoolteacher; Gertrude "Trudy" Berry, a washerwoman; young Fannie Ricks, a recent Oberlin graduate who explained why she wanted to go to Kansas this way: "All the men at home think I'm too intelligent to marry. It seems no one wants a smart wife."

Sitting next to Fannie was Zora Post, a twenty-five-year-old widow who'd gone from selling pepperpot on the streets of Philadelphia to owning three Chicago boardinghouses. She wanted to go to Kansas, she said,

"To have the babies I wasn't able to have because of my late husband Chester's untimely death."

Following Zora were women named Viola, Maggie, Georgia, and Susan; there was a Lena, a Priscilla, an Eleanor, and a Tamar. A Sylvia stood; a Pauline stood. Wilma Deets was a hairdresser, and Rhea Hancock bragged that she made the best dandelion wine north of the Mason–Dixon line. The introductions didn't end until every face had a name.

All in all, the women impressed Grace as good choices. They seemed eager and friendly. Other than the Mitchell sisters, there didn't seem to be a complainer or whiner in the lot.

Once the introductions were completed, Loreli Winters asked, "Is Mr. Blake joining us tonight, Miss Atwood?"

Grace answered with a shrug. "I thought he would be, but—"

"He certainly is a handsome devil," the teacher, Ruby O'Neal, tossed out.

"That he is," someone echoed. "If the men in Kansas turn out to be toads, can we draw straws for Mr. Blake instead?"

More laughter followed. Grace sensed the group growing closer, except for the Mitchell sisters. The seamstresses were sitting there with sour looks on their faces, but she didn't worry; they'd come around.

Next, Grace had everyone assemble around the large and very crudely drawn map she'd sketched on a large piece of brown butcher's paper. The map showed the valley and how she envisioned the camp might be set up. "How many of you have driven teams before?"

The spectacled Daisy Green shyly raised her hand as Grace had expected. She hadn't expected to see Oberlin graduate Fannie Ricks's hand, though. The woman looked too cultured. "My papa owns a livery," she said by way of explanation. "Didn't I put that on my sheet?"

Grace shook her head. "No."

"Then I'm sorry, Miss Atwood. I've been around horses all my life. Drove my first team at the age of ten."

A few of the other women raised their hands, including Loreli Winters. "I was owned by a colonel in Kentucky before the war. Horses, drinking, and gambling were all he knew."

Sarah Mitchell couldn't seem to contain her distaste any longer. "Miss Atwood, I must ask, are we really going to be subjected to a gambling woman in our midst? What type of man would want her as a bride?"

Before Grace could respond, Trudy Berry cracked, "Probably not the same man that'll want to marry you, so don't worry."

A few muffled giggles were heard, and Sarah drew herself up in outrage. Trudy looked back at Loreli and winked. Grace saw Loreli smile in reply.

Grace knew she had to quash this dissension before it began to fester. "Miss Mitchell, if you and your sister would rather not be a party to the journey—"

"Oh, no," Molly spoke up quickly, "I'm certain that isn't what Sister meant, is it?"

"Well—no," Sarah admitted, in response to her sister's pointed look. "Molly and I wish to go to Kansas. We're hoping to find two men able to meet our exacting standards."

Somebody snorted.

Grace fought to keep her smile from peeking out. "Then you won't mind traveling with the rest of the ladies?"

"No."

"Are you certain?"

"Yes."

"Good. Now, let's get back to the map."

They talked about a configuration for the many tents that would be their temporary homes and the equal division of chores. One of the women thought it would be nice if they had common meals in order to get to know one another better. Grace thought that a marvelous idea. The others did as well.

The washerwoman, Trudy Berry, asked, "For those of us who need extra money, can we take in laundry?"

"From outside the camp?" Grace asked.

The dark-skinned Trudy nodded.

Grace didn't see why not. "There's a small township nearby, and I see no reason why that can't be explored. The men in Kansas have sent me ample funds for outfitting the trip, but it never hurts to have coin of your own."

"Amen," someone declared.

As she was winding up, Jackson walked in. He was dressed in his usual black attire beneath the sweeping black duster, and his dark handsomeness touched every woman in the room. "Evening, ladies. Miss Atwood."

Grace nodded. "Mr. Blake."

The rest of the ladies greeted him with hellos and smiles.

Grace looked up at the man who'd kissed her so tenderly and she tried to put the lingering echoes out of her mind. "I thought maybe you'd forgotten about us."

"Forget about my brides? Never. I just had a hard time making my way across town. Couldn't find a hack anywhere, wound up walking part of the way. What did I miss?"

Grace filled him in. "We're five women short. We can account for one—she got married this weekend."

"Really? What about the others?"

Grace shrugged. "No idea, but if I don't hear from

them by Friday, I'll contact the alternates."

"That's all you can do," he said. He looked around. "Is it too late for introductions?"

Before Grace could reply, the women rose one by one and gave Jackson their names. Even the Mitchell sisters were smiling broadly. He responded to each bride with a nod or a hello.

"When will we be moving to the camp?" one of the women asked Grace.

"Monday morning, unless you hear otherwise."

"So soon?" Loreli asked.

Grace nodded. "We've much to do and to learn before we leave Illinois and the sooner we begin the sooner we can get underway."

Grace looked around. "Are there any more questions on the campsite?"

No one had any. "Then I think it's time you ladies met the men who are wanting to be your husbands."

From a large portfolio Grace withdrew the stack of photographs and portraits of the Kansas men and spread them out on the table. "By all means, please take your time in deciding. There are short biographies on the backs of each man's likeness. If you see someone you feel strongly about and wish to make your decision now, go right ahead. If some of you prefer to wait until we get to the camp to decide, that's fine also."

That said, Grace stepped back out of the way as the women descended upon the pictures. While the brides viewed the choices, Grace and Jackson took a seat at a table away from the fray.

He told her, "All the ladies seem to be real fine choices. I think you chose well."

Grace appreciated his comments, but she did have a few misgivings. "I'm a bit concerned about the Mitchells. They wanted to know if they were really going to have to be subjected to a gambling woman in their midst all the way to Kansas."

"Which one's a gambler?"

"Loreli Winters."

He turned to view Loreli for a moment. "Why'd you pick a gambler?"

She shrugged. "My instinct says she might be a valuable addition."

"Your instincts," he echoed doubtfully.

"Yes, I've always wanted to learn to play poker."

He shook his head and smiled. "And the Mitchell sisters objected to her coming along."

"They did until I asked if they wanted to stay behind."

"Good for you. What did they say?"

"No."

"Well, if they get too offended, we can always drop them off at a town somewhere on the way."

"Let's hope it won't come to that."

As their gazes held, Grace could feel herself succumbing to his spell again. She swung her attention away. "I need to see how the women are doing."

She hastened over to the gathering and therefore didn't see the knowing look in his eyes as he watched her depart.

Putting Jackson out of her mind for now, Grace meandered through the group listening to myriad conversations and stopping here and there to see how the choosing up was going. The Kansas men were letting the women do the selecting and vowed to honor whatever choices were made. Grace found the plan a lot more satisfying than having the women looked over like slaves on a block once they reached Kansas.

Schoolteacher Ruby O'Neal asked, "What if we don't find a man to suit, Miss Atwood?"

Grace hadn't really dealt with that possibility. "Well, I suppose any woman who can't will have to pay her own way. The Kansas men are only sponsoring women who'll marry."

"So the choice has to be made by when?"

"The day we arrive at the camp."

Ruby scanned the faces of the two portraits she held in her hands. "Okay, Miss Atwood, I'll decide."

Grace smiled sympathetically.

The women spent another thirty minutes or so evaluating their choices. More than half went over to Grace to state their picks formally and have the names of their chosen mates written into her ledger.

"Can we keep the portraits of the men we've picked?" asked one woman as she scanned the photograph in her hand.

"Certainly," Grace replied. "It'll be a good way to recognize them once we get to Kansas."

In response to Grace's words, a soft rustle of excitement flowed from the group as women compared photographs. Tess Dubois stuck the small face of her chosen mate down into the well of her ample bosom. "So he'll get used to sleeping there ahead of time," she told the group. The women howled, then Grace howled, too, when she realized Tess had chosen Grace's cousin, Price!

Most of the other women who'd made choices held the photographs and likenesses as if they were made of gold. Grace even saw a few women give a kiss to the men they'd chosen before carefully placing them in their handbags. All in all, it had been a productive and winning meeting. Grace was not naive enough to think the women were going to get along like a happy family all the way to Kansas; issues and arguments were certain to arise, personalities were going to clash, and feelings were bound to be hurt, but right now everything seemed to be proceeding smoothly, and she vowed to do everything in her power to keep it that way for as long as she could.

Proceeding less smoothly were her efforts to distance herself from the heady effects of one Jackson Blake. Just looking at him made her want to be kissed again. She knew she shouldn't be having such thoughts, especially in a church, but he was impossible to ignore. He stood talking to a group of the would-be brides, and all she could think about was how tall he was and how handsome. She watched the way he moved, the way he smiled, the firm set of his chin, his vivid eyes.

"You're going to give yourself away."

Grace snapped back to reality to see Loreli Winters standing beside her. Grace stumbled to speak, "I—I'm sorry. What did you say?"

"I said, you're going to give yourself away. You keep looking at him like he's the last piece of chocolate on earth, and he's going to know for sure that you're interested in him."

Grace's first instinct was to lie and deny having any interest in the Texan, but the gambler had such a knowing look on her face, Grace decided to go with the truth. "Was I that obvious?"

"As a skunk standing next to a bright red barn."

Grace chuckled. "Then thanks for saving me."

"You're welcome. We girls have to stick together."

That said, Loreli Winters walked back over to the group and Grace congratulated herself for having invited Loreli along.

Grace let the women visit for a few moments longer, then looked over at Jackson. "Do you have anything to add before we close?"

"Yes," he replied, and turned to address the gathering.

"Ladies, when you're deciding what to take to Kansas, remember—the teams can pull only so much weight. I know you're probably wanting to bring armoires and sideboards and other kinds of furniture, but if you could get your folks or a friend to ship you some of the heavier pieces after you're settled in Kansas, our going will be easier. Any questions?"

No one had any. Grace looked around the room. "Any last concerns?" No one seemed to have any of those, either.

"Then Mr. Blake and I will be in touch with you, hopefully no later than this Friday with final details, like maps and such, so get your packing started."

The women were buzzing with excitement as they gathered up their coats and other belongings and headed for the door. When they were gone, Grace looked over to Jackson. "Everything went wonderfully."

"Yes, it did. You're very good at this."

"Thank you. We seem to do well together."

"I agree."

Grace could feel him tempting her, but she fought her response and began gathering up her things. "I meant, we *work* well together."

"It's what I meant, too," he lied, and followed her to the door.

Outside, the night air held the chill of early spring. "How're you getting home?" he asked her, not sure he was ready to part from her just yet.

"A hack, as soon as I can hail one."

"At this time of night?"

"It's only half past nine, Mr. Blake," Grace pointed out easily. "It isn't awfully late."

"It's too late to be out here alone."

"I appreciate your concern, but I'm accustomed to it. Sometimes I'm at the bank much later than this."

Jackson didn't like hearing that. She was a beautiful woman who probably knew little about defending herself. It made her ripe pickings for someone intending her harm. "I'll see you home."

"That isn't necessary."

"Yes, it is."

Grace sighed with frustration. "Mr. Blake, I am a grown woman, and as a grown woman, I—"

Jackson listened as she went on and on about women, society, and a woman's place in it, and when he'd heard enough, he pulled her to him and kissed her so thoroughly and completely, Grace melted like a rose in heat. She saw sunsets, heard bells ring, and when he finally turned her loose, he looked down at her lying limp across his arm and asked, "You were saying?"

Grace couldn't remember what she'd been saying.

"Shall I hail us a hack?"

Still tottering, she nodded.

A smile flitted across his dark eyes. "I'll be right back."

As they rode in the seat behind the driver through the dark Chicago streets, Grace used the cover of the shadows to openly observe the man at her side. Less than four months ago she'd sworn never to risk her heart again, yet her attraction to Blake seemed to be sending her down that slippery slope once again.

In spite of all her pledges and vows, his kisses left her wanting more. Of course, she would never admit that fact to him; she was certain females had been falling over him since primary school and he didn't need another notch on his bed post, but how did she combat the pull of such an overwhelming man. *You just ignore it*, her inner voice declared. *It doesn't matter if his kisses make you see sunsets and hear bells ring, Nothing good will come of it—nothing. You don't need a man in your life, and you certainly don't need to journey all the way to Kansas with a broken heart.* Sighing with rightness of the advice, Grace grudgingly admitted to herself it was true.

The driver stopped the hack in front of her house. Jackson helped her out, then escorted her up to the porch. As they stood there in the darkness, she looked up at him outlined against the moonlight. *Lord, he's gorgeous.* In direct contrast to the sage advice she'd given herself only moments ago, some unknown part of herself wanted to throw caution to the wind and act upon the wild call that seemed to be arching between them.

Jackson knew that he should say goodnight and head back to the hack, but he couldn't move, didn't want to. He realized he could stand here all night just looking at her. As the need for her broke through his defenses, he husked out, "Aw hell, one more . . ." and he gathered her back into his arms. He kissed her again, this time so long and well, her knees turned to butter. When he eased away, her eyes were closed and her body echoed with a pulsing, yearning heat.

"Goodnight, Grace," he whispered, watching her, wanting her. "I'll see you in a few days."

As Grace stood braced against the door, her senses still echoing, she remembered whispering goodnight in reply, but had only a hazy recollection of his departure.

Entering the house, Grace found a note from the aunts saying they were out with the Henderson twins again. In a way, she was glad to find the house empty. This way nothing would intrude upon how she felt.

As she prepared for bed, her lips and senses were still tingling. Standing before the mirror in her muslin nightgown, she touched her mouth wondrously. Before meeting Jackson Blake she'd no idea that a man's kisses could leave a woman so singed. When she and Garth were courting, they'd shared quick pecks on the lips, but she'd never caught fire as she had with the Texan. In just a few days, Jackson Blake had turned her sedate, controlled life upside down and she wasn't sure how she felt about it.

*His kisses are magnificent, though,* came another voice in her head. The volatile feelings and sensations Blake had somehow planted inside her were as tantalizing as they were shocking. Grace wondered how it would be to have him kiss her without inhibition, then forced her mind away from that thought. Well-raised women weren't supposed to speculate on such things.

Grace turned down the lamps and plunged her bedroom into darkness. Crawling beneath the quilts, she decided that thinking about Blake would bear no fruit. It was obvious to her that he was practiced around women, and probably viewed her as just another conquest. As she'd stated to herself earlier, she'd no plans to be another notch on his bedpost, and she didn't need to journey to Kansas with a broken heart, no matter how well he kissed.

The next morning, Grace had breakfast with the aunts.

"How was the recital last night?" she asked them, as she sugared her coffee.

"Dreadful," Dahlia proclaimed. "The singer supposedly sang on the stage, but we're not sure where this stage might've been."

"I think it might've been a stage*coach,*" Tulip offered. "She was truly dreadful."

Grace chuckled. "How are the Henderson twins?"

"Old," Dahlia declared.

"Old and boring," her sister added. "I don't know why we keep stepping out with them."

"Because presently, they're the only fish in the sea."

"I suppose you're right."

The aunts had been seeing the seventy-year-old Henderson twins for about a month now, and the men made it no secret how much they wanted the aunts to be their wives. In the eyes of widowers and pensioners, her aunts were quite a catch because of their education, good health, and financial independence, but Tulip and Dahlia had married and buried six husbands between them, and they'd been putting old codgers like the Henderson twins through paces for nearly two decades now.

Dahlia said, "Enough about our evening—what about yours? Are you ready to set up the camp?"

"Yes. We took care of the remaining details last night."

"And how is Mr. Blake?" Tulip asked.

For a moment, Grace didn't respond, as she turned over the dilemma of Jackson Blake in her mind. Whatever was she going to do about him?

Dahlia and Tulip shared a speculative look, then Dahlia leaned over, peered into Grace's face, and said softly, "You're going to stir a hole in that cup, dear."

The remark brought Grace back to the present. "I'm sorry. Mr. Blake is fine. I just wish he'd stop kissing me."

Both aunts paused, then Tulip asked, "Is there something wrong with them?"

"Oh, no," Grace offered hastily. "They're wonderful, frankly, but—"

"But?" Dahlia cajoled.

"I know he isn't serious. I mean, it isn't as if we're going to be married when all is said and done. Not only are we from two different worlds, but when we reach Kansas, he's going on to Texas, and I'll be coming back here."

"Then where's the problem?"

"If I keep letting him kiss me, he's going to think I'm some type of hussy."

"Enjoying a man's kisses and his company doesn't necessarily make you a hussy, Grace," Tulip pointed out.

"So what does it make me?"

"Human," Dahlia said succinctly over her raised coffee cup. "Just like the rest of us. No more, no less."

"Surely you're not suggesting I encourage him?"

"I'm not suggesting anything," Dahlia pointed out, "but there isn't a woman alive who hasn't experienced a stolen kiss or two."

"Or three," Tulip added with a merry twinkle. Then she said dreamily, "His name was Luis."

Grace and Dahlia shared a mystified look.

"*Whose* name was Luis?" Dahlia asked suspiciously.

"A man I stole kisses with."

Grace's eyes widened.

"Ah, Luis . . ." As she spoke his name, Tulip's whole presence seemed to glow. "The week we spent together were the most memorable seven days of my life."

A startled Grace looked over at Dahlia, who appeared just as surprised. Dahlia then turned to her sister and asked, "Why haven't you ever mentioned this Luis before now?"

Tulip's reverie seemed to fade in reaction to her sister's pointed question. "Because it was none of your business, Dahl, and besides, the subject never came up until now. Remember when I ran that ferry service to the gold fields in California back in the 'forties?"

Dahlia nodded.

"Well, I met him around that time, a year or so after Barney died."

Grace knew that Barney had been one of Tulip's four husbands, but didn't know which number he'd been.

"I met him in Mexico City. We danced, we dined,

we—well, never mind. Suffice it to say, we all need a
Luis in our lives, Grace dear, even if it's only for one
week."

Still a bit stunned by her aunt's revelation, Grace
asked, "What happened to him?"

"After he finished his business in Mexico City, he
sailed home to Spain and I never saw him again. I can't
believe that was almost forty years ago. I wonder what
ever became of him and if he remembers me as fondly?"
She smiled briefly. "Oh well, it doesn't matter, not really. I'll always have the memories."

Grace had always known about the unconventional
lives led by her aunts. Tulip, a true Prescott female, had
sailed all over the world and done everything from running the aforementioned ferry service during the gold
rush to rafting cotton to market through the estuaries of
the Carolina Sea Islands after the war. Dahlia, a highly
successful mortician before and after the war, had traveled with a band of actors at one point in her life, and
according to Grace's mother, had been dueled over by
two besotted Haitian counts during a visit to Paris back
in the 'fifties. Grace liked to think that same free-spirited
Prescott blood flowed in her veins, too, but to hear Tulip
acknowledge having taken a lover was truly startling.

Tulip seemed to have read Grace's mind. "Have I
shocked you, Grace dear?"

Grace had to confess, "A bit, Aunt Tulip."

"Well, I haven't been old all my life. I was young
once, too, and when you're young, your whole life is
before you. When you're old, you want to look back
upon your youth and smile—not wonder 'what if.' Do
you understand?"

Grace did, or at least she thought so.

# Chapter 4

$\sim\!\!\approx\!\!\circlearrowright\!\!\oslash\!\!\sim$

Grace spent the rest of the week turning over the reins of the bank to Lionel and the other clerks, packing for her trip, and trying to keep her mind off Jackson Blake. She hadn't seen him since the night on the porch and she'd decided to take her own advice and distance herself from the Texan and his fiery kisses.

Although Tulip and Dahlia supported the idea of the wagon train, it didn't stop them from being sad about losing their niece's company, if only for a few months. Monday morning was more than forty-eight hours away, but Tulip was already in tears.

By Saturday night, Grace had most of her belongings secured. Unlike the brides, she would be traveling light. Since she planned on returning to Chicago once the adventure ended, she had no need to include household goods or furniture. Her godfather, Martin Abbott, had agreed to give her a ride to the site where camp would be set up. Because he and his fleet of his wagons would be delivering all the supplies she'd ordered to the camp late Monday, he thought it made sense for her to make the journey with him and his men.

By now, most of her customers were aware that she'd be leaving town with the wagon train and many of them stopped by her office to wish her luck and Godspeed. Grace admitted to being a bit nervous about the undertaking, but she wouldn't trade the upcoming adventure for all the gold in the world. She had no idea what the next two months had in store, but she was willing to meet the challenge head on.

On Sunday morning, Grace and the aunts walked to church. Grace and her family were members of the local Episcopal church and had been all of Grace's life. Black Episcopalians had their roots in the first Black Episcopalian church founded in Philadelphia by Absalom Jones. Jones and his followers named that first church the African Church of St. Thomas, and it was dedicated, August 12, 1794. Grace knew the date because it was one of the many facts she learned in Sunday school while growing up. Her own small parish, St. Mary's, was not so historic, but it catered to a mostly Black representative congregation and had a strong commitment to the needy throughout the community.

Before the morning service started, Grace and the aunts took their regular seats in a pew in the middle of the sanctuary, then knelt a moment to say the traditional silent prayer. Grace gave thanks for the blessings she'd received for the week past, and asked blessings for the journey ahead. She spent a few more minutes in quiet reflection before rising from her knees and retaking her seat.

As the church began to fill with worshippers, Dahlia

poked a gentle elbow into Grace's rib to alert her to the arrival of Beatrice Young. Beatrice Young, a loud, overbearing widow who seemed to believe her late husband's fortune entitled her to be that way, was, as always, attired in a costly dress that may have fit her short wide frame a few seasons ago, but didn't anymore. Add to that the ill-fitting auburn wig and she reminded Grace a lot of Sarah Mitchell.

Dahlia whispered, "I know we're in church and I should be having only Christian thoughts, but you'd think Beatrice would simply concede and buy gowns that fit."

Trailing Beatrice were daughter Amanda and Amanda's husband, Garth Leeds, Grace's former fiancé. Grace hadn't seen the married couple since they'd returned from their Cincinnati honeymoon, and in reality, she'd been dreading encountering them socially, thinking her heart might still be in mourning, but surprisingly she felt nothing.

The tall, fair-skinned Amanda, as badly dressed as her mama in a very unflattering shade of purple, seemed to be making an elaborate show of holding onto the arm of the grim-looking gray-suited Garth. She was smiling around at anyone and everyone as if showing off a prize at a fair, and Grace silently prayed for strength. Amanda had dressed the prize well, at least. The suit Garth wore looked new, as did the white shirt and the large gold cuff links.

Still clinging possessively to Garth, Amanda gave Grace and the aunts a regal inclination of her head as she passed them by on her way to the Young pew up front. Grace had known Amanda most of her life and was surprised the new Mrs. Leeds hadn't stopped to gloat.

Tulip whispered sarcastically, "Garth certainly looks happy."

Grace scanned his tight-lipped face. She smiled and then stood as the organist began the processional.

The time after service was usually a social event, a time for gathering, refreshments, and talk. Most of this Sunday's conversation revolved around Grace and her upcoming trip. After receiving lots of well wishes from many members of the congregation, Grace planned on making a fairly hasty exit, due to her plans for tomorrow's leaving, but she and the aunts were waylaid at the door by Beatrice, Amanda, and a Garth who wouldn't meet Grace's eyes.

"Well, hello there, Grace. Mrs. Mays, Mrs. Kingsley. How are you all?" Beatrice trilled.

Everyone said they were fine.

Amanda asked, "Grace, what is all this nonsense we've been hearing about a wagon train of mail-order brides? Now, I knew you were upset about losing Garth to me at the altar, but to leave town? Has the whispering become that bothersome?"

Grace dearly wanted to rip Amanda's well-coifed hair from her head and show the world that the tresses were originally equine, but she calmed herself and said in an even tone, "This has nothing to do with you or Garth, Amanda. I'm doing this as a favor to my cousin."

Amanda breathed an audible sigh of relief. "I'm so glad to hear that. Neither Garth nor I wish to be responsible for you being hounded out of town. Do we, darling?"

"No," he replied frostily.

The terse response seemed to coincide with the gossip Grace had been hearing. Was there really trouble in paradise so soon? The two had been married only a short while, but Garth's Adonis-like face certainly didn't reflect a man flush with the happiness of his honeymoon.

Amanda's nose crinkled with distaste. "But why would anybody in his right mind want to be a mail-order bride?"

Dahlia drawled, "Not everyone is fortunate enough to find a man like your Garth, Amanda."

Grace coughed to cover her reaction to Dahlia's cutting remark, and saw Garth's eyes flash angrily.

The dig seemed to sail right over Amanda's head, though. "I suppose you're right, Mrs. Kingsley."

She then lovingly linked her arm through Garth's. "Garth and I are the happiest couple in the world, aren't we, darling?"

Garth's gray eyes flashed angrily. "Yes, Amanda, we are."

"Well, we should be going," Tulip said. "Grace has to get an early start in the morning."

Beatrice wasn't done yet, however. "Grace, are we going to see you at the society meetings when you return?"

"No, Beatrice. I'm going to resign."

Beatrice looked outraged. The society in question was the Lucie Stanton Literary Society of Chicago, named after Lucie Stanton, the race's first female college graduate. Although Grace had enjoyed the gatherings in the past, lately there'd been little incentive to attend due to the way things were being run and whom they were being run by. The society's former leader, Minnie Sanders, a friend of Grace's mother, had never let personal feelings enter into any of the decisions affecting the group; committee assignments had always been handed out honestly; and the primary missions had always been to help those less fortunate and to promote an appreciation for literacy within the race. But not any more.

When Minnie died last spring, Beatrice Young had

become the new president, and the group had been going to hell ever since. Instead of taking on community projects that would benefit the poor and needy, Beatrice preferred to, as she put it, tout the achievements of representative Black Chicago society by sponsoring elaborate invitation-only dinners, outdoor band concerts, and boat cruises on the lake.

The Stanton Society members hadn't sewn socks for the needy, collected monies to pay death benefits to the indigent, or been treated to the works of any new novelists or poets of the race since Minnie's death. As a result, attendance at the meetings had plummeted as members voted with their feet and joined organizations elsewhere in the city. Grace's mother, Vanessa, and her peers had worked hard to establish the Lucie Stanton Literary Society of Chicago and to give it a strong foundation; it rankled Grace knowing that the once prominent organization would probably be dead before the new year.

The still outraged Beatrice snapped, "Well, once you resign, we won't take you back, you know."

Tired of the encounter now, Grace turned to her aunts and said, "Are we ready?"

"Yes," they said in unison.

Grace gave Beatrice and the others a polite nod of departure, then she and her aunts left the church.

As soon as they stepped out into the Sunday sunshine, Dahlia snapped, "With all that money she's supposed to have, you'd think Beatrice'd employ a dressmaker capable of creating gowns that didn't make her look like a cased sausage."

"Amen!" Tulip proclaimed.

With that settled, the three grinning Prescott women turned their steps toward home.

\* \* \*

As a favor to Sunshine, Jackson drove her buggy over to the train depot Sunday afternoon to pick up a crate of possessions belonging to one of her girls. He'd just put the heavy crate in the back of the buggy and was preparing to head back when he stopped at the sight of what appeared to be a familiar face.

The man, Dixon Wildhorse, caught Jackson's eye at about the same time, and a wondrous smile spread across his dark face. The two men hastened through the throng outside the depot, and when they came together, greeted each other with grins and manly back-slapping hugs. "Is it really you?" Jackson asked, looking his friend up and down.

"Yep," Dixon replied.

The last time they'd been together, Dixon Wildhorse had just been appointed a U.S. deputy marshal in the wild and woolly land known as Indian Territory, and Jackson, on the run from the law, was using a false name as a member of the all-Black 24th Infantry. That had been almost ten years ago. Wildhorse lived in the Territory and was a member of the Black Seminole tribe. His people had waged a long thirty-year war against the U.S. government for the right to stay on their Florida lands, but the Seminoles, like the other major tribes of the south and southeast, had been stripped of their way of life and forced west. "What in the hell are you doing in Chicago, Dix?"

"Tracking a varmint."

"Anybody I know?"

"Yep. Bart Love."

"The old con man?" Jackson asked with a smile.

"One and the same."

Jackson knew the character Dix was referring to. Love lied so much and so often, folks weren't even sure his name was Love. "What's he wanted for this time?"

"Stealing my herd and selling it to the U.S. Army."

Jackson whistled appreciatively.

Dix nodded. "No kidding, I've been trailing him almost two months now. He's supposed to have family here in the city somewhere, but so far he's managed to stay one step ahead of me."

"Where're you staying?"

"Boardinghouse."

"Well, you know, Sunshine Collins is here in Chicago, too. I've been bunking at her place the last six months or so. She's going to be mad that you came to town and didn't let her put you up."

"Is she still in the business?"

"Does it snow in Chicago in January?"

The two friends laughed. They spent a few minutes catching up on the past and the fates of mutual acquaintances. Jackson had confided in Dix long ago about why he'd fled Texas, and Dix asked if the problem had ever been resolved.

"Not yet, but hopefully soon."

Dixon went silent for a moment. "You're not thinking about going back down there, are you? Rivers are running with blood in some places."

Jackson nodded grimly. "I know."

The newspaper reports coming out of Texas were bleak. As the hate of the Redemptionists spread like wildfire across the south, Black folks were paying the ultimate price. "You'd never know the Rebs *lost* the war, the way we're suffering and dying," Jackson added with bitter sarcasm.

"I know, which is why you've got no business going back."

"Have to."

Dix searched the eyes of his friend. "If Lane Trent's

still alive, I doubt he'll just let you waltz in and have him arrested."

"I know, but my daddy's owed justice," Jackson replied, his eyes hard.

"Yes he is, but what's the sense in you dying too? Jack, look. Why don't you come and live in the Territory? Start over, men do it all the time. As long as you stay within the law, no one will bother you."

"I want my star back."

Dix held Jackson's serious eyes. They both knew a wanted man could never in good conscience put on a star again, not if he were really dedicated to enforcing the law.

"I was a damn good lawman, Dix. Lane Trent took that, too."

Jackson decided to change the subject. He'd be facing his future soon enough. "Have you heard anything from my brother Griffin?"

Dix let loose with a seldom seen smile. "Your little brother has made quite a name for himself. He's wanted in five states for train robbing. Last time I checked, the reward on his red head was in the five-figures territory."

Jackson chuckled. Who knew the wisecracking orphan who'd become his brother would wind up a notorious train robber. "Have you seen him?"

"Yeah, I have. Since he isn't wanted in the Territory he stops in every now and again, but the women always wind up fighting over him so I always end up running him out of town just to restore the peace."

Jackson shook his head. "My daddy Royce's probably spinning in his grave."

"No doubt. He's a handful, that little brother of yours. So tell me this, what are you doing in Chicago?" Dixon asked.

"Trying to stay one step ahead of the bounty hunters."

"It's been a long time, Jack, I can't see anybody still tracking you after all these years."

"The moment I say that, somebody'll knock on my door. Lane Trent's daddy Roy was a pretty powerful Reb back then, you know. Lane's probably still trying to find me if for no other reason than to keep me from telling the truth about what really happened the day his daddy died, and about his hand in Royce's death."

Again pushing aside the dilemma posed by Lane Trent, Jackson asked the lawman, "What're you going to do if you can't find Bart Love?"

"Head back to the Territory and wait for him to show up. He'll head home eventually."

"Well, I just signed on to be wagon master for some folks going down to an Exoduster colony in Kansas. Sure could use a scout, if you're interested."

Jackson didn't dare tell him the trip would be an all-woman expedition because he knew Dix would never agree.

"If I can't find Bart, I don't see why not. It's a bit out of the way, but—" He shrugged.

They spent a few more minutes talking about the pay, possible routes and the estimated date of departure for the wagon train. Dix promised to stop by Sunshine's later and the two old friends parted. By the time Jackson drew the team to a halt in front of Sunshine's Palace, the need to return to Texas echoed inside him like a heartbeat.

After spending eight hours on a hard wagon seat, Grace could barely climb down to the ground. She ignored the chuckles of her godfather Martin Abbott watching her as he held the reins. Her behind felt as stiff as the wooden seat, and her legs had been turned to stone.

"Sure you're ready for this trip?" he teased.

Grace shot him a warning look, but it was filled with all the love she felt for her father's lifelong friend. "Yes, I am," she lied confidently, finally making it to the grassy ground. Lord, she wondered if she'd ever be able to walk again.

"Bit stiff, are you?" Martin asked, getting down from the wagon with experienced ease.

"Just a bit, but we were on the road all day," Grace said in defense of her condition.

"That we were, but you'd better get used to it. This is going to be your life for the next month or so. Remember?"

She did, and for the first time began to wonder if this whole expedition was really such a good idea. Her legs were just now regaining some semblance of feeling, but because Grace had never been one to wallow in self-pity, she buried the doubt-filled second thoughts about the upcoming journey and forced herself to take a few halting steps.

The tall, burly, gray-haired Martin laughed aloud. "You look like you're made out of metal and gears."

"You'd better be glad I love you so much," she tossed back with merry eyes. "Metal and gears, indeed!"

Grace could finally feel her blood flowing again, but had no idea when her behind would recover. Putting her physical discomfort aside for now, she looked around the sun-filled valley and felt the silence and peace fill her soul. She could almost envision how the camp would look once everything was in place, see the activities as the brides went about their day.

"Thanks for letting me use this spot," she said, scanning the budding trees and the blue sky.

"You're welcome, but when have I ever been able to deny you anything?"

Grace turned and looked at him with such seriousness he raised an eyebrow. He asked, "What's the matter?"

"When I told Aunt Dahlia and Aunt Tulip about this trip, they said the same thing. I'm blessed to have people who love me so."

Since her parents' death, the love of Martin and the aunts had done much to ease her pain.

"You're very special, Gracie. Folks can't help but love you."

Grace gave him a watery smile. Then, because she knew Martin would understand, she let the tears fill her eyes as she whispered, "I miss Papa so much, Uncle Marty—so much . . ."

He came over, eased her against his big barrel chest, and held her tight. "I do too, baby girl, more than I ever thought I could. He was a good friend. A *damn good* friend."

She cried for a few moments longer and they consoled each other silently. Grace had no reason to hide her misery, Martin had loved her father too; so when Grace glanced up and saw Jackson Blake mounted atop a big black stallion positioned behind them, the pain she felt was vividly portrayed on her face.

Before she could speak or move, he drew out the longest gun Grace had ever seen and then called out in a low, sinister voice, "Let her go, mister!"

Grace's eyes widened as Martin, still holding her, instinctively spun to the commanding voice. When he came face to face with the armed and mounted stranger, his eyes widened, too, then he barked, "Who the hell are you?"

Jackson's eyes were wintry. "Back away from the lady, old man. Grace, are you hurt?"

"Old man!" Martin shouted, and thrust Grace from him with such force, she almost lost her balance. Fire in his eyes, Martin bore down on Jackson like a maddened grizzly.

Jackson calmly raised the Colt, hoping the man would have the sense to stop before he put a bullet in his leg, but Martin kept coming, saying, "You'd better put that peacemaker to good use, boy, because once I get my hands on you, you'll be having it for supper."

Grace stared at them as if they'd suddenly grown cow's heads, then shouted, "Dammit, stop this now!"

Both men froze.

She wheeled on the Texan first. "Jackson Blake, put that gun away. Have you lost your Texas mind?"

"I thought you were in trouble!" he snapped.

A stunned Martin asked her, "You know this outlaw?"

Too angry to answer questions, Grace turned on her godfather. "And *you*. He has a gun, for heaven's sake, and you don't have the sense the good Lord gave a rock to worry about being killed. I've already buried Papa. Are you trying to make sure I bury you, too?"

The men looked chastened.

"Now," Grace huffed, as she attempted to calm herself. "Martin Abbott, this is the wagon master, Jackson Blake. Mr. Blake, this is my *godfather*, Martin Abbott. Both of you, say hello."

Grumbles were exchanged.

"Good. Now, if you two will excuse me, I have a camp to set up." And she stormed off. She was so mad with them both she couldn't see straight.

Watching her retreat, Martin said, "She's something else, isn't she?"

Jackson was watching her too. "Yes, sir, she is that."

"Her mother, Vanessa, had that fire, too, and that red hair. She raised Grace to be strong and brave and to speak her mind. She learned well, I think. Most men don't appreciate it, though."

Jackson nodded. He appreciated her, but had no idea how much until now. Seeing her with Abbott and thinking the man was assaulting her had filled Jackson with both dread and rage.

"Grace's daddy and I grew up together, escaped from Maryland together, and when he died last year, I swore to him I'd take his daughter on as my own. It wasn't necessary though because I'd walk through hell's fires for that girl. Loved her since the day she was born. Did you know that her great-great-granddaddy was a pirate?"

Jackson was watching her too. "No, but it explains a lot."

Martin chuckled.

Jackson supposed he owed the man an apology. "Sorry I drew on you, I thought she was in trouble."

"Reasonable mistake, I suppose," Martin offered. "Would you really have pulled the trigger?"

"If I thought you were harming her? Yes."

Martin then looked Jackson straight in the eye and said, "When she first came up with this cockamamie idea about this wagon train, and going to Kansas, I was worried about her being out on the road. Now, I won't have to, will I?"

Jackson told the truth. "No, sir. You won't."

Martin gave a short nod of approval, then walked over and stuck out his hand. "Glad to meet you."

Jackson leaned down and returned the shake firmly. "Same here."

The brides began arriving late that same evening in all manner of conveyances, bringing with them trunks, crates, and furniture. What had been a deserted glade was turned into a valley bustling with people, supply wagons, and belongings. Many of the women came alone, while a few were escorted to the camp by parents or other family members. Most of the families were friendly and as excited about the journey as their daughters and were helping the women with the unloading of their things. When Grace explained to the family members that she would not allow them to stay at the camp with their daughters, most saw no problem with her stance. They understood the bonds she was trying to forge amongst the brides and thought the idea a sound one.

The Deetses, however, were an exception. Mr. and Mrs. Deets were the parents of hairdresser Wilma Deets, and were not pleased when Grace told them no, they could not stay on site with their daughter until departure for Kansas.

"But we insist," her mutton-chopped father insisted. Dressed in a fine gray suit, he appeared to be someone accustomed to having his orders followed without question, but Grace had been dealing with men like him most of her life.

"Mr. Deets, I understand your concern, but the women will not become the strong, cohesive unit they will need to become if there are outside influences."

Deets sputtered, "Outside influences! I'm her father, for heaven's sake."

The fashionably dressed Mrs. Deets stood silently at his side. The way in which her eyes were darting back and forth between her husband and Grace made Grace wonder if she'd ever seen him challenged before.

"Who's in charge here?" Deets demanded, looking around, presumably for a man.

"I am," Grace told him, "so unless you're planning on taking Wilma back with you, I suggest you leave us and let us get on with things."

"Impertinent young woman, how dare you talk to me that way!"

Grace turned on her heel and walked away.

"Damn you, don't you dare walk away from me!"

Holding onto her temper, Grace spun back and said, "Mr. Deets, this is private property, and in a few moments you will be trespassing. Either get, or I will have you removed."

He looked on the verge of choking. Mrs. Deets's eyes were wide as saucers. Wilma stood behind her parents with a secretive smile on her thin brown face. She seemed to be enjoying her father being bested.

Grace continued tersely, "If you and your wife wish to stay and see Wilma tonight before you leave, I've no quarrel with that, but tomorrow will be the last day for visits. There is a boardinghouse in the town nearby. I'm sure they can offer you accommodations."

Grace then turned her attention to the now openly smiling Wilma. "You should come with me so we can get you set up."

The words seemed to be the only encouragement Wilma needed. She gave each parent a quick peck on the cheek, then fell in beside Grace. As they headed toward the women gathering in the clearing, Grace could feel Deets's eyes boring into her back. She ignored him and hoped none of the other relatives would be as bullheaded and boorish as the ill-mannered Mr. Deets.

Grace didn't see much of Jackson Blake. He and Martin spent most of the day overseeing the unloading of the supplies along with Martin's small army of men, then checking everything against Grace's inventory list. She still couldn't believe this morning's incident, but it pleased her to see they'd worked out their earlier problems and seemed to be getting along.

The now emptied wagons would serve as the women's sleeping quarters tonight, but tomorrow they'd all get a chance to learn how to properly pitch a tent. Those same tents would be their homes until Blake deemed them ready to head the wagons to Kansas.

By nightfall there were almost thirty women in camp, and when the work for the day was done, family members headed for the town's boardinghouses, Martin bedded his men down on the far side of the valley (they'd be heading back to Chicago in the morning), and the brides picked out their wagons, then said goodnight.

After offering her goodnights to them in turn, a tired Grace decided she was still too wound up to seek sleep, so she grabbed a blanket from her wagon, draped it around her shoulders to ward off the night's chill, then headed for the fire the men had built earlier in a cleared area. Bathed in its red and orange glow, she sat down on the big felled log that served as a seat and pulled the blanket closer.

It had been a long day, and she knew tomorrow would be just as long, if not longer. Quiet had settled over the camp. Grace could see the glow of lanterns shining softly inside the canvas of some of the wagons as the women prepared for bed, and over on the far end of the valley she could see another small fire around which some of Martin's men sat, but there was no one else close by to intrude on her solitude. She'd done it, she congratulated herself, she'd gotten Price's brides, ordered the supplies and the first day had been completed. Grace couldn't think of anything else she needed to make the day more winning.

She sensed his presence behind her the moment he walked up. There was no need to turn and visually verify what her senses already knew. She felt him there as real as she felt her heartbeat. "Good evening, Mr. Blake."

"Miss Atwood," he voiced quietly.

For a moment, Grace felt a bit awkward and tongue-tied. The last time they'd been alone together, his kisses had made her melt, and even though she'd vowed to keep their relationship focused on the business at hand, her mind kept reliving being in his arms. "Thank you for coming to my aid this morning. Even though it wasn't needed, I appreciate your concern for my safety."

"Martin and I sorted it out."

The silence resettled, broken only by the sharp crackling sounds of the wood in the fire.

Grace gathered her courage. "Please, sit if you'd like," she offered, turning so their gazes could meet.

"Nice night, nice fire, beautiful woman. I probably shouldn't come any closer—"

Feeling her heart begin to pound, Grace turned back to the calming effects of the blaze. "We're both adults, Jackson. Surely we can talk without—"

"Kissing?" he asked, finishing her thought. It pleased him having her address him by his given name.

"Kissing, yes."

"I don't know," he replied softly. "Something about you makes me want to do that more and more."

His every word affected her like a stroke from his hand. She nervously clasped her hands together. "You're a lot more forward than I'm accustomed to."

"I understand that, but my daddy raised me to speak what's on my mind . . . and you are, Grace Atwood. When we get to Kansas, I'm going to head down to Texas and you'll be coming back here. We'll probably never see each other again, but you're not a woman easily put out of a man's mind."

Grace turned back and looked up at him again. He was pretty vivid himself, came the thought. "I'll not forget you easily, either."

Then she confessed softly, "I don't really mind the kissing, you know, but I think if I were better prepared for them, I wouldn't be so—so woozy afterward."

"You think so?" he asked, both amused and fascinated by her innocent assessment.

She nodded. "Yes. Don't you?"

Jackson shook his head. "No."

She studied his dark presence. "Why not?"

"Because it doesn't have anything to do with being prepared, it has to do with passion and sparks between two people."

"And is that what you think we have—passion and sparks?"

He nodded. "It's starting to look that way."

Grace pondered that for a moment, then said, "Well, I think you're wrong. Kiss me again, and I'll prove it."

Jackson went still. "Excuse me?"

Grace couldn't believe she'd asked that. It was as if she'd somehow been transformed into one of her outrageous aunts, but the cat was out of the bag now, and it was too late to do anything but row. "It's the only way I know to prove to you that my theory is correct."

Jackson looked down into her fire-flecked face. "This theory being, that if you know a kiss is coming, you won't be woozy afterward."

"Yes," she concurred quietly.

"I can't just kiss you out here in the open like this. Folks'll talk, and your godfather would have my hide."

Grace scanned the darkness. "How about those trees over there? If anybody asks what we were doing, I'll say we were scouting for a place to rig up a shower."

He laughed softly. "A shower?"

"Do you have a better lie?" she asked, eyebrow raised.

"Not off the top of my head, no."

"Then mine will have to do. Besides, everyone's so tired, they're probably asleep."

He reached out a hand. "Come, then."

Grace placed her hand in his and he gently assisted her to her feet.

They walked away from the camp and into the moonlight darkness of the trees. Once they were alone, hidden from prying eyes, they stopped.

He looked down at her and asked, "How's this?"

Grace had never done anything like this before and a part of herself demanded to know if she'd lost her mind. But another part knew this had nothing to do with theories; being in his arms took her to a realm so tantalizing and tempting, she wanted to enter it again, if only for a few moments.

Savoring the heat of her closeness, the faint scent of her perfume, Jackson stood unmoving a moment. He then used a guiding finger to gently raise her chin so he could feast his eyes on the lush dark bow of her mouth. "Are you ready?" he whispered.

"Yes," she managed to reply with more bravado than she felt. The nearness of him was already making her woozy; her inner bells were chiming like Easter morning, her heart racing like a rabbit in full flight.

He lowered his mouth to hers and brushed his lips ever so faintly across her own. "Are you sure?"

Grace's eyes slid closed of their own accord and the initial heat of contact made her walls begin to crumble like Jericho. "Yes," she whispered back.

Jackson eased away, then rubbed a slow thumb over her parted lips. Watching her closed lids flutter in response to his touch filled him with desire. "I dreamt about this mouth last night."

He kissed her gently; faintly at first, then again and again using the same lingering motions. Grace, holding onto his strong arms, fleetingly acknowledged the blanket slipping away but paid it no mind.

Wanting more than just a brief taste of her, Jackson

drew her closer until her womanly curves nestled intimately against his hard, lean frame and her arms came up to hold him tight. Satisfied, he deepened the kiss, feeling her lips part under his passionate conquering. For a moment he nibbled on the sultry fullness of her bottom lip, then darted his tongue against her mouth's tender corners. What had begun as a simple test had turned into something else entirely for Jackson Blake. Murmuring his kisses across the small brown shell of her ear before recapturing her lips, his desire to have her rose and flared. He wanted to lean her back against the big tree behind them and watch her eyes fill with heat as he opened the buttons on her gray dress, and hear her soft intake of breath when he brushed his lips across the perfumed warmth of her throat and the tops of her breasts. He imagined slowly raising her skirts so he could fill his hands with the sculpted ripeness of her hips, then showing her how the erotic touch of the right man could make her burn hot as the Texas sun.

"What's the sum of thirteen and nine?" he husked out against her ear. He needed to distract himself lest he turn his fantasies into reality.

Grace was caught up in such a whirlwind of new sensations she couldn't even recite her name. His previous kisses had been chaste compared to the winds buffeting her now and he wanted her to recite sums? "Um, twenty-three," she breathed, "no, twenty-four."

Smiling, he pulled back so he could look down at her braced in the circle of his arms. "Remind me not to put my money in your bank. Since when is thirteen and nine ever twenty-three, or twenty-four?"

Grace tried to clear her faculties of the haze clouding them, but had great difficulty doing so. She'd never been kissed with such intensity before.

"That wasn't fairly asked," she whispered, still shaken

by her strong reaction to his heady magic.

"Why not?" he questioned lightly, raising her chin so he could see for himself what his kisses had done to her. "You said being prepared wouldn't leave you woozy."

Unable to resist the lure in her, Jackson ran a finger down her velvety cheek. Once again, he hadn't gotten nearly enough of Grace Atwood. "Doing sums should be second nature for a banker lady like yourself. Still believe in your theory?" he asked in a voice that stroked her.

She focused on his night-shrouded eyes. "Yes," she lied softly, baldly.

"Lightning's going to strike you, lying like that."

She turned her head away to hide her smile.

"I'm glad I didn't shoot your godfather this morning," he said, turning suddenly serious.

"I am too."

"I saw the tears in your eyes and I thought you were in trouble."

Only now could Grace acknowledge how moved she'd been by his attempt to defend her honor. She'd never had a man champion her before. Reaching up, she stroked his cheek in silent thanks. "The tears were for my father, but if I'm ever in trouble, you'll be the very first person I'll call for."

"I'm holding you to that." He turned her hand to his lips and kissed the soft center of her palm.

The possessive intimacy of the gesture made Grace see stars. So far, he'd kissed nothing but her lips and her palm, yet every inch of her body seemed to be alive and pulsing.

He said, "We should probably get back before someone sends out a search party."

She agreed, but she didn't really want to go. Being with him under the stars this way made her feel reckless and daring, something the usually level-headed Grace had never felt with any other man, not even the traitorous Garth.

Jackson wasn't ready to let her go either. He could hold her this way until dawn. But they had to get back, so he picked up her blanket, draped it about her shoulders, and walked her back to the main camp.

When they reached Grace's darkened wagon, she looked up at him and said, "Goodnight, Jackson."

But he still didn't want to leave her. "Suppose I wanted another kiss—would I get one?"

His voice was as hushed as the night and the power of him seemed to touch her everywhere. "My experiment covered one kiss."

"The experiment's over. This one will be for pleasure . . ."

She'd never had a man promise her pleasure before, and the anticipation made her senses rekindle all over again. They were drowning in each other's eyes. Grace could feel her lips parting of their own accord and Jackson could feel his desire unfurling for want of her. The air became even more charged as he reached out and slowly traced a crescent over the silken brown skin of her cheek. A man of some experience, Jackson knew that if he moved any closer or touched her in any other way but this he'd wind up carrying her off, and to hell with the consequences. "I'm about two seconds from carrying you off like one of Hannibal's raiders, Grace Atwood."

The whispered declaration rippled over Grace, and everything that made her woman responded to the sensual call in his eyes. "And I'm about two seconds away from letting you, so go to your wagon, Jackson."

Wondering how much longer he'd be able to keep from spiriting her away and making slow, sweet love to her, he touched her cheek once more. "Goodnight, Grace."

"Goodnight, Jackson." And she went inside.

Jackson was whistling softly as he headed over to the end of the valley where Martin Abbott and his men were bedded down. Their fire had burned down to almost nothing, but a pipe-smoking Martin Abbott was hunched before it, feeding it wood. The barrel-shaped man turned to appraise Jackson for a moment, then went back to adding sticks and twigs to the growing flame.

"You know, son," Martin declared sagely, "the last time my Gracie slipped off in the dark with a fella, he left her at the altar with a broken heart."

He then turned to Jackson and let him see the seriousness in his fire-bathed face. "Did you know that?"

Jackson found himself taken by surprise. "No, sir, I didn't."

"Promised her aunts if it ever happened again, I'd settle up with the man myself. You following me?"

"Yes, sir."

"Then enough said."

Martin stood. "Goodnight, Blake."

"Goodnight."

Jackson watched him disappear into the dark. Martin Abbott had just handed him another piece of the puzzle known as Grace Atwood, but he wasn't certain what to do with it or where it should be placed. He did know that any man capable of leaving Grace on her wedding day had to be a fool.

The next morning, Grace said good-bye to her godfather and his men and thanked them for their help. Grace waved wildly as the two wagons began to roll. "Thank you, Uncle Marty!"

"You're welcome, baby girl. I'll be back for the big

send-off," he called back. "Take care of yourself."

The wagons rumbled up the valley's rise, then headed toward the road.

As Grace rejoined the women, the sight of Jackson walking up made her remember last night, but she had no time to savor the vivid memories. He put everyone right to work. First order of business—raising their tents.

With the aid of a few of the women he demonstrated the tent-raising process by erecting one. He took questions, gave answers, and then stepped back.

Using hammers and horseshoes, the women drove the spikes into the spring-soft earth and began. Grace had assigned two people to each tent, which meant fifteen tents had to be erected. Since she'd opted for no roommate, that brought the number to sixteen. Tent number seventeen belonged to Jackson, but he'd already erected his tent early this morning before breakfast. The three tents designated to house the supplies had been put up yesterday by Martin and his men, but the boxes of cooking utensils, spare wagon wheels, water barrels, rope, and the like had to be put inside. That would be the next order of business.

Right now, they were concentrating on the tents. They worked in teams, and the women who'd never raised one before found it a bit more difficult than the experienced Jackson made it appear. Some had their canvas inside out, some hadn't sunk their stakes in the right spot, others had no aptitude for the task at all and would've thrown up their hands had Jackson and the other brides not given them encouragement.

While they worked, the women wiped the sweat from their brows and talked about where they'd string the many clotheslines that would be needed and where the trestle tables might be set up for their common meals. Oberlin graduate Fanny Ricks and Loreli volunteered to help Grace put together the duty roster. Everyone agreed a roster would be helpful in keeping the campsite clean and in divvying up chores like laundry and cooking.

In the end it took nearly three hours to get all the tents raised, and when the women were done, they wiped their brows, stood back, and viewed their accomplishments with pride. This section of their green valley now resembled a small tent city, and they'd built it with their own hands.

Jackson walked through the canvas city, checking ropes and stakes. He made a few of the roommates retie some of the knots that held the corners of the tents to the stakes—they weren't taut enough. The perspiring work crew didn't mind relashing them because no one wanted their tent blown over by a strong wind in the middle of the night.

When the general seemed reasonably assured that the tents would last the duration of their stay, he gave them the go-ahead to move in.

Shouts of jubilation and hallelujahs filled the air and the women hastened to get their belongings.

The afternoon saw them spend another few hours loading up the supply tents. They carried tack and barrels and blankets and rope, then went back for shovels and tarps and wood for building a corral for the animals. There were water jugs and cooking stoves, shoes for the horses, straw and feed.

*Why in the world did I order all this?* Grace wailed to herself, after making what felt like the fiftieth trip. Her poor arms felt like rubber, and having on a tight corset beneath her simple blouse and flowing skirt certainly didn't help her breathing.

Once the women got everything stacked inside the three supply tents, they wearily trudged over to the two long trestle tables to enjoy their first dinner together—

Zora Post's highly seasoned pepperpot. The stew, made chiefly of tripe and dumplings, had never been one of Grace's favorite dishes, but after a day of hauling goods, moving crates, and tackling tents, Grace would've eaten boiled shoes, she was that hungry. All the women were hungry; hungry, weary, and sore from the full day of physical labor. That night, when Grace's head hit her pillow, she went right to sleep.

# Chapter 5

Grace awakened tired and stiff. Thoughts of Jackson Blake had filled her dreams. Now, as she lay in her bedroll listening to the dawn silence, she came to the conclusion that regardless of how well Jackson Blake kissed or how tempting being reckless with him appealed to her inner woman, it had to stop. Yes, she'd had this talk with herself before, and no, she hadn't followed her own advice, but this time she planned to chisel it into stone, mainly because she was developing feelings for him, feelings that had to be nipped in the bud before they grew any stronger.

He'd said it himself, they'd probably never see each other again once the wagon train reached its destination, he'd return to his life and she to hers, but the more time she spent around him the more time she wanted to spend around him, and that made little sense to a woman as well known for her good sense as Grace.

She'd been devastated when Garth Leeds backed out of the wedding, but now she could admit that a small part of herself had been glad. Even though Garth had been courteous and gentlemanly while courting her, she sensed that their married life would never equal her parents' union in intensity and passion because Garth hadn't shown himself to be a passionate man. He never would have kissed her the way Jackson had the night outside the church, or leave her as breathless and stupefied as Jackson had last evening.

Garth had treated her like a china doll, but Jackson treated her like a woman, and there lay the rub. She sensed the passion in him, could feel the sparks, but there was no future in it. He'd go his way and she hers, and when he left, he'd take with him the spark and passion she'd always envisioned sharing with her heart's mate. So from now on, she'd stick to business when it came to dealing with Jackson Blake, and this time she would keep the vow come hell or high water.

After taking care of her morning needs, Grace dressed and set out to go meet Loreli. The gambler and a few of the other ladies had volunteered to help set up the duty roster, and to Grace's way of thinking, the sooner a roster could be posted, the smoother the camp would run. As it were the Mitchell sisters had yet to lift a finger to help with setting the table for meals or aiding in the clean-up. Grace couldn't wait for Mr. Drain to deliver all the horses tomorrow so she could put the two siblings on mucking detail. A good dose of humility would do them good.

Even though it was an overcast May day, the camp was bustling with life. Grace received and called back many hellos and good mornings as she walked through their small tent city. Some women were hanging clothes-lines while others were dragging large vats to the spot where the laundry operations would be. Hotel owner and pepperpot maker Zora Post had taken it upon herself to organize the kitchen, and had commandeered a group of willing women to open the crates and barrels of food-stuffs so they could inventory what the camp had on hand. Seeing such initiative made Grace smile.

Grace, Loreli, and the rest of the roster committee had agreed to convene at the trestle tables and had just begun sharing ideas when the black-clad Jackson Blake walked up.

He touched his hat. "Morning, ladies."

The smiling ladies returned the greeting.

His eyes moved to Grace and she fought down her reaction. "Miss Atwood, can you spare me a few moments? We need to figure out where we're going to put Drain's animals once they're delivered."

"Certainly."

She excused herself and walked with him over to the supply tent that doubled as his office. Once inside, Grace looked around. Like the other supply tents, the place was stacked to the gills. Wagon wheels were piled up next to cooper's barrels. Harnesses and tack were piled high in a corner, along with shovels and wagon axles. There were buckets and knee-high coils of rope; tarps and hooded rain slickers. They packed the tent so tightly one could barely turn around. She saw that he'd turned the top of one of the larger crates into a makeshift desk. Spread atop it were opened maps and scattered sheets of supply lists.

When she became aware that he was watching her, Grace plunged right into the business at hand. "What were your thoughts on the animals, Mr. Blake?"

"So, we're back to Mr. Blake now?" he asked evenly.

The memories of last night's kisses rose in her mind. She buried them so that her plan wouldn't go awry. "Yes."

He studied her a moment. "Why?"

She wouldn't meet his eyes. "It's necessary."

"Why?" he asked again, watching her closely.

"Because you and I need to establish a business relationship, and we can't do that if we're—"

"Kissing?" he asked, finishing the sentence.

"Exactly," she replied, avoiding his eyes again.

Jackson smiled to himself. Admittedly she made a lot of sense—loving and business didn't often mix well—but he was certain she could feel the sparks between them, he certainly did. He wondered if she knew that putting them out would be a lot easier said than done. "I agree, business is more important at the moment, but—" and he paused dramatically.

"But what?"

"There's a very passionate woman inside you, Miss Atwood. What are you going to do about those sparks we talked about?"

"Ignore them," she responded confidently.

He chuckled softly.

Grace wondered if she was supposed to be offended. "You don't think I can?"

"Nope."

"Why not?"

"I was the one you were kissing last night, remember?"

She did, and forced herself to keep her voice light. "Sharing a few kisses with you doesn't mean I'm in danger of throwing myself at your feet. No offense intended."

"None taken," he replied, even as he wondered if her sleep last night had been as fretful as his own. He awakened this morning still hard from the remembered scents, tastes, and the feel of her softness pressed against him under the moonlight. "If you want this to be a business partnership, so be it, but it may already be too late."

"Meaning?"

"The first thing I thought about this morning was kissing you."

Grace's whole world swayed. "Jackson, I—"

It pleased him to hear her slip up and husk out his given name. "You said you valued truth, so I see no sense in lying about it. I want you, Grace Atwood, and in every way a man could possibly want a woman."

Grace wondered if she'd ever breathe again. "We aren't supposed to be having this discussion."

"Why not?" he asked easily. "You said it yourself last night. We're both adults."

"But you're just looking for a toss in the hay."

"You're wrong. I'm looking to share passion with a beautiful woman."

His penetrating gaze was so filled with desire, Grace felt as if they were the only two people in the world. The high collar of her blue blouse suddenly seemed tight and restrictive around her throat. The parts of herself that he'd awakened last night were slowly coiling to life and she hadn't a clue as to what to do. "I'm not that kind of woman," she confessed, eyes filled with honesty.

It was an honesty he respected. "I know that, but it still doesn't stop me from wanting to take you in my arms."

"You're too forward," she whispered over her pounding heart.

"I know that too, but the truth remains."

Grace wanted to know why he was doing this. Where she came from, women didn't hop into bed with a man just because he desired she do so. There were rules and protocol to be observed first, mainly a wedding. His realm seemed to be void of such conventional restrictions, though, and the parts of herself that were attuned to him boldly wondered how it might be to walk there, if only for one night. Shocked by her scandalous thoughts, she refocused her attention his way.

"What were you thinking?" he asked. He'd been watching her thoughts pan across the planes of her small face.

"Nothing," Grace lied. Last night she'd admitted to being susceptible to his kisses, but she would not confess to desiring him.

"Do you ever let your hair down?"

Grace's hand went unconsciously to her severely pulled back hair, then dropped hastily back to her side. "Not in mixed company."

"You should try it sometime."

Grace imagined herself letting her hair down for him and just the thought made her senses quicken and her blood warm. "Let's get back to the issue at hand. Are we in agreement to stick to business?"

"Yes, we are." Jackson wasn't really, but as he'd mused earlier, business first—the rest would take care of itself.

"Then let's talk about animals."

"I still want to kiss you, though."

Grace looked up into his eyes and felt herself going woozy. "Jackson, you have to behave if this agreement is to work."

He reached out and lightly traced the tip of his dark finger over the small spray of freckles dusting her left cheekbone.

As the moment rippled over her, he said in a voice as soft as his touch, "You have my word that I will not kiss you or touch you again, until I'm asked. How's that?"

Grace, in the midst of melting, realized he'd used the word "until," and not "unless," as if he knew she wouldn't be able to master her attraction, at least, not for very long. She admitted that he could be correct. He was practiced in this game, she was not. She'd never even been kissed properly until he came into her life, she knew that now. Everything about him seemed to promise this would not be the last time they'd visit this subject, and the knowledge filled her with both a thrilling anticipation and a modicum of distress. Wondering how on earth she'd accomplish being around him for the next few months and remain unmoved, she ducked away from his hand and turned the conversation back to the less volatile subject of animals.

After she and Jackson were done, Grace made her way back to the tables just in time for the end of the roster committee's meeting. She was handed a draft of the schedule and asked to look it over. Grace promised she would. Fanny and the other women left to rejoin the main group, but Loreli stayed behind.

"May I speak with you privately for a moment?"

Grace had no idea what Loreli was about but replied, "Of course. Let's use my tent."

Once they were inside the canvas walls, a curious Grace asked, "What did you wish to speak with me about?"

"I want to give you my fare. You said anyone who doesn't pick a husband will have to pay her own way, so I want to give it to you now."

Grace stared, confused.

Loreli offered an explanation. "I've been around enough to know that no farmer is going to want a woman like me for a wife, and that suits me fine, because Lord knows I'm not cut from wife cloth."

"Then why are you going along?"

"To get away. I need a change of scenery."

Grace looked into her golden brown eyes and wondered how much truth Loreli was really revealing. "Have you been to Kansas City before?"

"Numerous times. It's not bad, as cities go, but I'm looking to head west. California maybe."

"Then why not just get on a train and go?"

"I thought this might be more fun."

Grace smiled.

Loreli then reached into the side pocket of her gray skirt and withdrew a tied-up red handkerchief. She undid the knots and handed Grace ten double eagles. "Will that cover me?"

Grace couldn't hide her surprise. "It's more than adequate."

Loreli's two hundred dollars would be useful, should they need to purchase additional supplies or should an emergency arise. Grace put the coins in her pocket. "Thank you, Loreli. I'm looking forward to knowing you better."

"Same here," Loreli offered genuinely. "So, how're you and Blake getting along?"

"Fine, I guess." Grace didn't know Loreli well enough to confide in her and so kept her thoughts on Jackson to herself.

Loreli must've sensed her reluctance because she didn't press. "Well, if you ever need a shoulder, it's here."

Grace nodded. "Thanks."

Loreli gave her a smile and left through the tent's open flap.

With Jackson's blessing, the women had the rest of the day off. After the physical challenges of yesterday, having nothing to do gave them the opportunity to rest their sore muscles, continue fixing up their tents, and visit with their neighbors. To distinguish the tents from one another, some of the women fashioned address signs from the wood of discarded crates and placed them outside their residences. Others decorated their entrance flaps with ribbon or scraps of colored cloth. One tent even had a flowery hat tacked over the entrance. Grace thought it was a wonderful and creative way to tell one tent from another.

That evening, as Grace sat at her makeshift desk writing a letter to the aunts, she heard Jackson call to her from outside, "Grace, someone here to see you."

Puzzled, she got up from the crate she'd been using as a seat to see who Jackson had with him.

The young woman standing on one side of Jackson was not someone Grace knew. She did know the man in the cleric's collar, however, and the sight of him surprised her greatly. He was Reverend David Petrie, the father of Grace's late friend Nan, and a man who'd not spoken to Grace or any member of her family since Nan's tragic death thirteen years ago. The Reverend Petrie had pale-as-ivory skin, and at one time had been a very robust man, but over the years the bulk had wasted away, leaving behind a paper-thin husk of the man he had once been. Rumor had it that he was dying.

"Evening, Grace," he said hesitantly.

"Reverend."

"This here is Belle Carson."

Grace nodded a greeting at the subdued young woman clutching a Bible. She was covered from neck to toe by a voluminous black cape that looked frayed and old, but the face above the collar was as dark and beautiful as an angel's.

"Hello, Miss Atwood," she said clearly.

Grace smiled at her, then turned her eyes back to Petrie. She introduced Jackson. "Reverend, this is Jackson Blake, our wagonmaster."

The two men nodded a greeting, then Jackson excused himself, leaving Grace and her guests alone.

Grace said, "I'd offer you a seat, but as you can see—"

She gestured around at her cramped, filled-with-crates interior. All supplies that wouldn't fit into the tent had been put in here with her.

"That's all right," Petrie said. "Hopefully, I won't take up much of your time."

"How may I help you, Reverend?"

"It's Belle who needs the help. I'm wondering if she can go on your wagon train?"

She scanned the silent woman at his side and wondered what her connection to the reverend might be. It didn't matter really, though, because she had all the brides she needed. "The women have already been chosen," Grace explained as gently as she could. "We don't need any more brides."

The girl's head dropped for a moment, then she looked up at Grace with a plea in her dark eyes. "Please, Miss Atwood, if you could reconsider, I'd be much appreciative."

Grace could hear the quiet desperation the girl seemed trying to hide. "We had a meeting last week, Belle," Grace said earnestly. "Why didn't you come?"

"I didn't know anything about the journey until yesterday."

Grace studied Petrie again. He met her eyes and then looked away as if he were uncomfortable. Grace decided she needed to get to the bottom of this. "Miss Carson, why don't you let me speak with the reverend alone for a moment, please?"

The girl nodded and went back outside. When the

silence resettled, Grace met Petrie's eyes. "What is this all about?"

He spoke frankly. "She's carrying a child, and the man is a deacon in her father's church. I—I don't want what happened to Nan to happen to her."

Grace studied his face and wondered why a man who'd put his own daughter out into the streets for the same sin would now take up the cross for someone else. "Is she kin?"

He shook his head no, then sighed, "As you've probably heard, I'm dying, and I think the Lord sent Belle to me so I could right things before I meet Him."

The pain in his eyes looked real enough to touch.

When he continued speaking, his voice was thick with emotion. "I didn't do right by Nannie, and it's been eating away at me ever since. I've prayed for the Lord to take away my guilt and shame, but so far He hasn't seen fit to do so. I've also prayed every night for you, Grace."

"Why?" she asked softly.

"Because you showed my Nan the love I didn't possess then. When she confessed her troubles to me, I was angry, proud, and too worried about what my bishop and congregation would think, but you and Elliot only worried about Nan."

"She was my dearest friend, Reverend. She had no one else."

"I know, and for years I held onto my anger and hubris to excuse what I'd done, but the Lord didn't excuse it. Deep in my heart I knew I'd failed, not only as a man of God, but more importantly as a father. However, it was far easier to blame Nan than to admit I'd been wrong."

He went silent for a moment, as if reviewing old memories. "But I *was* wrong, and I tell her that each and every time I visit her grave."

He looked to Grace. "Thank you for burying her and for the headstone. You were right to place on it that she was a loving daughter to me and her mother, because she truly was. I only wish now that I'd been more loving in return."

"Is this why you wish to help Belle?"

He nodded. "She has no money to speak of and her father is a lot like I was at his age, full of fire and brimstone but lacking the true sense of what it is most precious in life. He'll treat his daughter no better than I did my own."

Grace found his confession moving and knew that Nan would want Grace to help Belle too, so she didn't think twice. "Reverend, Belle can journey to Kansas with us, and Mr. Blake and I will make certain she stays safe. If it's needed, I'll even pay her way. When we arrive in Kansas she can pass herself off as a young widow, if that is her desire. She and her child can start a new life. I don't wish for her to end up like Nannie, either."

The reverend's grateful smile mirrored the tears of gratitude in his eyes. "Your compassion will bring you many blessings, Grace. My wife and I will pray for you."

"Thank you, and I'm glad you've made your peace with Nan's death."

He nodded tightly.

"Now, let's call Belle back in and give her the good news."

Belle was ecstatic. She hugged Grace and cried. Grace held her close and swore she could feel Nan smiling down from heaven.

It was agreed that Grace would stay in camp while the reverend went back to the city to try and convince her parents to pack up her belongings and bring them to her. The Carsons knew nothing about their daughter's condition and Petrie vowed to hold onto the truth and let Belle inform them in her own time. Belle suggested he talk to one of her aunts about her need for financial assistance. According to Belle, the aunt had always been supportive in the past.

Grace and Belle walked the reverend back to his buggy.

Grace told him, "You're welcome to stay the night and journey back in the morning."

"No, an old friend of mine lives just a few miles back up the road. I'll sleep there."

Before he climbed in, he turned to Grace and said, "Thank you again, Grace."

"You're welcome."

He then spoke to Belle. "Take care of yourself."

"I will," she replied. "How can I ever repay you for your help?"

"I've already been paid, child."

Grace and Belle watched him drive away, then walked back through the darkness to the camp. There were a few women standing around watching Grace's return and she knew they were curious about Belle's presence. She stopped for a moment to introduce Belle, and everyone welcomed her with a smile.

After securing Belle some bedding, Grace let the tired young woman bed down in her tent. In the morning, they'd make more permanent arrangements.

"Goodnight, Belle. Pleasant dreams. I'll be back later," Grace told her. She was leaving for a while so the young woman could have some privacy.

The dark-skinned Belle looked up from her bedroll. "Thank you so very much, Miss Atwood."

"It's Grace," Grace told her gently.

Belle nodded. She then asked seriously, "You won't tell anyone that I'm—"

Grace knew what the girl was trying to say. "No, Belle. Your business is your own unless you decide otherwise. I do want to tell Mr. Blake, though. He should know so he can keep your safety in mind."

Grace could see tears in Belle's eyes, and sought to reassure her. "Everything will be fine, you'll see. Now, get some rest. I'll see you in the morning."

The camp was bedding down for the night. Quiet had replaced the hustle and bustle. Small campfires could be seen dotting the dark, and around them sat small groups of women talking quietly. Tomorrow the horses and mules would be arriving and many of the brides would be learning how to drive a team for the first time. If things went well, they'd be on the road by next week this time.

Grace didn't realize her steps had taken her to Jackson's tent until she spotted him sitting in front of his own small fire. Her first instinct was to turn and go back the way she'd come, but never having been a coward, she moved toward the fire as if coming to see him had been her intent from the start.

"I've decided to take Belle with us."

Jackson was glad she'd sought him out because he'd been on the verge of searching her out. "Is that the young woman with the reverend?"

Grace nodded.

"I thought we were full."

"We are, but—she needs to begin life someplace new."

Jackson sensed a seriousness in her she'd not had earlier. "Something wrong, Grace?"

"No," she answered quietly. "It's just funny how life can be, sometimes."

She'd often wondered if the Reverend Petrie would ever admit that his own actions had been partially responsible for Nan's tragic end. It had taken thirteen long years and the plight of another young woman for him to act with the charity he'd been preaching all his life.

Jackson sensed she was miles away. "Do you want to talk?"

She shook her head. "No."

Jackson figured that was Grace the banker talking. The banker probably very rarely admitted needing help with anything. After all, the banker put the wagon train together, ordered the supplies and gathered the brides, and so far had not left one "t" uncrossed or one "i" undotted, but he didn't think she was the banker right now; right now she was a woman who he sensed needed to talk. "Sit," he invited softly.

Grace shook her head again. "I'm fine."

"Sit down, hard-headed woman," he scolded. "It's pretty obvious you have something on your mind."

Grace allowed herself a small smile. "And you called me bossy."

He simply smiled.

She sat.

For a moment she didn't say anything, then confessed, "I suppose the Reverend Petrie's visit is the reason I'm so melancholy."

"How do you know him?"

"His daughter Nan and I were best friends."

"You said 'were.' Did the two of you have a falling out?"

"No. She's dead, Jackson."

She said it with such detachment, he wanted to pull her into his arms and hold her. Judging by her tone and manner, the death of her friend must've affected her greatly.

"How old was she?"

"Seventeen, just as I was at the time."

"What happened to her?"

The memories came flooding back to Grace, bringing with them the pain of those times. "She was in love. I never knew his name. All she would tell me was that he was older, someone her father knew, and she was carrying his child."

Grace paused for another moment, thinking, remembering, then she continued, "She thought the man would marry her, but when she told him—"

Jackson finished for her, "He denied it."

Grace nodded grimly. "He told her she should talk to the other men she'd been with. But she hadn't been with any others."

"Quite the man."

"Quite the man," she echoed. "Nan was devastated, of course, and finally confided in me all that was happening."

She looked across the fire at him. "Society can be very cruel to women bearing a child out of wedlock and she was terrified about her future. I dearly wanted to help, but I couldn't because I didn't know how. I wanted to enlist my father's help, but I was certain he'd tell her folks. At the time, her father, Reverend Petrie, was the minister at the AME church."

"Did she have other family she could've gone to for help?"

"Not anyone who didn't breathe fire and brimstone like her father."

"So what did she do?"

"Gathered her courage and confessed everything to her parents."

Grace's cold voice matched her eyes. "He whipped her to within an inch of her life, then put her out on the street. Told her she was dead as far as the family was concerned and he didn't care what happened to her or where she went."

"Glory," Jackson whispered. "So where'd she go?"

"She showed up at our door in the middle of the night, bleeding and crying. My father immediately went for the doctor, and while the doctor was in with her, I told my father the whole story."

Grace held Jackson's eyes. "He said she could stay until she recovered and that he would talk with Reverend Petrie to see if a solution could be found. I think I loved him more than ever that night. He could've chosen not to get involved or been too afraid of the scandal it might've caused once word got out that he'd opened his home to Reverend Petrie's pregnant daughter, but he was genuinely concerned about her welfare and treated Nan with respect."

"Your father sounds like a fine man."

"The finest."

"What happened next?"

"About a week later, when she'd recovered sufficiently enough to be up and around, she said she had an errand to take care of and that she'd be back by supper, but she never returned. The next morning, some fishermen found her dead body floating in Lake Michigan." Grace's voice trailed off to a whisper. "The authorities said it was suicide."

Jackson watched as she used the backs of her hands to staunch the tears filling the corners of her eyes. He dearly wanted to take her in his arms, but knew if they were seen by anyone in camp, it would cause talk, so he forced himself to sit quietly and ask, "How did her parents react to her death?"

Grace's voice hardened. "The reverend told the authorities he didn't have a daughter named Nan and refused to claim the body, so my father and I did. We arranged the burial and paid for the tombstone. She must've been more terrified of the future than I knew—to take her life—" Her voice trailed off again. The pain of Nan's death was still fresh in her heart even after all these years because she hadn't been able to help.

"You shouldn't blame yourself. You did what you could. You and your daddy gave her a place to stay, even made sure she was buried properly. It was society weighing down on her—society and how folks view unmarried women who have children."

"I know, but I still feel as if I could've done more."

Jackson wanted to remind her that she'd been only seventeen, and seventeen-year-old females were powerless when facing the rigid dictates of society.

"So is Belle in a family way, too?"

Grace nodded. "I promised Belle you'd be the only person I'd tell."

Jackson's heart swelled in response to her trust, but he found Nan's story very sad. He now understood why Grace had agreed to take Belle on. "I'll keep her condition in mind during the training sessions."

"Thank you."

He leaned over and peered into her face. "Talking with me make you feel better?"

She nodded. He withdrew a clean handkerchief from the pocket in his black shirt and handed it to her. Grateful, she wiped at her teary eyes, then blew her nose.

Since they were on the subject of no good men, he wanted to ask about the coyote who'd left her at the altar, but now was not the time. He didn't like seeing her sad, he was beginning to realize.

Grace had a question. "Women always find you this easy to talk to?"

"Just those who want to talk."

Grace grinned and rolled her eyes. "And he's modest, too. Who'd have ever thought?"

The fire reflected on his smiling face.

She slowly rose to her feet. She thought back on their first meeting that night in his room and how angry she'd been upon leaving. Back then, had anyone told her that she'd end up talking with him this way, she'd've asked what they'd been drinking. "Thanks for listening."

"Anytime."

"I should be getting back. We've a full day ahead of us tomorrow. Goodnight, Jackson."

"Goodnight, Grace. Sweet dreams."

He watched her until she disappeared into the night. The first night they'd met, all he'd wanted to do was throttle her for nearly knocking him out cold with that lethal handbag—and now, now he wanted to teach her to ride the winds of passion and hear her whisper his name in the dark.

After breakfast the next morning, Mr. Drain arrived with the horses and mules. He had them strung together like a remuda and they were being watched over by three men on horseback. After close inspection, Jackson determined the animals were indeed the ones he and Grace had chosen and that there wasn't a ringer in the bunch. Drain and his men led the pack down into the valley and into the makeshift pen put up by Martin Abbott and his men before they left. Another pen would have to be constructed to hold the horses that wouldn't fit comfortably, but that could be dealt with later. A grateful Grace handed Drain the bank draft for the balance due and he and his men rode off with a wave.

For the rest of the morning, they were given instructions by both Jackson and their animal nurse, Daisy

Green, on the proper care and feeding of the fifty or so animals.

Jackson announced, "And you ladies should get used to stepping in pies, because by the time we head out this valley is going to be full of horse—" He caught himself just in time. "Well—you know."

They did.

He scanned the group. "So, are there any questions?"

There weren't any.

Under a grueling afternoon sun they tackled their next task, learning how to put the bridles and leads on the teams, and the proper way to remove them. The tack was heavy, the animals uncooperative, and Jackson made them do it again and again and again. Grace knew he couldn't help but hear the grumbling and the angry mutters the hot and frustrated women were offering up, but he seemed intent upon ignoring their fits of pique.

"The sooner you ladies can do this, the sooner we can move on to something new," he told them. Jackson wondered if they knew how angry they looked. From the tight jaws and the threatening eyes being shot his way, he decided it best to keep the question unasked.

Grace's patience had worn thin over an hour ago. "Jackson, we can do this in our sleep."

"Prove it."

She blinked. Once she got over the shock of his words, she asked, "How?"

Grace never learned the answer, because a half second later, the tall Tess Dubois crumpled to the ground like a wet sheet. Women sprang to her side, but Jackson got there first.

"Somebody get me some water, quick!" he barked, gently lifting Tess's head so he could cradle her against his arm. It was quite obvious she'd fainted from the heat. While schoolteacher Ruby O'Neal vaulted up the hill to the deserted church to get water from the pump to fill a canteen, he looked up, spotted Grace's concerned face, and said, "Get her out of this damn corset so she can breathe."

Grace thought that a brilliant suggestion and hastened to his side. She took on the chore of holding Tess's head and he backed out of the way while the women formed a circle around the fallen Tess. They all stretched wide their skirts, creating a shield around Loreli and Daisy as they opened Tess's clothes. Ruby returned with the now filled canteen and slid into the circle's interior.

Standing a respectful distance away, Jackson was admittedly impressed seeing them rally on behalf of a fallen companion, and he thought maybe they were beginning to form the camaraderie Grace had hoped for, but wondered where the women had learned to use their skirts in such a manner and if it was something females learned while growing up. He put that thought aside. He was about to announce his first real wagonmaster edict, and he knew they were going to go through the roof.

Once the groggy Tess was helped to her feet and escorted back to her tent by Daisy and Belle, Jackson looked out on the small sea of female faces and declared, "Ladies, from now on, it would be better if you went without your corsets."

For a moment there was a stunned silence, until a suspicious sounding Grace asked, "Why?"

"Because once we get on the road, we aren't going to have the time to stop twenty or thirty times a day to revive fainters. You're going to be working like men, and you need to be able to breathe like men. After driving six, eight hours a day, those teams aren't going to care whether your waist is eighteen inches or not, but your lungs will."

His voice and manner made it easy to determine that

this was not a request, but Grace spoke on behalf of her brides. "Jackson, we are not going without proper undergarments."

"I'm certainly not giving up mine," Sarah Mitchell huffed.

"And neither am I," her sister pledged.

The only woman who didn't appear angry was Loreli Winters, and she said matter-of-factly, "For what it's worth, I agree with him."

Silence descended, and in unison the women all turned to stare.

"I think corsets are the number one menace to female society," Loreli said. "You can't breathe, they leave you scarred. Who needs them? The first time I wore one was the *only* time I wore one. I can't abide the things."

The women looked at each other as if trying to decide whether to declare Loreli a traitor.

The well-endowed Trudy Berry said coolly, "That's all well and good, Loreli, but what about those of us who have a bit more to offer, shall we say? I can't bounce all the way to Kansas City!"

"Then bind yourself," Loreli encouraged. "We've all done it before at one time or another. Even bound you'll be a lot more comfortable."

Jackson could've kissed her, but his voice was firm as he added, "And ladies, any cheating, and you'll be on pie-shoveling detail."

Grace stared at him as if he'd lost his mind. Her hands went to her hips and she stood there a moment. Granted, he might have their health in mind, but to issue threats! He was not the type to blow smoke, so she had no trouble believing he would do what he'd pledged, but she swore if any brides decided to back out of the venture because of Jackson's methods she'd feed his ears to the mules.

Jackson could see the volatility in Grace's eyes but he paid it no mind. She hadn't hired him to mollycoddle these women. She'd hired him to get them to Kansas City, but they weren't going anywhere if everybody started dropping like flies. Preparing himself for a visit from the fire ant later, he told everyone, "Let's get finished up here."

So for another hour and a half, they put tack on, they took tack off. They threaded reins through the teams of horses, they unthreaded reins through the teams. They hooked teams to the wagons, they unhooked teams to the wagons. Only when they had him convinced that they could indeed do the tasks in their sleep did he dismiss them.

"The rest of the day is yours. Grace, I need to see you later."

"And I wish to speak with you, too," she said with a false brightness. "Now."

He had the nerve to smile her way, then walked back toward his tent.

When he was out of earshot, Sarah Miller asked, "Surely you are not going to let him run roughshod over us this way. What will he demand next, that we go without our drawers?"

The stout Sarah Mitchell turned her angry gaze Loreli's way. "I can't believe you took his side on the corsets."

"I'm probably going to do a lot of things you won't believe before we get to Kansas City," Loreli tossed back. "But that's what we no-corset-wearing, gambling women do."

Grace held up her hands. "Ladies."

Sarah Mitchell huffed and turned her head.

Loreli had a smile on her ivory face that did not reach her eyes.

Hoping this wouldn't lead to a serious spat, Grace said, "I'm going to speak with Mr. Blake."

"I'd rather he be boiled in oil," Fanny declared.

"Hear! Hear!" schoolteacher Ruby O'Neal called out. "I'm so tired, I'll probably never walk again!"

Everyone laughed at that and as the chuckles faded away, Grace looked out over the assemblage and saw the dirt-stained clothes and sweaty faces that verified how hard they'd worked. "You ladies did well today. Everything we learn and everyday that passes put us one step closer to Kansas. Be proud of yourselves."

She saw a few smiles, and that buoyed her spirits. "Now, our general has given us the rest of the day off, so go enjoy yourselves and we'll see everyone at dinner."

As the woman trailed away, Grace set out for Jackson's tent. He was behind it chopping firewood. "You were quite short with us back there."

He put down the ax, then wiped his brow on his sleeve. "Was I?"

"Yes."

For a moment he studied her silently, then asked seriously, "Do you want the women to be prepared for this journey or not?"

She thought that a rather silly question. "Of course I do."

"Then let me prepare them."

"But—"

"They won't be ready if I have to talk softly or kiss skinned knees all the time."

"No one's ask—"

"Grace," he said calmly, cutting her off.

She snapped her mouth shut. "What?"

"I'm going to be tough on everyone, including you, because their lives, your life, may depend on how well you learn. If I'm rude, it's because I want it done right. If anything happens, I don't want it to be because you and the ladies couldn't tie a proper knot, couldn't control your teams, or couldn't breathe . . ."

"You make it sound as if we're enlistees."

"In a way, you are, and I'm first in command."

Grace didn't think she liked his attitude at all. "You and I are going to fight a lot, if that's going to be your thinking."

"We've already conceded that point, remember?"

She did.

"If the thought of my doing something like forbidding corsets keeps someone from fainting and maybe injuring herself or the animals or someone else, so be it. You aren't paying me to be liked, either." He went back to his chopping.

"If I were, you'd already be shown the door."

He smiled and paused. "You don't like me in my general's hat."

She didn't lie. "No, I don't."

"Well, when we get to Kansas City, I'll burn it, but until then, this is the way it'll have to be. I'm responsible for this train, and I take that very seriously."

"Too seriously, I'm thinking."

He went back to chopping.

Jackson knew he wouldn't be nominated for any congeniality awards today, but he wasn't seeking any. All he wanted was to get the brides to the men in Kansas in one piece, and if he had to act like an overseer in order to accomplish his goal, then so be it. The women were rawer than the greenest army recruit. They were going to have to be toughened up, and if wanting to take a buggy whip to him for issuing orders about their underwear added to that toughness, he was all for it.

"You know," he said between swings of the ax, "I

respect your business sense and that razor-sharp mind, but neither of those attributes is going to mean much to the teams you and the other women are going to have to drive for hours on end, or to the rivers they may have to ford, or to the hundred other dangers that might lay ahead."

He paused and looked her way. "Even if this trip is smooth sailing all the way, it's still a very serious undertaking. I've got every faith that these women can make it."

"Even if you didn't think so at first?"

He wanted to kiss that sassy mouth of hers until she saw stars. "Even if I didn't think so when I hired on. The ladies worked hard today."

"Then you should tell them that," Grace pointed out. "It would mean a lot. When I left, they were talking about boiling you in oil."

He chuckled. "That bad, huh? Then maybe I should."

Grace was glad the tension had dissipated.

"Are you still mad at me?" he asked frankly.

"No. You're right about the corsets. We do need to be able to breathe."

"Good."

In the silence that followed, their eyes held. Grace could feel herself beginning to drown in his eyes.

"You know," he indicated softly, "There are certain advantages to not wearing a corset. Remind me to show you the next time you come around looking to be kissed."

Grace could've sworn the ground swayed beneath her feet. "That isn't going to happen," she somehow managed to retort.

His eye said he didn't believe her. Neither did her pounding heart.

Deciding now would be a good time to hoist anchor,

Grace said more hastily than she'd intended, "I'm going to my tent now. I'm glad we talked."

"So am I."

As he watched her head back the way she'd come, he said again, "So am I."

# Chapter 6

That evening after dinner, Jackson called everyone together. As the tired and weary women took seats at the trestle tables, Loreli leaned over to Grace and whispered, "Do you know what this is about?"

Grace shook her head. She hoped it had to do with her earlier suggestion that he say something positive to the women, but after his declaration this afternoon concerning their undergarments, who really knew why he'd convened the gathering.

Once everyone was settled, Jackson stood. "Ladies, I brought you together just to let you know what a fine job you did today."

A stunned silence filled the air.

Someone called out humorously, "What did you do with the *real* Blake, mister?"

Laughs followed, and even Jackson had to smile. "I'm

serious. I know I didn't win any prizes from you today, but you ladies won one from me. Oh, you grumbled and fussed and wanted to boil me in oil, or so I heard—"

He looked at Grace. She ducked, her head hoping he wouldn't see her grin. "But you worked hard, and I'm real proud of you."

Just as Grace had predicted, the women looked pleased as punch. Any animosity they might've been holding seemed to slip away.

"Does this mean tomorrow's a holiday and we don't have to work?" someone cracked.

Jackson replied through the resulting laughter, "Nope. We've got to start driving lessons and get that second horse pen built."

Mock groans filled the air.

He shrugged his wide shoulders and smiled. "Sorry."

As a group they spent a few more moments discussing tomorrow's agenda and then the meeting adjourned. The women drifted back to their tents with a bit more pep in their step than they'd had when the meeting had begun. Grace attributed it to Jackson's praise.

"Thank you," Grace told him, once they were alone at the tables.

"You're welcome, but I should've thought of doing that myself. Being decent is something I used to be fairly good at, believe it or not."

"I think you're pretty decent now," she admitted. "You don't think of yourself as decent."

"Not as decent as I once was. No." As a wanted man, he could never reclaim the man he used to be, the man decent enough to pin on a star.

Grace saw a bitterness in his eyes she'd never seen before. "Are you all right?"

He nodded. "Yep."

Grace sensed a darkness in him she wanted explained.

What secrets did he harbor? She realized she knew very little about him. "Will you tell me about it someday?"

The question surprised him. He searched her eyes for a moment and read the concern. "There's nothing to tell."

He'd lied because he didn't want her involved in his past. If she didn't know anything, she couldn't be drawn into whatever awaited him in Texas.

"You're lying, Jackson Blake."

That caught him off guard, too, and he chuckled lowly. "Says who?"

"Says me. You're not being fair, you know."

He wanted to ease her into his arms and give that very perceptive mind of hers something else to think about, like his kisses. "What am I not being fair about?"

"Remember last evening, when you made me tell you what was on my mind?"

"Yes."

"Well?"

"Well, what?" he asked with mock innocence.

"It's time for you to reciprocate."

"That's another one of those highfalutin words."

"And that's your attempt to keep from speaking the truth."

Jackson knew she was right, but he was a wanted man. How was he supposed to tell her that? He stated seriously, "Grace, if and when the time comes, you'll know."

That wasn't a lie. That was truth.

Grace realized he hadn't given her much, but she accepted it and let the rest be. "I'm holding you to that."

He nodded his understanding. Looking at her he realized that were he not a wanted man, he'd be giving serious consideration to the idea of courting her, plain and simple, even though she was probably destined for a man with a much higher social standing than he'd ever attain. He saw her with a doctor or a politician or some fancy Negro mortician with a gold watch in his pocket, not a Texan who couldn't even give her his name.

"A penny for your thoughts."

Her voice brought him back to reality. "Just thinking about you being married to some fancy doctor or politician."

Grace's face filled with mock alarm. "Whoa, cowboy. I'm not marrying anyone."

"Sure you will, eventually."

Grace shook her head. "No. Never."

"You sound pretty set."

"I am. When a man leaves you at the altar, you never want to be burned that way again."

Grace realized that thinking about that day no longer brought pain. She felt anger at Garth for being such a bounder, and at herself for being silly enough to think he actually loved her, but pain, no. "He assumed that because I was a banker's daughter I was worth a king's ransom. When he found out I wasn't, he threw me over for someone wealthier."

"What was his name?"

"Garth Leeds."

Grace wondered what he'd do with the information and how it would affect their future dealings, so she told him, "It's not something I'll enjoy being teased about."

"I understand," came his soft reply, "but was this Leeds loco?"

She smiled, grateful for his support. "No, I was."

"How long did he court you?"

"Almost a year."

Jackson could imagine how difficult it must've been for her to face her friends and acquaintances after the canceled wedding. Although he'd known her only a short while, he knew her well enough to be certain she wouldn't've hidden herself away in response to such a public embarrassment. No doubt she'd gone on with her social life and her charity work, and tried to close her ears to the gossip that probably greeted her everywhere she went. Beneath all that fire and bossiness beat the heart of a woman far more resilient than women of her class were supposed to be and she deserved a man who'd value that, not some two-bit coyote who only wanted her money. He hoped he'd get a chance to meet this Garth Leeds someday.

"What're you thinking now?" she asked.

"How I'd like to meet this Leeds, and how a strong woman like you needs a strong man."

"Like you, I suppose?" she asked knowingly.

Enjoying this soft banter, he shrugged. "Maybe, but women like you don't truck with men like me. Two different worlds."

"I suppose, but stranger things have been known to happen."

Grace and her father had often sat on the porch in the summertime talking about anything and everything under the sun until the wee hours of the morning, but those conversations differed from the conversations she'd been having with Jackson. This shared time felt more intimate, more personal. Even though he'd successfully evaded her attempts to get him to reveal more of himself, she still felt as if they'd become connected to each other somehow.

His voice interrupted her thoughts. "You know, that first night you snuck into my room, I'd no idea this is where I'd wind up."

"You were rude and arrogant and far too high-handed for me."

"I was hoping I'd scare you off."

"I don't scare easily," she said with pride in her eyes.

"I noticed. I thought you were the bossiest female I'd ever met. Still do."

She punched him in the arm. "I'm not bossy."

"Ha!"

"I am not. I'm—firm."

"You're bossy, woman, but that's part of your charm."

Their gazes met and held. Even though it was now dark, it did nothing to mask the sparks arching between them.

She asked playfully, "Can I get you to write that down and then sign it?"

"Only if you asked to be kissed . . ."

"I think it's time for me to go home," she responded wryly, softly.

"Are you sure?"

"Positive. Otherwise, we're going to be the talk of the town tomorrow."

"Why?"

"Because I'm about two seconds from asking to be kissed."

The air between them was hot and charged. One more spark and their world would burst into flame.

"Then let's get you home."

They made the walk silently, but each was as aware of the other as they were of their own breathing. More than once, Jackson fought down the urge to carry her off into the dark, but many of the fires and lanterns around the camp were still lit, signals that a good many of the brides were still awake. Yes, he wanted her, but he also cared about her reputation.

At her tent their steps slowed. The soft light shining from inside the canvas meant Belle was awake and probably reading her Bible, something she did every night before turning in.

"Belle's still up," Grace pointed out, in an effort to substitute small talk for her yearning and feelings.

As though cued, Belle suddenly appeared in the opening. She was dressed in her night clothes, and upon seeing Jackson at Grace's side, drew back a bit. "Uh— hello, Mr. Blake."

"Belle," he said pleasantly. "How are you?"

"Fine, Mr. Blake."

"Good. Miss Atwood and I were going to work on maps tonight, but she thought it best she check on you instead."

Belle looked to Grace who hoped the girl couldn't see the surprise on her face. *What maps?*

The girl smiled and said reassuringly, "No, I'm fine. You don't have to worry. Everybody's been so nice. If you two need to work, go on ahead. Loreli's already told me that if I need anything and you're not around, just to let her know. Is she really a gambling woman, Miss Atwood?"

"Yes, Belle, she is."

"Never expected a woman like that to be so nice."

Grace smiled, glad that Loreli had gone out of her way to make the young woman feel welcome.

"So, go on and do your maps. I'll be fine."

That said, she went back inside, leaving Grace to look up at Jackson and ask suspiciously, "Did you say you were once a sheriff or a confidence man? You led her exactly where you wished for her to go."

"I know, but I wanted to spend more time with you."

Grace wondered if there were some kind of root she could take that would make her less susceptible to him and all he seemed to promise.

He told her softly, "You can go on in or not, your choice, Grace."

Even though the banker in Grace protested loudly, the woman in Grace chose "not."

Since they'd told Belle they were going to look at maps, Grace and Jackson set out for the supply tent that also served as his office. Once there, he lit a lantern and the dark interior took on a soft glow. Grace looked over to him and realized that the vow she'd carved in stone this morning might as well have been written in sand. Being with him this way made her feel reckless and more than a little bit giddy.

"So, maps or kisses—which would you prefer to explore?"

Smiling, she had to turn away from his shadowy presence for a moment before turning back to say, "Whatever am I going to do with you, Jackson Blake?"

"How about this . . ."

And he pulled her in against him and kissed her languidly, deeply, and passionately. When she responded with a passion that rivaled his own, he deepened the kiss, nibbling on the tempting flesh of her bottom lip and tasting the opened corners of her mouth with the hot, seeking tip of his tongue. He vividly reacquainted himself with the lips he'd been craving for what seemed like an eternity and ran his hand up to the base of her neck to bring her even closer.

He savored her, ignited her, and Grace sought to do the same. She could feel the strong muscles in his back beneath her wandering palms and the hot, tempting pressure of his thighs against her own. As he brushed his mouth across her ear and over the edge of her jaw, she tossed aside all pretense of not wanting this man and let her desire soar.

Jackson wanted to touch her in all the ways a man

could touch a woman. His lips sampled the scented column of her neck, and again the delicate curve of her jaw. He brushed fire over the high collar of her blouse where it met her skin and Grace sighed in the rising heat. She could feel his hands roaming slowly over her back, and up and down her sides, but when his big hand cupped itself around her breast, the sensations were so strong she drew back for a moment in an effort to clear the haze.

In the interim, he stood before her dappled by the shadows of the lone lamp, pulsing for her, hungering for her. Jackson knew he'd die if she didn't want him to touch her again, but she was Grace, and not a cathouse whore. He had to give her a choice. "Do you want to go back?" he asked quietly.

Still breathing heavily, Grace shook her head. "No. I just need to catch my breath."

He smiled. "Woozy?"

"Very," she replied huskily. "You're giving me quite an education."

"Then shall we continue your lessons?"

His words were as hot as his eyes.

"Yes."

He pressed his lips to hers gently in reward for her passionate willingness, then drew her back into his arms. He spent a few more languid moments kissing her until her senses sang, then she felt his hand rise to her breast and begin to caress it slowly.

When he dipped his head and gently captured her nipple with his teeth, she moaned aloud. Grace's head dropped back and her virgin's body arched invitingly. She'd never had a man touch her this way and the sharp sensations were as brilliant as the sun. He gave her other breast the same bone-throbbing caresses and Grace swore her whole body liquefied.

Jackson raised his head to capture her lips again, then filled his senses with the feel of her hips in his hands. He knew he couldn't take her fully, not with all the risks it incurred, but he wanted to pleasure her in ways so vivid she'd never forget this night or him.

"I want to touch you, Grace . . . let me touch you . . ."

To that end, he slowly began undoing the buttons on her blouse. They were the only barriers standing between his lips and the silk-skinned treasures he wanted to explore. Grace knew she should not let him take the liberties he seemed intent upon; well-brought-up women did not encourage such scandalous behavior, but scandalous was how she felt and she didn't want his lessons to stop.

She reeled as he brushed his lips across the now bared expanse of her throat. His mouth was warm; his tasting tongue against the tops of her breasts made her arch even more. It took all she had just to breathe. The knowledge that he was slowly undressing her was heady enough, but when he parted the halves of her blouse and worshipped his palms over the hard, dark tips of her breasts beneath her thin camisole, she just knew her body had burst into flame. He eased her camisole aside. His kisses came next, dallying, masterful conquerings of her breasts that left each nubbin pleading and hot. The sensual suckling in tandem with the lingering licks from his tongue made her keen pleasurably. She didn't care that under the impetus of his big hands her skirt was circling higher and higher up the back of her thighs, nor did she care that the initial touch of his hand as it moved over her drawers scorched her waist and skin; all she cared about was this wanton desire burning in her blood.

Jackson wanted her more than any other woman before. The scents of her, the sounds of her passion and her warm silken skin made him want to find the nearest bed, lay her down, and fill her until the sun rose, but he couldn't, not without compromising her, so he contented himself with her pleasure.

Grace's whole world was spinning. His expert touches and caress made her ripple like summer heat on the horizon. She knew she shouldn't let him, but she didn't want him to stop, not even when he boldly undid the silken ties of her drawers.

Grace trembled as her drawers whispered open. The hot feel of his hands followed as they cupped her hips. When he possessively pulled her in against all that made him male, she drew in a sharp breath. Sensations were stacking up inside herself like thunderclouds on a stormy day, engulfing her, fueling her to part her thighs so he could make them climb even higher.

He rewarded her with a sensual touch that made her growl even deeper. Jackson never imagined she would be so passionately responsive. He could feel the age-old rhythms begin to claim her hips, and his own desires hardened further, seeing and feeling her virgin body gently straining for more. Unable to resist, he dropped his head to her bared breasts. Lingering there for a few silent moments, he made sure both dark-tipped nubbins would answer to him before concentrating on the damp, pulsing flesh between her thighs.

Grace had no idea how much longer she could hold up against this sensual conquering. She felt hot and swollen, but he continued, pleasuring her brazenly, masterfully; adding more to fuel the fire that engulfed them both. Jackson could hear her heightened breathing, see the rictus of passion on her face. Being a man of some experience, he knew she was only a heartbeat away from completion. "Let's get this first one out of the way . . ."

Grace had no idea what he meant, but when he wantonly circled his finger over the warm flowing shrine, then possessively slid a gentle finger inside, her being exploded. The force of it buckled her, shook her. It made her want to scream his name as she rode out the storm with her head against his chest. Nothing in her life had prepared her for such earth-shattering sensations—nothing.

Grace finally came back to herself, and as she looked up at him with both awe and passion, he bent to kiss her softly. "Is that the first time you've ever felt that, Banker Atwood . . . ?"

His mind-numbing kisses were interfering with the few faculties she had left, but she somehow summoned the will to answer. "Yes."

His hands were teasing her nipples again, boldly exploring her hips and thighs. She husked out, "Was that one of the advantages of not wearing a corset?"

Jackson was so hard with desire for her he didn't know he'd summon the strength to see her back to her tent. "Yes, one of them."

He wanted nothing more than to acquaint her with all the various ways a man could pleasure a woman as passionate as she, but he knew if he did that, she'd be here until morning, consequences be damned.

Grace's completion continued to send tiny pulsating echoes through her blood. Her hair had come undone, her blouse was still open, and her camisole lay twisted beneath her damp breasts. She looked scandalous and felt the same, but she'd loved every touch she'd been given. Whether she'd be able to go back to being the chaste and diligent Grace Atwood was debatable, after what she'd experienced in his arms. Also debatable was whether she really *wanted* to go back.

In the end, though, he slowly did up her buttons again, then brazenly retied the strings of her drawers. He gifted her with one last thrilling kiss, then said, "Let's walk you back."

When they reached her tent, there were no lights on inside. Belle had evidently gone to sleep.

He said, "I'll see you in the morning. Thanks for helping with the maps."

Smiling, she shook her head. "And thank you for the lesson."

"Anytime."

Neither of them wanted to part. The moments they'd shared in the supply tent were not easily dismissed. Neither would be able to deny their desire, nor could they go back to the people they'd been before. Tonight had changed things between them.

Grace wanted him to take her back into his arms, but she had to settle for saying, "Goodnight, Jackson."

"Goodnight, Grace. I'll see you in the morning."

As Jackson walked back to his tent on the far side of the glade, he realized that as usual, he hadn't gotten nearly enough of Grace Atwood. His manhood was hard as granite. In the past he'd never been one to be bowled over by a woman, any woman, but after holding Grace in his arms and tasting her passionate kisses, he was beginning to feel that way. Before meeting her, he'd been a solitary, brooding individual consumed with and by a past that had dogged his steps everyday for the last ten years. Now, after being knocked in the head by one Grace Atwood, his life seemed to be taking a different turn. He actually felt alive again. Admittedly, he'd always been a serious man, but he'd found even less joy in the world since fleeing Texas. The few pleasures he did find were ofttimes taken in temporary havens offered by women like the ones Sunshine employed, women who didn't mind his leaving before sunrise as long as he placed some coins on their nightstands before departing. Truth be told, because his life had become so joyless, he honestly couldn't remember the last time he'd laughed aloud before his hellion Grace entered his life, swinging that damned handbag and proposing he lead an all-woman wagon train to Kansas. Surviving on odd jobs and staying one step ahead of the Texas warrant had been all he'd known or cared about since his father's murder. Now he wanted to know Grace Atwood, even if there was no future in it.

Over the next few days, the valley became a beehive of activity as the encampment blossomed to life. The duty roster was implemented, the laundry lines were strung, meals were planned, and the brides' personalities and temperaments began to surface. As Grace and the Mitchell sisters learned, most of the thirty-five women were leaders, not followers.

The episode began with a suggestion from Zora that a constable be elected—"Someone we can all trust to keep the peace and settle disputes fairly," was how she explained it.

Grace thought it an excellent idea, so that night after supper she opened the floor for nominations.

Trudy raised her hand. "I nominate Loreli."

A surprised Loreli looked around, but before she could say anything, Molly Mitchell snapped, "That's like having a fox guard the chickens. I nominate my sister, Sarah."

Sarah smiled benevolently, "Why, thank you, sister, and if elected, I will stand for morality and reason."

There were a few loud snorts.

"Any other nominations?" Grace asked, trying not to roll her eyes at the Mitchells' airs.

Silence.

"Then I guess we have two candidates. Loreli, do you accept the nomination?"

The gambler looked over at the sneering Mitchell sisters and drawled, "Damn right, and I'll stand for fun and good times."

Trudy clapped vigorously.

Grace tried to hide her grin. "When do you want to have the vote?"

Before anyone could reply, Sarah stated self-importantly, "Some of us hardly know one another. I say we have the election next week."

A voice in the back cracked, "That's too long. You're not running for President."

Giggles greeted that sage reminder and earned stern glares from both Mitchell sisters.

Fanny spoke up, "Then let's compromise. How about we hold the election during dinner the day after tomorrow. That should be more than enough time for folks to make up their minds."

"And a secret ballot," Zora added. Her suggestion met with unanimous agreement.

So the vote was held. Jackson was drafted to count the ballots, and when he returned, announced, "Loreli Winters, twenty-five. Sarah Mitchell, five."

Bonnets were tossed in the air, congratulations were given, and the Mitchell sisters stuck their noses in the air and left the gathering along with their supporters.

That had been three days ago, and now, as Grace prepared for bed, she wished she'd trusted her intuition and found replacements for them when she'd had the chance. Now she seemed stuck with their judgmental, pompous personages, but she supposed it could be worse; there could be six or seven harridans in the group instead of just two.

Grace blew out her lamp and burrowed beneath the

quilts and blankets atop her bedroll. She still had not become accustomed to sleeping on the hard, unyielding ground, and as always, tossed and turned for a few moments, trying to find a spot that would not leave her body bruised for life and not wake up Belle while she searched. The bedroll offered a bit of cushioning, but only a bit.

Trying to take her mind off of her rigid accommodations, Grace turned her thoughts to Jackson. Since the night in the supply tent, they'd had no opportunities to slip away. She saw him and he saw her, but both were too busy to do anything more than share a glance or a few words. He'd worked them hard that next morning and the next day and the day after that, until every woman in camp was so weighed down by aches and pains of learning to drive they were ready to say to hell with Kansas City and go home. Loreli came to their rescue, though. She went to her tent and returned with a salesman's sample case. It was filled with little tins of a clear, violet-scented salve that she gave to everyone who wanted one, although the Mitchells declined. The case had originally belonged to a salesman Loreli had met over a poker table in Cincinnati. After Loreli won all of his money, he'd had nothing left to bet but the case, and he eventually wound up losing that too.

Loreli swore the salve worked like a charm and she was right. Once rubbed into the skin, it soothed the fire in their overworked muscles and joints. The next morning the women had risen ready to take on the world.

That had been two days ago; the same day a messenger from town brought Jackson a wire from Chicago sent to him by a marshal friend, Dixon Wildhorse. It seemed the marshal needed Jackson's assistance. When Jackson told Grace he'd asked the marshal to join the wagon train as a scout, Grace agreed that it was a good idea.

After pledging to send back word to the camp if the marshal's business took more than a day or two, Jackson, astride his chestnut stallion, had ridden out.

Grace would never admit it aloud to any of the brides, but she missed him. Although he'd been driving them like an overseer, she missed his smile and the way he sometimes looked at her as if she were once again half dressed in his arms. She'd grown accustomed to having him nearby, even if he did spend most of his time striding around barking orders as if they were army recruits. Truth be told, she and the brides had learned a great deal under his tutelage; they were stronger, fitter, and more confident. Admittedly, many of the women had yet to master the intricacies of driving a team, but that would come in time. Grace had miscalculated how long it would take for them to get ready, but now she had every reason to believe that by the first week of June, less than a week away, the brides would be ready to embark on their journey. It would all be because of Jackson Blake.

At breakfast a few mornings after the vote, the women listened as Loreli read off the names on the day's duty roster. Grace and the roster committee had broken the women down into groups and each group was assigned a particular job for three days. At the end of those three days the groups rotated. The main jobs were laundry, meals, and caring for the animals. The first two were a joy compared with the last. No one enjoyed being on pie detail or mucking out the pen, but it had to be done.

Grace had spent the past three days with the animals and was happy to be rotating to laundry. So what if the lye and the hot water stung her eyes and left her hands cracked and red? It was much better than shoveling manure.

Late that afternoon, as Grace and her group, which

included Fanny, Trudy, and Tess labored over the tin washboards, Trudy asked, "What are we going to do about our unwanted visitors?"

"I really don't know," Grace replied tersely. Trudy was referring to the townspeople who'd been gathering on the rise for the past three days to watch the camp's activities. The numbers seemed to be increasing daily and the women were beginning to feel like attractions at a fair. A good twenty-five people were up there now. Grace's Uncle Marty had warned Grace that the brides and their camp would probably generate the most excitement the little township had seen in a while, and evidently he'd been right. Whole families arrived at midday, set themselves up—complete with box lunches— and departed at dusk. So far, they seemed content to do nothing more than watch and occasionally heckle the women's bad driving, but Grace wanted them gone. She didn't like being gawked at.

She was just about to ask if anyone had suggestions about how to get rid of their unwanted visitors when the tall Tess straightened up over her laundry tub and said, "Well, look who's back."

It was Jackson. The sight of him slowly riding down the rise evoked a chorus of mock groans from women from all over the camp, but they appeared happy to see him. Grace noted that his dark-skinned good looks hadn't diminished during his absence. If anything, he looked even more handsome astride the stallion. When he rode over to the makeshift laundry, their eyes met and he touched his hat in greeting. She nodded in reply while trying to hide her true feelings.

"Afternoon, ladies," Jackson said to the women as he dismounted, but he had eyes only for his hellion. "Grace."

The front of her blouse and skirt were soaked from

the wash water and her hair was a mess, but she was still the most beautiful woman he'd ever seen.

"Afternoon, Jackson. Welcome back."

As usual, he was dressed in all black. "Thanks. How've things been going?"

"Fairly well," she replied. "How's the marshal?"

"Not bad. He and his wife are in town. They'll be along later."

Grace hid her happiness over seeing him again beneath her composed manner. "I didn't know he had a wife."

"They were married yesterday," he explained. "Her name's Katherine. They'll need a tent."

Grace nodded. In reality she wanted to greet him with a lot more intimacy than this public gathering would allow.

Jackson wanted to drag her away to some private place and show her how much he'd missed her, but instead, he called out, "Ladies, we've got driving practice in one hour."

Real groans greeted that announcement. He pointed out, "If you can't drive, we can't leave."

That said, he took the horse by the reins and headed to his tent.

On the heels of his departure, Tess sighed. "When I meet my man in Kansas City, do you think he'll look at me the way Jackson looks at Grace?"

Grace turned to her and chuckled. "Whatever do you mean?"

Trudy said, "Don't play dumb with us, Grace Atwood. He looked like he wanted to drag you off to his tent, and you know it."

Embarrassment heated Grace's cheeks, but she went back to her washboard without comment.

Grace and the brides had practiced driving during

Jackson's absence, hoping he'd be impressed with the progress they'd made, but he wasn't, mainly because there were more than a few near collisions and they couldn't form a circle or a straight line to save their lives. A few of the women hadn't secured their teams to the wagon properly and when they slapped down the reins the animals took off back to the corral, trailing the harnesses and leaving the wagon behind. Some of the male spectators up on the rise were laughing so hard at the chaos, Grace wanted them shot.

About an hour into the practice, a tall man and woman entered the camp. Grace assumed them to be the marshal Wildhorse and his new wife, Katherine, but Jackson's barking did not make Grace feel neighborly enough to get down from her seat on the wagon to meet them. She did want Jackson's head, however. He was standing in the middle of the clearing yelling at the top of his lungs, "A line, ladies! Can't you make a simple line?"

They'd been at this for almost two hours now and a few women had angry tears in their eyes after having been singled out for their ineptness. Belle was one of them. Grace looked over at the young woman's defeated face and decided she'd had it. Pulling back on her reins to bring her team to a halt, she hopped down and ignoring the onlooking marshal and his wife, lit into Jackson for all she was worth. "If you don't stop yelling, I'm going to punch you right in the nose, Jackson Blake!"

"Not if you have to drive over here to do it!"

Grace's eyes bulged. "How dare you!"

"You're driving like a bunch of women!"

"We are women, you stubborn, cowbrained jackass!"

Grace could see the Wildhorses staring as she and Jackson argued. She was certain she was making a terrible impression, but did she care? Grace told him hotly, "In ten minutes this practice is over."

"You're done when I say you're done," he replied.

"Ten minutes!" she snapped, then stormed back to her wagon.

Jackson threw his black hat to the ground.

True to her word, Grace called a halt to the madness ten minutes later and sent everyone back to their tents to rest up before dinner, then she and a few of the brides set out to erect a tent for the newly married Wildhorses.

The tent was erected with swift efficiency; after being around Blake, the women could erect a tent blindfolded and asleep. They moved in some empty crates for the newlyweds to use as makeshift furniture and bedrolls and blankets from the storage tents. Grace looked over the sparse interior and noted that it wasn't much of a honeymoon home but it would have to do.

As she stepped back outside, she found Jackson standing nearby talking to the Wildhorses. He introduced Grace to the tall, graceful Katherine and her handsome lawman husband Dixon.

"Glad you could join us, Mr. and Mrs. Wildhorse. If you're friends of Mr. Blake's, I'm sure he's been filling your ears with plenty of lies about me. Don't believe him."

Katherine Wildhorse grinned.

"We have your tent ready. Hope you don't mind that we put you over here, a bit away from the main camp. Mr. Blake says you're newlyweds, so we thought you might like whatever privacy we could manage."

Grace thought she saw amusement light the lawman's dark eyes for a moment, and that Katherine seemed a bit uncomfortable, but Grace blamed it on her imagination and introduced the new arrivals to some of the women who'd helped her ready the tent.

After receiving a sincere thanks for their efforts from the Wildhorses, Grace and the ladies walked back to the main camp.

That evening, as Grace sat in her tent writing a letter to her aunts, a familiar voice called, "Knock, knock."

Grace set her pen aside. "Come in, Jackson."

She rose from the empty barrel she'd been sitting upon and when he entered asked, "Are the Wildhorses settled in?"

He nodded.

Grace had been among the women who'd witnessed the lawman carry his wife over the threshold of the tent. The traditional romantic gesture had evoked hearty cheers from the brides looking on and been the talk of the camp at dinner. "They seem like a happy couple."

"They will be," he said.

Grace thought that a rather odd response but didn't press for more details. "What can I do for you?"

"We need to talk."

Grace observed him for a moment. "About what?"

"Us."

Their eyes held as she asked quietly, "What about us?"

"I missed you, Grace."

The soft-spoken statement made her heart spin. She looked away, lest he see the emotional response in her eyes. She missed him, too, but she was still simmering from this afternoon's driving lessons. "Two of the women want to go back to Chicago."

"Because of me?"

"Partly. They don't think they're measuring up."

He sighed. "Do *you* think they're measuring up?"

She shrugged. "You're the one in charge."

"Would it help if I spoke to them?"

"Not if all you're going to do is yell. Jackson, believe

me when I say everybody understands why you're so stern, but we are women. We take yelling very personally, and as my aunts are fond of saying, you get a lot more done with sugar than with vinegar."

He nodded his understanding, but added, "It's hard to be sugary when you have to explain the same thing fifteen times."

Admittedly, he had far less patience today and believed it stemmed from knowing they were just a few days away from pulling out. He wanted everything they needed to learn learned today, if not yesterday. Although Grace had warned him from the beginning that the women might be inexperienced, he thought they'd at least have rudimentary skills, but there were women who'd never handled a tool in their lives, women afraid of the mules, and women who spent most of the morning lessons brushing mud off their skirts, as opposed to listening to him explain, for the fifth time, how to adjust the tack. Yes, he'd yelled; any man would've. Any man with sense wouldn't've taken on this detail in the first place, but he'd been so mesmerized by Grace. Looking at her softened his mood.

"Can I have my kisses now?"

She smiled and shook her head. "What kisses?"

"The ones you've been itching to give me."

"I thought you wanted to *talk*."

"We did, now I want to kiss."

"I missed you too."

A heartbeat later she was in his arms and being kissed as if their separation had been weeks, not days. They shared kisses filled with longing and passion, kisses that lingered sweetly and swept them both away. When they finally came up for air, her hair had fallen and her heightened breathing mirrored his.

Jackson would've given all he owned for enough privacy to make love to her, but the camp held no such place. Were she his wife, such wishes wouldn't be necessary, he realized. Inwardly his eyes widened. Where in the world had that thought come from? He readily admitted to having some feelings for her, but that he'd actually contemplated wanting to take Grace as his wife hit him like a cold bucket of water in the face.

Grace noticed the change in him right away. "What's the matter?"

He shook his head. "Nothing, I just remembered I promised Dix we'd go over maps this evening."

Grace had a feeling he wasn't being truthful. "Then I'll see you in the morning."

"Yep. In the morning."

Without a further word, Jackson gave her a chaste peck on the forehead and exited. Grace stood there wondering what had come over him.

Jackson stalked across camp at war with his feelings. One part of himself wanted to go back and finish what he'd started, but other parts were asking him if he'd gone loco. The differences in their circumstances were bad enough, but having to clear his name made proposing to her out of the question. Yet he wanted her like the desert craved the rain.

Over the next few days, Grace found herself impressed by the way smart, witty Katherine Wildhorse fit into the group. She was a journalist, of all things. None of the women had ever met a newspaperwoman before. Everyone had advised her to ease into the work, after all, the brides had at least two weeks of hard labor under their belts and had grown the muscles to handle all that needed to be done, but she hadn't listened and paid the price. She had to be given some of Loreli's magic salve in order to drag herself back to her tent those first few nights.

Grace wanted the details of the journey chronicled and asked Katherine if she would write the wagon train's story. Katherine thought it an excellent idea and began interviewing the women at dinner that evening.

Grace saw very little of Jackson. He and Dixon Wildhorse were most often sequestered in the supply tents plotting the route the train would take, catching up on their friendship and making sure there were enough supplies. She sensed he might be avoiding her, but attributed his rare interactions with her to being too busy getting everything ready.

True to his word, however, he had changed his tactics somewhat. When the Mitchell sisters backed their wagon over the corral, he'd thrown his hat to the ground but he hadn't yelled. Instead he made them rebuild it. The sight of the fussbudgets struggling with the wood, hammer, and nails put smiles on the faces of every woman in camp.

Two of the women did go home and were soon replaced by two new candidates recommended by another of the brides. They were cousins named Beth Grimsely and Melody White. Melody was an accomplished pianist and arrived at camp with one of the biggest and grandest pianos Grace had ever seen. Jackson refused to let her take it along, citing the weight, and even though Grace tried to get him to change his mind, he refused.

Jackson really had been avoiding Grace, his hope that distancing himself would decrease his ardor worked as long as he didn't see her, but he couldn't avoid it. When she wasn't trying to convince him to take along pianos, she was marching around camp keeping the women's spirits up and everything else in order. Her energy amazed him, as did her optimistic outlook on life. The night they had the rabbit-gutting classes, she'd turned up her nose like most of the other women when confronted with the tasks of skinning and removing entrails, but she'd set her jaw and gone at it while encouraging the others to do the same.

As he watched her now striding across the glade intent upon taking tea to one of the women not feeling well, he remembered that night in her study when he'd thought her too refined and delicate for a trip like this. At that time he'd been unable to imagine her covered with dirt and sweat, but now? Every time he encountered her she had dirt somewhere on her face and her flowing skirts were always caked with mud, as were the boots on her small feet. As he watched her now, he envisioned her sitting in a large tub, with him, soaping her skin while he washed her hair. He could almost feel his hands playing over the tight buds of her breasts and how it would be to slide his touch down to the warmth between her thighs.

"Jack?"

Dixon's voice brought him back to reality. "What?"

"I asked if this route on the map would be faster."

Jackson looked down at the map spread on top of the crate. "Uh, yeah."

Dixon peered into the face of his old friend. "You really should talk to her, you know."

"Who?"

"The hellion."

"Grace?"

"No, Molly Mitchell," the sheriff replied sarcastically.

"Why do I need to talk to Grace?"

"Because you've been watching her like a puma watching a fat rabbit. You can't keep your eyes off her."

"Sure I can," Jackson said, rolling up the map and setting out another. "Grace is destined for a man who can buy her carriages and jewels, not a broken-down Texan like me. Besides," he added sagely, "since when did you become such an expert? Aren't you the one who had to force Katherine to marry you?"

"I wouldn't go so far as to say I forced her."

"Dix, you told the woman you'd throw her daddy, Bart Love, in jail if she didn't say yes to you. I call that forcing, even if you don't."

"Maybe so, but at least I'm not scared to talk to her."

Jackson tried to explain, "The situation with Grace is a lot more complicated."

"It's only as complicated as you make it. Believe me, I know."

The next day, Grace looked up from her laundry tub and stared at the man striding across the camp in her direction. *Surely that can't be Garth Leeds?* she said to herself. But it was. For the life of her Grace couldn't imagine what he was doing here.

He was dressed in a fine blue suit and a starched-collared shirt. His good looks drew quite a bit of attention. Women all over the valley stopped and stared as he passed. Grace looked around for Jackson. He and Dixon were working on the axle of one of the wagons and he'd evidently seen Leeds too, because he left what he was doing and began walking toward the laundry.

# Chapter 7

As Garth neared, Loreli asked, "Does anyone know this handsome man?"

"I do," Grace offered tersely. She noted he had the nerve to be smiling at her as he made eye contact.

Trudy cracked, "First Blake and now this one. How come you have all the luck, Grace?"

"Believe me, this one you can have."

Garth's steps slowed as he came abreast of Grace and the rest of the laundry detail. "Well, hello, Grace. I found you."

"Yes, you have. What do you want?"

Her chilly manner seemed to throw him off balance. "Why don't you introduce me to your friends?"

"Garth, why are you here?"

As if sensing Grace had no intention of thawing out, he said, "I'd like to speak with you, if I might."

"Concerning?"

Aware that the other women standing near Grace were eyeing him curiously, he declared, "It's a personal matter."

Grace didn't think she and Garth had anything even remotely personal to talk about, but she took the bait. "Follow me."

She led him up the hill to the old church. When they reached it, she was just about to ask Garth again why he'd come when Jackson walked up. She could see him viewing Garth suspiciously as he asked, "Problems, Grace?"

She shot Garth a baleful glance and replied, "No, Jackson, there's no problem so far."

As if he planned to make certain the situation stayed that way, he took up a position at her side. She was glad to have him there. "Jackson Blake, meet Garth Leeds."

The two men silently evaluated each other before sharing a brief handshake.

"So, Garth, again, why are you here?" she asked.

"Just thought I'd come and check on you, Grace."

Grace told him in an even voice, "There was no need, Garth. I'm fine."

She watched Garth assessing Jackson Blake before he asked pointedly, "May Grace and I have some privacy?"

Grace countered quietly, "No, we may not. If you've something to say, please do so in his presence."

Anger flashed across Garth's ivory brown features, an anger he directed Blake's way. In response, the dark Texan made himself comfortable against one of the church's weathered wood walls, then calmly folded his arms across his chest.

"Well?" Grace asked.

A tight-lipped Garth turned away from Blake to face Grace. "He your new beau?"

"That's really none of your business."

"You saying you don't care if people think you're carrying on with a cowboy?"

"Why do you care? Because of you I have very little reputation left."

He seemed to take a moment to think about what he wanted to express, then stated, "I should've married you, Grace."

Grace chuckled coldly. "And what am I supposed to say to that?"

"I just thought—" He seemed at a loss for words.

"You thought what?" she asked, in a voice as chilly as January.

"I—made a mistake walking out on you like I did. I just thought you should know, is all."

Grace did not pull her punch. "Is Amanda a bit more strong willed and forceful than you assumed?"

Squirming under the force of her steady gaze, he looked away, so she continued, "They're not going to let you anywhere near their fortune, Garth, I hope you're aware of that. Beatrice loved her husband very much, and when he died, she swore she'd go to her grave with his fortune intact. And when she goes, Amanda will get it all. I know this because my father and I handled the will."

When he didn't reply, Grace continued, "Amanda and her mother may be rude and boorish, but they are not fools. You underestimated them, Garth. *That* was your mistake."

His eyes sparkled with anger. He looked over at the now smiling Blake, then to the stiff-backed Grace, who told him, "I hope you and Amanda will be very happy. Is there anything else?"

"Well, yes," he replied tightly. "I came out here to

see if your bank would broker a loan for me. That clerk of yours, Lionel Rowe, refused."

"Are you gainfully employed?"

"Well, uh, no."

"Any collateral?"

"No."

"Then that clerk of mine was right to tell you no. Anything else?"

Evidently he had nothing more to say. He spun around and went back down the hill.

"Bravo," Blake crowed quietly, once they were alone again.

His support made her feel good. "Thank you. And to think I thought myself in love with that bounder. Mistake, indeed."

Blake's chuckle floated on the night breeze. "Remind me to stay on your good side. You sliced him up so politely, he didn't even realize he was bleeding until it was too late."

Grace allowed herself a smile as she felt her anger slip away. "The nerve of him, but he's getting his just desserts, mark my words. Now that he and his bride have returned from the wedding trip, Amanda's been parading him around like a farmer with a two-headed goat. There are going to be soirees, dinners, teas. I'm glad I'll be gone all summer so I won't have to attend. Once Amanda gets done with him, he'll wish he'd never met her or her mother."

"Is it really going to be that bad?"

"Trust me. I've known Amanda Young my whole life and she never wastes an opportunity to show off a new bauble. When we were seventeen, her papa bought her a bracelet from Paris, and I swear she wore it everyday for six months. She kept thrusting her wrist in our faces, saying, 'Have I shown you the French bracelet my papa gave me? Have I shown you the French bracelet my papa gave me?' Everyone grew quite tired of it right quickly, I must say."

"Sounds to me like maybe Garth ought to be gone one morning when Amanda wakes up."

Grace drawled, "Only in his dreams. Amanda will probably chain him in at night just to keep that from happening."

He laughed. "You have a real wicked streak, do you know that?"

She turned and gave him a dazzling smile. "I'm just a hardworking woman banker, Mr. Blake, nothing more."

"You're also a very beautiful one, Grace Atwood."

Grace fought to free herself from the powerful pull of his presence. She told him plainly, "Jackson, the last man who tried to convince me of that just marched back down the hill. Forgive me if I seem a bit skeptical."

He nodded his understanding, "But what happened between you and Sir Garth has no bearing on my thinking. You are a beautiful woman, Grace."

Grace drew in a shaky breath as his finger slowly traced her bottom lip. Bells chimed and she knew good and damn well that she should leave the rise as quickly as her feet could carry her because of the women staring up at them, but his caress made her feel so out of touch with everything but him she didn't want to flee.

Her blood was fairly singing with anticipation. "Don't you dare kiss me in front of all those women down there."

"Why not?" he asked in a husky but amused voice. "I'll bet if I asked them, they'd tell me to go ahead."

Before Grace could say a word in response, he hollered down, "Should I kiss her?"

The brides who were gathered below lifted their laughing voices in unison. "Yes!"

So he did.

And when he turned her loose, Grace had a vague sense of people cheering and hooting, but little else. "Wait until I get you alone, Jackson Blake," she managed to say threateningly, but smiling.

"I was thinking the exact same thing."

Grace playfully socked him in the arm and took off down the hill. The brides greeted her with more hooting and hollering and an embarrassed Grace could do nothing but grin foolishly as she retook her position at the laundry tubs.

Her laundry companions were all smiles as Trudy cracked, "Now, that's a man!"

Grace agreed.

During the days that followed, Grace and the others learned such things as first aid, harness mending, and how to make smokeless fires. They practiced tying down their wagon canvases in the middle of the night, and compass reading. True to his word, Jackson kept a lid on his temper and answered each and every question, no matter how silly.

As Grace lay in bed that night, she admitted that Jackson was making her crazy. He hadn't said more than two words personally to her since the day on the hill. One minute he was kissing her and the next minute he was avoiding her like she had the plague. Was he beginning to lose interest? She supposed it was possible and she found the prospect upsetting. After all, in society's eyes she was nothing more than a nearly thirty-year-old redheaded spinster. Did he see her that way too? Maybe he had lost interest. Grace willed herself not to think about it and drifted off to sleep.

It was now the last week of May and the weather had turned hot and muggy. Grace's work group had been rotated to the cooking crew. Because of that they had to get up at dawn in order to prepare breakfast.

On the morning of May 31, Grace was the first member of her group to arrive for duty. She was just about to fire up the cookstove when Jackson appeared. Determined not to let him anywhere near her already bruised feelings, Grace said emotionlessly, "Good morning. Coffee will be ready in just a moment."

"No hurry." He took a seat at the trestle table near her and watched her silently.

Ignoring him as much as was able, Grace set a fire beneath the big vat of water that would soon hold the grits, then began on the coffee.

"Grace, can you and the ladies be ready to leave in two days' time?"

His words caught her so off guard that for a moment she could only stare. Then she smiled. "Why, yes. Do you think we're ready?"

He nodded.

She was so excited she wanted to kiss him. "Can I tell the others?"

"Whenever you like."

"Thank you, Jackson, for everything."

"You're welcome."

After breakfast Grace made the announcement and the news was greeted by cheers that filled the valley. The prospect of finally getting on the road had everyone smiling, and the women began loading their belongings into their respective wagons. Even the Mitchell sisters were happy, although no one believed it would last for very long.

The women worked late into the night and many were assisted by family members who'd driven back to see their brides off. Belle Cannon's parents were among that group and according to Loreli, Belle's father had been adamantly opposed to Belle's leaving.

"So, how did Belle react?" Grace asked Loreli as they talked about it later.

"She was respectful but ignored him. Her parents spent the whole time bickering."

Grace sought Belle out the next morning and found her sitting outside her tent reading her Bible. "Morning, Belle."

"Hello, Grace."

"Are you excited about leaving?"

"Excited and a bit frightened."

"Why frightened?"

"Because I don't know what the future will bring."

"I heard from Loreli that your father doesn't want you to leave."

She looked sad for a moment. "No, he doesn't. He can't understand why I'd want to do this. Says I shouldn't be going so far away to marry a man I've never met."

"He's just concerned."

"His only concern is who's going to wait upon him once I'm gone. You see, I do all the washing, cooking, and cleaning. Mother hasn't lifted a broom or a pot in years."

Grace nodded solemnly. "So are you going to pass as a widow once we reach Kansas City?"

"I'm still pondering that."

"Is there any chance the baby's father will acknowledge his child?"

Belle shook her head. "No, he's married and has four children."

Grace wanted to take a buggy whip to the man. She remembered Reverend Petrie saying the baby's father was a deacon in Grace's father's church. "Whatever decision you make, you'll have my support."

"Thank you, Grace."

Grace gave her a pat on the shoulder, then left her to her reading. As she was walking across the camp she was stopped by Katherine Wildhorse.

"I wanted you to take a look at this journal entry just to make sure you approve. I'm going to wire it back to my editor, Geoff, hoping he'll send it on to newspapers across the country. I think this is an historic undertaking, and folks in other places may be interested."

Grace took the paper and read:

*Tonight, 35 women of the race prepare to embark upon a unique journey. They're bound for Kansas— not as Exodusters fleeing the madness in the South, but to become brides to men they have only seen sketched in a portrait. Some of the families are distraught over the idea of their beloved daughters and sisters traveling the vast plains alone to marry men they've never met, but the women are determined and resolute in their desire to go. There are only two men on this journey, the wagonmaster and the guide. While the men predict the journey would test the courage of even the strongest man, they are confident the women will succeed.*

*Your agent,*
*Brother K. Love*

"This is simply wonderful," Grace exclaimed. "But who is Brother K. Love?"

"Me. Some newspapers won't accept items from a woman, so at times I pose as a man."

Grace understood. "Well, one day things will change."

"I agree, but if I have to keep up the masquerade until then, so be it." Katherine smiled and headed off to continue her own preparations for departure.

The women spent the first day of June dismantling the camp. This would be the last night the tents would be used. Down came the laundry, the clotheslines, and Wilma Deets's makeshift hairdressing shop. The trestle tables were stacked and ready to be placed into one of the supply wagons. The weather was hot and muggy. The humidity had been building steadily for the last four or five days, making everyone wish for a good hard rain. The wish for rain was a double-edged sword, however; yes, everyone wanted it to rain, but no one wanted to begin the journey to Kansas hip deep in mud and soaked to the skin.

By the end of the day, Jackson went back to his tent one tired wagonmaster. He and Dix had spent every waking hour supervising the departure preparations. They'd scanned every inch of each and every wagon one last time in a search for damage or defects; helped the ladies load grandfather clocks, rocking chairs, and sea chests so heavy they had to be filled with rocks. He'd pulled and tested the tightness of the ropes lashing the water barrels to the wagons and made a few women redo the ones that failed his inspection. He'd loaded the supply wagons, fed the animals, and ignored the Mitchell sisters' complaints about their place in line; it seemed they didn't want their wagon anywhere near the one being driven by Loreli.

The remembrance of that encounter made him rub his hands over his weary eyes and once again wonder whatever had possessed him to think he could handle this. Admittedly the women had passed each and every test and he was real proud of them, but it was going to be a long, rough drive if he had to listen to petty whining from women like the Mitchell sisters the entire way.

And Grace, what was he going to do about her? Not being able to resolve the dilemma she presented was keeping him up at night. As much as he desired her, he already knew he couldn't have her the way he wanted her; not always, not forever, because he had too much pride. He couldn't give her the material things she'd grown up accustomed to having, and with Texas clouding his future, he couldn't make a commitment to her on any level.

The only logical thing to do was to stay away from her, period, but he didn't want to do that either. The prospect of not being able to take her in his arms and reacquaint himself with the sweet, hot rush of her kiss or hear her sigh when he brushed his lips across the tops of her breasts was keeping him up at night.

He had no business leaving her dangling this way, but he'd never been in a situation like this before. He'd always preferred cathouse ladies. No claims, no commitments. Six months ago, had someone told him he'd be mooning over a bad-tempered red-haired hellion of a lady banker with buccaneer bloodlines, he'd've taken away their tequila. Yet here he sat, wishing for some tequila of his own so he could temporarily banish his need for her.

In the end, his heart won out over his pride. He left the tent to seek her out. The sooner he talked to her, the sooner she could get on with her life and the sooner he could get some sleep.

A weary Grace had just changed into her nightgown in anticipation of a much-needed sleep. She'd spent the day loading her wagon, helping other women load theirs, and overseeing the dismantling of the camp. Now, all she wanted to do was sleep. She was just about to blow out her lantern when she heard, "Knock, knock."

She stilled at the familiar sound of Jackson's voice and the familiar lurch of her heart. "Just a moment," she called back in reply. She put on her robe. "Come in."

As he entered her firsts thoughts were, *Why did he have to be so handsome? If he'd had the face of a goat maybe he wouldn't move her so.*

"Evening, Grace."

"Jackson. Is everything coming together?"

"Yep. We should be able to leave on schedule."

"Good."

The air between them was thick as the humid night.

"I need to talk to you about something."

"Go ahead."

Wondering what this might be about, she steeled herself and waited for him to find the words.

Jackson's whole being screamed that he not do this, but his mind was made up. "You and I have had a good time these past few weeks and I—"

"You want to bring it all to a halt," she stated.

He went silent.

"I'm no naive ingenue, Jackson. If you've lost interest, fine."

"Grace—"

"No explanations are needed," she told him. "It's been fun, really, and I see no reason why we can't remain friends."

Her heart was breaking, but she'd be damned if she'd show it.

Jackson was a bit taken aback by her emotionless acceptance. He'd expected—hell, he didn't know what he'd been expecting. It was as if she were the one intent upon ending things between them. She'd accused him of losing interest, and although that had nothing to do with his reasoning, he couldn't help wondering if she were the one who'd lost interest instead. That thought didn't sit well.

"Is there anything else?" she asked pleasantly.

A bit stunned by the turn of events, he shook his head. "No."

"Then I'll see you in the morning."

Grace swore she'd pluck out her eyes before letting him see her cry. But before he could depart, an ominous rumble of thunder shook the silence. They stilled. A loud crack of lightning sounded. Suddenly, strong winds buffeted the tent. More thunder followed, and then the rain began hitting the tent like rocks. The tent began to sway in the rushing wind. "We need to get to the animals!" Jackson yelled, and ran.

Grace rushed to follow.

Outside, the wind and rain were so fierce it momentarily stole her breath. Flashes of lightning turned night into day and she could see women running helter skelter to secure their wagons and flapping tents and to help Jackson. Barefoot and in her nightgown, Grace was soaked through to her skin before she'd run two yards, but she ran as fast as she could.

At the corral she imitated Jackson's actions as he yelled and hit the animals on their rumps to move them inside the corral. The Mitchell sisters hadn't done such a good job rebuilding it, but the small roof Dixon and Jackson had added a few weeks ago served to shelter the animals as much as it could. Other women ran over to lend a hand, as did the Black Seminole lawman, Dixon Wildhorse. Once the animals were reasonably secured, Jackson screamed at her over the clashing elements, "Go back to your tent!"

"I'm staying!"

"Stop being so damned stubborn and go! I can handle it from here!"

The other women and Dix didn't have to be told twice. Dashing off through the storm, they went back to their tents to seek shelter. Grace peered through the pelting rain in an effort to make sure everyone reached safety.

"Dammit!"

The next thing Grace knew, she was being picked up and carried at a run back toward her tent. She couldn't protest because the wind kept stealing her breath, so she placed her head against his storm-drenched chest and prayed they didn't get struck by lightning on the way. Tents were being blown around like tops and Grace prayed hers would be still there. It was, and once inside, he set her on her feet while the wind whipped at the canvas. No longer able to share his body heat, she stood there drenched and shivering from the cold rain. Although the darkness made it hard to see, he evidently sensed her distress. "Get out of those wet things before you catch pneumonia."

Taking his own advice, he stripped off his wet shirt and dried himself with it as best he could. The intermittent flashes of lightning lit the interior long enough for her to spot her sea chest and she searched inside for a dry gown. She found one by touch and without hesitation reached down and dragged the soggy gown up over her head and off.

Jackson turned her way just in time for a flash of lightning to reveal her nakedness, and his manhood hardened instantaneously. Their eyes met and she paused. Time stood still as heated memories arched between them, then the interior was plunged into darkness again. Another flash showed her quickly donning the dry gown.

Haunted by the touch of his eyes, Grace took the thin blanket from atop her bedroll and wrapped herself in its warmth. "This is the only blanket that isn't packed," she told him. "We can share it if you're cold."

"No thanks," Jackson replied, his back to her now. If he went anywhere near her, all bets would be off. He wondered how long it would take him to recover from the stirring sight of her lightning-lit body. "Are you still shivering?"

"Just a little."

The storm continued to blow and the thunder and lightning continued to call and respond. Grace wondered how everyone else in camp was faring. She hoped no one had gotten hurt. The howling wind seemed to be doing its best to rip the tent from its moorings, but the guide ropes and stakes held. She now appreciated Jackson's rigid training. Had he not taught her so well, the tent might have already blown away.

Ten minutes later the rain slackened and the rumbling of thunder grew fainter. Thankfully the storm had moved on.

In the darkness, she blindly searched for her matches atop the crate that served as a nightstand. Once the flame caught, she found his eyes waiting, watching. Grace looked away lest he see how he affected her. "We should go out and assess the damage," she said, dragging on the brogans most of the women had taken to wearing.

When she looked up he was still watching her with hungry eyes.

"Is something wrong?"

For a moment there was silence as Jackson thought to himself, *Yes, there is. I want you so badly I can almost taste the rain on your skin, your lips, your breasts.* But aloud he said, "No. Let's go see what's still standing."

She followed him out.

Grace was glad for the ugly boots on her feet as she

slogged through the mud. The valley was littered with
downed tree limbs, damaged tents, and blown-over
empty barrels and crates. Led by Loreli, many of the
women had taken shelter in the shell of the old church
at the top of the rise and they were now descending to
see what the storm had done. Very few of the tents were
still upright. The weight of the contents in the wagons
had kept them from being blown around, but things like
bedding and unpacked clothing were soaked.

"You ladies without tents should probably sleep up in
the church," Jackson told the bedraggled women. "We'll
right everything in the morning."

The women gathered up as much dry bedding as could
be found, then trudged up the rise to the church.

Grace and Jackson were left in the clearing alone.

"I'll walk you back," he told her.

"That's not necessary. I'll see you in the morning."

She walked off into the night.

As he watched her leave, Jackson realized that declaring himself free of her was going to be a lot more
difficult than he'd imagined. His previous efforts had
failed, but he was determined to succeed this time. Grace
deserved better than a broken-down cowboy, and because she did, he'd just have to be that much more dis-
ciplined in her presence. But as he headed over to his
own tent, all he could think about was making love to
her while thunder roared and lightning flashed around
them.

Jackson woke up the next morning in a surly mood.
He'd had yet another sleepless night and he blamed it
squarely on Grace. Were she as ugly as the Mitchell
sisters he wouldn't be having this problem. Getting up,
he washed up in the water from his bucket and got

dressed. He stepped out into a beautiful blue-sky day, but his mood was gray and dank.

Grace rose that same morning thinking of Jackson and pledged that after this she would avoid handsome men at all costs. Her heart had now suffered at the hands of two such individuals and it would not happen again. Although she'd promised herself she wouldn't dwell on the matter, she again wondered if Jackson had set his sights on someone else. He'd promised not to prey on the brides, but as handsome as he was, he was probably accustomed to sampling women as if they were chocolates in a box. Her declaration that she wouldn't be going to Kansas City with a broken heart now rang hollow.

Thoughts of Jackson dogged her morning and put a damper on her excitement over leaving. After breakfast she went back to her tent to ready the last of her possessions for transport to her wagon. She'd just closed her sea chest when she looked up to see him standing in the entrance of her tent. There was a scowl on his face and he appeared as if he'd had a restless night.

"Is there something you need?"

"Yes," he said, striding over to her. "This . . ."

And he pulled her to him. With his arm locked across her back, he looked down at her with dark blazing eyes and said, "Thought you might like one last kiss."

He then kissed her so possessively and thoroughly she melted into her brogans. The kiss was at first angry, then tender, overpowering and dazzling. Any thoughts she might have had about protesting his actions turned to ash in his fiery embrace. She found herself responding with such fervor he groaned and dragged her closer. For a few hot moments all their pent-up passion and need exploded like a blast of lightning, and when he turned her loose, she was breathing heavily. "Now, *that's* how to say good-bye."

And he stormed out.

For a moment Grace stood there stunned, then became so angry she wanted to throw something. How dared he keep jerking her heart back and forth this way!

She was pacing and muttering curses when she looked up and saw Katherine Wildhorse standing in the tent's opening.

With concern in her voice, Katherine asked, "Whatever is the matter?"

Grace shot her a look and said, "He makes me so angry I could scream."

"Who?"

"Jackson 'pigheaded' Blake." Grace said, then added tartly, "A more stubborn and arrogant man has yet to be born."

"What has he done now?"

Grace stopped her pacing, held Katherine's eyes a moment, and said, "He kissed me! Again! In his arrogance, he believes I enjoy it!"

Katherine chuckled, "Well, do you?"

Grace admitted slyly, "Just between you and me? Of course. His kisses make me see sunsets."

Grace looked into Katherine's smile. "Stupidest, damnedest experience of my life."

They both grinned.

Katherine asked, "So what are you going to do?"

"Pray I make it to Kansas without killing him or falling in love with him. Do you have any idea where I had to meet him to ask about him mastering the wagon train?"

"No, where?"

"A whorehouse outside of Chicago known as Sunshine's Place. He mistook me for a whore named Lilah."

To Grace's surprise, Katherine confessed, "Lilah's quite nice, actually."

"You *know* Lilah?"

Katherine nodded, "Sure do. Miss Sunshine, too. In fact, Dix and I were married there."

Grace couldn't believe her ears. "You were married in a *whorehouse!*"

"Yes. The preacher mistook *me* for one of the girls. I was horrified."

Grace put her hands to her mouth and stared at Katherine with widened eyes. "Katherine, I know it's impolite to pry, but this sounds like a dime novel, and I can't wait for us to know each other better so I can hear the whole story."

Katherine laughed.

"I'm serious. How long do we have to be friends before I know it all?"

"I think you are as outrageous as I, Grace Atwood."

"And I think you and I are going to get along famously, Katherine Wildhorse."

They shook hands to seal their pact.

Grace felt unbearably short standing next to the statuesque Katherine and said, "You know, I always wanted to be tall like you, able to look a man in the eye and sock him in it if need be. A good kick in the knee is about all I can give from down here."

Katherine's grin showed even white teeth. "Well truthfully, I've never wanted to be any shorter, at least not since becoming full grown. Though you tiny ones always make me feel clumsy, awkward. You take dainty little steps; we giraffes stride."

Grace disagreed. "But the carriage and confidence. I envy that."

"Really?"

"Yes, you and that husband of yours complement each other well, both being so tall."

Katherine confessed. "He's the tallest man I've ever

known. I'm accustomed to looking down at men. I've never had to crane my neck up. It can be disconcerting at times."

"I've seen the way he looks at you."

Katherine chuckled. "What do you mean?"

"His eyes follow you a lot when he thinks you're not looking. Passion eyes, if I can be frank. It's the way Blake looks at me sometimes—makes me feel like my clothes are about to catch fire. Like I said, stupidest damnedest experience of my whole life."

"Well, it's obvious he moves you. Do you love him?"

Although she knew she was lying, she said, "Lord, I hope not. Do you love your husband?"

"I haven't known him long enough."

Confused, Grace asked, "What does that mean?"

"I wed Dix to satisfy a debt."

Katherine then gave Grace a brief account of the how and whys of her marriage.

When she finished, Grace stared in amazement. "Your father stole the property of a United States Deputy Marshal? And you had to marry him!"

"Or watch my father be thrown into prison or hung."

"My goodness, Katherine, and you agreed?"

"What choice did I have?"

"In reality none, when it comes right down to it—but my, what a choice. Although it didn't hurt to have Dix turn out to be such a handsome specimen. If he'd had the face of a mule, my father might've been up the creek without a paddle."

They both laughed, then Grace asked, "Is he as kind as he seems?"

"So far."

Grace noted the wistful look on Katherine's face. "Well, a man as magnificent as that shouldn't be too hard to love."

"Look who's doling out advice," Katherine cracked. "What about Blake?"

"Jackson Blake had undoubtedly broken a lot of hearts in his lifetime, but his streak stops here."

"So you say."

Grace added truthfully, "So I hope."

# Chapter 8

❦

On the morning of June 3, 1884, the women prepared to leave. In spite of the gray day, townspeople and relatives of the brides descended on the valley to witness the departure, and at precisely 8 A.M., all bowed their heads as Belle recited a prayer to bless the journey. After the amens faded, the atmosphere lifted when to their surprise a five-man band from the town appeared on the rise and broke into a rousing tune. The elated women mounted their wagons, and while the onlookers cheered heartily, expertly guided their teams up the rise. Grace was so moved by the outpouring of support she had tears in her eyes as she drove past her waving godfather, Martin Abbott. He'd come to see her off and to deliver some letters from the aunts and her friends at the bank.

"The aunts send their love," he shouted. "Keep yourself safe, baby girl!"

"I will," she yelled back. "Tell the aunts I love them too and I'll write as soon as I can."

Her heart full, Grace Prescott Atwood set her eyes forward. She and her brides were finally on their way.

The ladies knew from Jackson's talks that he wanted to cover at least sixteen miles a day. Only a few women like Loreli and Fanny, whose father owned a livery back in Ohio, had ever driven such a distance, but they were all determined to accomplish the wagonmaster's goal. Interactions between Grace and Jackson had been polite during the morning's festivities. He looked as though he were still angry, but she didn't care. She doubted his anger surpassed her own.

Taking her mind off the handsome but maddening Jackson Blake, Grace concentrated on her driving. The women were two to a wagon: the Mitchell sisters were together, as were Fanny and Zora, Tess and Trudy, and Loreli and Belle, to name a few. Grace and Katherine Wildhorse brought up the rear in the supply wagons and were amongst the few women driving alone.

In his role as scout, Katherine's husband Dixon had ridden ahead before the brides broke camp to see if he could secure them a farmer's field to camp in for the night. He rode back to the wagon train late that afternoon with good news. A farmer about ten miles outside of Aurora had agreed to let them camp.

"How much will he charge us?" Grace asked the mounted Dixon and Jackson as they matched their pace to the pace of her wagon.

"Six dollars."

She thought that a bit exorbitant, but—"Jackson, what do you think?"

"Sounds fine."

In the past she would've questioned such a short, clipped response, but she reminded herself that Jackson

Blake and his moods were no longer any of her concern. She told Dixon to ride ahead and make the arrangements. Dix nodded, touched his hat, then headed his coal black stallion north. Jackson met her eyes and looked on the verge of saying something, but instead rode away without a word. Grace shook her head then returned her attention to her driving.

They arrived at their destination just as night fell and the bone-weary brides reined their teams to a halt. They'd covered ten miles, a fair piece for the first day, according to Jackson, but everyone knew they would need to pick up the pace if they wanted to reach Kansas City on schedule.

To the surprise of everyone, the farmer's apple-cheeked wife had a sumptuous meal waiting, one that must've taken all day to prepare because there were spitted hogs, corn pudding, and yams. Grace thought she'd died and gone to heaven when the woman brought out strawberries and ice cream for dessert.

"Women have to look out for each other, no matter what color we are," the wife explained sagely, as she set the desserts on the two trestle tables.

Evidently, her husband did not share her views. Grace was in her wagon preparing for bed when she heard, "Grace, we have a problem."

It was Jackson. She bent and made her way to the back of the wagon, swearing to feed him to sharks if this "problem" involved kissing. "What's wrong?"

"The farmer wants more money. He says he needs to cover the cost of the food." Grace could see the anger in the hard set of his jaw.

"No one asked him to feed us."

"I know."

"How much more does he want?"

"Ten more."

"Ten! Is he out of his mind?"

"Nope, just greedy. Says either we pay or we leave."

Grace sighed with angry frustration. "Where is he now?"

"Up at the house."

Grace hopped down from the wagon and walked with Jackson to the small whitewashed farmhouse. They found the farmer, Otis Burns, standing on the lantern-lit porch smoking his pipe. Dixon Wildhorse stood waiting on the steps. His jaw was as tight as Jackson's.

Grace stepped to the porch and asked in a falsely pleasant voice, "What is this about more money, Mr. Burns?"

"Just as I told them," he said, pointing with his pipe, "I need to cover the costs of the food."

"We didn't ask you to feed us."

"True, but you didn't think I'd feed the bunch of you just out of the kindness of my heart, did you? Vittles cost money."

Grace wanted to wring his beady-eyed little neck.

"Either pay me or move on. Don't make me no never mind."

Grace looked to the men flanking her and said, "Get everyone up. We're moving on."

Jackson smiled. He'd yet to meet any man capable of besting the hellion.

Burns's wife, Olga, stepped out on the porch. Drying her hands on an old dish towel she asked, "Did I hear you say you're leaving, Miss Atwood? This time of night?"

"Your husband's left us no choice, Mrs. Burns."

She turned confused eyes on her husband, then looked back to Grace. "What do you mean?"

"He's insisting we pay for the beautiful meal you provided. We weren't told about that part of the bargain beforehand."

"Neither was I." Turning blazing eyes on her husband, she asked, "Whatever is the matter with you, old man? Why are you trying to cheat these nice people?"

The farmer stiffened.

"And I don't want to hear any cock-and-bull explanations. We had a good harvest last year and we've more food stored than we know what to do with."

It was quite easy for everyone to see who held the reins in this household. Mrs. Burns then turned to Grace. "My apologies, Miss Atwood. I fed you because it was the Christian thing to do."

"No need to apologize. We appreciate your generosity."

"Well, you're welcome, and don't worry your head about more money. Otis here didn't mean it."

Grace nodded. "Goodnight. We'll see you in the morning."

"Goodnight."

As Grace and her men turned to leave, they heard Mrs. Burns tell her husband angrily, "You ought to be ashamed of yourself!"

They smiled.

Dixon parted from them and went off to his wagon and his wife. Jackson walked with Grace back to her wagon.

As they reached it he stopped and asked, "Would you really have rounded everybody up and headed out?"

She replied truthfully, "And have to listen to the Mitchell sisters whine about it? No. He had me over a barrel. Why do you ask?"

"Just curious."

For a moment there was an awkward silence.

Grace finally said, "Well, goodnight."

As she turned to climb back into the wagon, he stayed her with a gentle hold on her arm. "I'm sorry if I've hurt you, Grace."

His voice and eyes were genuine, so much so, she said, "I—have to go. Goodnight."

Without a backward glance, Grace disappeared into the wagon. Later, as she lay on her bedroll in the dark wagon, Grace thought back on what he'd said. Why in the world would he tell her that? Surely he didn't think to work himself back into her good graces? She'd had quite enough of his on-again, off-again attraction. If he didn't want to be with her, then fine. She didn't want to be with him either.

The train was now five days out and the journey was going relatively well. Their next landmark destination would be Fort Madison, more than two weeks away. Jackson planned for them to cross the Mississippi just south of there to enter the state of Missouri.

On the eighth day, they came across a lone covered wagon. At first, everyone thought it had been abandoned because of the broken right back wheel, but a dark-skinned young woman emerged and began waving frantically in their direction. Jackson held up his hand, signaling a stop. The brides pulled back on their reins, glad for the respite.

The woman's name was Yancey Fitzgerald. In the wagon were her three young sons. As Jackson and some of the women inspected the wheel to see if it could be repaired, Yancey told Grace her story. "My husband died about six months ago and his mother no longer wanted to support my boys and me, so she turned us out."

Grace wondered what kind of grandmother could turn her back on her own grandchildren. "Where are you headed?"

Yancey didn't know. "Someplace where I can start over." She was a cook and housekeeper by trade.

When Grace asked if she would like to travel with the brides, the woman nodded enthusiastically. "You'll have to let me cook, though, I don't cotton to charity."

So it was decided. Loreli and Daisy retrieved one of the spare wheels from Grace's wagon. With the help of a few other brides, they took off the busted one, replaced it with the new, and in under an hour Yancey and her young sons pulled their wagon into the line.

By the fifteenth day, the monotony of the drive and the sameness of the landscape were beginning to take their toll. A few of the women had gotten into arguments over nothing. The food, mostly jerky, potatoes, and rabbits, were making everyone crave a good hot meal, and the rumors surrounding Belle Cannon's condition were being fanned by the Mitchell sisters.

The next day, they were forced to alter their route because of a Reb farmer who refused to let them cross his land. This was the second such occurrence, and like last time, having to go around would not only add a significant number of miles to the journey and waste valuable daylight, it would also keep them from accessing any fresh water on his property. The brides groaned because most would've killed for a bath.

From where she sat behind her reins, Grace could see the displeasure clouding Jackson's face as he weighed what to do. In the end though they all knew they had no choice; they'd have to go around.

They drove until dark, then halted as Dix rode back to the wagons. The ever resourceful marshal had found another man who not only agreed to let them camp in his fields for the night but had a good-sized freshwater stream. Hallelujahs filled the night air.

The brides celebrated by washing in the farmer's stream and Loreli shocked the socks off of the Mitchell sisters and their supporters by stripping naked and wading into the stream. It had been many days since they'd had a chance to bathe fully and Loreli had done the same thing then. And just as then, many of the women imitated their constable and followed her into the cold water naked as the day they were born, the judgmental Mitchell sisters be damned.

That evening the brides relaxed around a large fire inside the ring of wagons to eat Yancey's rabbit stew and to enjoy each other's company, but the atmosphere changed when Sarah Mitchell stood and declared, "As good Christian women, I think we have a right to know if Belle Cannon is carrying an out-of-wedlock child."

Grace saw Belle stiffen as all eyes turned her way, but before Grace could put the sanctimonious woman in her place, Loreli asked coolly, "What business is it of yours?"

The tone and Loreli's cold golden eyes made Sarah pause as if she weren't sure she wanted to proceed, but she drew up her formidable bulk and plowed ahead anyway. "Because some of us don't wish to be sullied by such an association."

Trudy asked pointedly, "And if she is, what are you proposing we do?"

"Leave her at the next nearest town."

Grace stood. "We aren't leaving anyone anywhere."

Fanny said, "And besides, we don't even know if she is carrying. So she's been sick, so what?"

There were a few mumbles of support. Belle had been sick, so sick Loreli had been driving their wagon alone.

Suddenly Belle got to her feet and everyone quieted. She looked at the faces gathered around the fire and stated in a firm yet soft voice, "Yes, Miss Mitchell, I am carrying an out-of-wedlock child, but the only person I have to answer to is the Lord."

"Hear! Hear!" Zora crowed.

Grace smiled at Belle's words. In spite of Belle's solitary ways, she was well liked. Before the morning sickness claimed her, she'd always pulled her share of the load and Grace had never heard her utter an unkind word about anyone. That so many women seemed to be on her side filled Grace's heart.

Belle sat down.

Loreli scanned the crowd. "Anything else?"

"Yes. I say we take a vote," Molly Mitchell countered.

Daisy waded into the verbal fray. "Who put you in charge? The only person who can call a vote on anything is Grace, Mr. Blake, or our duly elected constable, *Loreli.*"

"I say we have one anyway," Molly challenged haughtily.

Grace had had enough. "We aren't calling a vote on anything. Belle stays. So unless anyone has anything of *value* to add, I say we adjourn to our respective wagons and see each other in the morning. We've had a long day."

Sarah's voice dripped with outrage. "I refuse to be around her."

"Nobody's asking you to," Loreli snapped back.

Grace used her most forceful voice. "Ladies, this discussion is over. Goodnight."

As the meeting broke up, many of the women gave Belle's shoulder a supportive squeeze as they left the fire, but others huffed past her with a sniff. The issue of Belle had split the brides into two factions. Grace hoped the rift didn't split any wider.

After everyone else left, Grace pulled her own weary self up off the hard ground and started back to her wagon only to have Jackson Blake step into the firelight.

"You handled that well," he told her.

For a moment, she forgot about her vow to remain unmoved. Having him so near caught her off guard and all she could think about was how much she missed him.

"Thanks," she said emotionlessly as she hastily rebuilt her defenses. Her mood was melancholy enough. She didn't need him adding to the weight on her mind.

Jackson looked into her fire-flecked face and wanted to tell her that he'd been wrong, again. Being around her all day and not being able to laugh with her or hold her in his arms was not only keeping him awake nights, but he couldn't eat either. Hell, he didn't even like short women, but she was turning him inside out. He had too much pride to get down on his knees and beg her forgiveness, but he was almost at that point. These past two weeks had been the worst two weeks of his life.

"If I told you I wanted to kiss you, what would you say?"

"I'd say, do you want *both* of your ears cut off and fed to the mules, or just one?" And she headed off to her wagon, declaring firmly, "Goodnight, Jackson. I'm too tired for this and of this."

"Grace—"

"Goodnight."

She tried to walk fast enough to lose him but because his legs were nearly twice the length of hers so he had no trouble keeping up.

"Grace—"

"Leave me alone, or so help me I'll feed you to the next shark I find."

Jackson wanted to laugh but knew she probably would cut off his ears. "Grace, please."

The softness of his entreaty made her stop. Had she heard him correctly? "What did you say?"

"I said, please."

She searched his eyes in the dark. "Have you ever said that to a woman before?"

He knew what he was supposed to say, but it was also the truth. "No. Not like this."

"Why now?"

He could see she was not going to give him any quarter, so again he told the truth. "Because you're turning me inside out, woman, I can't sleep, I can't eat."

Grace felt a smile come over her heart, but once bitten, twice shy, and he was not going to get off so easily. "What's to keep you from waking up tomorrow and breaking my heart again?"

Jackson winced inwardly, but knew he'd earned it. "Knowing that I'd hurt you again."

Grace looked away. The sincerity in his tone threatened to put tears in her eyes. On one hand his words were a tender balm to her hurt feelings, but on the other hand she wanted to yell at him for putting her through this turmoil in the first place. Loving a man could make a woman crazy.

"Grace, I'm stubborn, pigheaded, and yes, I got way too much pride, but these past two weeks without you have been hell."

She turned back to him then. "You make this very hard, Jackson."

"I know, darlin', and I'm sorry, but being around you makes me not know my own mind sometimes. That's hard on a man."

He reached out and drew a crescent across her cheek and the familiar sweet gesture closed her eyes. "Forgive me . . ." he whispered.

How could she stay angry at a man who'd opened his heart and let her look inside? "I should make you walk the plank."

He smiled. "If you can find one, I'll walk it."

She tried to remain firm, but a smile peeked out.

Seeing it, he picked up her hand. "I'm sorry, I really really am. Will you at least let me walk you back to your wagon?"

She nodded.

Still holding hands, they prepared to stroll away when a female voice rang out from one of the nearby wagons. "It's about time you two made up!"

"Sure is!" shouted another.

Grace's eyes grew round.

"Loreli, you owe me two bits! I told you they'd be back together before we left Illinois." That was Trudy.

"Pay you tomorrow!" Loreli yelled back.

An astonished Grace stood there speechless while Jackson's laughter split the night.

They made it back to Grace's wagon without further comment from the eavesdropping brides, and once they did, were reluctant to part.

"I should get to sleep," she said, wishing they weren't on a wagon train in the middle of the plains so they could spend the night in each other's arms and not have to worry about being heard or rising before dawn.

"If I promise not to stay too late, can we sit and talk awhile?" he asked, hoping with all his might she'd say yes.

The request pleased her immensely. "I suppose a little while wouldn't hurt, but let's find a place away from the choir."

He chuckled. "Any particular place in mind?"

Grace shook her head. "No, how about we just walk?"

"Okay."

So side by side they headed off into the darkness, away from the camp. Grace felt a contentment she'd thought she'd lost. No, she didn't need a man to make her life full; she'd been blessed since birth, but having him by her side did make the world seem brighter. Only time would tell how long they'd be together, but when the time came to part, she'd have no regrets because life would go on.

They slowed a good distance from the circled wagons and stood in the silence of a stand of trees partially bathed by the moon's pale light. A downed trunk provided a place to sit.

"What do you wish to talk about?" she asked.

Jackson thought for a moment as he searched his mind for a topic of conversation that wouldn't lead to another falling out. "Tell me about this pirate grandfather of yours."

The question surprised her. "How'd you know about that?"

"Martin Abbott mentioned it the day he and I met. He said that's partly why you're such a hellion."

He added, "I was born a slave. My daddy was sold at birth to a Texas planter on the eastern side of the Republic. He never knew who his parents were. I envy you being able to trace your line back so far."

She found the tribute touching. "Many in the race can trace their lines back, even some who weren't free."

"I know, but there are many more of us who can't, and I'm one."

Grace searched his eyes and saw an openness in them he'd never shared with her before now. "You're right of course, but I can't remember ever *not* knowing who my ancestors were. On my mother's side I'm a Prescott, descended from the Buccaneer, as we call him, and on my father's side I was an Atwood. He was a runaway from Maryland."

"Your daddy was a slave?"

She nodded. "The most resourceful, smartest, and

kindest man I'll probably ever meet in this lifetime."

He smiled at the love in her eyes. "That great, huh?"

She smiled in reply. "Greater. He was owned by an Annapolis sea captain and had been bred to the sea. That was how Black seamen slaves were described back then. Plantation slaves were bred to the land. Men like my father and his father were bred to the sea. He went on his first sea voyage at the age of eight."

"When did he run?"

"During the spring of 1852. He was twenty-four at the time and trusted enough by his sea captain master to be the quartermaster."

"Like a quartermaster in the army?"

"I suppose. He laid in the supplies, ordered provisions, handled the books. I don't know what an army quartermaster really does, but in the Buccaneer's day, the quartermaster was the man who saw to the equal divvying up of things like plunder and food, and made sure everyone, including the captain, got no more than his share. The famous pirate Captain Kidd had a Black quartermaster for a time."

"Really? Or are you making this all up?"

Taking mock offense, she punched him playfully in the arm. "No, I'm not making this up. The Buccaneer knew these men and he made his daughter, my Great-great-great-aunt Lilith write all his memories down before he died."

"Okay, okay, put your cutlass away, Pirate Queen Atwood. Who else did this old pirate granddaddy of yours remember?"

Her eyes were shining with humor. "Abraham Samuel."

"And who was he? Don't tell me he was the captain of an all Black pirate ship."

She shook her head, no. "There were no Black pirate

captains, as far as I know, but Abraham was a West Indian runaway and a quartermaster on the pirate ship *John and Rebecca.*"

"And?"

"And later the King of Fort Dauphin."

"Where was that?"

"Madagascar."

"Madagascar? Who in the world would make a pirate king?"

"Other pirates. It's said Samuel had a very powerful presence, was extremely intelligent and very strong—all the right attributes of a pirate king. He also had slaves and wives."

Jackson cocked his head. "Wives? As in more than one?"

"As in more than one."

Jackson stroked his chin as if contemplating the information. "Doesn't sound like a bad job, being a pirate king."

A grinning Grace shook her head. "You probably can't even handle *one* wife, let alone wives, plural."

"Be willing to give it a good-old Texas try, though."

"Men," she snorted.

For a moment, they settled into a companionable silence, then Jackson's thoughts changed direction. "The Mitchell sisters weren't real nice to Belle."

Grace's anger resurfaced. "The Mitchell sisters are harpies and I should've replaced them when I had the chance."

"Too late now."

"Yes, it is."

Grace sighed, "Well, they'll be someone else's problem once we get to Kansas City. Maybe husbands will temper their meanness."

Jackson snorted, "If they can *find* husbands. I'm

tempted to warn those men to head for the hills."

Her voice held amusement. "I've been considering that too."

He was glad they were no longer at odds. "So, is the journey all you hoped it would be?"

"In many ways, yes, the women have pulled together wonderfully, and I get to see the beauty of the country-side, but I doubt I'll ever travel by wagon again."

"No?" he asked, chuckling.

"Positive. My hips are going to be permanently black and blue from riding that hard seat."

She then looked at him. "Speaking of black, why do you always wear black?"

"Out of respect for my daddy. When his murderers are brought to justice, I'll quit mourning."

The bitterness in his voice was quite apparent. She searched his eyes in the dark. "Your father was mur-dered?"

"Yes, and once I get you and the women to Kansas, I'm heading back to Texas to hunt down the Rebs that did it."

A strong sense of fear came over Grace. "Alone?"

"Alone."

She wanted to tell him how dangerous that might be, but was certain he already knew. Now that the nation had turned its back on reconstruction, justice was barely alive in many areas of the country, but it was already dead in Texas; he would be taking his life in his hands if he journeyed there. "You can't go there alone."

"Sure I can." Jackson could feel her concern and it touched his heart, but going back to Texas was some-thing he'd already made up his mind to do. He owed it to his daddy and to himself. "It has to be done and I'm the only one who can do it."

Grace realized she knew very little about this man,

still. There were demons inside him that might cost him his life, and she didn't like the thought of that.

"But I will be careful. I promise."

She knew that no matter how careful he tried to be, he could still lose his life.

He must've sensed that, because he said, "I didn't bring you out here to weigh you down with worry."

"I know, Jackson, but—"

"No buts. Come on, I'll walk you back."

Grace wanted to try and convince him to choose another path, but knew how stubborn he was, and that in spite of her feelings for him she had no right. His father had been murdered; only he could decide how to alleviate that grief.

They walked back in silence, and once they reached her wagon, he said, "So, now you know why I've been having such a hard time with my feelings for you. I can't commit to anything or anyone until I can clear up things back home."

Jackson knew he hadn't told her the whole story. He still didn't know how to tell her he was also wanted in Texas.

"Don't worry," she told him. "We'll take the days as they come."

Jackson's heart swelled.

Grace reached up and tenderly cupped his cheek. "Thanks for telling me."

He turned her palm to his lips and kissed the center. "Thanks for not cutting off my ears."

Their smiles met and she whispered, "Goodnight. I'll see you in the morning."

"Goodnight."

And for the first time in many nights, they both slept peacefully.

She woke up the next morning to find a bundle of

wildflowers on her wagon seat and a note that said, *Hope you like them.* There was no signature, but she didn't need one. The fragrances of the multicolored bouquet filled her nose, and his kindness filled her heart.

Over the next few days, Jackson made it plain to everyone how he felt about Grace. Every morning when she got up, she found on the seat of her wagon a piece of paper weighed down by a beautiful coral-colored rock. Sometimes the notes were just a few lines wishing her a good morning or a good day, but others were so poetic and moving they put tears in her eyes.

One read:

> *In the old age, black was not considered fair,*
> *Or if it were, it bore not beauty's name;*
> *But now is black beauty's successive heir,*
> *And beauty slandered with a bastard shame.*

When the wagon train stopped that afternoon, Grace was so excited she hunted down Loreli and Katherine and showed them the paper.

Loreli looked at the well-penned words and said, "My goodness, Grace. I've known a lot of men in my life, but they've never written me poems."

Grace grinned as Loreli handed the small piece of paper over to Katherine.

As Katherine read, her eyes widened. "Grace, do you know what this is from?"

Grace hadn't a clue. "No."

"Honey, this is Shakespeare."

She handed it back. "And I think it's one of the sonnets that he supposedly wrote to a woman he called the 'Dark Lady.'"

Both Loreli and Grace stared.

"There are rumors Shakespeare had a Black mistress

named Lucy Negro and the poems were for her."

Grace read the lines again, now more amazed than ever.

Katherine added, "I worked at a newspaper in Virginia a while back and a woman I did a report on claimed to be a descendant of Lucy's."

Loreli shook her head and smiled. "Shakespeare. Grace, if you don't want that man, *I'll* take him."

The women laughed and a still stunned Grace went back to her wagon.

As the rest stop ended, Grace picked up the reins and slapped them down on the team's back to get them moving. She realized once again that Jackson Blake was proving to be much more complex than she'd ever imagined.

That evening after dinner, she found him playing checkers with Yancey Fitzgerald's two sons. Because of the lengthening days, dark was coming later and the boys, James and Solomon, were playing as one against Jackson. Since Yancey and the boys had joined the train, Jackson made it a point to spend some time with the boys each day. He shot marbles, challenged them to footraces, and even took them up individually on his horse and let them ride with him at the front of the train. As a result they worshipped the ground he walked on. Yancey did, too.

But as Grace stood behind the boys to watch the checker game, she could see they were losing badly. Jackson had enough kings on his side of the board to launch a medieval crusade.

"He's beating us again, Miss Atwood," the older boy, Solomon, said with a mock glumness.

"Looks that way to me too, Sol," Grace declared sympathetically.

Jackson simply grinned, then moved a king to swallow the boys' last checker.

The boys smiled in spite of their defeat and James asked, "Can we play again tomorrow, Mister Blake?"

"You bet."

The boys grabbed up the checkers and the board, and after saying good-bye, ran off to rejoin their mother.

Grace said, "You've been very nice to them."

"They're good boys," he said, watching their retreat. "Always hoped to have sons of my own someday."

Grace had always wanted children too, but knew now it would probably never be.

"Ever think about kids?" he asked, looking up at her from the barrel he was sitting on.

"I did, when I was young, but now?" She shrugged. "Not anymore."

"Why not?"

"I'm not planning on marrying. After that debacle with Garth, I think I'll just concentrate on being a banker."

"Well, you never know. Nothing in life is carved in stone."

Grace mulled over his words as she looked out at the camp. The wagons were circled up and a fire blazed in the center as it did every night. Women were slowly walking to and fro, seeing to animals, talking to friends. She found herself hoping their dreams would come true once they reached Kansas City and that the men awaiting them would treasure them for the fine, upstanding women they were.

Her voice was soft when she turned to him and said, "Thank you for the poem. Katherine said it's from Shakespeare."

"She's right. Sonnet 127."

"Jackson, where on earth did you learn Shakespeare?"

"My father. My mother died when I was young, but reading poetry was one of her favorite pastimes. After her death, when I grew older, my father made me learn some of the ones she liked best, so that I'd have a part of her in me."

"How old were you?"

"Nine-ten."

Grace found the story touching.

"Never expected a cowboy like me to know Shakespeare, did you?"

"Frankly, no."

"Well, I never thought I'd have a use for it outside of honoring my mother's memory."

Grace had no trouble deciphering his meaning. His confession made her feel very special indeed.

"And Grace, just so you'll know, I've *never* given poems to any other woman before."

She understood that too. "And I've never received any from any man before."

"Then how about we keep it that way?"

She nodded as her heart sang. "We have a deal."

"Wish we could seal that deal with a kiss."

"Me too," she whispered.

"How about I come to your wagon and see you tonight after everything quiets down?"

Grace grinned. That reckless feeling came over her again, as did the anticipation of what it might bring. "You'll come to my wagon?"

"If you'll let me."

"We'll have to be very quiet."

"I know."

She thought for a moment, but knew her reply didn't need much inner debate. "Then I'll see you later."

He winked and she left him smiling.

\*     \*     \*

Anticipation made it hard for Grace to sit still after quiet settled over the camp later that night. She kept peeking out of the back of the wagon's round canvas to see if he were coming. The two hours she'd been waiting had given her time to go to the nearby creek and wash away the grime and smell of the day's driving and to put on fresh clothes. She'd even tried to make the interior of the wagon more comfortable by moving some of the crates, barrels, and trunks out of the way so they'd have a place to sit. The crowded inside of a covered wagon didn't remotely resemble a place for a romantic interlude, but it had to do.

Then she heard his whispered call. *"Grace?"*

In her haste to greet him, she knocked the side of her knee against the edge of a crate and almost fell. The pain shot through the bone, evoking a very unladylike curse as she hobbled to the back of the wagon.

Outside, Jackson heard the commotion and glanced around quickly to see if anyone else had. When her face finally appeared, he asked softly, concerned, "Are you all right?"

"Hit my damn knee," she whispered back.

She limped out of the way as he climbed in, then waited and watched as he quietly pulled up the gate behind him and secured it closed.

It took a moment for his eyes to adjust to the dark interior, but he soon saw her standing a few feet away.

"You sure you're okay?"

Bent over and rubbing her knee, she said, "I think so."

"You should light a candle so you can see."

"No, the light might give you away. I'll take a look at it in the morning."

He ducked down a bit and made his way over to her.

Grace's pain was soon forgotten as he took her into his arms and held her close.

He said, "Never had a woman cripple herself trying to get to me."

She chuckled and their smiles met. He leaned down and touched his lips to hers and she kissed him back just as softly. Moved by all she was, he rubbed a slow thumb over the skin of her cheekbone while wondering again how he'd ever let her go. He gave her another faint brush across her mouth and she responded by using the tip of her tongue to lightly tease his bottom lip. For long heated moments they did nothing but kiss as if relearning the taste of each other, the shape of their mouths, and the mingling hush of their breathings. He took a moment to find a seat atop a crate, then pulled her onto his lap and began again.

Grace sighed pleasurably as his hands moved to cup her breasts. Her nipples rose and hardened, already divining the intense pleasure to come. He didn't disappoint. The top buttons of her gray shirtwaist surrendered without a fight and a throbbing moment later the bare expanse of her throat and the tops of her bound breasts were exposed to his lips and the warm night air. His lips paid tribute to her freshly washed skin and he drowned himself in her perfumed scent. She'd bound her breasts with a silk scarf the color of violets. His hands slid over the gossamer-thin covering and her hard nipples teased the center of his palms. He flicked his tongue against the trembling well of her throat, then descended to the silk to dally there until it dampened and clung to the berried flesh.

Grace wondered if any other pleasure on earth equaled this. Every pull of his lips on her breasts echoed sensually through her core. Each pass of his hands set her afire. Rising passions made her want to unveil herself to him fully so she could be taken here in the shadows. Fate had brought them together and destiny would set them apart, but she wanted memories. "Will you make love to me . . . ?"

Jackson's erection, already hard and ready, pulsed at the sound of her sultry entreaty. He kissed his way to her mouth, wanting to drag her beneath him and fill her until she screamed loud enough to be heard in Chicago. "You're a virgin, Grace, and we've no protection."

"I don't care . . ." Yes, there was the possibility that their joining might produce a child, but if it did, she wouldn't walk into the arms of an icy lake and end her life. This might be her one and only chance to know the true measure of the passion she'd been seeking from her heart's mate, and for better or worse, she considered him that.

"Well, I do. No . . ."

She countered with a kiss she hoped held enough heat to curl his toes. "Yes," she said softly.

To further tempt him into giving her what she wanted, she took off her blouse, then reached behind her and undid the violet silk binding her breasts. Knowing his eyes were on her, she removed it slowly, yet deliberately. The golden globes shimmered free and were caught by the faint glow of the moon. "Yes," she whispered.

She stood and began to undo the button on the waistband of her skirt.

In a strangled voice, he asked with alarm, "What the hell are you doing?"

"Seducing you."

His whole world reeled.

The skirt whispered down her body and pooled in the dark at her feet, exposing her firm legs encased in nothing but her drawers, hose, and shoes. He didn't have to see her eyes to know they held heat, he could feel it in every pore. Jackson's heart was racing and he fought to keep his sanity for just a few moments more. One of them had to be sensible and it was obviously not going to be the Pirate Queen. "I'll let you seduce me on one condition."

"That being?"

"That if my seed takes, you marry me."

She paused. Standing there only partially dressed in the heated shadows, she was Eve personified, and Jackson fisted his hands to keep from reaching for her. She slid herself between his slightly spread thighs and placed her arms around his neck. Her breasts were beautiful twin temptations perfectly positioned for his pleasuring.

"And if I say no?"

He ran a finger around the aureole of one nipple. "Then, you won't get this . . ."

And he suckled her in so possessively her legs turned to water. "Or this . . ."

The other nipple received the same erotic care, and he raised the stakes by sliding the loose cotton drawers seductively over her bottom until her skin warmed deliciously.

"Say yes, Banker Atwood."

He flicked his tongue over her nipples again and again and lustily again. She was aching for him, blooming for him, hot for him.

"You're not playing fair . . ."

"If I'm not cheating, I'm not trying . . ."

He made her stand, undid the tapes of her drawers, and dragged them down. The bold move set her spinning and she wobbled for a moment on unsteady legs. Without a further word he circled her heat brazenly with erotic fingers that knew far too much about a woman's pleasure, and she groaned thickly.

"I need your answer, Grace . . ."

She felt him slide two fingers gently into the swollen damp vent of her core, and the glory of it made her say, "Yes—no—whatever you wish me to say . . ."

He smiled. "Do you think you're ready for me?"

She couldn't speak. She was trembling on the edge of the night's first release, and his fingers moving so carnally were pushing her closer and closer.

Jackson knew how close she was to climaxing by the way her beautiful body strained and by the small, rhythmic thrusts of her hips, so he widened his fingers just a bit and she shattered with a lusty strangled cry.

Jackson kissed her back down to earth, then slid himself from her warmth.

The surroundings were not conducive to their making love the way he wanted to, but he eased her over to the pallet she used for sleeping and soundlessly directed her to lie down.

Even though Jackson had agreed to her request that he make love to her, he had no intention of honoring it. As much as he wanted to make her his own, he'd no intention of leaving her with a child, especially one who might never know him. His own father had played an important role in his life, and he planned on doing the same for any sons or daughters he might sire, but he wouldn't be able to if he didn't leave Texas alive.

He ran hot eyes over the glory of her ripe brown nudity, and his need for her crystallized even more. Unable to resist, he stroked her throat and then bent to place a tender kiss on the valley between her breasts. "You're so beautiful . . ."

His hands joined his kisses in a sensual exploration of her lovely brown body, and soon Grace was caught up in the throes of the storm once again. His touches were bold, brazen; his kisses thrilling. When he softly asked her to part her legs, she did so willingly, and he rewarded her with such torrid, dallying slides of his fingers over her soft, damp shrine that Grace's hips rose shamelessly for more. He bent and flicked his tongue across the shadowy nook of her navel, then brushed his kisses over the inside of her soft skinned thigh. Upon feeling the heat of his breathing near the pulsing spot his fingers had prepared so well, she pulled back in panic. Watching him with wide eyes, she choked out, "What are you doing?"

In answer he ran a lazy finger over the red-gold hair at the apex of her thighs and said, "Giving you another lesson . . ."

"But—"

"But what?" His bold touch slid over the heat of her once more—teasing her, inviting her to part her legs so he could continue her education. The bliss he evoked as he circled her and tempted her overrode all else. Not caring anymore, Grace surrendered and lay back.

And this time, as his lips and hands unveiled and then awakened the hidden treasure within her hair, shock warred with pleasure at his magnificent expertise. As his mouth found her, all she could do was groan erotically. His loving was masterful, skillful, and so totally wanton that when he brazenly suckled her, her world shattered once more and she had to grab up the bed pillow to cover her face lest her screaming completion awaken everyone in the state of Illinois.

Jackson was harder than he ever remembered being in life, and watching her ride out the turbulent winds of her orgasm only increased his need. Lord, she was lovely; everything about her demanded he brand her as his own now, as his throbbing desire ached to do, but he could not. He couldn't offer her a future, and until he could, he had no right.

He leaned up and kissed her, and as she returned his kiss, he realized he'd been right. She was the kind of woman a man would take to his grave. Everything about her made him want to keep her at his side always, forever.

Grace had never felt so dazzled, and as she kissed him softly, asked, "Are we going to continue?"

He ran a worshipping finger over her magnificent mouth and said, "No. We're not."

"Why not?" she whispered hotly. "I know my education may be lacking, but I do know that you're supposed to get a turn, too."

"If I were to have you the way I want to have you, Grace Atwood, you'll be having triplets in nine months."

She had the decency to be embarrassed by his frank statement. "But you said—"

"I know, but you're not ready to marry. You said so yourself, and I—I don't want a child of mine raised on the memories of a dead father."

Grace searched his eyes. "It's Texas again, isn't it?"

"Yes, it is. If I don't come back, it won't be fair to you and it won't be fair to the child."

Grace knew he was right.

"So just let me hold you for now, okay?"

She snuggled up against him and he draped his arm around her waist and pulled her back against him.

"I don't want you to go to Texas."

He kissed the top of her head. "I know."

Grace didn't remember falling asleep, but when she awakened the next morning she was alone.

# Chapter 9

On the twentieth day of the journey, the brides spent four hours ferrying their wagons across the Mississippi River and into the state of Missouri. They were wet, exhausted, and drained, but glad to be in Missouri at last. However, by the twenty-third day, their elation turned to misery as they were forced to travel through a cold, bone-chilling rain. The thick, deep mud slowed travel considerably and they spent more time pushing wagons out of the axle-deep mire than they spent driving.

"We look like a tribe of mud women," Grace called out over the blowing and driving rain, as she and a good many of the women set their shoulders against the back of the Mitchells' wagon to try and free it from the mud.

"Remind me why we're going to Kansas City again?" Fanny wailed in mock misery.

"I don't remember!" Tess Dubois shouted in response.

It rained for three long days, and in those three days they covered barely twenty miles.

Day 26 was a Sunday, and after a few Bible readings, the women gave thanks that no one had contracted a disease or suffered tragedy. They spent the balance of the day rearranging wagon loads and airing out and straightening up the interiors.

A few days later, three of the mules were stolen during the night. The two women on watch (members of the Mitchell contingent) had fallen asleep. An angry Jackson wasn't pleased by this turn of events and decreed that all night watch members from then on be armed. Those lacking firearm skills were given training by him and Dixon. Those who couldn't abide weapons armed themselves with cast-iron skillets instead.

The next day, Jackson had Loreli call the brides together. Once they were gathered, he and Dixon reported on four mounted men who seemed to be trailing the wagons.

"Do you think they might be the ones who stole the mules?" Grace asked, as many of the women shaded their eyes against the noonday sun to peer out at the horizon in hopes of seeing the mysterious riders.

"Hard to tell," Dixon said. "They're hanging back just far enough to keep from being seen clearly."

"Who else might they be?" Loreli asked.

Jackson answered, "Drifters looking for a meal—outlaws."

That word set up a buzz of worry.

"Now, I'm not saying they are, but if they are, you ladies need to be prepared to defend yourselves. Those confident with firearms, check your rifles and keep them close by. Maybe they're not trailing us, maybe they're just taking a parallel route, but either way, keep a sharp lookout. If you see anything unusual or suspicious, let someone know."

Dixon added, "Coyotes usually work at night, so if they are planning something, it'll probably be after dark."

For the rest of the day, the women each kept one eye on their teams and one on the horizon. The ride was an uncharacteristically quiet one. There was no calling back and forth, no visiting amongst those walking beside the wagons as they rolled, and no communal singing of hymns as they made their way. The thought that there might be men out there somewhere waiting to prey on them made everyone tense.

When they circled the wagons for the night and lined up for the dinner meal, the mood was still subdued.

Suddenly, they heard Jackson call out, "Ladies, here they come, they're riding in slow, get ready, and let me and the marshal do the talking."

Then Dix added, "If anything happens to us, do whatever it takes to protect yourself."

Loreli jumped up and ran toward her wagon, but no one knew why. Putting her flight quickly from their minds, the other women checked their guns, then sat at the trestle tables as if this was just another meal. Only they knew that there were long-nosed Colts nestled in skirt pockets, rifles hidden beneath tables and in the folds of skirts. A few of the women casually got up and walked to their wagons and sat quietly inside, rifles at the ready. They may have been women, but they were armed women, and most were not afraid to shoot if it became necessary.

Illuminated by the light of the fire, the four men rode slowly into the camp. They were some of the dirtiest men Grace'd ever seen. The soiled clothes were patched and worn, the boots in their stirrups mud caked and run over. They were looking around discreetly, as if assessing the encampment and the people in it. The women at the tables looked up at their entrance, but no one made a sound.

One of the men, a thin-faced White man who hadn't seen soap or water in some time, showed off a gap-toothed smile, then called out cheerily, "Evenin', folks. How you all doin'?"

Jackson, rifle held at his side, walked up, and nodded easily. "Evenin'."

Dixon came out of the shadows and stood a pace or two behind him.

"Name's Luke," he said, introducing himself as he eyed Dixon. "Luke Wordell."

Grace could see Luke's companions looking around at the women. The brides were watching them just as closely.

Jackson didn't offer his own name. "What can we do for you, Wordell?"

"Call me Luke, everybody does."

"All right, Luke. How can we help you?"

"Just looking for a meal, hoped you got a bit extra."

One of the companions, a Black man wearing a battered brown hat low over his eyes, asked around the toothpick in his mouth, "Where's all the men?"

Before Jackson could say anything, he heard, "There aren't any others."

Sarah Mitchell.

Two dozen sets of angry female eyes shot Sarah's way. Had she not heard Jackson say he and the marshal would do the talking? Grace wanted to know. Suppose the men thought they could outgun Jackson and Dixon and all hell broke loose?

"Well, we should tell them," Sarah said huffily, coming to her own defense. "If they know we're out here alone, maybe they won't bother us."

"There ain't no other men here?" This was from one of Luke's other riders. He was a young White boy with red, patchy skin. His clothing and hat looked as battered as the other's. "Well, hell, what're we waiting for? I'll take that shy-looking little thing over there," he said, indicating Belle. "I'll bet she ain't never had a real man."

Jackson and Dixon both raised their rifles, and Jackson voiced coolly, "Yes, what are you waiting for?"

The Black man said with a grin, "Mister, there's four of us and only two of you," and the four raised their guns in unison and aimed back. "Drop 'em."

Tension filled the silence.

Dixon, gun still aimed, said, "I'm a deputy marshal."

Luke, his smile gone, replied coldly from behind his own rifle, "Well, then, somebody'll make sure you have a fancy funeral. Lower that gun, *Mr*. Marshal."

He then told Jackson, "You too."

Grace could see the anger on the face of Katherine Wildhorse as she stood across the glade, powerless to help her husband. The two women shared a look, then Katherine made a gun with two fingers, intimating that she was ready, but Grace shook her head. Something told her to wait.

The tense silence was shattered by the distinct and deadly click of a trigger being cocked, and in response, a now wide-eyed Luke froze in the saddle, then straightened up like a board.

"Evenin', Luke," said Loreli's death-cold voice from behind him. "This here's a buffalo gun in your back, and it's loaded for bear. "If your friends even *breathe* in my direction, I will blast your foul guts all over the night."

Every armed woman in camp took that split second to draw her own weapon, and when Luke's companions turned back, they too froze. They were now facing raised colts and rifles, derringers, and pistols. There were armed women beneath wagons and leaning out the backs; women gripping frying pans and lengths of wood; and they all had fire in their eyes.

Luke and his men, overwhelmed by the odds, tossed down their weapons.

Jackson crossed his arms over his chest and chuckled. "Well, now. Looks like you boys picked the wrong camp!" He was so proud of Loreli.

Dix picked up their weapons. "And I'm not even going to arrest you, because Loreli's the duly elected constable here. I'm sure she can come up with a suitable punishment."

The men's eyes widened.

Dix handed the weapons to Grace and Katherine, who immediately began removing the bullets.

He then added, "But I am going to confiscate your horses."

"What?" they yelled.

"Would you rather I take you down to Fort Smith and have you talk to Judge Parker about your attempt to attack a wagon train full of women?" he asked in a quiet but steely voice.

They hastily intimated that they did not.

"Loreli, they're all yours."

As she stood in front of them, the contempt and anger in her golden eyes was plain to see. "When I was fourteen, I lost my virginity. It was not by choice."

Silence fell over the camp.

"I swore then that I would never let myself or anyone I love be taken advantage of in that way again."

Her blazing eyes then settled on the man who'd

wanted to harm Belle. "That little shy one you wanted to get your hands on is one of those people I love. Now, because the marshal probably won't let me *geld* you—"

All four men jumped.

"This is what we're going to do. Give me your clothes."

They stared at her with wide eyes.

"Now," she said. "And quickly. The ladies and I drove those teams sixteen miles today and we're ready to go to sleep."

The men looked to Dix and Jackson as if for help, but found no support there.

Dixon said, "Do as the lady says or it's Judge Parker. Hanging Judge Parker."

An angry Luke and his gang began undoing buttons.

Loreli turned to Grace and the other women looking on. "Anybody offended by the sight of *real* men had better head to their wagons."

Belle, a few others, and all of the Mitchell contingent chose to leave. Everyone else stayed to watch their constable dispense her unique brand of justice.

By now the gang were down to their filthy union suits.

"Those too."

"No!"

"Yes. Isn't that what you had in mind when you rode in and saw all these women, taking off your clothes? Why should it be any different now?"

Grace shared a smile with a grinning Katherine, and both women turned their backs. Neither had any desire to see "real" men.

Grace heard Jackson laughing, and the shocked, humor-filled squeals of the women who'd been bold enough to watch.

Grace heard Loreli say, "Now, I'm going to let you

put your boots back on, and then I want you boys to start walking."

"You can't send us out in the night like this!"

"Sure I can," she countered coldly. "I'm the duly elected constable here. Now, get!"

Grace couldn't resist and so turned just in time to see the cringing, naked men, wearing nothing but boots, disappear into the night.

Cheers went up as the women mobbed Loreli. She'd saved the day.

By the thirty-fifth day, they reached the small city of Kirksville. They camped outside of town and a wearier and dirtier bunch of women Grace had yet to see. Their lack of cleanliness made them ripe pickings for the mosquitoes and biting flies, and everyone was covered with red, itchy spots. Their only consolation was that Kansas City was only a mere hundred and sixty miles away.

The Mitchell sisters started the thirty-seventh day by demanding that a meeting be called. Accommodating their request was the last thing Grace wanted to do, but she grudgingly agreed.

That evening, after the wagons were circled up, dinner shared, and the first opportunity to wash in days taken advantage of, everyone convened around the fire to hear what the Mitchells and their friends, aptly named the Seven Deadly Sins by Loreli, wanted to discuss. Weariness showed plainly on everyone's face.

Since Loreli headed up these gatherings, she didn't waste any time. "What do you ladies want?"

The thin-faced Molly said, "We want to end this fiasco and find a train that'll take us the rest of the way to Kansas City."

Grace's jaw tightened. "How do you plan to get there?"

"By wagon, of course," Sarah said in a patronizing tone.

"No, you won't. The wagon you're in has been purchased by the men in Kansas. If you leave, you and your things leave without it."

Fanny's voice was filled with sarcasm. "Have you ever traveled Jim Crow, Sarah?"

"No."

"I didn't think so."

Fanny then looked to Loreli. "Permission to go back to my wagon, Loreli. I've no desire to even discuss the merits of riding in a cattle car filled with dung. I've ridden Jim Crow."

Loreli nodded her understanding. "Permission granted, Fanny."

Fanny rose, gave the Mitchells a disgusted look, then left the circle.

Zora weighed in. "Suppose we did agree to do that, Sarah. What're we going to do if the conductor decides to put us all off the train? What about our possessions? Where would we go? Who would aid us, out in the middle of nowhere?"

Neither Sarah nor Molly nor any of their followers seemed to have a ready answer.

Ruby O'Neal cracked, "You and your friends must have been living in a foreign country for the last few years. Do you have any idea how things are going here for folks like us?"

Molly looked offended. "Of course, we read the papers."

"Then why are we having this discussion?" Grace asked coolly.

Sarah snapped, "Because I'm tired and sore and sick of looking at the backside of a team twelve hours a day.

I want a real bed to sleep in, and hot water, and a meal that doesn't include rabbits!"

Loreli didn't buy it. "Grace told you how it was going to be before we left Chicago. We're all tired and sore and sick of everything you're sick of, but I agree with Fanny, Jim Crow is not an option—at least, not for me."

Then she added, "Yes, this is probably the toughest task any of us has ever had to do, but I refuse to have a bigoted conductor banish me to a cattle car or ask me to leave in the middle of the night simply because of my ancestry."

"Hear! Hear!" someone called out.

Grace, glad for the support of Loreli and the others, said, "So, if you and your group wish to travel to Kansas by other means, we can unload your belongings, leave you some water and food—"

"You wouldn't dare," Sarah challenged.

"Believe me, I would," Grace promised. She'd had it up to her eyebrows with them. They'd done nothing but complain and snipe and aggravate people the entire trip. They also were still refusing to speak to Belle, and for that alone Grace wouldn't think twice about leaving them behind.

Grace stood. "Let me know what you decide in the morning."

She then looked to Loreli. "Madam Constable, are we done here?"

"Looks that way to me. Have a good evening, everyone."

The women, tired after yet another long day, trudged back to their tents.

Muttering and cursing under her breath, Grace wanted to kick something when she returned to her tent. She planned to spend the rest of the evening alone, lest she run into the Mitchell sisters and slap them silly. Just as she came around the front of her wagon, her angry steps slowed. Jackson was up on the seat. When he gave her that bone-melting smile, her anger melted away.

"Evenin'," he greeted.

She wondered if a more gorgeous man had ever been created. "Evening, yourself."

He'd been gone all day, scouting the road ahead. He and Dixon had been alternating the task so that Dixon and Katherine could have a bit more time together.

"You looked like you wanted to run somebody through when you came around the corner just now. It isn't me, is it?"

She couldn't hide her smile. "No, it isn't you."

He made a show of wiping sweat from his brow, and Grace laughed, then replied, "It's those blasted Mitchell sisters. Do you think we've enough oil on hand to boil them in?"

He chuckled. "What've they done now?"

She told him.

When she finished, he drawled, "Is there any chance we'll really get a chance to leave them behind?"

Grace sniffed. "We've a better chance of teaching the teams to fly. Neither of them has the testicular fortitude to do anything but whine."

He laughed. "Grace, I'm surprised at you. Testicular fortitude?"

"Sorry, something I picked up from my father."

"I like it."

"So do I."

Enjoying the sight and sound of her, Jackson told her, "Missed you today, hellion."

"Missed you, too," she replied truthfully.

Silence crept in as their need for each other rose and curled about them like smoke.

He asked, "Think I can come by later and show you how much?"

"Only if I can do the same."

"You're an outrageous woman, do you know that?"

Grace could already feel her body blooming with anticipation. "You wouldn't want me any other way."

He winked, hopped down, and disappeared around the side of the wagon.

True to his word, Jackson entered her wagon a few hour later. Taking her in his arms, he kissed her leisurely, gingerly, making himself go slowly so that he could savor her. He reacquainted himself with the sweetness he'd been craving since the last time they'd been together this way, and then nibbled her sultry bottom lip. As he used the tip of his tongue to taste the passion parted corners of her mouth, desire flared between them like a match against the tinder. He gathered her closer and deepened the kiss.

The memories of his last visit had had to sustain Grace until now, but they soon faded as reality took hold. The first tempting notes of passion's prelude had begun, and her senses unfurled to the song.

His lips left her mouth to graze across her jaw. Grace's head fell back to accommodate the thrilling kisses playing against the tender skin beneath, and up and down the column of her throat. His hand moved up her spine, warming her skin through her clothing. She wanted to be free of her clothes; free to be caressed without inhibition by the only male hands she'd ever known. The lips she responded to so hungrily were as deeply familiar as the gentle teeth now nibbling the shell of her ear. Even though they'd been together like this only a few times before, the heat of his big palms sliding the back of her skirt so provocatively over her full hips made her feel as if she'd known his touch for a lifetime.

The buttons on her shirtwaist were now being undone and she didn't care. The opened halves of the shirt revealed the fine, lace-edged chemise she wore beneath, and the golden tops of her breasts swelling above. He brushed his lips over the satiny curves and she moaned deep in her throat. Each touch of his lips left fire in their wake.

"Let's take this off . . ." he murmured.

He removed her blouse and then her short chemise. Fueled by the heat he sensed in her eyes, he used a finger to trace slowly the softness of her throat, then her kiss-ripened mouth. As desire shimmered around them, he pressed his lips against her parted mouth and the scented hills of her breasts. He raised his head so he could run his palms over her already berried nipples, then hotly suckled each in turn. She arched in response to his magnificent loving and to the storm he set off inside her soul.

When he took her hand to lead her over to the pallet, Grace sought his lips as they moved. He halted in mid-stride to accommodate her, and for a while they did nothing more than savor their shared desire before resuming the short journey. After taking a seat on the crate beside the pallet, he undid the tie on the waistband of her poplin skirt. It pooled at her feet and her polished cotton slip soon followed. She was clad in nothing but her frilly drawers. He pulled back a moment to feast his eyes on her half-clad loveliness.

"You're beautiful . . ."

He slid a finger over her nipple and heard her purr. Enflamed by the sight and sound, he leaned forward and suckled the nubbin gently. When the purr became a sensual growl, he treated the other, then slowly drew away. He couldn't stop touching her though; not her mouth, not her breasts, not the soft skin of her waist, usually kept hidden by the corset. As his hand explored her, he touched what felt to be a series of small scars on her side. Mapping them gingerly, he felt his curiosity rise, and he asked quietly, "How'd you hurt yourself?"

"My corsets . . ." she breathed.

Jackson hated the things for many reasons; the scarring of a woman's skin was one. He made a mental note to let her know again how he felt about the damned contraptions later, but now he wanted to hear her purr. She was beautifully endowed for a woman of such small stature. He felt her trembling. "Are you cold?"

"No," came her whispered reply. Grace was so filled with the haze of desire, the air in the shadowy wagon could've been as frigid as the winds of January and she wouldn't've been able to tell. Passion kept her insulated from all else.

"Then let's make sure you stay warm . . ."

Jackson slid an intimate finger between her thighs. The slit in her drawers allowed him to be as brazen and bold as he pleased, so he pleased her until she was lush and flowing. As he played, he watched her eyes close and her head drop back; she purred and then groaned. His manhood was so heavy and hard it felt like a length of steel. Were she a woman of more experience, he'd ease her down on him right now and make her ride him until they were both too sated to move, but she was Grace and it would be her first time. Mindful of that, he wanted to initiate her slowly, gently. He'd teach her to ride next time.

This evening's tutoring centered on just what he was doing now: circling her, caressing her, preparing her. He could tell by her strangled breathing and the soft, rhythmic arching of her lovely little body that she was on the brink of the night's first climax, so rather than make her wait, he wantonly increased her pleasure and she shattered, hoarsely whispering his name.

Still resonating with the shuddering aftereffects of his magic, Grace came back to herself slowly. Gazing into his eyes, she saw passion, heat. He grazed a possessive knuckle over her still pulsing shrine. The sensations filled her core once more. Wanting him to stop until she could locate her mind again, but hoping he wouldn't, she moaned responsively.

"Such a sultry little pirate queen."

His voice was thick, hot. The dallying continued. Grace shamelessly widened her stance.

She wondered how in the world she was going to keep from wanting him after he left. "You're in my blood, Jackson . . ." she whispered.

He rewarded her with a soft kiss on the lips. "You're in my blood too . . ."

And she was, every luscious inch of her. It bothered him in a way, because he didn't know how to keep her with him, but he set the thoughts aside for now. He concentrated on sluggishly kissing her swollen lips, toying with her nipples, and generally keeping her warm. "Let's lie down."

Caught up in the rising heat, Grace didn't want to move and lose his bliss-filled touches.

"Gluttony is a sin, Banker Atwood . . ."

She couldn't hide her smile. "You're entirely too good at this."

"Aren't you glad?"

She leaned down and treated him to a kiss that showed him just how glad she really was, then took his hand and led him down to the pallet.

Jackson knew he might be courting danger by removing his clothes, but he wanted to feel her nude beauty against his skin.

Grace had never seen a naked man in the flesh before, but even in the moon-dappled shadows she could see that he was beautifully made. He appeared to have been chiseled from a dark exotic marble. She boldly reached out and ran a finger over the well-defined muscles below his ribs and in his chest. Her eyes brushed the part of him that made him male, but because she didn't want to be caught staring, she raised her eyes quickly to his face.

"That was a quick look," he told her softly.

The words and smile threw her off stride. "I didn't want to—ogle."

"Ogle all you like, because I'm sure ogling you."

She dropped her head to hide her smile. "This is all so new."

"I know, but it's fun. Isn't it?"

She had to admit it was, so she nodded.

"Then take a good long look this time. It won't bite."

Grace felt the heat of embarrassment burn her cheeks. Still refusing to look, she said, "Maybe I'm not as brazen a pirate queen as I thought."

"You're brazen enough. Come here . . ."

He gently pulled her closer so that her back was against his chest and he cradled her in his arms. "If you want me to get dressed again, I can."

"No, I like being with you this way. Does that make me brazen?"

"Yep."

Feigning outrage, she switched around and found him smiling. "You're supposed to say no."

"Why?" he asked, running a bent knuckle over the nipple closest to him. "You are brazen, but like you said, I wouldn't have you any other way."

He slid a finger over her lips and then dragged it slowly down her body to her nipple. "This is why . . ." And he circled it, and stroked it, and when he took it into his warm mouth, she arched sinuously.

"And this is why . . ."

He gave the other nipple the same intimate care, and she moaned.

"Oh, and add this, too . . ."

His fingers found the swollen bud between her thighs and plied it so languidly and expertly the groans spilled out of her throat like a song.

He eased a finger into her and her passionate response broke the quiet space with a strangled sound. He bit each nipple gently; then, after easing in another bold finger, kissed her mouth.

Grace had never felt such heat; never craved anything as much as she craved this. Sh didn't want him to stop. "Please . . ." she whispered. She'd no idea what her plea might be for, but Jackson did.

"Don't worry, darlin', I'll please you."

Now, Jackson had no intention of taking her fully, or at least, that's what he told himself, but she was so passionate, and when she whispered, "Make me yours . . ." the soft entreaty coupled with his own raging need made him want to grant her wish more than breathe.

He entered her slowly, making himself remember that her virgin state would not allow him to enjoy her with as much zeal as his desire demanded—at least, not this first time.

Keeping her lack of experience in mind, Jackson made his way inch by sensual inch. He was a big man and she was a small woman. The last thing he wanted was to cause her more pain than necessary. "Am I hurting you?"

Grace didn't know. It was all so foreign, yet so delectable. She could feel her flesh opening to receive him. "I don't think so, at least not yet."

"Good."

Fitting his hands to her hips, he held back on the urge to plunge his way to paradise and forced himself to maintain his slow pace. She was so warm and so tight, it took all he had. "Grace, if it's going to hurt, now will be the time, so hold on."

He thrust himself past her maidenhood and felt her tighten in reaction. "I'm sorry," he whispered, kissing her eyes, her nose, her brows. "It won't ever hurt again, I promise."

But it hurt now, and Grace wasn't sure she wanted to continue. The parts of herself sheltering him were filled with a searing pain.

"Let me make it better . . ."

"How?" she whispered, dearly hoping he could.

So he showed her.

Employing a slow, rhythmic stroking, he tempted her to rejoin him in life's most ancient dance. At first she couldn't respond; each and every movement made the pain resonate, but after a while her body began to warm and rise to that seductive rhythm and she was on the path to pleasure once again. "Oh, Jackson," she purred in response. "This is better, much, much better."

He grinned and lengthened his strokes. "Is it . . ."

"Oh, yes . . ."

Her confession pleased him; the sight of her rising to match his strokes pleased him even more. Grace Atwood was a sensual, hot-blooded pirate queen beneath her strict banker's veneer, and as he'd said, he wouldn't want her any other way.

While she met his thrusts, he brushed hot kisses over the hills and valleys of her soft, scented skin. He leaned back. Fired by the sight of her rising and falling beneath him amidst the shadows, he toyed wantonly with the slick, passion-swollen flesh hidden within her hair, and when she moaned, the sounds and sight fueled him to increase the pace and power of his strokes.

Grace could feel herself about to shatter. Nothing

equaled this. The velvet hardness of his desire moving like bliss between her thighs made her ravenous, greedy. She wanted all he could give her and more. Here in the fiery shadows, she could be any woman she wanted to be, and tonight she wanted to be his.

So Jackson made her his with all the fervor he could bring to bear. She climaxed twisting and trying to keep her pleasure from being heard, rising to meet his strong, possessive strokes. The sight and feel of her responding so passionately made him drop the reins on his own carefully paced control, and he shattered too, growling his pleasure as he rode to the end of the storm.

As he lay there in the aftermath with his arm behind his head, Jackson looked up at the darkness overhead and wondered what to do now. They'd made a child tonight, maybe two, judging by the intensity of the union; he could feel it. He turned his head her way. "So, when do you want to get married?"

"You said, *if* there's a child."

"There will be one, so when?"

Grace raised herself on an elbow and looked down at him. She sensed he'd withdrawn from her and she wasn't sure how to respond. "You can't be sure."

"I am."

"Jackson—"

He cut her off, "We already talked about this, remember?"

"I do," she said quietly, "but you don't want to marry any more than I do."

A part of Jackson secretly cheered tonight's outcome; now she would be his, but the other was appalled by this very decided deviation from the path he'd laid down. He was supposed to be going to Texas to confront Lane Trent, not succumbing to a passionate little pirate queen with a body lush enough to drown in. Because of his lack of discipline he might've just condemned her to having to raise his child alone, and his child to growing up without a father. Both of them would need his name, even if it was one gracing a wanted poster.

He got up and began searching for his clothes.

Grace tried to keep the hurt out of her voice. "You're leaving?"

"Yes," he said, pulling on his pants. Acknowledging the pain he sensed in her, he said softly, "Please don't think you've done anything wrong, Grace. You haven't. This is all my fault."

"I've no regrets."

"You will if I don't come back from Texas, and so will our child."

"Jackson—"

He found his shirt, thrust his arms in the sleeves, and started in on the buttons. "We'll get married in Kansas City."

She stood. "No, we won't."

He looked over at her and her nudity pulled at him so hard he wanted to toss off his clothes and spend the rest of the night hearing her whisper his name. "Don't fight me on this, Grace, you'll lose."

Grace didn't like his tone at all. "Excuse me? I gave you my virginity, not permission to tell me what I may or may not do."

In spite of the rising tension he smiled inwardly. *Lord, what a woman.* "I'll see you in the morning."

"Don't bet the farm."

Shaking his head, he walked over to her, and before she could protest, pulled her to him, kissed her long and hard, then turned her loose. When he exited, she was still pulsing and floating.

*     *     *

They'd been on the road forty days when they crossed paths with a group of mounted Black soldiers from the Tenth Cavalry. The soldiers were escorting a small contingent of Indians.

"They're being removed to government lands," Dixon explained.

Grace knew that Dixon was a member of the Black Seminole tribe, and as the members of the wagon train stopped to witness the silent procession, his usually stoic face reflected both pain and sorrow. This was Grace's first encounter with the nation's native people, and she saw that they were not the "dreaded savages" she'd been led to believe. The slow-moving group of about thirty individuals consisted of elders, women, and children. Many appeared weary, sick, and ill fed, and the sight pulled at her heart.

Grace watched Katherine move quietly to her husband's side and slip her hand into his. He squeezed her hand in silent acknowledgment, but never moved his eyes from the column until they passed by.

The wagon train reached Kansas City exactly forty-five days after leaving the outskirts of Chicago. The farm owned by Grace's cousin, Price Atwood, was their final destination and he waved them onto the property with a welcoming grin. Grace had never been so glad to see him in her life. As much as Grace had enjoyed the journey, she was very glad it was over.

The excitement of the arrival pushed aside all the weariness as the women jumped down from their wagons and hugged each other in celebration. They'd done it; they'd traveled over five hundred miles with no one to rely upon but themselves. In many ways they'd been altered by the experience; most were physically stronger and more confident inside and out. Grace hoped the grooms would appreciate the exceptional women and give them the love and respect they deserved.

As the brides left their wagons, they were told by Price that the grooms were staying at various boarding-houses in the area and that someone would be sent to alert the men of the brides' safe arrival. Grace insisted the women be allowed a few days to refresh themselves before meeting their prospective mates. Dresses needed to be unpacked and pressed. Hair had to be done and baths were sorely needed. None of the weary women wished to be seen covered with the dirt and grime of the trail.

Grace had been changed, too. She was in love with Jackson Blake. The idea of maybe having to raise his child did not frighten her; she already knew her aunts would lend her all the support she'd need, but she honestly hoped she was not with child, mainly because he didn't love her and she didn't want him forced into a marriage based solely on obligation. They hadn't had a chance to discuss the situation further, but she knew it would come, and she was not looking forward to it.

By evening, arrangements had been finalized for the brides to stay with members of the local A.M.E. church. The parishioners had graciously offered their homes. Hugs were given and tears were shed as the women prepared to leave with their various hosts and hostesses. They'd become a family during the trip, and for Grace it felt strange to no longer be together.

The Wildhorses said their good-byes, too. Katherine and Dixon would be spending a few days in Kansas City, and then it would be on to Indian Territory. Grace and Katherine parted tearfully. They'd become good friends and Katherine promised she'd write, even though they both knew they might never see each other again.

As Grace and Jackson stood on Price's porch under the twilight, watching Dix and Katherine disappear into the distance, she said, "It feels so strange, watching everyone go their separate ways after being together the way we've been."

"Yes, it does."

Grace's cousin Price joined them on the porch. "You two want something to eat? My housekeeper, Mrs. Trundle, fixed a good-sized meal before she left for the day."

Grace said, "Bath first, food second."

"Blake?"

"I'll wait and eat with Grace, if you don't mind."

The tall, thin Price shrugged. "Sounds fine. Come on in and I'll show you where you can bunk."

"Out here on the porch is fine for me," Jackson said. He knew he had no business sleeping in the same house with Grace. The thought of making love to her in a bed might tempt him into being indiscreet, and he didn't want to wake up with Price standing over them with a shotgun. Although that would settle the disagreement as to whether they should marry or not.

Grace dearly wanted to get Jackson alone so they could hash out this marriage mess, but she was afraid they'd end up arguing loud enough to be heard back in Chicago. Any argument would surely raise Price's suspicions, and she did not want him involved. Price was a teetotaler and a Bible thumper and had very strict morals. Being a good ten years older than Grace, he'd always been protective of her, and if he ever got wind of her true relationship with her wagonmaster, he'd make her marry Jackson so fast her head would spin off her neck. So after her bath, Grace had dinner and then went to bed.

The next morning Grace awakened at dawn. Although she'd planned to sleep in, habits were hard to break. For the first morning in a long time she didn't have to climb up behind a team, and that in itself made her fall back upon the fluffy feather mattress like a happy child.

Price's housekeeper, Mrs. Trundle, was a big, raw-boned woman of German ancestry. She and her husband were recent immigrants to the United States and had spent the last four years sharecropping on Price's land. She worked in the house to help make ends meet.

"So you brought Mr. Price a wife?" Helga Trundle asked in her thick German accent. She set out a feast of eggs, side bacon, flapjacks running with butter and syrup, grits, biscuits, and a strudel that melted in Grace's mouth.

"Yes," Grace replied, looking up at the woman's smiling face. "Don't you think it's time?"

Price grinned as he warned his cousin, "All right, Grace, don't start that now."

Price was one of the few male members in the Prescott line. He was the only son of an only son, her mother's eldest sibling, Dillard, and the aunts and every other female in the Prescott family had been pestering him for years to marry so there'd be more sons.

"Yah, I think a misses would be good for Mr. Price, but she better be a good girl. No whores," the housekeeper stated with a shake of a thick finger.

Price choked on his coffee and Grace picked up her own cup to hide her smile. She cast Blake a quick glance and found him smiling behind his cup, too.

Price used his napkin to wipe at his mouth. "Uh, Mrs. Trundle, I think we have everything we need now."

"Okay, I've windows to wash. Call if you need anything." And she hustled out.

After breakfast, Price hitched a team to his wagon and went into town to meet with the other bridegrooms. They had business to discuss, and he wanted to see if the wedding suit he'd ordered from New York's Bloomingdale's department store had arrived yet.

That left Grace and Jackson seated out on the porch alone.

"So," he said, "we're here."

Wearing a summer-weight skirt and blouse, she replied happily, "I keep thinking it's a dream and that I'm going to wake up and find I'm still on the trail."

She quieted a moment as she reflected on the past month, then looked his way. "You said you'd get us here and you kept your word. Thank you."

"You're welcome."

Then she asked the question she'd been dreading for weeks. "When are you leaving for Texas?"

"Soon. Need to get some gear and provisions first, though."

"I see."

Jackson couldn't imagine leaving her behind, but she couldn't go. He'd have enough problems watching his own back; taking her along would only make the venture that much more dangerous.

"So, do you want to get married with the brides, or have a separate ceremony?"

"Neither."

"Grace, we've already discussed this."

"I don't remember a discussion, just you telling me what I was going to do."

"You're carrying my child, it's all the same."

"No, it is not."

Admittedly, he hadn't given her a choice, but choice didn't enter into it. His child needed a name and a father, and Lord willing, he'd return so he could help with the raising. Once he returned from Texas, they could decide where to make their home. He didn't think he could live in Chicago. He'd tried fitting into a back east life and hated every day of it. She, on the other hand, had been bred to it, and he doubted she'd like being in Texas, where life lacked many of the luxuries she become accustomed to. There'd be no theaters, charity balls, or tea stores where he was headed. So that too would only add to the dissension. "So, again, when do you want to get married?"

"I'm not going to make you marry me."

"So, what? You planning on raising my child alone?"

"It's been done."

"You're right, but it won't be done by you."

"We're not going to get married, Jackson."

"Yes, we are. Do you remember the promise you made to me?"

She did, but hoped to shimmy out of it. "Jackson, that promise was made under duress and you know it. I'd've agreed to anything that night."

"We're getting married, Grace. No child of mine is going to be raised without me."

"But you don't want to marry me."

"The child needs a father. We'll marry, you'll go back to Chicago, and I'll come and get you when I'm done in Texas."

"You are not going to dictate my future, Jackson Blake."

"It's not your future I'm worried about. It's the baby's."

Their voices had been rising as they both dug in their heels, and soon they were in the midst of a shouting match that could be heard in St. Louis. Mrs. Trundle came running out.

"Whatever is the matter?"

Jackson's face was hard with anger. "She's carrying my child but she doesn't want to get married."

Mrs. Trundle's eyes widened and she put her hands to her mouth.

"Tell the world, why don't you?" Grace accused angrily.

"See if I don't!"

The next she knew he was saddling the coal black stallion. "What are you doing?"

"I'm going to tell the world. Maybe your aunts and your cousin can put some sense into that hard head of yours."

"Don't you dare wire my aunts!"

He hoisted himself in the saddle and picked up the reins. "I'll dare anything I damn well please because you're carrying my child!"

He turned the horse and headed it toward the road to Kansas City. Watching him ride away, Grace slapped her hand angrily against the porch post and stomped into the house to await the storm to come.

In Chicago, Tulip and Dahlia read the message: GRACE WITH CHILD. WON'T MARRY ME. NEED YOUR HELP. JACKSON BLAKE.

Tulip looked at her sister. Her sister looked at her and they were both so happy they locked arms and did a high-stepping do-si-do.

"You know what this means, Dahl?"

"I sure do, Tulip. Prescott sons!"

"Amen and hallelujah!"

"Let's leave on the first train in the morning."

"Let's start packing."

"Do you love her?"

Jackson looked into the steely gray eyes of Price Atwood. Jackson hadn't been able to find him in Kansas City so he'd waited until Atwood returned They were now sequestered in Price's study. "I do, yes."

Price hadn't been happy upon learning the news. In fact he was quite angry. He took his role as one of

Grace's male relatives very seriously. "Have you told her?"

"No."

"Why not?"

"Because she doesn't love me."

"That doesn't matter. The baby needs your name, and so does she."

"Not to her way of thinking."

"Then she'll just have to think again."

When Price entered the bedroom he'd given to Grace last night, she was seated in a rocker. Her eyes warned him away, but he came on in anyway. The angry argument that followed filled the house and rattled the freshly washed windows. Downstairs, a simmering Jackson listened and waited.

When Price stormed from the room, the furious Grace wanted to throw something. How dare these men try and run her life! Neither of them would give her any credit for being able to take care of herself and the baby; all they were concerned about was making her conform to society's norms. She'd not been raised that way. Granted, were her father still alive, he too would probably be trying to make her marry Jackson so the baby would have a name, but her child did have a name: hers. It was a very fine name, as far as Grace was concerned, and had served the family well since the eighteenth century. She'd no desire to be in a loveless marriage and she didn't think she or her baby should be doomed to such a fate. In her mind, Jackson would only end up resenting her, no matter what he claimed now, and she'd be the one he'd blame. No, she had no desire to put herself through such turmoil. She would not marry Jackson Blake and she planned to stick to her guns.

Grace spent the rest of the day in her room, alternately pacing and trying to come up with a solution to her dilemma. If Jackson had really wired the aunts, she expected they'd be in town no later than tomorrow afternoon. She'd no idea where they'd stand on the issue, but if they took Jackson's side, she would resist them too.

The aunts arrived late the next evening. Jackson and Price helped them bring in their valises.

"Where is she?" Dahlia asked, removing her gloves.

"Upstairs," Jackson told them. "I wouldn't be surprised if she's barricaded herself in by now."

"Angry, is she?"

"Past angry," Price responded. "Maybe you and Aunt Tulip can talk some sense into her. Morally—"

Tulip held up her hand. "Enough, Price. If you've been quoting chapter and verse, I'd barricade myself in, too."

The aunts then turned to Jackson. "Are you certain this is what you want?"

"For the sake of the child, yes. It shouldn't grow up being called a bastard."

"We agree."

Jackson sighed with relief. He'd no idea which side the aunts would take.

Tulip said, "She's going to be even angrier once we're done. Are you ready to take on a wife who will probably resent you for a very long while?"

He didn't hesitate. "I am."

"Then we'll talk to her."

Grace heard the knock on the door and snarled, "Go away."

Dahl snapped. "Open this door, Grace Prescott Atwood."

The voice put a smile on Grace's face for the first time since this war began.

When she opened the door, both aunts hugged her dearly.

"How are you, dear?" Tulip asked, after she and Dahlia closed the door and took a seat on the bed.

"As well as can be expected."

"How late are you?"

"I'm not late at all. Jackson *thinks* I'm carrying. At this point there's no proof at all. And even if I am, I'm not marrying him. It isn't necessary. I can raise a child."

"That's not the issue, dear. The issue is legitimacy. Children can be very cruel. Do you remember how angry you would get when your classmates called you 'Dot Face'?"

She did.

"Imagine being called 'Bastard' for the rest of your life."

"But Aunt Dahl—"

"Imagine it, dear. That's the name your child will wear. It won't matter that his or her mama is a banker, or that she's wealthy and smart as a whip. The child will still be 'Bastard.' "

Grace quieted.

Tulip asked, "And suppose the child wants to know why you and her father didn't marry?"

"I'll simply tell her the truth."

"What, that you made her a bastard by choice?"

Grace shot her aunt an angry look.

"There's no sense in cutting your eyes at me, missy, it's you making this choice."

"But I don't want to marry him, and he doesn't want to marry me."

"He does, Grace. Otherwise he wouldn't've wired us for help."

"It's purely out of obligation."

"He's an honorable man, Grace, and that means something."

"It means he wants to dictate my life."

"It means he doesn't want his child coming home in tears after being labeled a bastard. We Prescotts can trace our ancestry back to before this nation became a nation. What are his roots, do you know?"

"Yes, his father was a slave."

"Legitimacy means a great deal to those of the race whose families were torn apart."

She knew that.

"And though you may not like it, being with child means doing numerous things you might not want to do, that's why the good Lord put childbearing in the hands of women. Crying babies would be found strewn all over the road if men had that responsibility. They have neither the patience nor the temperament."

Grace had to smile at that.

Tulip's voice was soft. "Do it for the child, Grace dear. You had your father's name and your child needs the name of his father, too. And if you find that you're not carrying, you and Jackson can go your separate ways."

Grace could feel the defensive wall she'd built around herself crumbling under the aunts' even-toned reasoning. Grace sighed tiredly. She knew they were right. It didn't matter how modern a woman she thought herself to be; society would label her child regardless, and Grace hadn't considered that part of the balance sheet until now.

"Well?" Dahlia asked.

Grace sighed again. "Okay, I'll marry him, but don't ask me to like it."

The aunts smiled. Their work here was done.

# Chapter 10

The following evening, Grace tried her best to be cheerful while viewing the brides' mass wedding at the local AME church, but neither the celebratory air nor the happiness sparkling in the couples' eyes were enough to lighten her mood. Later on tonight she would be pledging to love Jackson until death too, and she was still adamantly opposed to the idea. It did please her to see the brides so happy, though, and the men looked proud and pleased as well, but she felt as if she had the weight of the world resting upon her shoulders.

While the brides and their new husbands danced their first waltz, Grace made her way outside, ostensibly to grab a bit of fresh air. She was soon joined by Loreli Winters.

"You've had a fake smile on your face all evening, Grace, what's the matter?"

Grace told the truth. "Jackson thinks I may be carrying his child and he's forcing me to marry him."

"Not happy about it, I take it."

"No. I don't like being told what to do."

The two women shared silence for a moment, then Loreli spoke. "Could be worse. He could be someone you can't abide."

"But he doesn't love me, and all I can envision is him resenting me somewhere down the road for giving me his name."

"You could be right, but you could be wrong."

"No, I'm right. He's marrying me only because it's the honorable thing to do."

"What's wrong with that?"

"Nothing, I suppose, but I don't want a husband. My life is fine as it is, and I can raise the baby alone."

"The baby should have a name, though."

"I know," Grace conceded. "I know."

"Look on the bright side."

Grace wished she could. "There *is* no bright side, Loreli."

"Sure there is. He could've denied responsibility and left you and the baby high and dry. This way, at least you'll have someone to help you with those midnight feedings new mothers are always complaining about."

"Thanks."

Loreli smiled. "Take it from a woman who's always wanted a steady man and babies. You're very lucky, Grace, don't let your pride keep you from finding happiness. Jackson is a good man. The poems alone make him a great catch. You'll see."

Grace cracked sarcastically, "Thanks again."

"You're welcome."

Setting thoughts of Jackson aside for now, Grace asked, "But what about you? What are your plans?"

"Tomorrow or the next day I'm hopping a train for California."

"None of the men here caught your fancy?"

She snorted. "Can you see me as a farmer's wife?"

Grace said genuinely, "Maybe."

She snorted again. "Right. One did ask me, but I turned him down."

"Why?"

She shrugged. "He seemed entirely too serious minded for a woman like me."

She quieted a moment as if she were thinking about the man. "Handsome as all get out though. Big shoulders. Taller than Jackson."

"Maybe you should reconsider. You did say you wanted a steady man and babies."

"Yes, I did and I do, but not him. Men like him want virgins. Once he finds out how 'experienced' I am, he'll run for the hills."

"You could be right, you could be wrong."

"Well, we'll never know. I've already purchased my train ticket."

"I'll miss having you in my life."

Loreli's voice was genuine. "I'll miss you too, Grace. Thanks for letting me tag along."

"You're very welcome. It was quite the adventure, wasn't it?"

"Sure was, but you know what's been the best part?"

"No, what?"

"Seeing Belle. The man she picked doesn't mind that she's carrying that cad's child. It was a love match at first sight. I was so happy when she told me, we were both in tears."

Grace had been moved by the sight of Belle and her new husband too. He seemed to be a godsend. "I hope she'll be very happy."

"Me too."

The hired musicians were now playing a lively reel and the music floated out of the church and over the night. "Well, I suppose we should go back in before Jackson comes out here to make sure his bride-to-be hasn't hopped a train and disappeared."

Loreli chuckled. "You two will do fine. Just give it some time."

"And you should consider that man's offer."

Loreli snorted again. "Let's change the subject. Did you hear about the Mitchell sisters?"

Grace nodded. "Trudy told me they were upset because none of the men met their high standards."

"That's the story they spread, but the truth is, they questioned those men so ferociously, the poor fellows fled and no one's seen them since. Talk is the Mitchells left for Chicago on this morning's first train."

"They shouldn't've left Chicago in the first place, if that's all they were going to do."

"I agree, but with any luck, they'll never marry and therefore never propagate."

Grace laughed. "You are so bad."

"I know, now let's go back inside."

At the end of the celebration the brides left with their grooms to share their first night together and Grace and Jackson drove back to Price's farm. He hadn't had much to say to her since she'd agreed to marry him and she was content to let things remain that way.

He said, "Everybody looked happy tonight."

"Yes, they did."

Jackson knew she was still angry, but he refused to let her have her way on this. The child was as much his as hers and he was determined to be a father. He owed it not only to the child but to his own father who'd raised him with much love. Jackson wanted the opportunity to raise his son or daughter in the same way. "I'll be leaving for Texas at the end of the week. You can ride back to Chicago with your aunts."

"And if you are killed?"

"Then you'll be a widow and all your problems will be solved."

It was a decidedly cold thing to say; so cold, in fact, they both rode the rest of the way in silence.

The justice of the peace was waiting for them when they returned. He didn't have to have second sight to see Jackson's tight jaw or Grace's flashing copper eyes. The aunts simply shook their heads at the two young people, then stood beside them in their role as witnesses. There were no smiles and no holding of hands. Jackson and Grace responded to the vows and that was it. When the justice pronounced them man and wife and gave Jackson the traditional permission to kiss the bride, he gave her a chaste peck on her forehead and turned and left the room. The aunts sadly shook their heads again. A furious Grace followed her bridegroom's example and went up to her room.

As Grace lay in bed later that night, it came to her that she was not going to let him go to Texas alone. Yes, they were at odds, and yes, his meddling in her life made her want to bury him in one of Price's fields head down, but she loved him, truly loved him. For all her anger and storming around, he was in her soul, and although she knew his feelings for her did not run as deep, she refused to have him shipped back to her in a plain pine box. He'd need her; she could feel it.

That next morning when she broached the subject of going with him, he told her in no uncertain terms just what he thought of her idea. "No, it's going to be too dangerous."

"I don't care. I'm going."

"No, you're not."

They were at the breakfast table. Price and his bride, the statuesque Tess Dubois, had spent the night at one of the Kansas City hotels and had not returned yet, so Grace, Jackson, and the aunts were enjoying Mrs. Trundle's morning fare without them.

Tulip said, "Grace, maybe Jackson is right. You don't want to endanger the baby."

"The baby will be fine. I'm going."

His voice was firm. "No, you're not. This isn't going to be a walk to church."

"I know that, but you insisted on making me your wife, and a wife follows her husband, no matter what."

"Not where I'm going."

"Well, you don't have a choice."

They were glaring at each other across the table.

"Why are you so damned hard-headed, Grace?"

"Because I have you as a husband. So, are we traveling by wagon or train?"

"*You* aren't traveling at all, so eat."

Grace's lip curled as she went back to her plate, but she knew this discussion wasn't over, not by a long shot.

After breakfast, while the aunts and Mrs. Trundle looked on from the porch, the brides and their new husbands came by Price's farm to say their final good-byes. They would be heading back to the Rice County colony tomorrow. With tears in her eyes, Grace gave them all fierce hugs and received strong tear-filled hugs in return. They'd become sisters in the months they'd been together, and as Grace had noted with Katherine Wildhorse, there was no guarantee she'd see any of them ever again.

Jackson had left for town right after breakfast and so missed the many thanks the women wanted to bestow, but Grace promised to relay them upon his return.

As she and the brides she'd grown closest to—Trudy, Fanny, Daisy, Zora, and Belle—walked back to the line of buggies, buckboards, and wagons where the husbands sat waiting, Fanny said, "Loreli told us about the marriage."

Grace looked around at their concerned faces. "Remind me to strangle her the next time I see her."

Smiles spread through the group.

Zora said, "Since we all know the problems between you and Jackson will be ironed out, we got you two something."

Zora waved her hand and Grace watched as Zora's husband, Barton, reached into the back of his wagon and lifted out what looked to be a cradle. As he neared, Grace's tears began anew. It was a cradle; a beautifully carved, dark wood rendering that would shelter her child lovingly while it slept. Barton laid it at her feet and a very moved Grace ran her hand over it gently. "Thank you," she whispered in a tear-choked voice.

They were all teary-eyed again too. "You're welcome."

Zora said, "Promise you'll write us and let us know when the baby's born."

Grace nodded. "As long as Belle does the same."

Belle walked up and gave Grace a hug that filled Grace's heart.

"Thank you," the young woman whispered with fierce emotion. "Thank you so very much."

Her friends left her then to go back to their husbands, and moments later drove away. With her cradle at her feet, Grace waved until they disappeared from sight.

Price and Tess returned a bit past noon and immediately began on their own preparations to leave. Since the founding of the colony, Price had been traveling back and forth between it and the property he owned here, but now that he and the beautiful Tess were married, he planned on leasing the farm to the Trundles and making the land he owned in the colony his permanent residence.

Mr. Trundle, who was as thin as his wife was large, had a grin on his face the size of Kansas when Price asked him into the kitchen to tell him the news. Price hadn't given them any inkling as to his plans for the land, and they were happy indeed.

The aunts spent the afternoon helping Price and Tess pack up the household items Price wanted to ship to the colony and getting to know Tess better. Grace pitched in too, because it gave her something to do besides think about her war with her husband.

He returned late that afternoon. As he entered the parlor he greeted the women emotionlessly, then asked Grace if he could speak to her.

Outside on the porch, Grace looked up at the beautiful day and wished her mood were as bright. "What did you wish to speak with me about?"

"I'm leaving in the morning."

Sadness momentarily touched her heart. "What time?"

"Eight on the Santa Fe."

"I see."

"I'll come back to Chicago as soon as I get things cleared up."

She was so still and unapproachable that to Jackson she looked as if she were carved from ice. Somewhere beneath that icy exterior lived the woman he'd made love to in a moonlit glade; a woman who'd burst into his life and made him alive again. He wanted her back, but she seemed so very far away. "Grace, the baby needs a name."

"I've already accepted that. Please, can we not talk

about this again?" The plea in her voice was mirrored in her eyes.

He nodded tersely.

Silence reigned for a moment, and Grace wondered where the two of them would be in a year's time. "You weren't here when the brides came by this morning. They wanted me to tell you good-bye. They gave us a beautiful cradle."

"I'd like to see it before I leave tomorrow."

"Okay."

Their gazes caught and held, and both saw the love of their life hiding behind emotionless eyes.

Grace asked him quietly, "Was there anything else?"

"No."

"Then I'll go back and help Tess and the aunts."

As she reentered the house, Grace had the information she needed. When he boarded the Santa Fe in the morning, so would she.

That evening, as Grace packed her essentials in a large carpet bag, the aunts looked on skeptically from their seats on her bed. She'd let them in on their plan, and they weren't sure whether they thought it was a good one.

"Are you sure this is the right thing to do?" Dahlia asked.

"Nope, but I'm doing it anyway."

Tulip shook her head. "Sometimes, I think you have too much Prescott blood in you, Grace dear."

"I'll take that as a compliment."

Grace planned on packing light; she knew Jackson wouldn't want to be burdened down by frivolous weight. "I promise to wire you whenever I can, wherever I can."

"You'd better," Dahlia countered.

"He's going to throw a fit," Tulip pointed out.

"I know, but he'll just have to."

"Do you love him that much?" Tulip asked.

Grace looked into the wise eyes and saw a softness there. "Yes, I do."

Dahlia sighed, "Then I guess we have to go along."

Once again, grateful to have them in her life, Grace smiled.

The next morning, Jackson awakened before dawn. Mrs. Trundle had promised to have his breakfast ready, and she did not disappoint. Everyone else was still asleep, he assumed, because he heard nor saw anyone else in the quiet house as he ate, then went out to saddle his horse. Leaving Grace behind tore at his heart and would delay the two of them working through their problems, but it couldn't be helped. He had to do this and he had to do it alone.

He went upstairs and knocked lightly upon her door. Hearing her quiet reply, he soundlessly entered. It didn't surprise him to find her already awake. She was dressed in a robe and was seated in a chair by the window. The sun was just coming up.

"Well, I'm heading out."

She stood. "Take care of yourself."

He nodded. "I will. You too."

An awkward silence developed.

"Wire me in Chicago when you can."

Jackson wanted to cross the room and take her in his arms, but didn't. He held his position by the door while his intense longing for her set off a tremendous ache in his heart. "Can I see the cradle?"

She gestured to where it sat near the wall. He silently admired the craftsmanship and the highly polished dark veneer. Knowing it would eventually hold their child tightened his heart even more. "I need to go. Say good-bye to everyone for me."

Grace fought down the urge to run to him and be held

against his strong chest. "I will, and you keep yourself safe. I'll see you soon."

He nodded and was gone.

Grace went to the window and watched him ride away. When it seemed certain he wouldn't return for anything he might have mistakenly left behind, she threw off her robe. Fully dressed beneath it, she hastened to the room the aunts were sharing and knocked. They called for her to enter and Grace went in and gave them both hugs. "I'll wire as soon as I can."

The tears in their eyes matched the ones standing in Grace's own. "Godspeed," they told her.

"I love you both." And she was gone.

Tess was already out front with the team hitched to the wagon and the reins in her hand. Grace climbed aboard. Tess slapped down the reins and they were off.

At the station, Grace, fashionably dressed in a navy traveling costume and wearing a hat with a veil, kept her shrouded eyes carefully peeled for Jackson as she made her way to the ticket window. She didn't want him to see her before she boarded the train. The depot was crowded with folks of all races waiting to be conveyed to their destinations. Grace hoped they'd mask her presence for as long as was necessary.

She purchased her ticket without incident. Now all she had to do was stay out of sight for the next hour until the train arrived.

It arrived in a hail of smoke, cinders and noise. As the whistle sounded, Grace stepped back to avoid breathing in the foul steam and to get out of the way of flying sparks and cinders which often burned holes in clothing. Burying herself in the mass of passengers that surged to the tracks, Grace slipped into line. A surreptitious glance toward the front showed Jackson in line about ten people ahead of her. Grace kept her head down so as not to draw attention to herself.

The conductor took her ticket, nodded a greeting, then said, "Just so you'll know, miss, we'll be riding Jim Crow once we cross the Texas line."

Angry at the news, but keeping her face emotionless, she thanked the man, then climbed aboard. Grace found her a seat near the back of the car. She could see Jackson seated two rows ahead. It took only a few more minutes for the rest of the travelers to board. As was the custom, none of the other passengers chose to sit next to a person of color, and so Grace had the seat to herself.

The whistle blasted one last time and she could feel the iron horse shudder to life. Folks on the ground were waving enthusiastically as the train moved slowly up the tracks but were soon left behind as it picked up steam and chugged out of the station headed west.

Grace decided she'd wait awhile before confronting Jackson, and to pass the time dug out of her carpet bag a copy of the book Tulip had given her to read on the train. It was titled *Clotel; or The President's Daughter: A Narrative of Slave Life in the United States*, published in 1853 by noted abolitionist and writer William Wells Brown, himself born in Lexington, Kentucky of a slave mother and a slave holder. *Clotel* held the distinction of being the first novel penned and published by a person of African-American descent, but unlike Harriet Wilson's 1859 novel *Our Nig*, which was the first African-American novel printed in the United States, *Clotel* was published in Britain. Grace had heard of the book but had never read it. According to Tulip, the story revolved around a mulatto woman named Currer and her two daughters, Clotel and Althesa. As a young woman, Currer served as a slave in the household of Thomas Jefferson, also the father of her daughters. When Jefferson goes off to Washington to accept his first government appointment, she and the girls are sold to another master.

Grace settled into the story and the tale was as melodramatic and tragic as Tulip had promised. When the story begins, Currer is forty years of age. The new master has died, and Currer and her daughters are put on the auction block in Richmond to be sold. A White Virginian named Horatio Green purchases Clotel as his concubine, but Currer and Althesa become the property of a slave trader who takes them south. He sells Currer to Reverend John Peck in Natchez, Mississippi, and the youngest daughter, Althesa, is taken on to New Orleans and auctioned to James Crawford as a house slave.

Grace read on, following the heartrending twists and turns in the lives of the three women, but she glanced up every now and again to make certain Jackson was still unaware of her presence.

The train had journeyed about an hour when Grace closed her book and decided to confront her husband. She expected him to be angry, but she hoped he wouldn't cause so great a scene that they'd both get tossed from the train. Still veiled, she left her seat and haltingly made her way to where he was seated. "Excuse me, sir. Is this seat taken?"

He looked up. "No." Then recognition widened his eyes.

Grace used the speechless moment to slide into the seat beside him. "Are you traveling far?"

Jackson couldn't believe his eyes. Looking around to see how much attention they were drawing, he whispered fiercely, "What in the hell are you doing here?"

She smiled. "The baby and I decided we didn't want to be left behind."

"Dammit, Grace." Jackson wanted to throttle her, but knew he'd never touch her in anger or commit violence against her person. Instead, he rested his head on the back of the seat and closed his eyes for a moment. Truth be told, beneath his anger, Jackson was elated. Leaving her behind had been one of the hardest things he'd ever had to do. No man in his right mind would take his pregnant wife into such a potentially volatile situation, but she was here. She'd obviously weighed the consequences and either hadn't believed him or hadn't cared. Grace Prescott Atwood Blake was fearless and untamed, and he should've known telling her no wouldn't be enough to deter her, especially once she made up her mind. Dammit! "I ought to take you across my knee."

Grace had no idea how much anger he might be hiding beneath his calm words, but his flashing eyes pretty much told all she needed to know. "The vows said 'til death do us part."

"You are so damned hard-headed."

"So I've been told."

Jackson loved her as much as he loved breathing, but she needed a keeper. "I've half a mind to put you off at the next stop."

"But you won't."

And he didn't.

The journey continued through Kansas, then cut through a portion of Colorado before heading south into Texas. True to his word, the conductor sent the few Black, Mexican, and Indian passengers to an empty car at the back of the train once they crossed the Texas line. The car's walls were made of evenly spaced horizontal slats, ostensibly to let in fresh air, but it still smelled of animals—cattle, to be precise—and everyone had to watch where they sat or walked because of the dung-filled hay littering the wooden floor.

Jackson hadn't had too much to say to Grace since she'd surprised him with her presence. His secret elation aside, he was still angry that she'd defied him and angrier still that she might come to harm. He planned on sending her back to her aunts just as soon as they reached Marshall, Texas, and if he had to put her on the train kicking and screaming, so be it.

Grace looked over at him sitting atop the fetid straw in a corner of the car and the tightness of his jaw told all. He wasn't happy about her being here, but now that she was, he seemed intent upon ignoring her. He hadn't said a word since they'd entered the car a few hours ago, and she was both angry and humiliated. The other passengers riding in the car with them, particularly a man and his two young daughters, and a salesman for a brush company, were trying to make the best of the bad situation by talking to each other, but Jackson hadn't said a word, so they gave up on trying to include him, and Grace did the same.

The man with the two daughters was on his way home to Houston after burying his mother, who'd died recently in Kansas City. His daughters, aged eight and twelve, were bright and charming. The brush salesman, possessing the gift of gab inherent in most salesmen, kept the girls entertained with simple sleight-of-hand tricks and by showing them his cases, which held not only combs and brushes, but hair ribbons, a variety of hair tonics, and toilet water for his lady customers. His name was Andrew Logan. He was a short, round-faced, brown-skinned man, and according to his nonstop talking, had spent a few years studying at Oberlin until he ran out of money and had to find a job.

Grace found him engaging.

"I too attended Oberlin," she told him, and they spent the next hour talking about the school and its traditions.

The brooding Jackson wished the talkative Logan elsewhere. It was easy to see the man was taken by

Grace and was going out of his way to impress her with his education and his case of goods. Every now and again Grace would glance over to where Jackson sat silent with his back against the car, as if waiting for him to enter the conversation, but Jackson had nothing to say.

When night came and everyone had no choice but to find a spot in the hay so they could sleep, Logan offered her his coat to sit upon.

"A lady like you shouldn't have to spoil her clothes."

Grace smiled, pleased to be in the company of such a gentleman, especially since the man she was traveling with seemed to have no manners at all, but she couldn't take his coat; she was a married woman now and she didn't want to seem to be encouraging his interest.

"No, thank you."

Andrew looked stung. "But—"

"You heard the lady," Jackson said coolly. "She said no."

Andrew Logan turned to Jackson and asked, "What business is it of yours, sir?"

"She's my wife, so that makes it my business."

Logan's brown eyes widened. "Your wife?"

One of the Mexican passengers who'd been silently observing the salesman's attempt to charm the lovely redhead chuckled at the surprising turn of events.

"Yes, my wife."

The salesman looked so disappointed, Jackson almost laughed too. "So, you'll have to sell your combs somewhere else."

Grace was not amused by Jackson's high-handedness, but kept her temper under control. Fussing at him the way she wanted to would serve no purpose. She thanked Logan again, then went over and sat down next to her husband.

Keeping her voice low, she said, "So, you're claiming me now?"

"Yes, and where I come from we shoot claim jumpers."

"He was just being mannerly."

"You've a husband for that, remember?"

"Oh, really? I hadn't noticed."

He grinned to himself, then surprised her by pulling her onto his lap. "Here, if you want something to sit on, sit on me."

Grace could see everyone in the car watching, but rather than give them a show, she placed her head on his chest and prepared to sleep in his arms.

Jackson held her tight.

For the rest of the journey, Jackson had nothing to say during the daylight hours but held Grace against his heart every night.

When Grace and Jackson finally departed the train near Marshall, she was stiff and smelly. Her blue traveling ensemble had not been designed to be slept in for over a week and as a result was dirty and creased. The hem of the skirt was now a dull brown due to the offal and dirt on the car's floor, but she didn't care. She and Jackson were together, even if he wasn't real happy about it.

"Wait here," he told her. "I need to get my horse from the end car."

Grace nodded and watched him stride to the back of the long train. Clutching her valise, she inclined her head at the other passengers of color who'd disembarked. They were on their way to be reunited with family and friends, but Grace had no idea where she and Jackson were bound or what kind of reception they'd receive.

He returned a few moments later, leading his horse by the reins. He checked the cinches on the saddle.

"How're you planning on getting around?"

The pointed question made her raise her chin. "I don't know. Is there a livery nearby?"

Finished with his saddle, he turned to her. It was quite obvious that she needed a bath and a good night's sleep. She was a mess. Her clothes were dirty, her hair disheveled. "You should've stayed in Kansas City."

"But I didn't, so where are we going?"

He wondered if his child would be as fearless as its mama. "Some friends of mine used to live about ten miles north of here. We'll head there first."

"Fine."

He mounted. "I should make you walk."

"But you won't," she countered dryly.

He pulled her up and set her in front of him in the saddle. They rode slowly away from the smoke-belching train and headed north.

At least he was speaking to her, Grace noted, as the horse ferried them across the desolate but beautiful countryside. It was a small comfort, considering he'd spoken to her as little as possible on the long train ride here. Not for the first time did she question her own sanity for wanting to accompany him, but she was determined to endure no matter what the future held. She owed it to the love she felt for him and to their growing child. No one was going to harm the father of her baby while she had anything to say about it.

They were soon passing small houses set near patches of what looked to her to be cotton fields. "Is that cotton growing?"

"Yes. Lot of folks, Black and White, sharecrop it around here."

"Do they make much money? The plots don't look particularly large."

"How much do you know about sharecropping?"

"Not much."

"Well, sharecroppers lease the land from the big owners, work the crop, and turn it in at the end of the year. The big landowner is supposed to deduct things like seed and rent and pay the sharecropper his profit, only it doesn't work that way. Most folks wind up owing such a large debt that by the end of the year they don't even make enough to feed and clothe their families."

"Then why don't they move on?"

"They're up to their necks in debt and can't. Most are former slaves, many go from cradle to grave on the same piece of land their parents sharecropped on. Farming is all they know."

Grace now understood.

Jackson continued, "The country made few provisions for its freed slaves, and it's real apparent around here. The few good agencies were dismantled right along with Reconstruction, so in the end, folks in the South that look like you and me are free, but only to eke out an existence sharecropping, or starve."

About an hour later, Jackson brought the horse to a halt in front of a small but neat whitewashed cabin. There were a few hogs and chickens milling about the premises and there was an old rusted buckboard next to the house. As Grace and Jackson dismounted, a tall, dark-skinned young woman came from around the back of the house. She had on a worn but well-patched dress, a pair of men's boots and carried a rusted hoe in her hand. She stopped and stared at them a moment. Jackson took off his hat as if to let her see him better and then her eyes widened in recognition.

"Jack!"

She came running and threw herself into his arms. He held her and rocked her in greeting and Grace, admittedly a bit green around the ears from jealousy, simply stood there and watched and waited for an introduction.

The woman and Jackson finally broke the embrace and the woman trilled happily, "I knew you were coming back to me, I knew it!"

Grace raised an eyebrow. She dearly hoped this woman was a relative.

Never one to be shy, Grace stuck out her hand. "Hello, I'm Jackson's wife, Grace. And you are?"

The woman's eyes widened and Grace could see Jackson's jaw tighten. Grace didn't care. She waited.

Jackson finally said, "Grace, this is Davida Craig. Davi, my wife, Grace."

"Pleased to meet you, Miss Craig."

The Craig woman looked Grace critically up and down. "How do."

She then turned to Jackson and there were tears in her eyes. Without saying another word, she ran back into the house, obviously distraught.

Grace asked, "A former lover?"

He rolled his eyes.

On the heels of that, another woman came out of the house. She was older, thin, and bore a strong resemblance to Davida. Her mother or aunt, Grace assumed.

Her tired eyes were shining with happiness as she approached Jackson with open arms. He held her tightly and they rocked slowly. "Oh," she whispered in a voice thick with tears. "It's so good to see you. *So* good!"

Jackson held tight to the woman who'd served as his mother after his own died. "It's good to be home."

They parted and the woman turned to Grace. The teary eyes were kind. "You'll have to excuse my manners. I haven't seen him in a long long time. I'm Iva Luckett."

"I'm Grace Blake."

A grin spread across her face. "Blake? Are you Jack's wife?"

Because of Iva's smile, Grace didn't believe the truth would draw as dramatic a response as last time. "Yes, ma'am, I am."

She turned to Jackson and said, "Now, ain't you *something* coming back here with a fine lady like this. No wonder Davida's inside stomping around."

She placed a hand on Grace's waist. "Honey, let's get you in and get you washed up. There's not much to eat, but what we have you're welcome to share."

As Iva propelled Grace forward, Grace looked back at her husband and for the first time seemingly in weeks, he smiled.

After Iva and Grace disappeared inside, Jackson looked out across the wild beauty of the land and felt a contentment he hadn't experienced in many years. Here the Texas blue sky stretched as far as the eye could see. Here there were no tall buildings to mar the view; no smokestacks to foul the air. There were no crowds, no noise, just the gentle passing of the breeze and the answering whisper of the grass and trees. He'd missed this; missed it a lot, and now that he was back, would find it hard to leave again.

After washing up at the pump behind the house, Grace felt infinitely better now that she'd donned clean clothes. The plain white blouse and dark skirt had been part of her wagon train wardrobe, so she knew the garments would hold up wherever travels with Jackson led.

However, whether her manners would hold up under the rude stare of Davida Craig was another matter. The younger woman began giving Grace the evil eye the moment Iva ushered her into the small two-room cabin. Now they were gathered around a small table eating a meal of salt pork and beans, and she was still shooting daggers Grace's way.

Evidently Grace wasn't the only one at the table who'd noticed, because Iva said, with a touch of irritation in her voice, "Davi, do you have something you want to say?"

"Yes. What does she have that I don't?"

Jackson looked up from his plate and drawled, "Manners for one."

She sat back in a huff. "Why'd you have to marry her?" she asked bluntly. "You were supposed to marry me, remember?"

"No, I don't. You were what, fifteen when Griff and I left here?"

"Sixteen, and you said you loved me."

"Like a little sister."

She folded her arms angrily across her chest.

Grace now had a clearer picture. Davida was not one of Jackson's old flames; she was merely petulant, obviously spoiled, and young.

Iva looked to Grace and said, "You'll have to forgive her, Grace. Davida's worked herself into believing that Jack would come back a rich man, make her his wife, and whisk her off to a fancy house up north somewhere."

The younger woman snapped, "What's wrong with dreams?"

"Nothing," Iva told her. "But there's dreams, and then there's nonsense."

Evidently Davida didn't like what she'd heard, because she stood. "I'm going over to Lucy's. We need to work on the quilt for the church bazaar. I'll be back in the morning."

Iva countered, "You'll be back tonight and before dark."

"Oh, all right." She stormed out.

Jackson quipped, "Not much has changed with her, I see."

"Not a leaf. I wish she could find someone to marry—take her off my hands."

"Is she your daughter?" Grace asked.

"Lord, no. She's my late brother's child. When he died, his wife brought her down here. Said she was tired of her. Haven't seen hide nor hair of her since. That was about ten years ago."

Grace couldn't imagine abandoning her child under any circumstances. Life seemed to have dealt Davida a cruel hand, but it was still no excuse for such blatant bad manners.

With Davi gone, the atmosphere in the cabin eased.

"How long you two been married?" Iva asked.

Grace remained silent and waited for him to answer. He did. "Little under a month."

Grace wondered if Iva could sense the troubles between them.

"That long?" the woman asked. "You here for a honeymoon trip?"

"No, I'm here to straighten out that warrant for my arrest. Lane Trent still own all the land around here?"

"Does the devil still rule in hell? Yes, he's still around. Richer than his daddy ever was. Folks like us are more miserable these days, too. Rent and seed are so high, you'd think everything around was made of gold."

"Whatever happened to Drew, Champ, and Isaac?"

"No idea. They left here a few days after you and Griffin lit out. Rumor says Lane paid them to leave so nobody could ask them about what really happened that day."

Grace had no idea who the men being referred to

were, or the part they'd played in Jackson's life here.

He must've sensed her curiosity. "Drew, Champ, and Isaac were my deputy sheriffs. They were with me the day Lane Trent's daddy was shot and killed."

"Will you tell me what happened?"

So he did, beginning with his father Royce's death at the hands of Lane and the Sons of Shiloh, and ending with the gunfight that resulted in Roy Trent's death.

"So you and your brother fled north to keep from being railroaded."

"Yes."

Iva added sagely, "Lane won't be happy knowing you're back. Why not just let things be?"

"Because he killed Royce, Iva. You of all people should be standing with me on this." Iva had been the love of his father's life for almost twenty years.

"And you of all people should know Royce wouldn't want you risking your life going up against Lane and his hate. *Vengeance is mine, saith the Lord.*"

"That's all well and good, but what about the warrant? Even if I could try and live with his murder, what's to keep Lane from hunting me down and getting me hanged?"

"A lion can't eat what's on the other side of the jungle."

"You're saying I should just head back north and stay out of his way?"

"Yes. Things are bad down here, Jack. Real bad. In some places Black men are hanging from trees like fruit. Don't make yourself be one of them, you have too much to live for."

Jackson could see the concern in Grace's eyes. "What would a Prescott do?" he asked her quietly.

"Stand and fight," she replied. "But that's from having the blood of the Old Buccaneer in our veins."

Iva had a confused look on her face. "The old who?"

"Buccaneer," Jackson replied, his eyes still on his wife. "Her family's founding father was a pirate."

"Like Lafitte?"

Grace found Iva's knowledge of the Frenchman surprising. "You know about Jean Lafitte?"

"Yep. My grandmother was a free woman and lived on Galveston Island when Lafitte owned the slave markets and everything else down there. She lost her husband because of that pirate and cursed him everyday for the rest of her life."

"What happened to her husband?"

"Lafitte sold him along with every other free Black living on the island back then."

"Really, why?"

"Well, back in eighteen hundred and nineteen, a hurricane came to Galveston—or as Lafayette called it, Campeachy—and wiped out everything. Sank all the ships, many folks drowned, and even parts of his big old red house with the cannons mounted on it came tumbling down. All the food stores were gone and he and his people were facing famine. He decided that the first thing he needed to do was have less mouths to feed, so he seized a schooner that had come from New Orleans and told his men to round up everybody that had African blood and put them aboard. Didn't matter if you were slave or free like my grandparents. Loaded them all up and took them to New Orleans and sold them. My grandmother managed to steal away and make her way back to Texas, but she never saw my grandfather again. Went to her grave still grieving."

"What a sad story," Grace said. She'd heard that Lafitte's settlement had included Mexicans, Indians, women of all races, free Blacks, and runaway slaves. She also knew that as a slave trafficker he'd sold members of the race for one dollar a pound, but she'd never met anyone who'd been personally touched by his greed.

"You two planning on staying the night, Jack?" Iva asked, after finishing her story. It was now very late. Davida had come in during the telling and was seated in the shadows of the other room.

"Hoped to."

"Well, all I can offer you is the barn. That old milk cow of mine won't mind sharing the place if you two don't."

They didn't, and so Iva walked them out to the barn. Grace found the ramshackle space infinitely cleaner than the accommodations they'd been forced to endure on the train, and besides, after being on the trail with the brides, she could sleep just about anywhere.

Leaving them the lantern that had lit their way to the barn, Iva said her goodnights and left to return to the cabin. This was the first time they'd been alone together in over a week and as a result there was a decided awkwardness between them.

In an effort to fill the looming silence, Grace said, "I like Iva. Is she related to you in some way?"

"No," he replied, unfurling his bedroll and laying it down on the barn's dirt floor. "She was my father's ladyfriend. His death nearly killed her."

Grace thought it must be awful to lose the man you loved to violence. In her mind one could better accept death if it stemmed from disease or natural causes, although she knew from her father's grief that even that could alter one's life forever, but to lose a loved one to hate? It would probably eat away at her just as it must be doing to Jackson.

"You take the bedroll. I'll bed down over here."

He indicated a spot a few feet away from the bedroll. After sleeping with him on the train, she'd grown accustomed to his presence. She swallowed her disappointment that he obviously preferred another arrangement tonight. She settled in and he doused the light. In the darkness she sensed him covering himself with a blanket and settling in too.

For a moment the silence returned, and then he said, "Grace, I wish you'd stayed with your aunts."

"I know, but I couldn't let you come alone. Sorry."

Silence again.

She had a question. Although she had no idea if he'd answer, she asked anyway. "Do you know how you're going to accomplish what you need to do here?"

"Thought I'd try and find the men who were my deputies at the time first, then go from there."

"Will they be able to prove that you didn't kill Trent's father?"

"They'll be able to tell a judge that Trent's daddy's men opened fire first. I was after Lane, not his daddy."

"And Lane was a member of this Sons of Shiloh gang?"

"Yes, they would dress up in sheets and pretend to be the dead spirits of the soldiers killed at the Battle of Shiloh. No one was afraid of the sheets, but they were of the men beneath. Sometimes they'd pretend to be ghosts who hadn't had a drink since their death. Had one old Black man spend a whole night drawing them buckets of water from his well. He did it because he was terrified they'd turn to something else, like killing his sons or burning his house down. They'd ride through the countryside at night shooting up cabins and using axes to break down doors."

"And you tried to arrest them?"

"I did, several times, even took them in, but the county had the only secure jail and they never had room, or so they always claimed." His tone was bitter. "So I had to let them go. I warned my daddy not to get involved, I'd written a letter to the governor, hoping he'd intervene in some way; after all, the township citizens both Black and White had elected me sheriff, but I never received a reply, and my daddy went to see Lane and his friends over my objections. Less than an hour later he was dead. I should've made him stay at home."

Grace's heart went out to him. Judging by the bleakness in his voice, the death continued to be a painful memory. He also sounded as if he blamed himself.

"You shouldn't blame yourself. Your father was a preacher, Jackson. He was going to rely on faith and the Word regardless of the danger."

"I know, but if only he'd listened..." His voice trailed off.

Silence resettled again, and a few moments later, he said, "Well, goodnight, and Grace, even though I'm still angry, I am glad you're here. See you in the morning."

A stunned Grace lay there in the darkness, then a smile spread across her face. "I'm glad I'm here too. Goodnight, Jackson."

"Remind me to paddle you after the baby's born, though."

She grinned in the dark. "I will."

The next morning, Grace and Jackson rode over to visit another friend. The man's name was Riley Borden. He was a blacksmith and owned a livery. Two old friends greeted each other warmly.

"When'd you get back?" Riley asked, as they broke the embrace.

"Yesterday. This is my wife, Grace."

The thin little man with the light brown skin and the muscular arms turned to her and gave her a gap-toothed smile. "Pleased to meet you, Grace. What's a fine woman like you doing with this old rattler?"

Grace smiled.

"Come on inside so we can get out of this sun," he urged. "It's not even ten yet and it's blazing already."

Grace agreed. Texas in July was much hotter than Illinois. Her blouse sticking to her skin was enough to prove it.

He ushered them into his large parlor and they took a seat. Grace noted the coolness of the interior and portraits on the wall. One held the likeness of Riley, a woman, and a child. "Is that your family?" she asked.

"Yep, that's my wife, Ann, and my boy, Riley the second. They're down in Austin visiting her mother. Miss them terribly."

The conversation then turned to the reason for their visit.

"We need a wagon and a team," Jackson told his old friend.

"I've a few you can look at, but first, have you seen Iva?"

"Spent the night at her place last night."

Riley nodded. "So are you back for good?"

"Depends on how things go."

Riley stared into Jackson's eyes. "You're not here to take up with Lane Trent again, are you? It's been a long time, Jack. Best to leave it alone. You got a wife now."

"I know, Riley, but I can't have it hanging over my head for the rest of my life."

Riley looked to Grace. "If you love him, you'll take him back north, Grace."

The seriousness in his eyes made the hairs stand on the back of her neck.

"I mean it. All he's going to find down here is death. Lane Trent is Satan. Not even his wife can stand him."

Jackson interrupted him. "He's married?"

"Yep. Married a young thing from Abilene about a

year after you left. Gossip had it that when he first asked for her hand she refused, so he bought up the note on her daddy's land and threatened to call it in unless she agreed, so she did. The folks who work for him say she hates his every step."

Grace was disliking this Lane Trent more and more. "Do they have any children?"

"No, she can't seem to carry to full term. She's lost at least three, according to the rumors and he's fit to be tied. He thinks she's taking something that's causing it."

"Is she?" Grace asked.

"Nobody knows but her."

Grace couldn't imagine hating a man so much that you'd abort your own children. If Trent's wife were indeed ingesting something so foul, her hate must run deep.

Riley then asked, "How's Griff, Jack? Have you heard from him?"

"Not in a while. He's still robbing trains, far as I know."

Riley smiled and shook his head. "That brother of yours always was a handful."

"Yes he was. I just hope he doesn't wind up in prison."

"Knowing him, that's probably the only thing that'll stop him."

Jackson nodded. "That, or the shotgun of some woman's irate husband or daddy."

Riley grinned. "Come on, let's go see if we can find you a wagon and a team."

Riley took them out to the livery and she and Jackson looked over the conveyances he had for rent. They decided on a buckboard that looked to be in fair shape and a two-horse team.

Jackson asked, "Have you heard anything about

Champ, Isaac, or Drew? Iva said Lane paid them to leave so they wouldn't reveal the truth."

"I heard that too, but no one's seen them since, far as I know."

"Their folks still around?"

"Drew's daddy died about eight months ago, but Isaac's mother and Champ's sister are still living in the same place."

"I need to talk to them."

Riley shook his head sadly. "Go back north, Jack. Folks around here are not going to like you stirring up the past."

"I don't care what they like or don't. I owe it to Royce and I'm tired of looking over my shoulder."

Riley turned to Grace. "Try and talk some sense into him, Grace."

"Jackson has to follow his heart."

"He's gonna follow it right to a lynch rope, mark my words."

With their business concluded, the men spent a few more moments talking about acquaintances still living nearby, then she and Jackson left with a wave and a promise to come to dinner when Riley's wife and son returned from Austin later in the week.

"So, where to now?" Grace asked, as she drove the wagon while he kept pace on his mount.

"I want to see if I can get some information on my deputies. Let's go and see Champ's sister."

The journey took them a few miles north to a small farm. There was a mixed race crew working in the cotton field. The White woman Jackson pointed out as the sister looked up at their approach, stared at them, then bent back over her hoe. She didn't appear to be happy.

He left the horse with Grace and walked out to where the crew worked. Before he could speak, Champ's sister

Maybelle said, "Get out of here, Jack. I don't want no trouble from Lane."

"I'm not here to cause trouble. I just want to know if you know where Champ is."

"No."

"Maybelle, please, this is real important."

She straightened and snapped angrily. "Important? Having my brother by my side is important, but he disappeared right after you did and nobody's seen him since. Go on back to where you've been and leave my family in peace."

She went back to her hoe.

A tight-lipped Jackson turned and walked to his mount.

"Let's go," Jackson said angrily, as he swung up into the saddle.

Grace slapped down the reins and followed him back to the road.

# Chapter 11

❦

Jackson stopped them a few miles away and slid from the saddle. He'd expected resistance, but not from folks like Maybelle Champion. Jackson, Maybelle, and her brother Champ had grown up together; they'd hunted frogs together, swum together, and tipped over privies together. He and Champ had been such good friends, there'd been no question about him being named deputy when Jackson was elected sheriff. Jackson trusted Champ with his life, but now Maybelle treated him like a Reb.

How would he get justice for his father in the face of such fear? If she did know her brother's whereabouts, she'd given one hell of a performance, but the desperation and anger in her voice and eyes seemed too real to be an act. Had Lane really paid Champ to leave town? More than likely he'd threatened Champ or Maybelle's life to get him to comply. During the height of the killings during Reconstruction, Texas rivers had run red with Black blood, yet he'd come here, one lone Black man trying to bring down single-handedly someone as powerful as Lane Trent. Like Iva said, there's dreams and then there's foolishness.

Grace watched her husband staring off into the distance and imagined him weighing all that had occurred since his return. Everyone seemed to think Jackson would find only death in this quest to avenge his father and to clear his name. Grace had no trouble admitting that she too felt wary of being here. This was the South, after all, and the stories of the hate and killings were well known by members of the race nationwide. Were it not for Jackson, Grace would not have willingly journeyed here. The idea that at any moment a group of men could ride up over the next rise with the intent of taking her life and do so without fear of reprisal scared her to death. She'd vowed to follow Jackson into hell, and now it appeared that she might be forced to do just that.

"Where to now, Jackson?"

He turned back and the bleakness in his eyes tore at her heart.

He shrugged. "If Maybelle won't talk, there's no sense in going to see Isaac's mother. She lost her Reb husband during the last days of the war and holds the race responsible. Never heard her say one kind word about Black folks. Always made me stay outside whenever I came to see her son."

"What about the man you called Drew?"

"Drew's daddy was the last of his kin. With him dead there's no telling where Drew went. Probably north. He was my only Black deputy, and like the others, a real close friend."

Grace wanted to find a way to raise his spirits, but couldn't think of anything.

He asked her, "Is all this talk about me being lynched or killed scaring you?"

She held the eyes of the man who'd stolen her heart and fathered her child and did not lie. "Yes."

He walked back to where she stood and for the first time in a long time took her in his arms and held her close against his beating heart. "Don't let it. Your aunts will be real angry at me if you return home a widow."

"So will I."

He drew back and looked down at her. "Really?"

"Do you honestly think I'd come to Texas with a man I cared nothing about? Being here scares me to death. The sooner we head back north, the happier the baby and I will be."

He ran a gentle hand over her still flat stomach. "How's he doing in there?"

Grace shrugged. "It's hard to tell. Since I've not done this before, I've no clear idea on what's supposed to happen or when. I'm assuming I'm going to get big and fat, but at what point, your guess is as good as mine."

He smiled down at her.

"I can't imagine you big and fat."

"Neither can I, but it's going to happen, so be prepared."

"Do you think you'll get so big you'll have to sleep in the barn?"

A show of mock outrage claimed her face and she punched him in the shoulder. "If I do, I'm going to make you sleep beside me so I can roll over and squish you in the middle of the night."

The amusement in his eyes faded and was replaced by love. "I've missed you, Banker Atwood."

Her heart began to tighten and expand all in one motion. "It's Banker Blake now," she responded softly. "I've missed you too."

"Then how about we make up for lost time."

"How about we do that."

The kiss was the sweetest they'd ever shared; sweet, tender, and filled with longing, silent apologies, and most of all, love. Her arms slid up his arms as the kiss deepened and he gathered her in possessively. Neither felt the heat beating down upon them from the hot Texas sun; they were too engrossed in one another. Grace wanted to make love to him right here and now, but knew she probably couldn't convince him because she was the wanton one and he was the one with sense. "I want to make love to you, Jackson."

He chuckled as he eased his mouth away. "Out here?"

"Out here, over there, it doesn't matter."

Her sultry reply matched the fire in her eyes and in-stantaneously hardened his manhood. He drew a slow finger over her parted lips. "Let's see if we can't find a more secluded spot but first . . ."

He looked around for anyone approaching, but seeing nothing but miles and miles of rolling land and silent blue sky, slowly began to undo the buttons on her blouse.

"I thought you wanted to go somewhere hidden?" she said, feeding on the heat in his eyes as that same heat touched her in all the places she knew he'd touch. They'd not made love since leaving the wagon train.

He opened her blouse and filled his hands with the soft, soft yielding flesh. When he brushed his lips across their tops and teased his thumbs over the nipples, they hardened as if on command, and she sighed as her inner fires began to climb.

He asked huskily, "Tell me about this man who made you change your name . . ."

He pulled her camisole down and sensually helped himself to the twin goblets of her breasts. "Does he do this . . . ?" He suckled one dark tip.

"Oh, yes . . ."

"And this . . . ?" He gave the other the same torrid treatment.

"Yes," she breathed. "And he's very good at it . . ."

"Good as this?"

He toyed and lingered until waves of desire filled her core.

Grace moaned low in her throat.

"Does he like it when you moan that way?"

Grace's breathing heightened. "Yes, but he likes this as well."

She boldly reached down and ran her hand over the hard bulge of his manhood. Two could play at this game. A brazen Grace slowly slid her hand over him again and again. This time the moan was his.

"Let's get out of here and go someplace where you can show me what else he likes . . ." he murmured against her mouth, but instead they spent the next few moments silently arousing each other with heated kisses and roving hands. They eventually parted but most reluctantly. He tied the reins of his horse to the buckboard, then drove them away.

They were like two adolescents in love, stopping the buckboard again and again to share kisses and intimate caresses. By the time they reached their destination, an old abandoned cabin, they were both fairly bursting with need. They never made it inside, however; he pulled the buckboard around to the back of the structure and took her right there on the seat of the buckboard, and she rode him until completion shattered them like glass.

Once they came down to earth, he left her to try and find a way inside the cabin. Still pulsing from her lusty ride, Grace asked, "Was this the home of someone you knew?"

"Yep," he told her as he grabbed at a piece of the plywood covering one of the small square windows and pulled it free. "Me. This is where the Blakes lived."

Grace sat up and looked at the wooden cabin in a whole new light. Holding her still opened blouse closed with one hand, she hopped down from the buckboard to join him. They were at the back of the place. To the right stood a small corral that must've held animals originally, but from the look of broken-down crossbars and the overall weathered condition of the wood, it obviously had not served that purpose in a long time.

Across the hilly field she saw two weathered crosses sticking up out of the red earth. "Who's buried out there?"

"My parents. Griff and I buried my daddy two days before we left."

He peered into the dark interior through the now freed window. "Looks fairly clean, from what I can see. It doesn't look like varmints have taken over."

A few well-placed kicks from his booted foot brought down the flimsy plywood door and she followed him inside. It was as silent as a tomb. There were a few pieces of furniture in the gloomy two-room place: a small table, a few chairs, a sideboard with a broken glass front. Everything was coated with a thick layer of dust.

The breeze followed them in and began to ruffle the air. "How long did you live here?" she asked. She could see what appeared to be bedding in the other room.

"All my life. I was born here, right over there in that corner. It's where my ma's bed was, according to my daddy."

He watched her look around. "Pretty humble place compared to what you're used to, isn't it?"

"Yes, it is," she admitted, and tried to imagine spending her whole life in a two-room place such as this. "Were you happy here?"

He nodded and smiled. "Yes, I was—very happy. We didn't have a lot, but I never went hungry and Daddy gave me and Griff lots of love. Of course he worked us like the devil in the garden and on his carpentry jobs, but once he turned us loose we fished, hunted, chased the girls."

Grace grinned.

His eyes became serious. "Do you mind staying here until we get this mess settled? We could probably find us a room to let in Marshall that would be more in line with what you're used to, but the less people know I'm here, the safer we'll probably be."

She didn't lie. "No, I don't mind where we stay, as long as we're together."

She yawned.

"Sleepy?"

"Yes, and I don't know why. I tire out so easily these days, and all I want to do is sleep."

"It's the baby you keep saying you're not having."

"I'm not having a baby, because Lord knows you'll be impossible to live with if I am."

He smiled. "Well, how about I bring in the bedroll and you lie down while I go hunt us up a few rabbits for dinner?"

"Sounds fine."

He left her with a rifle and a lingering kiss. Smiling, a content Grace snuggled in and went to sleep.

A few hours later, as the mounted Jackson came over the rise, he looked down on the cabin where he'd been born. He remembered the good times he and his brother Griffin had had: the marble games and the duck hunting; the swimming and the tree climbing. Although they hadn't had much materially, their father Royce had made sure they were well fed and clean. He made them go to school when the town had one and taught them at home when it was burned down by angry Rebs a year or so later.

And now he was back after ten years of drifting and hiding because he was tired of doing both. He had a wife and a child on the way. This mess with Trent had to be settled one way or another because he had to move on with his life.

The rabbits he'd caught for dinner hung on a string from his saddle, and he was heading down to the cabin when he heard the sound of horses. Turning in his saddle to investigate, he spied four riders bearing down on him like spectres from hell. He didn't know how, but instinctively he knew that they were after him. His first thoughts were of Grace, but trying to outrun them back to the cabin would be fruitless, and more important, alert them to Grace's presence. He also refused to run, because doing so would only add to their fun; they'd love to be able to hunt him down like prey. Yes, he was afraid, but he drew out his rifle and waited.

When they rode up and surrounded him, Jackson did not recognize the four riders, but the familiar face of the man driving the fancy buggy was one that had haunted his dreams. *Lane Trent*. He'd gotten older but no taller, and the fancy gray suit looked expensive. The blond hair was streaked with gray and there were weather lines at the edges of the ice blue eyes, eyes that held Jackson's smugly and triumphantly. Seated beside Trent was a small, distant-eyed woman dressed in black. Jackson wondered if she was the wife Riley had mentioned.

Lane smiled with malice. "Well, if it ain't our former sheriff. Heard you was back."

Jackon replied coolly, "Trent."

One of the riders, an older man with gray stubble on his face, snarled, "It's *Mister* Trent to you, boy."

Jackson turned a cold eye on the man before his attention slowly swung back to Trent. "I see you're still traveling with trash, Lane."

Jackson knew addressing Trent by his given name would only infuriate the old Reb more, but he'd no plans to be meekly led to the slaughter.

Trent's eyes flashed with a mild humor. "Never did know your place, but we're going to fix that in a few minutes."

Jackson's insides tightened, but he kept his face even.

Trent said, "We got a new sheriff now. It's ol' Box over there."

Jackson directed his eyes to the grinnning hyenalike features of the man Trent indicated, then looked away.

"You're still a wanted man here, Blake. Did you know that?"

"I assumed I would be."

"Then what the hell're you doing here?"

"Came back to try and clear things up."

Trent guffawed. "Clear things up. Nigra, don't you realize that we could string you up right here and now for killing my daddy that day?"

"I didn't shoot him and you know it."

"Yeah, I know it. Shot him myself."

Jackson stared with surprise.

Trent chuckled, "Surprised? Got tired of him lording it over me, telling me what to do. When those bullets started flying that day, I knew I'd never get a better chance, so—" And he shrugged as if that were explanation enough.

"And framed me for it," Jackson spat.

"Sure did. Still got the warrant, in fact, cos I knew you'd come back someday. You got too much pride, too much honor to stay gone like you should've."

The beady-eyed man named Box tossed out, "Maybe he'd like a tour of the place to welcome him home. What do you think, Mr. Trent?"

Trent's eyes, cold as Satan's, said, "Tie him up."

Jackson knew struggling would be futile, but he tried nonetheless. Because they outnumbered him, they made short work of the task. With his hands and ankles tied, Jackson prayed Grace was still asleep and would stay that way so she wouldn't witness the horror to come.

Grace awakened to what sounded like gunshots, men yelling, and the thunder of galloping horses. Groggy, she shook off the dregs of sleep and fought to remember where she was. The whooping and hollering rang louder now, and her first instinct was to look for Jackson. He was nowhere to be seen. Except for the sounds of the celebrating going on outside, the small cabin was quiet.

Walking over to the window Jackson had pried loose earlier, she looked out and saw a group of men riding and shooting and seemingly having a good time. For a moment she watched curiously, wondering what they were about. Only then did she see the man being dragged across the scrub-littered ground behind the fast-galloping horse. It was Jackson. Heart in her throat, hand to her mouth, she stared frozen with horror. He was tied by his wrists to a rope leading to the saddle. His face was covered with red dirt and blood, and his body bounced over the hard ground lifelessly as the rider whipped the horse into another wide circle.

"Bring him around again," she heard a male voice call out. The closeness of the sound made her think he must be standing on the small porch out front. He then uttered a laugh so filled with evil the hair stood up on her neck. Filled with a fear that equaled her rage, Grace grabbed up her rifle, fed it some shells, and went out the back way. She'd no idea what she, a lone woman, could do, but she was going to make them cut him loose or die trying.

Quietly making her way around the side of the cabin, she stopped short at the sight of a young woman seated in a fancy buggy. As the woman turned and looked her right in the face, Grace froze. Hoping she wouldn't raise the alarm, Grace held her breath and waited. They eyed each other for a silent moment and Grace noticed that the woman's eyes were filled with tears. Looking away from Grace, she cast a furtive glance toward the porch as if to see if anyone else had noticed Grace's approach. Evidently no one had, because she gave Grace an imperceptible nod, then turned back to the macabre show.

Blessing the mysterious woman for her silent aid, Grace pressed her body close to the wall of the cabin and crept ahead, all the while praying this would work for her as well as it had for Loreli that night Lucas Wordell and his gang came into their camp. She paused at the corner. Peeking around it, she saw the man on the porch. He was a short man, dressed in an expensive suit, standing with his back to her. He was laughing so hard and was so intent upon enjoying the sight of Jackson being dragged to his death, he didn't know she was behind him until Grace stuck the barking end of the rifle into his spine and said coldly, "You must be Lane Trent."

He stiffened, then slowly raised his hand above his head. "And you are?"

"Grace Blake, Jack's wife."

"Well, Miss Blake, you're obviously not from around here. Otherwise you'd know the gravity of this mistake."

"There's no mistake. Either tell them to untie him or I'll send you straight to hell."

By now the celebration had slowed as the riders became aware of the drama unfolding on the porch. "Tell them," she snarled angrily.

He let out the beginning of a chuckle. "Gal, have you lost your mind?"

Grace moved the rifle to the base of his skull. "I can shoot you high, or I can shoot you low. Your choice."

He quieted real quick.

"Have them drop their guns and untie my husband, or you're going to learn firsthand just how lost my mind is."

The riders were now staring stonily at Grace. Jackson lay unmoving on the ground. Grace could feel the sweat running down her back inside her blouse. She was so brittle with tension she thought she might snap.

Trent finally called out, "Throw down your guns, boys, and untie him. His uppity wife's got me by the balls."

He then added sarcastically, "For the moment."

Grace wanted to shoot him just for his arrogance, but held off for the moment.

They cut Jackson loose from the lead, then did the same to the ropes around his wrists and ankles. Grace could barely contain her urge to run to his side, but she had to get rid of some trash first. "Now, tell them to get!"

Complying, he yelled out, "Go on back to the house. I'll meet you there."

When they hesitated, he told them, "Go on."

Showing great reluctance, they turned their mounts.

After they rode away the surroundings grew quiet once again.

Grace's voice still held its deadly edge. "You may leave now too, Mr. Trent. Walk straight to your buggy and don't turn around."

Grace was certain he didn't like being ordered about,

but since she was the one with the rifle, he did as he was told.

He climbed into the buggy and took his seat next to the silent woman. Picking up the reins, he ran his cold blue eyes over Grace for the first time and they malevolently looked her up and down.

With hate in his voice he promised quietly, "I'll be back, gal, and when I do, I'm going to let my boys have you for as long as they want, and then I'm going to kill you."

"You have a nice day too."

He slapped the reins. Grace and the woman shared a speaking glance, then Lane Trent drove away. As they headed toward the road, Grace flew across the field screaming Jackson's name.

He was so still she thought he might be dead. Carefully raising his head to her lap, she called to him softly. When he answered with a barely discernible groan, happy tears streamed freely down her cheeks and she sent her thanks up to the angels above. Placing him gently back on the ground, she ran for the buckboard.

When she returned, she knelt beside her barely breathing husband and whispered, "Darling, you're too heavy for me to move, you're going to have to help me get you in the board."

He didn't move.

Fighting panic, she shook him gently. "Jackson, sweetheart, please open your eyes."

He did, but barely. "Grace?" he breathed.

"Yes. You have to get up so I can get you to a doctor."

Grace looked around. She didn't put it past Lane Trent to send his men back to finish their foul play. She had to get Jackson to get away from here. She stood and tried to lift him under the arms. Her tears made it hard to see. "Help me, Jack, please."

He stumbled to his feet, and the hissing sound he made in reaction to his great pain increased her anger and fear. "Come on, darling, just a few steps."

Using her body to lean against, he dragged himself the few steps to the wagon. She knew it must have cost him greatly to have to climb into its back, because once he did, he lost consciousness.

Grace slapped the reins forcefully and headed east, praying that the angels above would keep her from becoming lost on the unfamiliar terrain. Grace drove the horses with the reins and her yells. As the landscape began to look familiar, she increased the pace and hoped Iva was at home.

She was. In response to Grace's urgent calls for help, both Iva and Davida quickly came out of the house. "He needs a doctor."

"Dear Lord," Iva gasped, as she looked at him lying so still in the wagon. "Trent do this?"

Grace nodded, anger flashing in her eyes.

"We've got to get him to the swamp," Iva said with an urgent calmness.

"He needs a doctor, Iva."

"I know, Grace, but he has to get away from here first. Trent and his men will be hunting him down soon, if they aren't already. Davi, get the medicine kit."

A teary-eyed Davi ran back inside and got what Iva'd asked for. Iva quickly ran her hands over his limbs and he groaned sharply. "He's got some busted ribs, but the blood trickling from his mouth means he might be bleeding inside."

Iva turned to the tensely watching Davida. "Davi, hustle yourself over to Riley's and tell him I'm taking Jack and Grace into the swamp to M'dear, and I'll be back as soon as they're settled. In the meantime, if anybody asks where I am, tell them I'm gone to see my sister in Shreveport."

"Okay."

"Don't tell anybody but Riley where I've gone, and tell him I want you to stay with him until I come and get you. I'm depending on you, now, and so are Jack and Grace."

Davi nodded to show that she understood.

"Now, get going."

Davi looked at Jack lying so motionlessly, then at Grace, and whispered thickly, "Godspeed, Grace."

"You too, Davi."

Davi took off at a run to get her horse. She rode away at a full gallop.

Iva was all business. "I'll drive, you get in the back with Jack."

Grace climbed into the bed and Iva said, "You should probably get under this blanket here. Lie down."

Grace snuggled close to the unconscious Jackson and draped her arm across his barely moving chest. The blanket came down and Grace held her husband tight.

They traveled until the sun went down and night claimed the sky. Once the stars came out, Iva allowed Grace to toss off the blanket. Grateful, Grace sat up and drew in deep breaths of cool night air.

"How's he doing?" Iva asked, as she continued to head the team northeast.

Grace placed her hand on his battered forehead. "He's burning up with fever, and his breathing's still slow."

"I hope he can hang on."

"Who's M'dear?"

"Someone I hope can help him."

Grace did too.

&ast;  &ast;  &ast;

When dawn broke they were still traveling. Grace had managed to catch a few winks of sleep, but they had been filled with dreams of the laughing Lane Trent and the sad eyes of the woman in the buggy. Grace wondered if she was Trent's wife.

The land had changed during the night. The surroundings now looked marshy. Cattails were standing in pools of water and she spied towering willow trees ahead.

"Where are we?"

"Getting ready to enter Caddo Swamp." Iva then pulled back on the reins and brought the team to a halt.

"Why're we stopping?" Grace asked with concern.

"Need to blindfold you?"

"What on earth for?"

"Where we're going they don't like strangers knowing where they are or how to get there."

Grace didn't pretend to understand, but sat quietly as Iva covered her eyes with a long, clean rag, then tied the ends tight.

"Can you see?" Iva asked. "I need you to be truthful with me, Grace. Jack's life might depend on it."

"No, Iva, I can't."

"Okay. It might be best if you lie down the rest of the way so you don't lose your balance trying to sit upright. We'll be there in a little while."

So taking Iva's advice, Grace lay down next to her shallow-breathing husband and let Iva drive them into the swamps of Caddo Lake.

Throughout the trek, Grace had whispered words of encouragement to the man she loved; she talked to him about their baby, their future, and told him again and again just how much she loved him. It didn't matter that he didn't respond; she sensed he knew she was there.

Still blindfolded, Grace had no idea how much time had passed, but she could hear birds calling, and the smell of water now filled her nose. The air seemed cooler, too. Were they now in the swamp? Insects buzzed by her ears and she swatted at the few quick enough to bite her bare arms and neck. Sightless, she fanned her hand over Jackson's face, hoping to keep the little beasties from lighting on him, because he couldn't keep them away on his own.

They finally stopped. The eerie quiet echoed. The buzz of insects sounded loud and the occasional bird call made her turn her head in an effort to discern its location.

"We're here," Iva told her quietly. "You can free your eyes now."

Grace reached behind her head and untied the knot. She looked around. They seemed to have entered a different world. Trees, mostly mossy cypresses, climbed as high as the eye could see, effectively cutting off the sun and making the surroundings glow with a gloomy dimness. They were on the edge of a murky amber waterway that twisted its way off into the distance. Some of the giant cypresses were growing right out of the water. She saw a large fish suddenly break the surface to feed on the insects hovering above. But the silence was what that affected her the most. It was an echoing, resonating silence that seemed to permeate her soul. It felt forbidding, yet oddly welcoming.

Grace turned her attention to Jack. The fever still had him in its grip and he'd been murmuring nonsensically for the last few hours. As she caressed his head with a loving hand, she wished she could somehow give him some of her strength. "What now, Iva?"

"We call."

"How?"

Iva went over to a large hollow tree and reached inside. "With this."

She pulled out a large, tall drum and a small mallet.

Amazed, Grace smiled. The drum looked very old. Judging from the intricate carvings and bits of color left on its sides, it might've come from the Mother Continent and had probably been very beautiful once.

Taking up the small mallet that had its head covered with cotton and soft moss, Iva struck the head of the drum, first six times, then six times again, then twice. Done, she secreted the drum back into its hiding spot.

"Now, we wait for M'dear. She'll be here soon."

"Who's M'dear?"

Iva paused for a moment, and as she held Grace's eyes, Grace had the impression Iva was trying to decide how much to tell her. In the end she didn't reveal much, saying only, "She's a healer."

"And she lives here?" Grace asked, looking around at the exotic surroundings.

Iva nodded. "Most of her life."

"Do others live here, too?"

"A few, but during slavery these swamps were full of escaped captives. The patrollers and their dogs usually left folks alone, though. This swamp and the lakes that flow in and out of here cover hundreds of thousands of acres, there's nearly sixty-five miles of water alone."

"Easy to get lost."

"Real easy. It's like a maze. Parts of it will take you right into Louisiana if you don't know where you're going."

Grace glanced around again and wondered how it might've been to live here. There looked to be plenty of fish and birds to eat. Wood from the trees would've provided materials for cabins and furniture. The swamp prevented the catchers from hunting you down. It undoubtedly would've beat slavery hands down.

"So how long will our wait be?" she asked, turning her attention to the prone Jackson.

"Not much longer," said an elderly voice.

Grace's head shot up and she saw a very old woman moving with the aid of a mahogany cane walk slowly out of the trees. The braided hair was snow white, the ebony face unlined, but she had the stooped stature of the aged. Her purple gown had the shape of those seen on the Mother Continent and flowed around her as she neared. Accompanying her was the largest man Grace had ever seen. His height rivaled the cypresses. Unlike the woman, his skin was white, his hair dark, his face very badly scarred. His eyes were black and so blazing cold that when he turned them Grace's way she felt a chill crawl over her skin.

The woman must've noticed Grace's reaction, because she said, "He only hurts those who hurt me. I'm M'dear. And you are?"

Grace looked into a pair of wise old eyes that were as clear and as lively as a child's. "Grace."

"Welcome to Sanctuary, Grace," she said, smiling. "The boy behind me is William."

Grace nodded at William. His great size contrasted sharply with M'dear's youthful description.

"Pleased to meet you."

She expected to receive the same skin-chilling gaze, but he surprised her. He smiled, then resumed his solemn stance.

"Who have you and Sister Iva brought me today?"

"My husband. He's injured."

M'dear came over and looked in the bed of the wagon. As she laid eyes on Jackson, she peered at him for a moment, then looked up at Iva. "He looks very familiar. Do I know him?"

"He's Royce's oldest son, Jack."

M'dear placed a thin hand against her lips. Concern on her face, she then felt his head. "Help me up into the wagon, William."

The giant stepped forward and lifted her slight weight into the bed. She knelt with difficulty, but was soon opening Jackson's eyes, peeling back his lips and running her hands over his ribs and limbs. "He is almost gone," she said, then her eyes softened. "But you brought him here in time. What happened?"

"He was dragged behind a horse."

"Lane Trent's men," Iva added tightly.

M'dear looked into Grace's worry-filled eyes and pledged with kindness, "We will save him. You and I."

M'dear then withdrew from the pocket of her dress a small leather pouch. Opening the strings, she extracted a tiny leaf and placed it in Jackson's mouth. "It will ease the bleeding inside and help him to sleep. In a few hours we will give him something for the pain and fever."

Grace nodded. "Thank you."

"You're welcome, Grace. Once we get him settled we will let you rest. You and your babies need it."

Grace went stock-still. For a moment, she searched M'dear's brown eyes and then whispered, "Babies?"

M'dear simply smiled and William lifted her down from the wagon bed.

Grace's shocked eyes went to Iva.

In response, Iva shrugged. "I've never known her to be wrong."

Grace's hand went to her still flat stomach. *Babies?*

William picked Jackson up as if he were a fragile child and carried him the short distance down to the water's edge. There, a large wooden raft bobbed waiting, anchored to a large cypress. The big man gently laid him down on a large pallet. Once Grace, M'dear, and

Iva got aboard, William freed the rope; then, using a long pole, he pushed the raft away from the grassy bank and guided it upstream.

Once again Grace felt as if she'd entered a strange new world. She feasted her eyes on the many strange but beautiful birds, the wild, thick vegetation and the occasional small deer. She could've done without the horde of insects, though; she spent a lot of time slapping her arms and neck.

Jackson seemed more restful, she noted with relief, looking down at him as he lay with his head resting in her lap. The babbling had ceased but his breathing remained soft and shallow. She tenderly ran her hand over his forehead.

They reached M'dear's sprawling cabin later that afternoon. William secured the raft to the trunk of a cypress, then carefully carried Jackson toward a smaller log cabin set back from the water's edge. Grace followed him while M'dear and Iva went to her cabin to fetch the items M'dear would need to aid Jackson.

The cabin Grace entered was clean and neat. There was a small, beautifully carved table and chair, and against the wall, a large short-legged bed covered with a crisp, clean saffron-colored sheet. He placed Jackson's unmoving body atop it.

Once William backed away, Grace knelt at her husband's side and stroked his bruised and battered face. Tears slowly filled her eyes.

"I love you," she whispered.

A few hours ago he'd been at death's door, and now M'dear pledged he'd have a fighting chance at life. Grace dearly hoped so because she had no desire to stand over his grave. He meant too much.

She whispered fiercely, "Don't you dare die on me, Jackson Blake. Don't you dare."

The sound of someone entering behind her drew Grace's eyes to the door. It was M'dear and Iva.

M'dear said, "I've brought the things we'll need to bring down his fever and to wrap his ribs."

"Thank you."

With Iva's help, Grace got Jackson undressed. His skin had been scraped from his chest and shoulders by the dragging, leaving him as raw and bloody as freshly ground meat. Grace mentally cursed Lane Trent as she gently bathed away the dirt and the dried blood. Jackson's answering grimaces and strangled moans let her know just how much pain he was in and she cursed Trent even more.

Once his chest looked sufficiently clean, M'dear applied a light salve to the area, covered it with a lightweight cloth, and then wrapped his broken ribs. "That should ease his breathing a bit."

"Now for the boots and trousers."

That task proved a lot more difficult because his ankles were so swollen from his injuries, but between Grace and Iva they managed, causing him minimal additional pain.

Upon seeing how raw the fronts of his muscular thighs and chest were, Grace bit down on her lip to keep her emotions under control.

"Glory," Iva murmured sympathetically.

M'dear simply shook her head sadly, then began cleaning the wounds. She also treated his rope-burned wrists and the scraped backs of his hands.

M'dear then handed Grace a small wooden bowl filled with a warm dark liquid. "Try and get as much of that into him as you can. It's for his fever."

Using a small spoon, Grace dribbled the liquid across his lips. Most of it ran down his chin, but she kept at it. She somehow managed to empty the bowl, but it took time. When she was done, Iva handed her a blanket.

"We should let him sleep."

Grace draped the blanket over him and caressed his forehead. "Thank you both for all your help," she said to Iva and M'dear.

"He's grown in to a fine man," the old woman said.

Grace smiled softly as she scanned his quiet form. "How long has it been since you've seen him?"

"He'd just turned three, and such a little thing. Is he still bossy?"

"As the dickens."

Iva chuckled. "He got that from his father Royce. The two were like peas in a pod."

M'dear then placed a comforting hand on Grace's shoulder. "Sister Iva and I are going to get something to eat. I'll have William bring you a plate."

Grace nodded.

"I'll stop in and check on you later," Iva promised, then she and M'dear exited, leaving Grace and her husband alone.

Jackson was dreaming. He was at Grace's house in Chicago, looking for her, calling for her, but all he kept finding were hordes of brown-skinned, redheaded children laughing and playing and running all over the place. They were on the stairs, in the closets, underneath the big desk in Grace's study. He searched everywhere for her, but all he kept finding were more and more children.

Suddenly, the front parlor turned into a river, and the children, both boys and girls, were floating by him in little sailboats, waving child-sized cutlasses. Next he knew, a dragon rose up out of the water and in its bloody mouth were Black people screaming and trying to get free. Their anguished and tortured cries filled his head but he could only look on helplessly because he was afraid.

The dragon, now with Lane Trent's face, began moving toward the children in their little boats. Jackson began calling to them, telling them to turn back because he knew Trent would harm them. But the flotilla continued to bear down upon the monster. The children, seemingly intent upon the battle, raised their swords.

He began to call for Grace, hoping she could rescue the children, but she didn't answer. He called again and again. He was still calling when the dream faded and he was dropped back into the black depths of sleep . . .

Grace bathed his head with the cool lake water and prayed it would help keep his fever down. They'd been here three days and nights now, and every night she'd sponged him down and every night when he finally quieted she slept by his side in the bed. But this night seemed to be the worst. He'd been tossing and turning and croaking out her name for hours. M'dear had looked in on him before she turned in and said he was restless because the fever was breaking. She advised Grace to keep sponging him down and that by daybreak he should awaken.

In the wee hours of the morning he finally quieted and Grace was relieved to feel the coolness of his forehead. Hoping the fever had left him for good, she snuggled in beside him, draped her arm protectively across his chest, and slept the sleep of the dead.

When Jackson opened his eyes that next morning, he'd no idea where he was. Looking around the small cabin, he scanned the unfamiliar surroundings and for the life of him could not remember being here before. He noticed Grace sleeping silently beside him and that gave him a measure of familiarity, but where or what was this place, and why were they here? He moved to sit up, but pain crackled over his body like lightning and he instantly went still. The pain echoed and he had to draw in a series of quick, shallow breaths until it faded and he could relax again. That he'd somehow been injured only added to the puzzle. *What the hell happened to me, and where am I?*

"Grace?" His mouth felt as dry as a desert and he was thirsty enough to down an ocean.

"Grace, get up."

Grace came awake slowly. Seeing his eyes open and clearly holding her own, she smiled broadly. "You're up!"

Happy tears filled her eyes and she began kissing him all over his face. "I'm so glad, so glad!"

Her enthusiasm was infectious and he found himself smiling too, but—"Grace, where are we?"

"The Caddo Swamp."

His eyes widened. "Caddo Swamp? Why?"

"You don't remember." She posed it as a statement.

"No."

"Iva brought us here after your run-in with Lane Trent."

Everything came flooding back then; being caught by Trent's men on his way back to the cabin, being trussed up and tied to the horse, then being dragged until he'd lost consciousness. He had no memories after that. "How long have we been here?"

"This starts the fourth day. You've been unconscious since we arrived."

Grace could barely contain her joy. He was alive and well. It might take awhile for him to fully recover, but recover he would, just as M'dear had promised. "I'm so glad you're back with me. You gave me quite a fright, Jackson Blake."

He reached out and wiped away the lone tear sliding down her cheek. "My apologies."

He felt like the luckiest man in the world, having Grace to wake up to. She was strong, brave, and true. She looked like hell, though, but that had become part of her charm. "How'd I get away from Trent? He swore he was going to kill me."

"Well, when I stuck a rifle in his back and promised I'd send him to hell if his men didn't untie you and let you go, he had a change of heart."

Jackson stared, amazed. "You took on Trent, alone?"

"Yep. Told you you'd need me, didn't I?"

Grace then revealed the full story of what had happened on the porch that day and how the woman Grace had assumed to be Mrs. Lane Trent had silently aided her efforts. "She had tears in her eyes watching them hurt you. She could've alerted her husband, but she didn't. I'll owe her for the rest of my life."

Jackson couldn't get over the part his beautiful redheaded Grace had played in his liberation. "I'll owe you for the rest of my life. How's our baby doing?"

"Babies, Jackson. M'dear says I'm having more than one."

He stared. "More than one?"

Grace nodded. "That's what she said."

"Who's M'dear?"

"The woman who helped you heal. She knew your father."

"I owe her too, then."

"We both do."

"More than one?" he asked again.

Grace nodded with a smile. "More than one, but I'm still waiting for real proof."

Over the next few days, Jackson worked on getting his strength back while Grace and M'dear clucked over him like two mother hens. His appetite returned and he ate all the fish and game and roots and fruit William put before him. He and M'dear had become fast friends, playing checkers, slapping dominoes. Grace looked on with love in her eyes but wondered how'd he react when she told him she was going home and planned to insist he come too. She understood why he'd come here, but trying to bring down Lane Trent was not worth losing his life.

# Chapter 12

By the first week of August Jackson's wounds had healed well enough for M'dear to pronounce him whole. The skin on his chest, shoulders, and thighs no longer resembled raw meat, and the swelling and bruising had faded. In spite of the still-mending ribs, he'd become his old vibrant self again and Grace couldn't've been more pleased.

It also pleased her that by all indications she was indeed carrying a child.

"So, you've accepted the fact," he asked, as they sat on their porch eating dinner at a small table.

"It wasn't so much accepting the idea, I just wasn't sure."

"And now you are?"

"Yes. M'dear says I have all the signs: I can't stay awake. My courses haven't come, and I'm eating everything that moves. Do you want that last piece of fish?" she asked him, indicating the piece on the platter between them. Grace had never really liked fish prior to coming to the swamp, but now it seemed as if she couldn't get enough.

Across the table Jackson shook his head at her and her burgeoning appetite. "No, go ahead."

He watched her fork the last piece of the grilled bass onto her plate and consume it with delicate gusto.

He chuckled and shook his head again. "If you're eating like this now, what'll you be like six or seven months out?"

"I've no idea, but M'dear says fish is good for the babies and that it won't make me particularly fat."

"That's good to know, otherwise we might need to hire a circus strong man to get you in and out of the buckboard."

She shot him a quelling look that held a smile. "Get all of your jokes out now, funny man, because I guarantee when I do get big and fat, I might not be of a mind to entertain them."

"No?"

"No."

"Will you be of a mind to entertain me?"

His double-edged question made her remember past entertaining encounters and she gave him a sultry smile. "For as long as I can."

"You're outrageous, do you know that?"

She pointed to herself and asked with wide, innocent eyes, "Me? I'm just a stiff-necked lady banker from Chicago."

"Eat, woman, before I show you something a whole lot stiffer than that neck of yours."

"Soon?"

His laughter filled the cabin. A grinning Grace went back to her meal.

Although Grace had yet to approach Jackson about returning north, she did reveal her thinking on the matter to M'dear one morning a few days later.

"I'm afraid he'll lose his life if he goes hunting for Trent again."

"That's a real fear," M'dear responded sympathetically, looking up from her knitting.

"But how do I convince him to leave?"

M'dear shrugged. "Have you told him how you feel?"

Grace shook her head, "No."

"Then maybe that is where you should begin."

Grace looked out over the rich, verdant paradise she now called home and supposed that would be the logical approach, but she didn't want to cause another rift. Her anger over being pressured into marrying, his anger over her following him to Texas, had faded, and in the aftermath of his injuries, they'd found true peace, not only here in M'dear's Sanctuary, but in each other. She didn't want that jeopardized, but on the other hand, his quest for justice and her desire that they return north were destined to clash.

Grace turned back and found M'dear watching her with understanding in her old eyes.

M'dear said softly, "Leave it for now, if you must, but the longer you put it off, the harder it will be."

"I know."

But for the next few weeks, Grace kept her fears unspoken, preferring to bask in her husband's recovery. He'd grown strong enough to help William with the hunting and fishing. William hunted with a bow, but since Jackson showed little aptitude for that method of hunting, he concentrated on the fishing, something he'd learned to do as a child. In addition to bringing in strings of fish, he often returned bearing bouquets of flowering plants and long-stemmed exotic blooms for Grace as well. The simple gifts brought her pleasure, increasing her love and deepening her feelings of peace.

One afternoon as she, Jackson, and M'dear sat on the porch of M'dear's cabin, trying to escape the heat of the late August day, Grace asked M'dear about her past.

"I've lived like this all my life," she replied as she fanned herself with a large rattan fan. "Born in the Carolinas, though. A placed called the Great Dismal Swamp between North Carolina and Virginia. My parents made it their home after they escaped captivity."

The story brought up memories for Grace, too. "I remember my father saying he stayed in the Virginia swamps for a while after he escaped from Maryland."

M'dear nodded. "The Great Dismal was home to several thousand runaways before Emancipation."

"How'd you wind up here, so far away?" Jackson asked.

"Love." And her soft smile seemed to hold memories. "His name was Jupiter and he was a healer. Learned all I know from him."

She paused for a moment, as if reflecting. "We went from the swamps of the Carolinas to the swamps of Florida and Louisiana, healing, learning, loving. Finally wound up here and set down roots. He built this house. There was a good-sized community in here at that time, but after the war, things changed. Folks started leaving for the outside. In the last few years, night riders have pushed folks back, but they don't stay very long. They hide for a while and then find a way to head north or east or west."

"What happened to your man, Jupiter?" Grace asked softly.

"Died three years ago," she said sadly, then quieted

for a moment before adding softly, "Miss him. Even though his spirit's here, it's not the same."

Staring off into the distance, she said, "I will see him soon, though. Promised me he'd be here to help me cross over when the time comes, and that time is almost here."

Jackson and Grace shared a concerned look.

A worried Jackson asked, "Are you sick?" She'd saved his life. He wanted the time to get to know her better.

"No, Jackson, I'm not, but the time is near."

In sharp contrast to the humid heat, Grace felt a chill cross her soul. Did M'dear really know her death date? Grace glanced over at William standing sentinel-like beside the door to gauge his reaction, and saw the sadness in his dark eyes. Did he know what M'dear was alluding to?

"In the interim," M'dear said, rising to her feet with the aid of her ebony cane, "First thing in the morning, William and I will be leaving to tend to a sick child. Her family lives a ways down river, and if she's as sick as William says she is, we'll probably be there a few days. Will you two be all right here alone?"

Upon seeing Jackson's and Grace's grins, she answered her own question. "Of course you will, you're in love."

Leaving them with a twinkle in her eye, she slowly made her way into the cabin.

The next morning Jackson helped William load M'dear's things onto the raft while M'dear and Grace spent a few minutes talking about the food on hand, which of M'dear's many plants would need watering, and other things, like what might ripen and need to be picked from the vast garden behind the house. Grace mentally noted each item, then walked with her out to the raft.

William gently lifted M'dear's tiny frame up into his arms. Boarding the raft, he set her down in a big rattan chair that resembled a throne, then poled the raft away from the bank. Jackson and Grace waved and watched until the raft rounded the bend and disappeared from sight.

In the soft silence that descended, one could hear the ever present hum of the insects.

Jackson slipped an arm around her waist and pulled her gently into his side. "Well, we have this paradise all to ourselves. What do you want to do first?"

He waggled his eyebrows.

She grinned, then asked saucily, "Are you sure you're up to such strenuous activity?"

He turned her so that they stood facing. He'd intended to give her a quick quip in response, but he paused. Gazing down, he saw the face of a redheaded pirate queen who'd taken on Satan himself to keep her husband from entering death's door, and his heart swelled. "Have I said thank you for saving my life?"

She smiled softly. "I don't remember."

He traced her mouth wondrously. "You are one amazing woman."

"It's the lioness who hunts after all," she replied, her heart full too.

"I'm glad she does . . ."

He kissed her, the first real kiss they'd shared since his recovery, and time slipped away. As her arms moved up his back to hold him close, there were no memories of hurt, pain, or fear, just a slow, passionate recommitment to relearning each other.

"How about I heat us some water for a bath," he whispered against her ear.

Grace purred contentedly, "That sounds wonderful." After yet another stifling hot night, Grace couldn't wait for the opportunity to feel his lips gliding over her clean, fresh skin.

Tub bathing was done in a spot behind M'dear's cabin. The unique bathing room was actually a large latticed bower thickly covered with the curling tendrils of M'dear's thriving grapevines. The riots of vines provided a natural screening for complete privacy.

Seated on the bower's bench, Grace watched Jackson pour the last bucketful of warm water into the large clawfoot tub. "Do you think Jupiter built this for M'dear?"

"Maybe," Jackson said, straightening and gazing around. Being the son of a carpenter, he really would have liked to see how it had been constructed, but because of all the vines curling over the latticed wood one could see only the large arch overhead and the two tall walls it rested upon.

"It is a nice spot," he remarked, marveling at the beauty surrounding them. He then turned his attention to another beautiful sight. "Are you ready?"

They were both fully dressed, but he planned on rectifying that directly.

Grace rose slowly and went to where he stood beside the tub. The anticipation of making love again after what seemed like an eternity had her fairly shaking.

He freed the top button of her blouse and then the one below it. Still holding her captive with eyes that promised to fulfill her every sensual wish, he undid the rest, then brushed the halves aside, his palms grazing her nipples so enticingly, she swooned and closed her eyes.

He kissed her mouth, teasing her lips with the tip of his tongue. While she stood there seeing sunsets, he eased the garment from her to reveal her thin chemise. Enjoying her reactions, he slowly traced a finger down her trembling throat, then whispered it over the top of each breast. While the sensations rose and rippled over Grace in the thick silence, he leaned down and offered a soft kiss of tribute to each golden crest. He slid the camisole down and suckled each nipple so magnificently that her growl rose against the quiet air.

He straightened, then husked out, "Now you can get into the tub . . ."

Smoldering, Grace put her hands to the button on the waistband of her black skirt. Knowing that she had his full attention filled her with an odd sort of power. The wanton woman inside her enjoyed the way his eyes followed the path of her skirt as it slowly slipped down her legs, then glided up over her firm brown legs and thin drawers for the journey back to her face. Holding his hot gaze, she lifted the camisole up over her head. As she slowly discarded it, he smiled. Her nipples tightened in response and Grace had never felt so brazen.

She leaned up for a kiss, during which he untied the tapes of her drawers, then worked them down. Still kissing him, she stepped out of them and he took a moment to savor her curves and planes with his worshipping hands.

He picked her up in his arms and lowered her into the water. There was so much heat arching between them, Grace half expected the water to begin to boil.

"Where's the soap?" he asked softly.

Grace pointed to the small ironwork table nearby. On it were a variety of scented soaps, salts, and oils M'dear had given her after their arrival. He sniffed a few, found one he seemed to favor, and came back to the tub.

She reached out to take the soap from him, but he wouldn't hand it over, saying, "Not so fast."

Confused, she watched him wet the soap on the washcloth. With her still looking on, he soaped it into a lather, and she wondered if he was intent upon what he looked to be intent upon.

"Stand up for me, darlin'."

He was. Anticipation made her tremble as she slowly rose to her feet, and as if rewarding her, the soapy cloth slid down her back and over her hips in such a suggestive and provocative manner, her eyes closed. He washed her in all the places that he planned on loving later—her breasts, shoulders, hips, then up and down her legs and thighs. She stood there, glowing in the silence, with her nipples hard and her core yearning and knew that every bath she took from now on would remind her of this very special place.

He rinsed her clean, wrapped her tenderly in a drying towel, and carried her the short distance to the pallet on the far side of the bower. He dried her so slowly and so well that when his dark fingers began to circle the citadel hidden in her damp copper hair, her legs parted and her hips rose ardently. Pleased, he kissed her mouth and then suckled her pleading breasts until they sang. He kissed his way down her fresh, scented body, and then under the soft hum of their surroundings placed a kiss on the inside of each satin-skinned thigh.

When he brushed his lips across the soft copper hair, Grace thought she'd dissolve and die. She also thought that this time, she'd be better able to handle his sweet conquering, but she was wrong. His warm mouth and its intimate seekings set off thunder and lightning. His lips played, his fingers lingered, and in the end, her screaming release startled the birds out of the trees.

Moments later, he gave her a soft kiss. "I'll be right back. Don't move . . ."

And she didn't. She couldn't—hell, she had no desire to. She lay atop the sheet-covered pallet throbbing and pulsing with the echoes of his magnificent loving, hoping he would hurry.

And he did. Jackson took the fastest bath he'd ever taken in his life. Clean now, he came back and knelt beside her.

She lay right where he'd left her, nude and beautiful. He traced her mouth and she opened her eyes. For a moment they fed themselves on the desire in each other, silently speaking the way only lovers can, and then he lowered his mouth to hers and began again.

By the time he entered her, Grace was so ready, his first few possessive strokes almost sent her over the edge again, but she held off so she could enjoy him to the fullest.

Jackson knew he wasn't going to last long, not this time; she was too hot, the paradise sheltering him too lush. The sight of her rising so passionately to match him thrust for thrust was also sending him toward the top. The silky weight of her hips in his hands as he guided her in a bliss-filled rhythm made him drop his head back and increase the pace of strokes. Soon they were both rising and falling in sweet battle. She shattered first, twisting and clutching his strong waist, her voice rising in song. He came next, face tight, and growling.

In the aftermath, they lay side by side, looking up at their vine-covered ceiling.

Jackson said, "Well, if you weren't pregnant before, you sure are now."

Grace snorted with humor and playfully punched him in the side. "I hope my children aren't going to be as arrogant as their father."

"Me?" he accused, turning over so they were facing. "Who is more arrogant than you, Miss Pirate Queen?"

"You," she said, smiling.

He dragged her atop him. Resting a hand on each hip, he squeezed her lightly and said, "Our child, or if M'dear is right, our *children,* will be wonderful, who-ever they favor."

"You really think I might have more than one?"

"Anything is possible, I suppose. Are there any twins in your family?"

She shrugged. "Not that I'm aware of. I'll have to ask the aunts when we get home."

She searched his eyes for a moment, then asked qui-etly, "When *are* we going home, Jackson?"

He knew this subject would come up eventually, but in light of the good times they'd been having lately, he hadn't wanted to be the one to spoil everything by bring-ing it up.

So, in answer to her question he replied just as quietly, "I am home."

Grace dropped her head for a moment. "Jackson, I have to go back to Chicago."

"I know, but I've got things to do here."

"What more can you do?" she asked, trying not to get upset.

"I want to go back and talk to Maybelle."

"Didn't she say she didn't know anything about her brother, Champ?"

"I think if I can talk to her again—"

Grace rolled away and sat with her back to him. There was silence for a moment as she tried to put her feelings into words. "Jackson, this Texas of yours scares me to death. Call me a northern coward, or whatever you wish, but I can't live here, not knowing that while me and my babies are sleeping, night riders could barge in and take our lives, and nobody would care."

She looked at him over her shoulder. "Is that so selfish of me?"

"No," he admitted, not liking how this conversation would eventually end or the actions they'd probably be taking as a result. "I'm not going back to Chicago, at least, not right away."

She looked into his eyes and he met her gaze steadily. *This is the beginning of the end*, she said to herself. "Jackson, I understand that you want to do this for your father, but—"

"It's not just my father. Trent bragged that he has the warrant for my arrest. If I can get my hands on it, I can start over, *we* can start over."

"We can't do anything if you're dead."

"I didn't ask you to follow me down here, remember?"

"And if I hadn't, you would be dead, *remember*?"

He looked away.

Keeping her mouth shut lest she say something she shouldn't, she picked up her skirt and put it on. "I'll fix us some lunch."

Grabbing up the rest of the clothes, she draped a clean towel around her torso and left him alone in the bower.

Jackson wanted to throw something, but he knew it wouldn't change things. She'd mapped out her position and he'd done the same. He knew he had little chance of getting his hands on that warrant or bringing Lane Trent to justice, but his pride refused to let him give up. Trent and his friends had murdered his father, he couldn't just walk away from that. He also owed Trent for the dragging. Grace shouldn't've had to witness such horror and Jackson owed Trent for that, too.

Grace had spent quite a bit of time around her father's adult friends, so she knew a bit about men and pride. For some men pride was their driving force, and Jackson was one of those men. She wanted to grab him by his shoulders and shake him for placing his life in danger this way, but she knew she had no say in how he chose to handle his life. She, on the other hand, had the well-being of her child to consider and she had no plans to raise it in hell. If he didn't want to return to Chicago with her, she'd go alone.

Lunch consisted of leftover wedges of roast duck between slices of the bread she had made yesterday. It was eaten in silence.

When they were done, he stood and said, "I'm going back to the outside when M'dear and William come back."

Since he'd said nothing about getting her to the train station or even escorting her back to the outside, she supposed she was to make her own arrangements for home. She wondered if he could see the ache in her heart.

He could. "I told M'dear I'd finish chopping that wood I brought in the other day. I'm going to go take care of it now."

He noted she hadn't asked to be escorted back to the train station, or even back to the outside. Independent to the end. Without another word, he stepped off the porch and walked away.

For the next two days they moved around each other like ghosts. He slept in the hammock outside and Grace went to the bed alone. She refused to cry. They argued fiercely.

"Explain to me," Grace asked him one afternoon, "what it is you're seeking here. I want to understand."

"Justice."

"Jackson, it's 1884. There is no justice for us. Maybe in seventy-five or another hundred years."

"I know what year it is, Grace, but should I just give up? Should I just walk away and maybe let Trent kill another child's father?"

"Your death is not going to bring your father back into your life. It's not."

"I know that too."

"Then why don't you turn your back on this and walk away? Why let Trent control you like this?"

"He doesn't control me."

"Sure he does. You are so much in his control that you're actually helping him by placing yourself within his reach. That doesn't make sense to me."

"Then go back to Chicago, where things make sense."

Grace's lip tightened. "Fine."

She walked back to the cabin with angry unshed tears in her eyes.

When M'dear and William returned, the old woman looked tired as she used her cane to aid her onto the porch.

Grace, sitting on the porch, snapping beans, smiled for the first time in days. "Welcome home."

"Thank you. It's good to be back."

"How's the child?" Grace asked.

"Doing well, doing well. Snakebite. How are you?" M'dear countered, sounding weary as she eased down onto the cushioned seat of her favorite rattan chair. "Where's that man of yours?"

"Fishing downstream. Said he'd be back later." Grace tried to keep her voice light.

M'dear wasn't fooled; she leaned over and peered into Grace's face. "You two spattin'?"

Grace's lip tightened. "He's going back to the outside. I'm going back north."

For a moment there was silence as M'dear searched her eyes. "I see. Almost losing his life wasn't enough of a sign for him?"

"I guess not."

M'dear sighed. "Some folks have to follow the path to the end."

"Trent's going to kill him."

"You don't know that, child."

Admittedly, Grace didn't, but when this whole mess had started, she'd pledged to follow him into hell, and she had. Now she was ready to leave. Lane Trent would not have the satisfaction of killing off another generation of Blakes. She was taking her baby home.

She did want to stay here a while longer, though. She'd need to grieve once Jackson left her, and she'd rather shed her tears here, surrounded by familiar peace and tranquillity, than on the long, impersonal train ride home.

Grace turned back and looked to M'dear. "I would like to stay on a few days, if I might."

"Stay as long as you wish. William will see you to the train when you're ready to go."

Jackson decided he'd head down to Austin and see if he couldn't find Jeb Randolph. Randolph had been a Texas Ranger back during Jackson's sheriff days and had always been a man of integrity. He was probably the only man who could help Jackson reconnect the strings on a ten-year-old killing and offer advice on how to go about it.

As he packed his gear, he tried to avoid thinking about Grace, but couldn't. He understood why she wanted him to leave. She was afraid for his life, and Chicago was decidedly safer. But if Jackson didn't try and right his past, he'd spend the rest of his life with the injustice of his father's death burning in his heart. Soon he'd wind up blaming her for being the cause of his discontent and he didn't want that. If he did return to her, he knew he risked having her turning her back on him and not letting him back into her life, but it was a chance he'd have to take.

On one hand, he'd forced her to marry him because he hadn't wanted his child to grow up without him, but on the other, how could he look his child in the eye knowing he'd done nothing to avenge his own father's death? For Grace, going back to Chicago was a simple, logical decision, but for him it was much more complex.

So he would leave her in an effort to find his own peace, and hope she still loved him when he returned. *If* he returned.

Later that afternoon, Jackson loaded the last of his gear onto the raft, then went into the cabin to say good-bye.

"Grace?"

She had her back to him and turned. He could see the tears standing in her eyes.

She whispered fervently, "Don't do this . . ."

He felt his heart break. "I'll come to Chicago as soon as I can."

He walked over to where she stood and stared down into her watery eyes. He traced a finger across her freckles and wondered if he'd ever see her again. Hastily burying that thought, he pulled her into his arms and rocked her silently. She held him just as tightly.

"I love you so very, very much, Grace."

"I love you too, Jackson."

She looked up and whispered, "Come back to me."

He wiped at the tears rolling down her cheeks, then kissed her eyes. "I will, darlin'. Don't worry."

In spite of their differences, neither wanted to part in anger. And so the kiss they shared was filled with sweetness, love, and a bittersweet good-bye.

When they parted, he left without a word.

Grace stood in the doorway and watched William pole

the raft away from the bank and take Jackson out of her life. She was sad, angry, and most of all, fearful, wondering if she'd ever see him again.

That evening, after dinner, M'dear handed her a folded piece of paper. "He wanted me to give you this after he left."

Grace unfolded the note and read:

> I lov'd thee from the earliest dawn,
> When first I saw thy beauty's ray,
> And will, until life's eve comes on,
> And beauty's blossom fades away;
> And when all things go well with thee,
> With smiles and tears remember me.
>
> I'll love thee when thy morn is past,
> And wheedling gallantry is o'er,
> When youth is lost in ages blast,
> And beauty can ascend no more,
> And when life's journey ends with thee,
> O, then look back and think of me.

When she finished reading there were tears in her eyes.

After leaving the swamp, Jackson headed his horse south to Austin, and Grace spent the week helping M'dear in her garden, listening to her stories of times gone by and missing Jackson.

Although she tried to convince herself that if she didn't think about him she wouldn't worry, it didn't work. He was the first thing she thought about in the morning when she opened her eyes, and the last thing she thought about at night before going to sleep. Questions of where he might be and if he were safe were with her constantly.

It was now the end of September and it had been almost a month now since Iva had brought Grace and Jackson to M'dear's Sanctuary. Grace continued to enjoy the solitude and peace, but knew the weather would be changing soon and if she didn't head for home shortly, she might be forced to stay the winter. With that in mind, Grace and M'dear prepared for her departure.

Grace had decided to leave in two days' time, but problems arose that afternoon when the faint call of the drum echoed on the air. Six beats sounded from a long way off. Six more beats followed and then two.

As the pattern repeated itself, William quickly went to the raft and Grace looked to M'dear, who said, "The two sixes announces a friend, the two alone means there's trouble."

Grace remembered Iva pounding out the same drum beat when Jackson was first brought here. She wondered whom it might be this time and how M'dear could help?

M'dear said, "William will fetch them. No sense in worrying until he returns."

William returned less than an hour later with Iva. When Grace saw the awful bruises on the woman's face, she quickly called for M'dear, then ran to meet Iva as she came up the bank.

"What happened?"

"Trent," she managed to spit angrily. Her lips were so swollen they were twice their normal size. One eye was black and blue and swollen shut. She'd taken a tremendous beating, it appeared.

"Where's Jack?"

"Gone."

Iva stopped. "What do you mean, gone?"

"Gone."

"Where?"

"I've no idea," Grace admitted.

Iva scanned Grace's face, then she shook her head. "Let's hope he's somewhere safe."

After M'dear saw to Iva's injuries as best she could, Iva told her story. "Trent and his night riders are terrorizing the county looking for you and Jack," she said, turning her battered face toward Grace. "Paid Riley a visit night before last and me last night, and as you can see, he didn't believe me when I said I didn't know where you two were."

Grace felt awful. "Iva, I'm so sorry."

"Don't worry about me. It'll take more than a bunch of cowards in sheets to put me in the ground. And if they do, I'll be going to Glory anyway, so to hell with them."

Grace smiled.

Iva turned to M'dear. "He's turned over every rock and privy in the county; burning houses, questioning folks. Common sense says he'll look here next. This is all that's left."

M'dear looked to William. "We'll be fine. If Lane Trent brings his hate to my front door, the next door he enters will be Satan's."

It was agreed that in order to circumvent the problems that might arise should Grace return to Marshall, William would raft Grace into Louisiana and she'd get a train there. Iva said there were rumors that Trent had men posted at the Marshall train station with hopes of catching Jackson and Grace should they try and leave town.

Iva then asked, "So where did Jack go?"

Grace shrugged, and the uncertainty made her irritation with him surface again. "Other than that he was going to try and talk to Maybelle Champion about her brother, that's all I know."

"I don't think he realizes how much things have changed since he's been gone. Trent will kill him."

"I don't think he's thinking at all."

Iva nodded. "Well, we'll just pray he stays out of Trent's way."

"I don't think he has the sense to do that either."

Iva spent the night, and the next morning she and Grace shared a parting embrace.

"You take care of yourself now, Grace," Iva whispered fiercely. "And if I see that stubborn husband of yours, I'll crack him over the head, put him in a crate, and ship him to you."

Grace smiled. "You do that, and take care of yourself."

"I will. Davi and I are going to visit my cousin in California for a while until this blows over."

They parted and Grace said, "Well, you're both welcome to come to Chicago with me."

"Oh, no," Iva chuckled. "I hear it's so cold up there even the birds wear coats."

Grace grinned and then became serious. "I can never repay you for all your help."

"You just get yourself and those babies home safe. That'll be payment enough."

Iva shared a farewell hug with M'dear, then stepped onto the raft where William waited to take her back to her buckboard.

That night, as Grace drifted off to sleep, her last thoughts were of Jackson and home.

Grace awakened to a nightmare. Dogs were barking, men were yelling, and the horns of hell were blowing shrilly. The smell of smoke hung heavy in the air. Groggy with sleep, she stumbled to her door to see

M'dear's house in flames, and mounted, white-sheeted specters out front, riding back and forth, shooting pistols and blowing horns. With her heart in her throat, her first instinct was to run to the house, but upon hearing footsteps entering her cabin by the back door, she turned, eyes wide with fear.

It was William. "Come!"

He grabbed Grace by the hand. His big hand felt strong as she ran with him into a nearby stand of trees.

"Up there!"

He linked his hands together and held them low, and she put her foot in them. He propelled her up until she could grab onto a sturdy branch. Once she had a secure grip she began to climb.

"Stay until I come back for you."

Her terror overrode her long held fear of heights and she climbed as high as she could. Once she found a sturdy perch, she hugged the trunk and looked down on the chaos below.

The four riders were now circling her small cabin. One tossed in a lit torch. It did not take long for the dry logs to begin to burn in earnest, and soon the flames were growing and spreading. The dogs were baying incessantly, the sound mixing with the eerie calls of the horns and loud gunshots. Grace prayed William had taken M'dear to safety and prayed also that they'd survive this night.

All of a sudden, a male scream pierced the air, quieting the sounds of the ghoulish cavorting, and one of the men slowly tumbled from his horse to the ground. Before his companions could react, another man gave a tortured gasp and crumpled lifelessly across the back of his mount, his torch slipping slowly from his hand.

An unearthly silence fell over the scene then. Even the dogs had ceased their awful baying. As the two remaining riders turned their mounts this way and that in an effort to determine the origin of the invisible attacks, Grace could sense their fear. She scanned the night, wondering if William were somehow responsible, but saw nothing.

One of the men tore off his sheet and looked around. Although the moonlight offered only a faint illumination, coupled with the strong light from the blazing cabin, the face of Lane Trent could be plainly seen. As soon as he revealed himself, the man by his side let out an anguished cry, clutched his face, and fell to the ground, leaving the now visibly agitated Trent the only night rider still alive.

The dogs seemed as affected as Trent. Whimpering fearfully, they ran off into the darkness.

Now, all alone, Trent raised his pistol and fired into the darkness as if attempting to scare off the unseen assassin, but his bullets were wasted. Nothing happened. Nothing moved.

To Grace it seemed as if the entire world was holding its breath, waiting for whatever might happen next.

It came swiftly. Grace heard Trent's loud cry of pain and saw him clutch his shoulder. He tried to turn the horse, but froze as the assailant struck again. In the resulting silence he keeled over and fell to the ground.

Grace noticed the tears rolling down her cheeks for the first time and dashed them away. Her fear and dread had abated somewhat, but she still didn't know if M'dear had survived the attack.

Grace heard William call out, "Come down, Grace. It's safe now."

Grace made her way back down through the branches. William stood at the base and helped her to the ground. Only then did she see the quiver across the big man's chest and begin to understand. Trent and his men had been dispatched by arrows. No wonder they'd been unable to retaliate. William was an excellent marksman.

"How's M'dear?"

"Still with us, but not for long. Come."

Not wanting to accept what he meant, Grace followed him back into the night. His steps slowed at a spot hidden in the forest behind the bower. M'dear lay on a pallet bathed by the now rising moonlight. Her long white braids hung down across her shoulders. Her eyes were closed and her fragile frame so still, Grace feared she might be dead.

Grace looked up at William. He replied by nodding sadly.

Grace knelt low. Taking the old woman's hand tenderly in her own, she whispered, "M'dear?"

The eyes opened tiredly and then she gave Grace a weak smile. "Did William take care of those brigands?"

"Yes, ma'am, he did."

"All of them?"

"Not a one left."

"Good," she whispered, and squeezed Grace's hand. "Good."

Grace wanted to help but didn't know how. "Can I get you something, water—"

"No, child. Time's running out, that's all. Too much excitement tonight," she said with a soft chuckle. "Never did like a whole lot of noise."

Grace bit her lip as she smiled through a fresh sheen of tears.

M'dear added, "William will get you to Louisiana. Then you get yourself on home, you hear?"

"I hear."

"Babies don't like a lot of excitement either."

Grace nodded.

M'dear was silent for a few moments and then said,

"Don't worry about that man of yours. His heart's good. He'll come back to you. Just like Jupiter's coming back to me."

M'dear then raised her other hand for William to take. He knelt without a word and raised her hand to his cheek. She smiled up at him with love in her eyes. "I'll tell Jupiter you send your love, William."

Tears in his eyes, he nodded. "Take care of yourself, M'dear."

"I will, son. I will."

Then she smiled and said softly, "Ahhh, my Jupiter's come, just like he promised. Good-bye, William. I love you."

"I love you too, M'dear."

Her eyes closed, and a second later she was gone.

They buried her near the bower right after sunrise. When they were done, Grace and William stood together over the freshly turned earth and said their prayers.

There was not much left to salvage after the fires. A few charred pieces of broken china, a couple of heat-bent spoons. M'dear had lived in her cabin for over forty years and one horrible night of hate had reduced it to a pile of smoldering ash.

William had disposed of the bodies of Trent and his men, sometime before dawn. Grace didn't know what he'd done with them and she didn't ask. All she wanted was to get home, but even that had become a problem now. She'd lost everything in the fire, too, including her money. She had only her life and the clothes on her back. How was she to get home?

"Are you ready?" William asked.

"Yes, but I have no money."

"Trent did."

William pulled out a gold money clip choked with

bills. Grace didn't hesitate. She hoped Trent was spinning in his grave, knowing his money would pay for her journey home. Taking the clip from William's hand, she stuck it in the pocket of her wrinkled, dusty skirt and when she did, her hand closed over a folded piece of paper. Curious as to what it might be, she pulled the paper out and recognized it immediately. It was Jackson's poem. So she hadn't lost everything. Smiling now, she put the treasure back in her pocket and walked down the bank to the raft.

About an hour into the journey, she told William, "You know, I never heard you speak before last night. I thought you were mute."

"Didn't have anything to say," he told her, as he effortlessly guided them through the waters.

"How long have you lived with M'dear?"

"All my life. M'dear was midwife to the woman who birthed me. When she died a few days later, the husband blamed me for her death. Told M'dear if she didn't take me with her, he'd kill me for sure."

Grace thought that absolutely horrible. "So, she did?"

"Yes, she and Jupiter raised me as their own. He taught me to fish and hunt, and she taught me to read, and that color doesn't matter if your heart is good."

Grace wished Trent and his companions had been taught by M'dear. "What are you going to do when you return?" she asked.

"Probably rebuild the cabin and spend the rest of my days there until it's time for M'dear and Jupiter to come get me and take me to the other side."

And he said no more.

Grace caught a northbound train in Louisiana. The conductor made her ride Jim Crow, but she didn't care. With Trent's money she'd been able to buy enough food from the vendors outside the station to make sure she didn't go hungry on the long trip. And as soon as she reached a town large enough, she planned to buy a change of clothes and wire the aunts.

She forced herself not to think about Jackson.

# Chapter 13

E vidently, Grace's babies didn't like riding Jim
   Crow anymore than she, because as soon as she
headed north, the morning sickness caught up with her
and she was sick and nauseated the rest of the way. To
make matters worse, at an Indiana border stop, a change
in conductors resulted in all passengers of color being
asked off the train because of one woman's complaint
about Grace and the others riding. The woman's tender
sensibilities couldn't tolerate them riding anywhere. She
wanted them off the train and the conductor concurred.

For two days, Grace and the others waited alongside
the track for a train that would let them ride. When one
finally did, its conductor refused to draw the color line,
and so, for the first time since leaving Louisiana, Grace
had a seat. She didn't care that none of the other passengers wanted to sit beside her. Their disdain made it

possible for her to stretch out, and as soon as she did, she fell asleep.

When the exhausted Grace finally stepped off the train in Chicago, the sight of the aunts waiting for her was almost too much for her to bear. She began crying almost immediately. They didn't seem to care that she was dirty and smelled of mules and cattle. Dahlia and Tulip folded her in their loving arms and Grace's tears flowed like rain.

The aunts rocked her and Tulip whispered fiercely, "Oh, Grace, when we didn't hear from you we were so worried."

"No more than I," she admitted. She was so glad to be home, she swore she'd never leave Chicago again.

"That's the last time we let you go gallivanting across the country," Dahlia said, wiping at her wet eyes with an embroidered handkerchief.

Tulip scanned the other passengers disembarking. "Where's Jackson?"

Grace bit her lip to keep fresh tears from flowing. "I don't know," she said softly.

Both aunts looked surprised.

"It's a long story. Let's save the telling for home."

"Whatever you say, dear."

A familiar but repellent voice sounded at their backs. "My lord, Grace, is that you?"

A tight-jawed Grace turned to see Garth's wife, Amanda Young Leeds. She was wearing a sunshine yellow gown that had been designed for an ingenue, a title the plain-faced Amanda hadn't been able to claim for a decade.

"Why, it *is* you!" Amanda stated with wide eyes. She scanned the very dirty Grace up and down, then gasped, "What happened to you?"

Grace wondered what she'd done to deserve such a

fate. First she'd been forced to endure the train ride from hell, and now everyone in town would be gossiping about her again, all because she'd had the misfortune to run into the badly dressed Amanda not more than ten minutes after stepping off the train.

Grace finally answered the rude question by saying distinctly, "It's none of your business, Amanda."

Amanda drew back as if stung. "Well, excuse me, I'm sure everyone will be quite interested to know you're home." And she huffed off.

Grace shook her head, then looked at her aunts. "Can we leave now?"

"Certainly," Dahl responded, shooting a malevolent glance at Amanda's departing back. "We've a hack waiting."

When Grace first entered the house, the familiar pictures, furniture and feel of the place tore at her heart. Had Lane Trent gotten his way, she would never have seen her home again. She wanted to pinch herself to make certain she wasn't dreaming.

Looking over her shoulder at her aunts standing so silent behind her, Grace fed her eyes on the sight of them. The night Trent and his men came, she didn't think she'd ever see them again either. "I missed you two, very much. Very much."

Both aunts were teary, but gave her a smile.

"And we missed you, too," Tulip said, love in her eyes. "Are you hungry?"

"Am I?"

Dahlia said, "Well, you just go on up, get you a nice hot bath, and Tulip and I'll fix you something to eat."

Grace loved the sound of that. Weary in mind, body, and spirit, but thankful to be home, Grace and her babies climbed the steps to her bedroom.

While the water heated on the grate in her bathing

room, Grace slowly peeled off her soiled clothes. She planned on burning each and every item the first thing in the morning. Because she'd had to travel in cars that often sported vermin and filth, she had no idea what might be living in her clothing and had no desire to find out. Remembering Jackson's poem in the pocket of her skirt, she retrieved it, placed it on her dressing table, then went to start her bath.

After washing her hair three times, Grace lay in the tub surrounded by warm, scented water and soaked and soaked and soaked. When the temperature cooled, she added more hot water and resumed her reclining position. She stayed in the tub for quite some time, letting the heat and silence drain away her aches and anxieties, but when the skin on her toes and fingers began to wrinkle like dried apples, she thought it time to get out.

Later, after she'd oiled and braided her hair, she put on a soft, clean gown and started in on the plate of food brought up by the aunts. She had to force herself to eat slowly and not devour the green beans, yams, and smoked turkey as her ravenous stomach demanded. Instead, she ate slowly. She didn't want to be sick.

For the first time in many days the babies seemed to enjoy the food their mama had eaten. Later, a grateful Grace lay down on her bed and savored the soft mattress beneath her back.

She hadn't slept on a real bed since leaving to set up the wagon train. The wagon train seemed to be a lifetime away. She'd gone through so much since then. Her unguarded thoughts naturally swung to Jackson, and she wondered where he was, what he might be doing, and if he were safe.

Getting up, she unfolded his poem and tucked the edge of the open paper into the top corner of the dressing table mirror.

*. . . And when all things go well with thee,*
*With smiles and tears remember me.*

Grace kissed the tips of her fingers and placed them lovingly against her husband's written words. "Goodnight," she whispered. "Stay safe."

It took Jackson nearly three weeks to travel to Austin and track down former Texas Ranger Jeb Randolph. The man had moved five different times in the years Jackson had been away, and Jackson was just happy to find him alive.

When Jackson rode up to the small spread outside of Austin, Jeb was out front chopping wood. He had his sleeves rolled up over his meaty caramel-colored arms, and seeing Jackson, he stopped and stared.

"Jack! Is that you?"

Jackson smiled and dismounted. "Yep, it's me."

Jeb hastened over and the two old friends embraced.

"How've you been?" Jeb wanted to know, but before Jackson could answer, Jeb hollered into the house, "Mary, come on out. Somebody here I want you to meet."

A pretty young woman came out onto the porch, drying her hands on a dish towel.

Jeb said, "Jack, I want you to meet my wife, Mary. Mary, this is Jack Blake, one of the finest lawmen ever to wear a star."

Jackson nodded at Mrs. Randolph. "Pleased to meet you, ma'am."

"Same here. You two want something cold to drink?"

Jeb answered, "Yeah, that'd be nice."

He then beckoned Jackson up on the porch. "Come on, sit a while. Tell me what you've been doing."

So Jackson told him, starting with the death of his father.

Jeb interrupted. "I wondered why you suddenly disappeared. Lane Trent, huh? Never liked him or his daddy. Dealing with them was like dealing with rattlesnakes."

"Well, that snake is still alive. Wanted to know if you'd help me try and cut off his rattler."

Jackson then related the story of his most recent run-in with Trent.

Mary appeared with glasses of lemonade. When she departed, each man helped himself to a glass, then Jeb said, "Wish I could help, but I can't. Those fools at the capitol took my star. I'm not a Ranger anymore."

"Retired?"

Jeb shook his head sadly. "No. Black men can no longer be Rangers, Jack. It's against the law. They took my star in '76, probably around the same time you left."

Jackson found this hard to believe.

"Time's slipping back. They're rewriting the laws everyday, it seems. Can't vote, can't testify against Whites, no matter the circumstances; can't do this, can't do that. Why did we fight the war?"

Jackson stared off across the open land. Would he have to give up and swallow his quest for justice simply because he was a man of color?

"If I were you, Jack, I'd go on with my life and let the past lie."

"But I can't, Jeb. Trent shot my father down like a wild dog."

Jeb nodded his understanding. "I know, but what can you do? Times won't allow you to bring him to trial. Do you have family, a wife, children?"

A vision of Grace rose in Jackson's mind. "Yes, a wife. Children on the way."

"Then live for them. Someday—and it may not be in our lifetime—times will be different. Our children and our grandchildren will be able to petition the courts and receive the justice they seek. They'll be able to vote, Jim Crow will be dead, and who knows, maybe one of your descendants will run for President."

Jackson allowed himself a smile.

Jeb looked him in the eye. "Live for the future, Jack. Don't give men like Trent the satisfaction of lynching another Black man. Go back to your family. Get your revenge by raising strong, beautiful children who'll give these crackers a run for their money someday."

Jackson knew Jeb was offering sound advice, and at this point he supposed he was ready to take the words to heart, but how many other men like him would have to go to their graves with the bitter pill of injustice in their souls until the country righted itself and gave every man and woman, no matter the color, the right to life, liberty, and the pursuit of happiness? He thought about Grace again. She'd tried to tell him the same thing, yet his pride had prevented him from hearing her. She'd saved his life, but it hadn't stopped him from leaving her and his children. Was she in Chicago? he wondered. Were she and the aunts just sitting down to dinner? Were his children thriving and growing? He knew of only one way to answer those questions.

Jackson drained the last of his lemonade from his glass and stood.

Jeb looked disappointed. "You leaving already? You just got here."

"I know."

"Well, where you heading?"

"Up north to try and make peace with my wife."

Jeb smiled pleased. "Well, when you get there, give her a hug for me. And Jack?"

Jackson turned back.

"There's no shame in this, none whatsoever. Given a choice between living and dying? I'd pick living every time."

Jackson nodded. Mounting his horse, he gave Jeb a parting wave, then headed north to Grace and the future.

It took Jackson four days to reach Marshall. He wanted to stop off and see Iva before heading to Illinois. He decided it might be better to visit her at night, so as to avoid a confrontation with Trent, but she wasn't at home. In fact, the way the windows were boarded up, it appeared as if she'd abandoned the place. He found that odd. Puzzled, he got back on his horse and rode over to Riley's. Maybe he'd be able to get some answers there.

Riley opened his door cautiously, but when he saw Jackson standing against the night, he smiled and invited him in. "Sure wasn't expecting to see you 'round these parts again. Where've you been?"

"Austin, but I'm heading back north. Wanted to say good-bye to you and Iva first before I left, but her place is all boarded up. Do you know where she is?"

Riley shook his head sadly. "She and Davi are gone to California. After Trent went on the rampage, she had to leave. He and his thugs beat her up pretty bad."

"What?"

Riley then told him the story of all that had transpired since the last time he and Jackson were together. While Jackson listened, his jaw tightened upon hearing about the terror and the fear spread by Trent and his men in their search for Jackson and Grace, and about Riley's own beating.

"They beat me up pretty bad, too."

Jackson felt terrible. He'd no idea his old friends had suffered so much on his behalf. At least Grace had been safe with M'dear.

Riley said, "Funny thing, though. No one's seen Trent or his riders in over a month. Some folks are saying he went into the swamp and never came out."

Jackson felt a chill cross his soul. "When did he go into the swamp?"

"Rumors said a day or two after Iva and Davi left here. Why?"

"Grace was still with M'dear when I left for Austin."

Riley looked worried. "You think Trent might've found her?"

Jackson headed for the door. "I hope not. Lord, I hope not."

"Where're you going?"

"To see M'dear."

"You want me to go with you?"

"No, you've already proven what a friend you are. You stay and keep an eye on things here. I'll let you know in a few days if I find out anything."

So Jackson rode off, heading east. He prayed with every fiber of his being that Grace and M'dear were okay. He knew William would do everything in his power to keep the two women safe, but William was only one man. Even someone of William's immense size could be overpowered if the enemy brought enough troops. Jackson spurred his horse on. He needed to know.

From his travels with William through the winding waterways, Jackson knew that he and M'dear had a few rafts hidden in the undergrowth in various locations, so when he entered the area, he tied up his horse and searched one out. He dragged it to the water's edge, pushed it in, then used its long pole to move away from the bank and out into the silent water. He'd've preferred a faster mode of transportation, but since this slow drifting was all there was, he forced himself to be patient.

When he finally came in sight of the spot where M'dear lived, he thought he might have made a wrong turn somewhere on the river and gotten himself turned around because there were no cabins here, but as he poled closer, the piles of charred wood came into view, and his heart stopped. What happened here? Where were the cabins, where was M'dear? More important, where was Grace?

Even before he could maneuver the raft closer, Jackson yelled out, "Grace? Grace!"

Once he secured the raft, he stepped onto the bank and began to call again. His heart in his throat, he looked around the silent surroundings and began to call again. Dread rising, he didn't know what to do.

Then William appeared with his arrows and a string of birds. "Welcome back."

"Where's my wife?"

"I took her to Louisiana and she caught a train home."

Jackson felt so relieved he had to sit on a stump to wait for his heart to stop pounding. She was safe.

He asked then, "M'dear?"

"With Jupiter."

Jackson knew what he meant. The woman who'd given him back his life lived no more. "It wasn't Trent, was it?"

"Indirectly, yes. They came that night, but it was her heart. I got her and your wife to safety and then sent Trent to hell."

Jackson sat up. "Trent's dead?"

"Yes, and so that you may be certain, I will show you."

They took the raft and journeyed about a mile and a half downstream. As they rounded a bend, the grisly sight of four corpses hanging from the trees stopped Jackson cold. The arrows William must have used to bring the men down were still implanted in skulls, throats, and hearts. The bodies had begun decomposing and the birds had feasted on their eyes.

"They will serve as a warning to others," William offered simply.

That said, he turned the raft around and headed back the way they'd come.

Grace spent her first week at home, recuperating and catching up on her sleep, but by the second week the boredom got the best of her, so she went back to work at the bank. She hadn't heard from Jackson and was starting to wonder if she ever would. The aunts now knew the full story of what had happened to Grace while in Texas, and they too said prayers for his safe return each night.

As the days turned into weeks, Grace's stomach began taking on the roundness usually associated with her condition, but she didn't let it slow her down. She joined a new literary society, went to church, talked to her forming babies at night about their father, and tried to keep herself busy.

On the night of one of Black Chicago's most famous charity events, Grace viewed herself critically in the mirror. The black velvet dress looked stunning on her, she had to admit. The empire lines effectively camouflaged her burgeoning stomach, and the almost too daring neckline would give the gossips something else to talk about besides whatever tales Amanda had been spreading about their chance meeting at the train station.

Grace walked over to her dressing table to put on her jewelry, and as always, her eyes settled on Jackson's poem. *Where are you*? she asked him silently. Her worry was fast becoming irritation. He hadn't written or wired. Did he believe he could come back any old time and still find her waiting with open arms? Noticing that she was becoming upset, she set the thoughts aside and finished the business at hand.

Grace had been going to the Charities Ball for over a decade now. The first one had taken place in 1865, right after the end of the war. At that time she'd been far too young to attend such an adult-oriented gathering, but her parents had gone and it had become a tradition. In those days most of the money raised went to build Black schools and to defray the costs incurred by members of the community as they agitated for the right to vote on behalf of the city's Black male citizens because before the war free Blacks were barred from the process. The vote came in 1870, and the schools were desegregated four years later, but the need to raise money continued to be necessary.

Presently there were nearly fifteen thousand Black residents of Chicago, and more were arriving everyday from the states bordering Illinois and from upper southern states like Kentucky and Missouri. Most were employed as domestics and servants and denied access to the many jobs that were available in such an industrial city.

Grace wondered what the founder of the city, Black Frenchman Jean Baptiste DuSable, would think of the spreading metropolis that had grown out of his small settlement. She thought he would be proud of how it had risen like a phoenix after the devastating fire of October 1871. During those three terrible flame-filled days, four-fifths of the city had burned. Over thirteen thousand homes had been destroyed and three hundred and fifty thousand had been left homeless. A year later, the city was well back on its feet.

But she thought DuSable would be saddened to see the deplorable conditions many of the race were forced to live in, and further saddened by the city's discriminating policies. Most of the Black residents lived in mixed neighborhoods next door to Italians and Germans just as poor as they in an area framed on the north by the Chicago River, on the south by Sixteenth Street, and on the west and east by the south branch of the river and Lake Michigan, respectively. The area now being called the South Side Black Belt lay narrowly sandwiched between the railroad yards and the industrial factories east of the big, fancy homes of Wabash Avenue, and west of Wentworth Avenue.

The low wages made it hard for people to get a leg up on life and even harder on their children. Many families had no extra money for schooling or doctors, or, in some cases, burying. Events like the Charities Ball and others were held so that the race could take care of those who needed help until they could make it on their own.

Most of the representative Blacks also lived in mixed neighborhoods in places like Morgan Park, Hyde Park, Woodlawn, and Englewood. Many had ties to the White community by way of their services and businesses. Henderson Pratt, one of the city's wealthiest Black tailors, was this year's ball chairman and the event was being held at his spacious home.

As she stepped down from the hack and paid the driver the fare there were coaches parked up and down the street. Grace could see elegantly dressed men and women making their way to the door.

Inside, the mansion was so filled with guests one could hardly turn around and the noise of three hundred plus voices assaulted the ears. Grace didn't see their host in the crush, but could see blue-liveried waitpeople, employed by the city's finest Black catering establishment, wading in and out of the fray, offering the guests finger foods and refreshments from their trays. She helped herself to some of the deliciously prepared appetizers, then tried to make her way to a less crowded spot. As she did, she paused to share a few words with the prominent Frederick L. Barnett, who in 1879 founded Black Chicago's first newspaper, the *Conservator*, and was now a very important voice in the community's fight against Jim Crow and disenfranchisement. Barnett smiled upon seeing Grace. Barnett promised to send a reporter over next week to interview her about the brides and the wagon train so he could run a feature in his paper about the brides. Grace thanked him, then headed for the stairs in a quest for familiar and friendly faces. She dearly wished the aunts had come along but they were dining at home with the Henderson twins tonight.

On the steps Grace paused a moment to greet the pastor of Quinn Chapel AME, Chicago's oldest Black church, and the man at his side, the rector of St. Thomas Episcopal's Black congregation. The city's Black churches were the main beneficiaries of the monies that would be pledged this evening so they could carry on their work with those impoverished folks given short shrift by the White social agencies of the city.

Grace moved through the gathering like a ghost. After spending time with M'dear, she found it hard to be in crowds now. She'd gotten used to the silence and serenity of a solitary life, and all the noise and tightly packed throng were starting to make her head ache.

After spending an hour smiling falsely and talking with people who simply wanted to know if the tales Garth had been spreading about her having taken up with an illiterate Texan on the wagon train were true, Grace had had quite enough. A nosy old woman, a good friend of the Youngs, had been politely grilling Grace for the past quarter hour. Grace was just about to say something rude to the woman in response when silence settled over the gathering.

Grace turned to see who could be responsible for quieting so many guests and her eyes locked with Jackson's. Her legs went weak, and had she been the fainting type, someone would've been yelling for smelling salts then and there, but she wasn't. Dressed in his hat and duster, denim trousers, cotton shirt, and boots, he stood in the center of the room, an exotic contrast to all the other men in their formal suits. She didn't know whether to shed happy tears or sock him for the worry he'd caused her, but ever the Texan, he didn't give her the choice.

While the rest of the guests stared on, he crossed the room, picked her up in his arms, and headed toward the door. The thought came to Grace that the gossips were going to talk about her and Jackson forever, but she didn't care. Placing her head against his heart she let herself be carried past hundreds of wide-eyed guests and savored every moment.

As he placed her in the buggy he'd rented, she said quietly, "You know I'm mad at you."

He took his place on the seat and picked up the reins. "Figured you might be."

Without another word, he set the team in motion and directed them up the quiet street. As they traveled on, they left the gas lights and the fine homes behind and entered the rural stretch of trees and meadows that led back to the city. The stars were out and the quietness of the surroundings made for a perfect drive.

"It's a nice night," Grace remarked softly.

"Yes, it is."

They seemed to be the only two people in the world. The lights of the city could be seen in the distance up ahead, but it lay at least another thirty minutes away.

Grace asked, "Do you suppose we can stop and just enjoy the moon for a few moments?"

Jackson did as she'd asked and soon they were beside the road surrounded by silence and the moonlit darkness.

"So, how are you?" he asked.

"Fine. Babies are fine, too."

He looked over at her and tried to form the words. "I'm sorry I wasn't there when Trent showed up."

"Had you been there, you might not be here with me now," she responded softly.

The silence settled for a moment, then she asked, because her heart had to know, "Are you here for good?"

"Yep. Ready to face the future with you. If you'll still have me?"

Grace knew they had much to talk about, but that could wait. "On one condition."

"And that being?"

"That you tell me who wrote that beautiful poem you had M'dear give me."

He grinned. "Man's name was George Moses Horton."

"Was he English?"

Jackson chuckled. "With a name like Moses? No, he was a slave in North Carolina for about sixty years. Published over a hundred fifty poems in his day."

He draped an arm around her and kissed the top of her hair. "Is that really your only condition?"

"Yep, the babies and I are satisfied."

The darkness shadowed his smile. "You look very beautiful tonight, hellion."

"You are quite a sight yourself, Mr. Blake."

Jackson hadn't planned on kissing her (he thought they should talk more first), but he wound up doing it anyway because he couldn't wait. Passion rose slowly, coursing through them like the warmth of a fine June day, making the kisses deepen and linger. He slid his tongue into the sweetness of her mouth and she answered in kind. He pulled her closer and she answered by kissing his throat above the bandanna tied around his neck, then slowly worked her way back to his lips. "I missed you . . ."

"Not half as much as I missed you."

Jackson dragged her onto his lap. He fed her kisses and she savored them responsively. His hands caressed; her hands explored. The sounds of their heightened breathing rose against the cool night air.

Unable to resist any longer, he opened her cloak and brushed his mouth across the warm swells of her breasts. She arched sharply in response while he groaned in pleasure, smelling the deep, fragrant tones of her perfume. "Damn, you smell good . . ."

He slipped his fingers into the bodice of her gown and teased an already taut nipple. Rolling it back and forth, he slid his tongue over the provocative band around her throat and thrilled to her purring response. All he wanted was to strip her bare and make slow, sweet use of the buggy's seat, but she'd freeze to death and so would he.

"Darlin', we need to move on before we both catch our death."

But he couldn't resist the lure of her mouth, nor the nipple now peeking out of her dress. When he bent his head and dallied with it brazenly, Grace melted all over the seat.

"You have on too many damn clothes . . ." he growled passionately.

Because of the waves of passion she was riding upon, Grace dissolved under the feel of his strong hands gliding her dress up her thighs. The slit in her drawers offered him splendid access to a woman's paradise and he plied the gates expertly. "I was wrong," he husked out. "You're dressed just right . . ."

Seated on his lap, Grace purred as his finger found

her, and the wantonness began to rise. His bold touch set her afire. Grace thought she had on too many clothes, too, but the strokes and circles making her hips rise with an all too familiar rhythm set the mundane thought aside. Her whole world centered on the splendor flowing from his touch and the heat propelling her upward.

Jackson had never made love to a woman in a fancy ball dress before, and the sight of her all disheveled, her body ebbing and flowing from his touch, made him hard as a railroad tie. He wanted her like nobody's business, but he kept reminding himself that no matter how warm and damp and hot she was, they needed to be doing this somewhere inside.

"Grace, I'm going to bring you to pleasure and then we're gonna go get warm, okay?"

Grace didn't care; she didn't care at all. Sitting atop his lap, with her expensive black dress rucked up and down, she found that his dallying was making her so senseless, she'd've gladly flirted with frostbite if it meant the pleasuring would continue. The thick, hot promise in his voice as he whispered just what he intended to do fueled her passions even higher. When he boldly put words into action, her sighs escaped and her legs parted shamelessly for more. As she shattered with the climax, she had to use his sheltering shoulder to muffle her screaming release.

Later, after her clothes were righted and her pulsing abated, she asked, as they drove through the darkness, "How'd you know where to find me tonight?"

"Stopped by your house and your aunts told me, but not before giving me hell about not writing or wiring."

Grace grinned. "Good, then I won't have to later."

"Do you know how much I love you?" he asked then.

"Not half as much as I love you. Where do you want to live after the babies are born?"

Starting over fresh somewhere new had been something he'd spent a lot of time thinking about the last few days. "I don't want to live in Chicago."

"I know."

He tried to see the expression on her face. "That bother you?" he asked quietly.

She shrugged. "I'm not going to lie and say it doesn't. I've never lived anywhere else. My home is there, my job, but I know you can't abide the place."

"You're right, I can't. So how about Denver?"

Grace was surprised to say the least. "Denver?"

"Yes, that way you can have your snow and I can be west of the Mississippi."

"Denver?"

"Sure, there're theaters and stores for shopping. We'd be right on the rail line if we wanted to go and visit the aunts or if they wanted to visit us. It's settled, but not too."

"Could I start a bank there?"

"I don't see why not. The Black community is small, but growing."

He looked at her. "So, will you think about it?"

"Sure."

A second later, she said, "I've made up my mind."

He chuckled. "Already?"

"Yep, and the babies and I vote yes. Where you go, we go. If you want to live in Denver, so do we."

He grinned, stopped the buggy, and gently traced her freckled cheek. "Have I ever told you how much I love you?"

"No, I don't think you ever have."

"Well I do, very much, and thank you for saving me from Trent, and thank you most of all for being you. I was wrong to think you needed to be wrapped in cotton."

She smiled up. "Yes, you were, but I forgive you."

He kissed her gently, and she settled in against his side for the rest of the ride home.

The aunts met them at the door and showered them with hugs and tears. That next evening as they ate the big welcome home dinner for Jackson the aunts had prepared, Grace finally told the aunts about M'dear's prediction that she could be carrying more than one child. For the first time in her life, Grace saw that her aunts were speechless.

In the weeks and months that followed, Grace continued her job at the bank and began to look more and more like a woman on the road to giving birth. Jackson began doing carpentry work around town, and once word got around about his skill, he had more jobs than he could handle.

In late November, Grace received a letter from Belle announcing the birth of her daughter. Belle had named her Loreli Grace. Grace found the tribute so moving, she cried.

The new year ushered in 1885, and Chicago hunkered down for the winter as the snow flew and the winds froze the hairs in people's noses. The aunts returned home to Grand Rapids after the holidays, but pledged to be back in the spring in time to see the babies born. After their departure, Grace and Jackson made slow and gentle love in every room in the house.

Mid-March brought no significant change in winter's hold on everything, but it did bring a letter from Katherine Wildhorse. She'd given birth to a daughter and named her Jenny Rachel. It seemed Katherine had insisted upon Dixon being present at the delivery. She wrote:

*Hell, he was there at the beginning, I wanted him there at the end!*

Grace read further and laughed upon reading that Dix had fainted while observing the birth and had had to be carried from the room.

At the end of April, Grace gave birth to twin boys. M'dear had been right. Although they were small, the midwife declared them healthy. The proud parents named one of the squalling babies Griffin Elliot Blake, after Jack's brother and Grace's father, and the other Royce Prescott Blake, for Jack's father and the Old Buccaneer.

That night Jackson tiptoed into Grace's room. He expected her to be asleep after such a tiring experience, but found her lying in bed, holding and smiling down at her sleeping sons. At his entrance, she looked up, love shining in her eyes.

"How are you?" he asked, as he came and sat on the edge of the bed.

"Tired, but glad."

She looked down at her sons. "M'dear was right, there was more than one, and they're perfect, Jack."

"It's too bad they'll never know her."

"We'll just have to tell them about her, and on our way to Denver, we should stop off and see Iva, too, maybe."

"I'd like that."

There was silence then as they observed the sleeping babies. Jackson leaned down and kissed each small brown forehead. "Thank you for my sons," he whispered to her.

"The aunts will probably erect a statue in your honor. Boys are rare in our family."

He then placed a kiss on her brow. "I'll love you always, Grace."

With tears in her eyes, she whispered, "And I'll love you always, too, Jackson. Always and forever."

# Author's Note

*Always and Forever* is another story generated by you, my fans. After the 1997 publication of my fifth Avon novel, *Topaz*, the mail began rolling in. Most of you wanted to know what happened to Jackson Blake and the redheaded hellion Grace Atwood, so as usual, your wish is my command. I hope you enjoyed the ride.

William Welles Brown, the author of *Clotel; or the President's Daughter,* lived from 1815 to 1884. He escaped from slavery on New Year's Day, 1834. During his fifty years of freedom, he wrote more than sixteen published works, ranging from a chronicle of his own escape titled *Narrative of William W. Brown, Fugitive Slave, Written by Himself* (1847) to the first drama written by an American of African descent, titled *The Escape, or a Leap for Freedom* (1858). He also authored a number of Black history books. Two that I'd love to get my hands on are *The Black Man, His Antecedents, His Genius, and His Achievements* (1863) and *The Negro in the American Rebellion, His Heroism and His Fidelity* (1867).

Interestingly enough, when *Clotel* was finally published in the United States, almost ten years after the British edition, the title was changed to *Clotelle: A Tale of the Southern States,* and Currer's daughters were no longer fathered by Thomas Jefferson, but by a senator. The original version was not published in the United States until *1969*!

Here's a list of some of the books I used to help with the telling of Grace and Jackson's story; some are old and out of print, but others are readily available. Please consult with your bookseller or local librarian if you need help with your search.

Bolster, W. Jeffrey. *Black Jacks: African American Seamen in the Age of Sail.* Harvard University Press. 1997. Cambridge, MA.

Franklin, John Hope. *Runaway Slaves: Rebels on the Plantation.* Oxford University Press. 1999. New York.

Magill, Frank N., ed. *Masterpieces of African-American Literature.* HarperCollins. 1992. New York.

Mullane, Deirdre, ed. *Crossing the Danger Water: Three Hundred Years of African-American Writing.* Anchor Books. 1993. New York.

Rogers, J. A. *Sex and Race.* Vol. 1. Rogers. 1967. St. Petersburg, FL.

Sherman, Joan R., ed. *African-American Poetry: An Anthology: 1773–1927.* Dover Publications. 1997. New York.

Spear, Allan H. *Black Chicago.* University of Chicago Press. 1967. Chicago.

Webster, Donovan. "Pirates of the Whyda." *National Geographic* (May 1999).

A special shout-out to all the ladies, and the three husbands who attended my pajama party last May. Thanks for such a marvelous time. Yes, we're going to do it again—I just don't know when. Special thanks also to the fans in Australia, Canada, England, and the Islands for their wonderful letters. Welcome to the fan family.

In closing, I want to *give* thanks for all the prayers, letters, and words of encouragement that continue to flow my way. Sista fans of all races and denominations—you are the best. I am blessed by your support. Until next time.

Peace.

## Coming in October from Avon Romance

Breathlessly anticipated by her fans . . . it's the latest in Suzanne Enoch's WITH THIS RING series . . .

## Meet Me at Midnight

He's known as the infamous Lord Sin; she's been called "Vixen" by the *ton* . . . together they enter into a most unexpected marriage.

.....................................................................................................

And don't miss this book by a rising star of romance, Adrienne deWolfe

## Always Her Hero

He's the man she couldn't forget . . . but is he the man she fell in love with? Or has he changed?

"A jewel of a find!"
Christina Dodd